The Path Beneath Her Feet

A Novel

JANIS ROBINSON DALY

[signature: Janis Robinson Daly]

Black Rose Writing | Texas

ISBN: 978-1-68513-472-3
LIBRARY OF CONGRESS CONTROL NUMBER: 2024937345
PUBLISHED BY BLACK ROSE WRITING
www.blackrosewriting.com

Printed in the United States of America
Suggested Retail Price (SRP) $24.95

The Path Beneath Her Feet is printed in Sabon

*As a planet-friendly publisher, Black Rose Writing does its best to eliminate unnecessary waste to reduce paper usage and energy costs, while never compromising the reading experience. As a result, the final word count vs. page count may not meet common expectations.

Cover design by Author Bytes
Cover photos by Marj Warnick Photography
Map Illustration by Dana Gaines, Island Graphics

For my parents,
who came of age during the Great Depression and served upon
the seas and at the home front during World War II.
The Greatest Generation.
Their history is ours. Let us not forget it. Let us learn from it.

PRAISE FOR
THE PATH BENEATH HER FEET

"A historically compelling, engaging ode to a cadre of formidable women."
–*Kirkus Reviews*

"In this sequel to *The Unlocked Path*, we continue to learn about remarkable early women doctors. Meticulously researched and beautifully written, Janis Robinson Daly gives us the story of a life well lived. Kudos to the author for this compassionate look at these extraordinary women, brought to life through the fictional Dr. Eliza Edwards."
–Kathleen Grissom, *NY Times* Bestselling Author of *The Kitchen House* and *Crow Mary*

"*The Path Beneath Her Feet* offers a fascinating look at medicine in Depression and WWII-era America. Women doctors in particular—still a tiny minority in the profession—faced significant challenges even as the need for care increased. These challenges and the dauntless women who overcame them form the foundation of this sweeping yet intimate novel. Rich in historical details, this story transports the reader back in time while remaining highly relevant to today's world."
–Amanda Skenandore, Award-winning author of *The Second Life of Mirielle West*

"Readers will love adventuring through Eliza's mature years, as she encounters repeated setbacks in personal and professional ways. She is strong and accomplished, but still has much life left to learn. With a blend of fortitude and compassion, Eliza faces loss, heartbreak, and the burdens of aging. *The Path Beneath Her Feet* reminds us to never stop learning and believing in our dreams."
–Kerry Chaput, Author of the award-winning *Defying the Crown* series

"Spanning the historic and tumultuous 1930s-1940s in Boston and Appalachia, Janis Robinson Daly's expansive *The Path Beneath Her Feet* lures readers into a complex web of familial and professional drama centered on a female physician seeking acceptance in a male-dominated field while fulfilling roles as a wife, mother, grandmother, colleague, mentor, friend, and lover. Impeccably researched and detailed, this captivating novel is sure to garner acclaim. A triumph!"
–Ashley E. Sweeney, Award-winning author of *Eliza Waite*

"An inspirational story of a woman doctor in the early 20th century, battling misogyny at every turn in order to serve her patients and fulfill her calling. Eliza Edwards is a true original, and this novel is full of heart."
–Gill Paul, *USA Today* best-selling author of *A Beautiful Rival*

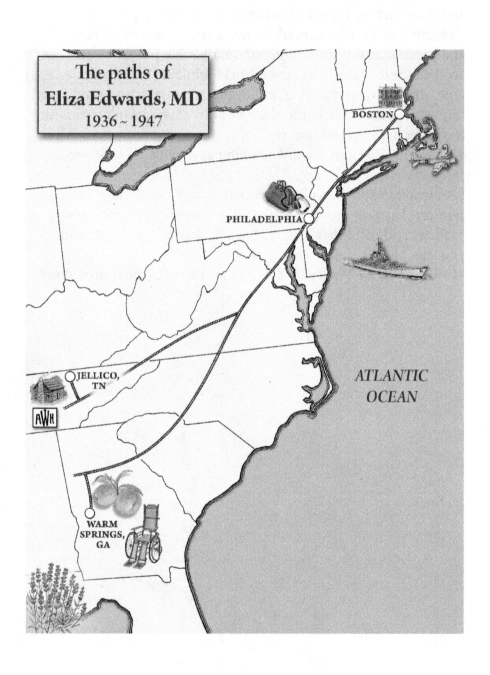

The paths of
Eliza Edwards, MD
1936 ~ 1947

BOSTON

PHILADELPHIA

JELLICO, TN

AWH

WARM SPRINGS, GA

ATLANTIC OCEAN

The
Path Beneath
Her Feet

PART ONE

"The purpose of life is to live it, to taste experience
to the utmost, to reach out eagerly and without fear
for newer and richer experience."
–Eleanor Roosevelt

CHAPTER ONE

Spring 1936
Boston, Massachusetts

"I'm sorry, Dr. Edwards."

Seated across the desk from the hospital administrator, Eliza Edwards stared into Dr. Miles's steel-gray eyes. His blank expression offered no sympathy.

"Surely, you must understand. The Peter Bent Brigham Hospital cannot add a position to our payrolls in this economic climate," he said, running his index finger down a list of names and dates. He shook his head in defeat. "I've double-checked. No one is retiring this year from the maternity ward. Dr. Gallagher's date is closest, although he may decline. He may be unable to give up his wages. He lost a great deal in '29 and I've heard his daughter and her four children moved in at Christmas."

Eliza sighed with an audible groan. *I'm sorry.* That short phrase had become a constant refrain as it reverberated around the country and in her ears over the past six months. *I'm sorry*, said every administrator she spoke with about a position. *I'm sorry*, said the landlord as he reminded Eliza that she and Olga Povitsky owed rent on their office space. *I'm sorry*, replied the druggist when Eliza asked him to reduce his prices on prescriptions that she wrote for her patients who struggled to buy groceries, let alone a month's supply of pills to ease menopausal symptoms.

Eliza stood. She should have worn higher heels, not for the extra femininity they would present, but for a taller stature they could provide than her five feet two inches. Although she doubted that even an Amazon woman standing before Dr. Miles could alter the facts on his staff sheet. She offered her hand. "I'm sorry, too, Dr. Miles. I believe my years of experience would be a great asset to the Brigham."

As Eliza headed toward the door, Dr. Miles's voice halted her reach for the glass knob. "I've a thought. It's radical, but I have enough sway around here to make an exception."

Eliza turned to hear his idea. At this point, she could manage radical.

"Every year, like clockwork, it happens," he continued. "Our new hires, with the ink barely dry on their certificates, find themselves with a diamond on their fingers soon after, which means many of them disappear off to birthing their own children before they get started. I realize you're married, but we could make an exception given, well, I don't suppose you'd be coming in to announce a pregnancy?"

Her eyebrows shot up as he suggested her child-bearing years had passed. She had taken great care to conceal her fifty-seven years. She had fought enough battles in her life to prove her abilities as a woman. She didn't need to pile on proof she still had all her faculties about her.

Dr. Miles's face colored to the same red as the bowtie at his chin. "Would you consider a nursing position?"

Eliza's cheeks flared to match his, not from embarrassment, but from fury. She doubted that he offered the same alternative to the young man, with his freshly minted Harvard degree, whom she had met in the waiting area.

"As I said, Dr. Miles, thank you for your time. However, may I remind you, again, I hold a degree from the Woman's Medical

College of Pennsylvania and have run a successful private practice with Dr. Povitsky. I am a doctor. I intend to remain one for many more years."

She wasn't sorry.

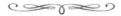

The day following her meeting with Dr. Miles, Eliza stood on the stoop of her office. The pale buds on the cherry trees lining Irving Street pressed against their bound petals, waiting. Spring in Boston seems to arrive later and later every year, Eliza thought. Perhaps the season also felt the defeatism which hung in the air and infected the walls of American homes and workplaces. A light breeze sent the sign over her head into a sway. For sixteen years, the sign's lettering had welcomed women to step inside the office of Edwards & Povitsky. When had she and Olga last repainted the black lacquer for a fresh shine?

Eliza's knotted fingers, which had soothed countless foreheads of women in the grips of labor, stroked a rabbit's matted white fur to settle it in the crook of her arms. A highly unusual form of payment by a patient, Eliza had relented and accepted the rabbit when Mrs. Luchetti resorted to a public plea on the sidewalk. Eliza pushed the door open. Their office space in Olga's apartment remained stocked with supplies of their trade. Thermometers, sanitary pads, blood pressure cuffs, speculums, and womb veils, or diaphragms as women now preferred their prescription sheets read. Syringes, sponges, and gauze lay in neat piles. Dark blue and brown bottles of morphine, chloroform, and ether stood capped in rows behind locked glass cabinet doors like soldiers awaiting orders. She took down a sterile porcelain bowl with a red rim from the top of the cabinet. The rabbit would fit. If she wasn't scrubbing her own hands for an examination, she might as well use the bowl as a rabbit bathtub.

Strands of gray hair fell from her up-do. Her battle to retain her natural auburn tresses had ceased a year ago. Eliza finger-waved the loose hairs back into place. The door swung open. Olga ambled through the entrance. She sized Eliza up and down and stopped on the white bundle in Eliza's arms.

"What in God's name?" Olga said.

Eliza lifted her chin to the ceiling. What new reprimand would Olga snort this time? Bringing her head back to an even level, Eliza turned to Olga. "It's a rabbit," she said.

"I can see that. But what is it doing here?"

"Don't worry, I don't need your help. Mrs. Luchetti caught up with me on the sidewalk just now. Poor thing. She's been beside herself, not paying for her last two appointments. I couldn't refuse when she thrust it into my arms, pleading if I'd take it as partial payment. How could I say no?"

"Easy. 'Mrs. Luchetti, like everyone else, we need fees paid in cash. The electric company, nor the Medical Board, will accept payment in the form of rabbit stew.'"

"Stew? I'm not boiling this sweet creature in the bowl. I only mean to clean it up, tie a ribbon around its neck, and give it to the grand nieces and nephews for Easter."

Olga tossed her briefcase to a side table and plopped onto her desk chair. The indents on the worn leather inset matched her form. Resting her chin on the heels of her hands, she massaged her temples in rhythmic circles. Since 1929, the creases in the corners of her eyes had deepened. She drew her lips in, tight and motionless. Eliza settled into her matching chair after depositing the rabbit on the floor. With a twitch of its nose, it set off to explore the vastness of a room after a life spent piled in a hutch.

Olga extended her hand across the expanse of the two desks. "Eliza. My dear, my innocent *podruga*. Mrs. Luchetti had no intention of that rabbit wearing a pink bow. She wanted to pay you with something she thought would be valuable, putting a meal on your table the way she does."

As year after year unfolded since the Great Crash, a hearty meal became an all-consuming task for millions of families like the Luchettis. Unemployment rates matched the lengths of soup lines and numbers of shanties erected under highway overpasses and along riverbanks of outlying towns alike. Eliza picked up the pen laying across the appointment calendar. Blank spaces covered the page. Before 1930, names had filled the weeks, giving Edwards & Povitsky busy days and frequent nights at the hospitals for deliveries. She rolled the pen between her fingers. From its nib, she had inked prescriptions and care instructions. Women who entered their office desired not only medical professionals but also the empathy and sympathy which only women doctors could provide. Their trust in Eliza and Olga never failed them.

Now, if a pregnancy or ailment required a medical professional, women sought midwives or checked into hospitals when a situation became dire. Eliza understood a decreasing ability to pay private practice fees. But, when she probed one patient about a canceled appointment, her sympathy dissolved, hearing that the woman's husband refused to pay a woman doctor's fees. If he made any payment, those monies would go to a male doctor, the head of a household like himself, trying to support his family. Eliza could offer no rebuttal. She and Olga carried no such responsibilities.

"I know Mrs. Luchetti's intent, Olga," Eliza snapped. "For just a moment, I guess I slipped into a place where rabbits hop about as a child's pet. Or a Nivens McTwisp."

Even at fifty-seven years old, Eliza would often reference her favorite childhood book. The copy sat on the bottom shelf of their bookcase, its gold lettering on the red leather spine and cover erased by thousands of children's fingers. While Eliza and Olga treated and counseled their mothers, the children flipped the pages, their fingertips gliding along the lines as Lewis Carroll's adventures carried them to a land of rabbit holes, tea parties, and a screeching queen playing croquet.

"We'd all like to escape from the mess around us. But I'm afraid, despite what your fine President Roosevelt says every day on his campaign stump, that day is not around the corner. It's not down the street, past the Charles River, and out into the countryside of Acton. It's nowhere, just like this office. A hole as dark and unending as Alice's but without secret potions to change our predicament. It's time, Eliza. We must discuss the date we'll announce my departure. I've barely seen a client in two years, and I doubt any request me over you. We owe them full disclosure of the state of the practice."

Eliza closed her eyes, their ocean blue deepening as a storm roiled. Mimicking Olga, she rubbed the crevices around her eyes and forehead. Olga's leaving and closing their office weighed on Eliza with a dull ache in her heart. She shouldn't be surprised. The mechanics of change had crept into their lives with the darkness of the depression. By 1933, when every month brought more closed business doors, a steep decline in patient counts sent Olga in search of another source of employment.

Franklin D. Roosevelt, keenly aware of the impact of polio, mandated his New Deal would include additional funding for overburdened public health departments. Infections invaded the masses as hunger wormed its way through empty bellies, taking advantage of weakened immune systems. Diphtheria, tuberculosis, and pertussis ravaged the young and the old. Poliomyelitis outbreaks claimed limbs and lives every summer. As a result, Olga had found a part-time position at Boston's Department of Health, where she buried her head amidst slides, petri dishes, microscopes, and copious notes in the solitude of research. Her extra wages covered their rent and kept the sign swinging outside their door.

Eliza opened her eyes. Throughout the years of assisting her patients in the last stages of labor, she had taught how controlled breathing could calm the mind. She inhaled deeply. The suspension of her exhale compelled the tension in her neck and shoulder to exit when she released the slow stream from her mouth. "I know, Olga. I know. We, or rather, I, have delayed the announcement. It's hard to admit a loss," Eliza murmured.

"We can't call it a defeat. Look at how long we've stayed open. How many women have we tended to over the past sixteen years, giving them the care and respect they may not have found elsewhere? We've done a remarkable job. I haven't lost. Neither have you, neither have they. We took nothing for granted. We've won, Eliza." She gathered a stack of papers strewn across her desk, tapped them into a neat stack, and headed to her bedroom off the back of the office.

The sense of loss enveloped Eliza on a personal level, not a professional one. She would miss her confidante, her classmate, her partner, her sister. Only Olga could lift Eliza's spirits and dress down her worries. In three weeks, Olga would board a train at South Station, heading to a spare bedroom in her sister's home, and a full-time position with the New York Department of Public Health in Manhattan. She had plans for a new beginning. Eliza had none.

Although the Boston hospitals hired a select few women for their residency positions each year, the administrators would scoff at an application from a woman thirty-five years out of medical school. A woman in medicine presented enough challenges. A box on an application form filled in with the number fifty-seven, male or female, would head straight to a corner basket. Thirty-five years of experience crumpled into a ball of worthless waste.

But did Eliza truly need a position? Her few shares in the Edwards Wool Company provided a small income. Her husband, Harrison Shaw, from whom she had separated seventeen years ago, paid for their sons' educations and when he moved to Washington, D.C., he gave her their home on Beacon Hill. Despite its empty rooms, it put a roof over her head. While millions suffered and struggled, her basic needs for food and shelter were tended to with relative ease. She should be grateful for her blessings. Why then couldn't she slow her pace like other women her age, content to pick up knitting needles or cross-stitch? Pearl Buck's entire trilogy lay stacked on Eliza's nightstand, its matching leather spines uncracked. An imaginary trip to China in *The Good Earth* could carry her away like when she had escaped as a child with the adventures penned by Jules Verne. Yet, sitting idle by a hearth with a shawl draped over her shoulders never entered an adult Eliza's mind.

Ever since meeting Anandibai Gopal Joshi in the library of the Woman's Medical College when Eliza was a young, directionless, eighteen-year-old, Anandibai had inspired many of Eliza's decisions in life. She adopted the words from Anandibai's application essay as her own. *My soul is moved to help the many who cannot help themselves.* The way to help was to act.

But how? And where?

CHAPTER TWO

A woman strode with purpose toward their office. Her camel-colored linen suit, belted at the waist, fell mid-calf, showing toned muscles from an active life. On the top of her head, a deep chocolate brown felt beret sat at a jaunty angle over a short chestnut bob. A powder blue and dusty rose striped silk scarf wrapped once around her neck, with the ends flowing free down her back, complemented the beret. Her elbow squeezed a leather cream fold-over clutch against her side. A ray of sunshine appeared on the stoop. A gloved hand waved to Eliza in the window.

With a spring in her step, Eliza rose from her desk to open the door.

"Bessie, what a treat! Come in. I'll put on a pot of tea. I've looked forward to hearing about your trip to North Carolina."

"The trip was exhausting. I'd love to tell you more, but maybe later?"

Since graduating from Radcliffe, Bessie Edwards, Eliza's niece, had followed her childhood dream of becoming a journalist. Eight years later, after a string of cub reporter roles, she had joined Lorena Hickok's team of writers working for the Federal Emergency Relief Agency. Bessie Edwards merited her wage of thirty-five dollars a week, delivering fresh perspectives with provocative reports through forceful prose.

Bessie dropped her voice, "I stopped in, hoping you'd be free for an appointment?" she asked.

"I think we can squeeze you in," piped up Olga, having opened her bedroom door when she heard Eliza's exclamation over Bessie's arrival.

Eliza considered her niece's request. Her outward appearance, cheery greeting, and quick remarks revealed no signs of illness. Bessie stayed active with tennis and golf and never over-indulged in sweets, or liquor, or cigarettes, at least to Eliza's knowledge. She didn't need rouge like other girls. Her creamy face bloomed ruddy with health. She loved the belted look of the latest fashions, which accentuated her trim figure, not like so many unfortunate girls with their gaunt bodies, who pressed their noses up to a bakery window, wishing for a single loaf of bread.

Did an illness lurk inside that trim figure? Had Bessie been faithful to Eliza's teachings of how to conduct a self-examination on her breasts? Early detection saved breasts and lives. To this day and forevermore, Eliza regretted that those teachings had come too late for her mother. Eliza whispered beneath her breath, *Dear God, no, please, not my darling.* Losing Olga to New York dealt a blow hard enough to send her reeling. She could not, she would not, consider the possibility that cancer was an inherited gene.

"I've more packing to get done," Olga said. "I'll leave you two alone."

Eliza looked into her niece's soft hazel eyes. How alive they sparkled, filled with anticipation, awaiting her next assignment, and a bright future of promise. She enfolded Bessie in her arms, inhaling the undertones of coconut oil skipping through freshly shampooed locks, and sensing Bessie's steady pulse and even breath.

"Let's sit. Now, tell me. Why do you need an appointment? Is your elbow bothering you again?"

Eliza began her assessment by probing more comfortable areas of inquiry. The tennis-playing members of the Edwards family each suffered from nagging pain after a match. A heavier dosed prescription of aspirin should relieve a returning ache.

"Shoulder is fine, Aunt Eliza, er, Dr. Edwards. In fact, did Will tell you I sent him to his knees in our match last week? Probably not. That son of yours can be a rather poor loser. Such a man. I do, however, need a prescription."

Prescriptions indicated a previous diagnosis. Bessie's spring allergies must be raging. Plumes of pollen had coated car windshields and hoods, streets and sidewalks, and every black wrought-iron railing which graced the Beacon Hill neighborhood like a thin layer of bumblebee dust. She could write Bessie a prescription for amphetamine tablets, the newer form of decongestant on the market.

Bessie continued, "Or, rather, a prescription for a medical item. I need a cap."

"Hmm. I'm guessing by cap, you're not referring to one found mixed in with the felt and fabric softies hat table at Jordan Marsh?"

"No, Aunt Eliza. I'm set with this spring's fashions."

Eliza leaned back in her chair, her eyes widening to see Bessie, no longer the sassy girl with a tea set or an inquisitive teen with a notebook. Firm, full breasts pushed against the bodice of her suit jacket. Her hands lay flat on her thighs, resting gently and relaxed. Confidence gleamed from her eyes, searching for her aunt's reaction. Bess Edwards embodied a modern woman with modern ways. An unmarried woman who wanted a cervical cap.

"Well, I wasn't prepared for this type of conversation. And, thankfully, I guess in some respect, not the symptoms I feared. But I hope you'll tell me your news. Who is he? Have you set the date? Fall weddings are gorgeous. You know, mine was in October. Sprays of asters in every color, garlands of ivy draped along the church pews. I'd offer you my dress, but I doubt the outdated style, or the result of my marriage, sets the tone for the beautiful bride you'll be. Do you know if Harvard allows Radcliffe graduates to use Memorial Church? Cambridge is lovely in the fall..."

"He's married," Bess interrupted.

The pen in Eliza's hand dropped and rolled over the desktop's edge and slipped to the floor.

"I'm sorry to spring this on you. I certainly haven't told my mother, or God forbid, Father. Mother would faint dead away. Dad? He may beat me with a fireplace poker into my bedroom, lock the door, and toss the key out the window. But you, Aunt Eliza. You, I hope, will understand. Jack's a photographer for *Harper's* magazine. FERA wants to send photographers down South, too. He'll be joining me on my Georgia trip."

From her request and the blush on Bess's cheeks, Eliza expected Jack would be doing more than accompanying her on interview rounds.

Bess continued, "Our editors think we're a good team. They suspect nothing. We've been very discreet. We met on assignment last year, covering the aftermath of Black Sunday. Do you remember his photos of Guymon, Oklahoma? The one nearly completely black, with the dust clouds bearing down on a farm? I nearly fainted dead away when I saw that one, knowing how close he had stood to the approaching beast. We learned I can write to what he shoots, and he shoots to what he knows I can write."

"Sounds like you and Jack have a shared eye for what works in a magazine article," said Eliza.

"Oh definitely. But it's more than that. I felt a surge of electricity the moment I met him. It's more powerful than a journalist's sense of time and place; more visceral than a woman's intuition. It's something deeper. A need we both recognized and realized."

She leaned forward in the chair across from her silent aunt. "Please, Aunt Eliza."

Bess's smiling face clouded with worry. The sparkle in her eyes faded. "I can't go through another month looking for a red spot to know my life is mine, and mine alone," she pleaded.

Eliza frowned as the notion of history repeating itself unfolded before her. A woman loving a man who could not commit to her. Eliza knew how a broken heart could change a person. When grief and revenge ceded to impulse and regret. She couldn't bear to think of Bess heading down the same path, making the same mistakes Eliza had made. Perhaps more devastating, what if Bess caught herself in a situation where she'd be left alone, making even greater life-changing decisions.

"Bess, I cannot tell you to stop seeing this man, nor will I preach to you about having sexual relations outside of marriage," Eliza said. "But I'm concerned about your health. If this man is having relations outside of his marriage, how do you know he's not seeing other women? Condoms would be easier and put some responsibility on Jack. They would also protect you from venereal disease."

Bess blanched and stared at the floor. "We have used condoms. But you won't find a Rexall on every corner in the rural South. And safe to say, all those Baptists wouldn't look kindly on stocking them in their local country goods store. I'm trying to be responsible. Honestly, I'm a bit put off you think I would get involved with someone who runs around. I know I'm the only one." She raised her head and looked directly at Eliza. "If you won't help me, I'm sure Olga will."

A well-trained journalist knew the fine art of persuasion. She practiced it daily, ensuring she would glean the information she sought through deep truths. Eliza shook her head. *Well done, Bess. Well done*, she thought.

"Bess, as your doctor, not your aunt, I will fit you for a diaphragm and pick it up from the druggist myself. There's a new pharmacist at Rexall's Drug on Tremont Street. I'll write a prescription for Mrs. Harrison Shaw and forge Harrison's signature on the acknowledgement form."

Eliza stroked her chin, wincing as her fingertip slid over the stubble of hairs which seemed to sprout every morning, despite her nightly plucking assault with tweezers. "On second thought," Eliza paused. "Normally they don't question me, but it's been over a year since I last purchased one on behalf of a patient. I definitely need some root touch-ups. Most men won't ask a woman her age, but let's not give the druggist any reason to question my need for the prescription."

Bess sprang from the chair, radiant with new hope. "You never cease to amaze me, Aunt Eliza. Thank you so much. I knew you'd help. If you'd like, I could pick up a box of Clairol tonight and we can tackle those grays together."

Eliza held up her hand to prevent the approaching embrace. "That's a good idea. However, I need you to do something else for me."

"Anything! Do you need help in choosing a new suit for Teddy's graduation? Of course, you must wear navy blue. We can find one with a broad white collar and wide, red belt. A perfect patriotic mother for our Naval Academy boy."

"I can manage my own shopping," Eliza said curtly. "Just promise me you'll consider whether you'll ever have a future with this man. Don't waste years of your life yearning for someone who may never fully be yours. I don't want your heart broken."

Damn you, Patrick Callahan.

Dr. Patrick Callahan had been the love of Eliza's life. How many nights over the past twenty-four years had she fallen asleep with the memory of his tender touch on her fingers? The way his piercing eyes held her gaze while his hands guided hers through a patient examination. His sympathetic support of her desire to practice medicine, in the same way Bessie's paramour appeared to encourage her journalism career. Those moments had never left Eliza from the day she received a letter from Ireland, announcing he had yielded his sensibilities to the land of his birth. On that day, Eliza let loose with the first of many utterances of: "Damn you, Patrick Callahan."

Bess's eyes widened as she sat up taller. Eliza's candor served her well with her patients, but she rarely spoke freely of anyone with an air of contempt.

"Aunt Eliza," Bess leaned in to place her hand on Eliza's arm. "I never knew. Was there someone before Uncle Harrison? What happened? Who was he?"

"Not today," Eliza said. "Let's not relive the ancient history of a Greek tragedy. All I'll say is, don't pin your future on a man whose other relationships will always have the upper hand and own his heart. It's a battle you'll never win."

CHAPTER THREE

June 1936
En route to Annapolis, Maryland

Train steam hissed into the tunnel, mixing with Eliza's damp eyes. She blinked away the swell of drops. Today was not goodbye, but merely a "see you again soon, my friend." A throng of warm bodies jostled towards the open train doors. Rucksacks and carpetbags bumped against Eliza and Olga, standing on the platform at New York's Pennsylvania Station, two of the few women in sight. The ten o'clock departure would deliver another mass of men to jobs awaiting them in Virginia and points south for the Civilian Conservation Corps.

The conductor called out to the platform. "Newark, Philadelphia, Wilmington, Baltimore, Washington. Final notice. All aboard!"

"All right then, get yourself moving," said Olga as she pushed Eliza back from their embrace. "You've got exciting days ahead. I won't be the cause of your tardiness. You tell our boy Teddy how proud I am of him. And Will. He'd better behave himself. This is his brother's weekend to celebrate."

"I'll give them both your best. You take care of yourself, too. I'll want a full report on your new assignments as soon as you're set up in the lab."

"And I'll want all the details about your talk with Harrison," said Olga, narrowing her eyes into a line of concern as she nodded Eliza toward the train steps.

Eliza's husband, Harrison Shaw, would meet her in Baltimore and drive them to Annapolis for Teddy's graduation ceremony from the Naval Academy. Although she dreaded an hour alone in the car with him, Eliza admitted to herself it would be preferable to a bus ride. His closing remark when they had discussed their travel arrangements, however, had put her on edge. He wanted the time to speak with her *privately*.

Over the past seventeen years of their separation, Eliza had orchestrated distractions when her husband came home from Washington. During the summer, she sent the boys off to Cape Cod with him where he worked for Massachusetts' Congressman Gifford during the House summer hiatus. Harrison kept them busy during the day with sailing regattas and swimming and baseball games in the evening. As they entered their teen years, he secured jobs for them at a local inn as busboys and servers. Eliza filled Christmas vacation week with gatherings at her brothers' homes. She offered an impromptu fraternity house for the boys at her home, while she escaped to stay with her Aunt Florence. The ploy worked. She avoided sharing a bedroom with her husband. Not that he would miss her. He was more likely to be passed out in their marital bed than to reach for her.

Eliza glanced over her shoulder to see Olga's fingers caress a cameo brooch hanging on a short chain at her throat. Eliza swallowed a sob. Her mother had given the gold filigree and ivory carving to Olga on their graduation day from Woman's Med. The gesture had forever endeared them as sisters.

After settling into her seat, she patted her breast pocket to make sure Olga's envelope was safe and secure. Folded inside, Olga had included a gold necklace with a ruby pendant, one of her last heirlooms from Imperial Russia. Before placing them in the envelope, Olga had read the note to Eliza on their last night together. They finessed the words and tone to convey their shared anguish over the crisis facing Woman's Med.

May 25, 1936
Martha Tracy, M.D., Dean
Woman's Medical College of Pennsylvania
1300 Henry Avenue, Philadelphia

Dear Dean Tracy,

As a proud member of the Class of 1901, I wish to send my unwavering support of Woman's Med. We must not allow these economic times and the whims of the AMA's governing board (filled with men) to dictate the future of our esteemed institution. Trying to limit our graduates from positions in favor of hiring men by revoking Woman's Med's membership in the AMA is despicable. I think you know by now, I'm not one to mince words, nor silence my opinion.

Our students work too hard to be denied their rights to an accredited diploma. Therefore, as a means to help contribute to the cause, enclosed you'll find a necklace I have entrusted my dearest friend, Dr. Eliza Edwards, to deliver to you. I hope you can locate an honest jeweler on Sansom Street to give you a fair price. Please do not accept less than five hundred dollars. Unfortunately, many jewelers are gouging sellers during these trying times. This sum should assist in funding another full-time position, which you can present to the AMA as evidence of our commitment to saving our beloved school.

I would like to keep my donation anonymous, but you may share my words and work with current students. Advise them to study everything thoroughly and never stop discovering new fields to explore. There are many ways that they can contribute to those fields, and therein lies progress for all. I look forward to hearing of their success. And, I will be happy, should the occasion arise, to have any one of them join me at the New York Department of

Health in my bacteriology work. The scourge of Disease claims too many. But we will prevail.
    Sincerely yours,
    Olga Povitsky, M.D. '01

Once Eliza arrived at Philadelphia's Broad Street, she would be returning to the city of her birth and childhood. There she had found her passion to become a doctor. In the halls of Woman's Med and West Philadelphia Hospital, she studied and trained, surrounded and supported by those she loved and who loved her. A city which once held the bounties of her life now offered another armful of emptiness, no different from the closed office and empty home she had left behind in Boston. She would stay one night in Philadelphia to squeeze in her appointment with the Dean and to visit Laurel Hill Cemetery.

Too many ghosts skulked the streets of Philadelphia. A college teetering on closure. Classmates scattered to all corners of the country and around the globe. Dead and buried grandparents, parents, and aunts. The grave of her classmate Edith Haskins, whom Eliza's mother had insisted be buried next to Aunt Estelle in the family plot, declaring partners should remain together into eternity. And the dark shadows of lost love from a man who had encouraged her passion to treat and care and who awoke other passions within her.

At Calvert Street Station in Baltimore, Eliza motioned for the Red Cap to leave her valise. The sun's rays bounced against the brown leather case. She shielded her eyes from the glare and peered about the area until she noticed a man standing by the depot's door. His stooped posture carried a heavy and tired look. Yet, his weariness didn't appear as the result of a vigorous tennis match or eighteen holes of golf. The burden lay deeper than mere muscle ache.

She approached him when he lifted his head, giving her a slight nod. His once light brown hair, now gray, lay as thinning wisps against his scalp. Behind his wire-rimmed glasses, Eliza noticed a tint of yellow swimming in his soft brown velvet eyes. A scrap of tissue paper clotted with blood clung to his neck. She assumed he had slapped it on to staunch a shaving nick. In the six months since she had seen him briefly at Christmastime, his disease had surged.

"Harrison," she said. "I really shouldn't have put you out to pick me up in your condition. I could have taken the bus."

He shook his head. "I can manage, Eliza, I'm not in the box yet. Although, I do plan to pick out my plot when I get to Cape Cod next week."

"Honestly, I've never understood how you can make comments like that at the most difficult times," she huffed.

Without waiting for him to reach the door handle, Eliza opened the passenger door, placed her valise in the seat behind her, and slid onto the front seat. Tucking her clutch and doctor's bag on the floor under her feet, she watched Harrison wince, his hands trembling as he gripped the steering wheel. A spasm seized in her heart. The cirrhosis had latched on to his liver, the victim of decades of alcohol abuse. Buried deep in worry, Eliza wondered if blame also lay at her feet. Every time he had staggered home, she ignored or berated him. Her medical training rendered her helpless against alcoholism. When Prohibition began and his stark-raving mad rants scared her, she relented and wrote prescriptions for him to secure his medicinal Bottled-In-Bond whiskey. Did his consumption of one hundred proof Old Hermitage trigger the start of the end? She found little solace that once he was back in Washington after the 1920 winter break, like many other politicians and their staff, he had found bootleggers who kept their liquor cabinets well-stocked. They should shoulder blame, too, she thought.

She softened her tone. "What does your doctor say? Is that what you wanted to discuss?"

"In part," Harrison said, putting the car in gear as it jolted forward. "Dr. Allen has been blunt from the start. I like that in a man. So, I'll be blunt with you, too. He's declared ten months, maybe a year. He suggested I leave my position now and enjoy Cape Cod for the summer. I may not see it next year."

"Oh, Harrison. I'm so, so sorry." She reached for his arm, recalling a moonlit night on a cliff in Newport when he had slid her hand down to encircle his waist and placed his hand on the small of her back. Like the hinged halves of shells on the rocky shore below them, she had thrown her hope of Patrick returning to the churning waves below and walked with Harrison down a dew-covered path, ready to start her life anew.

"I could have read more, seen if there's new research. I know it's not a virus, but I could have asked Olga to investigate it for us. I could have found a Woman's Med alumnus who specializes in liver disease."

"What's done is done. At this point, I only want to address my regrets and make them right."

Eliza considered the plea she expected in his next breath. Only a frigid, heartless woman would deny a dying man the right to bare his soul and confess his mistakes. She pulled forth the memories of happier days. She heard laughter in her sons' voices as they tussled with their father, building Lincoln Log cabins and painting sailboats by the Charles River. She saw PAID on the tuition bills for boarding school and Will's college. Her fingers spun the gold wedding band on her left hand. She had never removed it in all the time that they had lived apart, divorced from a marriage, but not on paper.

"You'll come home to Boston with me," she said. "Then we'll look for a spot to rent on Cape Cod. I must admit I've been envious all these years, listening to the boys when they came home, raving about the beaches, clambakes, badminton, sailing on the Sound…"

The car slowed as Harrison veered it to the road's shoulder. He placed it in park, dropping his head on the steering wheel.

"Eliza," he said, his voice strangled and low. "What I wanted to discuss with you has nothing to do with you becoming my wife again. I want a divorce. I want to finish out my days with the woman who's been my confidante and companion for twelve years. I want to marry her. She's already said yes."

Cars whizzed by them on the highway. In the distance, beyond a split-rail fence, young shoots of corn undulated in a gentle flow on a summer's light breeze. A wave moved up Eliza's body, surging as it gained power from her heart. His words clogged her ears. Her shoulders shuddered. She must have misheard him. While she held no misconceptions that Harrison had flings in Washington, the idea that he had one woman in his life for the past twelve years played her as the fool.

Blood coursing its way upward settled in her cheeks. An uncontrollable rage gripped her senses as she flung open the car door. "Eliza, wait," Harrison said, reaching for her arm.

Eliza wrenched away from him.

"Wait? Wait for what? Waiting's been my mistake."

She had remained in her limbo marriage for sixteen years. Being a mother meant protecting Will and Teddy at all costs, including from the shame and dishonor which a divorce would bring upon a family. Columnists at *The Boston Globe* would relish reports of a prominent Boston couple's divorce. Hushed talk among her sons' friends and their parents would lurk on the edges of conversations. Parents did not divorce. They set examples of mutual respect and marital bliss. They stayed true to love, even after death. Boys needed to become men before they could endure headlines and whispers.

"I need some air," Eliza said, stepping out of the car. She headed toward the farm fence. Barriers placed before her had always summoned an inner resolve to jump over those fences. She had learned that lesson from her Aunt Florence, *Fearless Florence*, as she and her brothers had called their aunt. Overhead, a crow cawed as if claiming his row of corn to the others who flew behind him. Eliza rolled up the sleeves of her cotton dress and leaned atop the rough-hewn, weathered gray railing. Small splinters rubbed against her bare arms. Gazing out to the field filled with green stalks reaching for the sky, she collected her thoughts. Harrison may have started the conversation about divorce, but Eliza would claim her destiny and end it on her terms.

CHAPTER FOUR

June 1936
Boston, Massachusetts

After Teddy's graduation, Eliza returned to Boston with clear intentions. Today, Monday, June 29, 1936, in the Suffolk County Court, a family law and probate judge dissolved the marriage of Mr. and Mrs. Harrison Shaw. With Harrison's agreement, Eliza filed a claim that his past seventeen years in Washington constituted utter desertion. No news reporter would cover an inconsequential case which lacked the jazz of infidelity or intoxication as fodder for headlines.

The reality of the end of her marriage arrived with signatures at the bottom of a piece of paper. Her terms outlined simple requests. They would equally divide proceeds from the sale of their Mount Vernon Street home, along with its contents. Her new two-bedroom residence on the North Slope of Beacon Hill may lack grandeur and prestige, but made up for any of its shortcomings with the homey and welcoming comfort of living with her Aunt Florence. Eliza chose Number Five Smith Court for its location. At seventy-eight, Florence enjoyed visiting the West End Settlement House a quarter of a mile away. While her palsy kept her from teaching her painting classes, she enjoyed daily visits to read to the young children and critique the art students' work. Eliza would also be able to cover expenses until she secured permanent employment. What that position might be, where, and who would hire a fifty-seven-year-old woman doctor, eluded her. Living near Massachusetts General Hospital gave her hope that the proximity could be a talisman of good luck.

Upon exiting the granite courthouse in Pemberton Square, Harrison gestured toward The Parker House. "Care for a slice of pie? Nothing like dessert before dinner to take the edge off an unpleasant afternoon."

A slight smile spread across Eliza's lips. They had spent many evenings at The Parker House when Harrison courted her, promising a future as creamy and dreamy as the Boston Cream Pie's rich filling. One slice wouldn't hurt her thickened waistline. When menopause had hit, she increased the length of her daily walks to no avail in the fight against decreased hormones and metabolism.

"That would be nice, but isn't Helen waiting for you?" asked Eliza. Although she loathed saying the woman's name without a curse linked to it, Eliza accepted the existence of Helen Warner, the woman Harrison wanted by his side for his final days. Helen's position as a lawyer, a novelty as uncommon as a woman doctor, provided pure irony to the situation. Harrison's opposition to a woman's professional work apparently did not apply to women without children.

Harrison checked his watch. "I'll make the time."

Eliza slowed to match his labored pace as they turned onto Tremont Street. To their right, the Boston Common dozed in the summer heat. Eliza noted couples strolling the walkways, arms linked, and faces tilted in for private conversations. Despite the release from school weeks earlier, however, few children scampered through the fountains' spray, seeking relief from the humid afternoon. Nor did any cluster together in circles of *Duck, Duck, Goose*, tapping one another's heads or calling *send Johnny right over* to break through ropes of clasped hands in games of Red Rover.

Summer had descended on the city, playing on a parent's fear. Poliomyelitis. The prior summer, polio cases had spiked with sixty-one deaths in Boston. Eliza had sent silent thanks heavenward that year and others before then that her sons had spent their summers on Cape Cod with Harrison. Will and Teddy, away from the city, swam in well-circulated ocean tides, not stagnant city pools or rural swimming holes. They escaped the plague of the crippling virus which had attacked thousands, including a classmate of Will's, leaving the boy forever sidelined from stickball games and tennis matches. Will had told his mother the boy's leg brace was as bulky and ominous as Jacob Marley's chains. She had admonished Will for his gloom and told him his friend needed his support now more than ever.

Inside Parker's Restaurant, a tuxedo-clad maître d' seated Harrison and Eliza at a back corner table. Eliza welcomed the privacy, enhanced by the dark mahogany paneling on the walls and the cool stream blowing down from the overhead air-conditioning vent. A meal at Parker's, one of the few establishments which had installed air conditioning units, was worth the high price for relief on a stifling Boston summer day. Before the maître d' could beckon a waiter, Eliza ordered two slices of the restaurant's signature pie, coffee for Harrison and sherry for herself. He pulled her chair out, his jaundiced hand shaking like the palsy in Aunt Florence's aged, arthritic ones.

"Have you heard from Teddy?" Harrison asked as the waiter poured coffee into the gold-rimmed, cobalt blue china cup.

Eliza re-pinned her Panama-style hat, fingering the grosgrain ribbon at the hat's base before she tugged the wavy brim into a dip over her right eye. A wide brim provided enough of a shield to hide the glimmer in her eye. She had heard from Teddy. Her pride swelled to know that he corresponded with her regularly, more so than with his father.

"They made it to Guantanamo in five days, as expected. He noted he's sent you a box of cigars. They should catch up with you on the Cape by next week. Sounds like the *Mississippi* is in fine shape after her refitting in Newport News. Guess we'll have to trust those shipbuilders," Eliza said. She paused, picking up the crystal cordial glass of sherry. The orange-gold liqueur danced on her tongue, its hints of apples and raisins tart against the sweetness of the pie.

She continued, "I'm quite anxious though about the trip through the Canal. They won't let them off the ship, do you think? The malaria rages down there. I can't imagine those flimsy mosquito nets do much good. I wish they'd hurry with the research of that new chloroquine I've read about. If he's going to be stationed with the Pacific fleet for a while, it's imperative that they find better treatments, or preventative measures."

Scooping a bite of pie onto his fork, Harrison smirked. "Eliza. Our son is not the first Navy man in jungle environs. If you can trust the shipbuilders, trust the brass that they won't put our men in any unnecessary danger, including Ensign Edward Shaw."

"I suppose you're right this time," she winked.

As the hour wore on, the ornate crystal chandeliers sparkled, spreading their light across the room. "It's getting late," Eliza said, reaching for her purse.

"Yes, of course, but I have one other item I wanted to mention to you. Five more minutes?"

Now what? she thought. Beyond their sons, with the ink dry on the divorce papers, what else needed discussion? Would he have the gall or idiocy to invite her to his wedding next week? She re-settled in her chair and drained the final drop of sherry.

"I understand you have no immediate employment plans. Have you thought of retiring?"

Before she could shudder at the mention of the dreaded word, *retirement*, Harrison interrupted her thoughts, "Or might you be interested in a special case?"

Over the course of Eliza's years of medical practice, Harrison rarely asked about her work. He had preferred to interact with

Mrs. Harrison Shaw, or Will and Teddy's mother, not Dr. Eliza Edwards, as she presented herself to her patients. Eliza leaned in towards him, the small table cleared of the pie plates.

"What type of special case?" She emphasized *special*, suppressing the horrid idea that Helen, the new wife, needed maternity care.

With a chuckle deep in his throat, he laughed as she dropped her eyes to her lap. "Seriously now, you don't think this feeble man has much left in him for that type of extra-curricular activity, do you? No, it's not I nor Helen who needs your services. It's Congressman Morrison. Or rather, his daughter. She's expecting her first child, Morrison's first grandchild. They're all thrilled, of course. They were, that is, until she contracted polio last month. Her right leg is completely paralyzed."

"Oh, how dreadful, the poor thing!" Eliza exclaimed. First time pregnancies escalated worries for any woman, but the clutch of poliomyelitis ratcheted fear to a whole new level of anxiety. "Morrison," she pondered. "Isn't he the Black man from Chicago? A city like Chicago has plenty of fine doctors; I expect even Negro ones. Why would they need my services?"

"Congressman Morrison has arranged for the absolute best care for Kay. But the polio causes an ugly wrinkle. She's just started her fourth month, so it's safe enough for her to travel. He'd like her to go to Warm Springs. He hopes the treatments might help her out of the wheelchair. He wants a trained maternity doctor to accompany her. Someone to monitor the pregnancy and consult with the therapists. He can't find anyone in Chicago. Either they don't want to leave their practice, or they don't want to step foot in Georgia. I thought of you. He'll pay you well and will cover all your travel and lodging expenses."

Typical Harrison. Dropping a bombshell when Eliza thought she was done with him. Yet, the image of this congressman's daughter flashed before her. A young woman paralyzed by fear in her mind and her legs. A mother-to-be seeking the power to strengthen her body before its most arduous labor and job began. A father wanting to help his daughter through any means available to him to give her a full life.

Then another image in her mind crowded the young woman aside. An older woman, gray streaks invading her auburn hair, a doctor sitting idle in an empty office, staring out a window. A letter opener lay on the desk next to her, waiting for letters—any form of communication and connection. The hand-carved oak opener, etched with a North Star design, had been a gift from Daniel Dangerfield, a runaway slave whom Eliza's grandfather had defended in court to win his freedom. When her grandfather spoke of the opener, he reminded Eliza and her brothers of his defense work for men like Dangerfield by stating, *Those that have, and can, must care for the defenseless and the powerless, for they have no one else.*

"When do they need me?"

CHAPTER FIVE

July 1936
Warm Springs, Georgia

Atrickle of sweat pooled between Eliza's breasts. She wriggled against the vinyl train seat as she lifted a lock of hair off her neck and let it fall. Between the humidity and reading two-hundred pages of Margaret Mitchell's instant bestseller, the pull on her eyelids tempted her to rest. Ten more minutes before they'd reach the station. She'd have to pick up her pace. Her inquiring mind needed to know. What awaited Scarlett O'Hara in Atlanta?

"Warm Springs!" the conductor announced, passing down the aisle of the first-class passenger car. *Gone with the Wind* would have to wait.

Eliza disembarked at the small clapboard station, walking straight into a Georgia oven, its coils searing every inch of exposed skin, from her cheeks to her wrists. She stood alone, waiting for Kay Morrison Clark and her husband, John. Squinting into the noon-day sun, she caught movement at the end of the cars. A conductor placed a wooden ramp against the edge of the baggage car's doorway. Eliza left her bags by the bench and headed toward the rear of the train. Tall, broad-shouldered, and as hale as any young man in the prime of his life, John Clark jumped to the platform with a valise in each hand. His linen suit fell in wrinkles.

He placed the bags down and hopped back up into the car. Walking backward down the ramp, he guided a wheelchair. Kay, in a cream gossamer dress dotted with blue delphiniums and loose at the waist to cover her small bump, grasped the armrests of the chair. A thin cotton coverlet lay across her lap and draped over her legs. It took them several minutes to cross the short platform, as John pushed the chair and juggled the valises.

"Please, let me help," said Eliza, gesturing for the smaller suitcase, which John willingly ceded to her outstretched hand.

"I'm so sorry," she said. "I wish I had pressed that conductor in Atlanta. His behavior is inexcusable. Placing you in the baggage car. There is absolutely no risk of contagion. I'll be sending a letter off to Southern Railway tomorrow morning with the conductor's name and his repulsive treatment of you well noted."

Kay shook her head with a slight toss. Her blue hat with a skimmer of an ivory veil bobbed against her dark waves. "Dr. Edwards, we appreciate your concern, but my polio has nothing to do with him putting us there. It's not the first time we've met someone like him. I daresay, here in Georgia, you can't throw a rock without coming close to hitting a man like him."

"You learn how and when to pick a battle, Ma'am," John added. "He wasn't worth either of our time or trouble. We're just grateful to Mr. Morrison for securing a spot for Kay. He won't admit it, but I'd bet a shiny dime he finagled a meeting with Roosevelt himself. Only the President could direct Warm Springs to make an exception. They have had no other Black patients, nor staff that we know of. There's been talk of starting a center at Tuskegee, but Lord knows when or where they'll find the funding."

When Harrison had told her about Kay, Eliza focused on the care she could provide for a pregnant woman. John's comments about the segregation issue at Warm Springs made Eliza think she might have to contribute more than fetal monitoring. Kay would require a physical therapist to work with her daily. If the staff refused to help a Black woman, they might ask Eliza to assist. In that moment of realization, Eliza acknowledged Harrison knew she would have no qualms in treating a Black woman. At the settlement houses of Boston's West and South Ends, Eliza had never shied away from caring for the patients who came to her: African, Lebanese, Chinese, Slavic, and others from around the world. Treating them brought her joy and purpose.

But physical therapy? She lacked any training in the specialty. She would have to learn on the job. Worse yet, would she have to wear a bathing suit to accompany Kay into the pools? Eliza glanced down at her pear-shaped body. The days of her shapely figure had slipped away as slowly as the sand in those hourglasses.

Kay interrupted Eliza's thoughts of body shape despair. "The train ride wasn't a complete disaster. My brilliant architect husband fashioned a comfortable chaise from a pile of carpetbags. Pray that the passengers don't catch wind that a Black polio patient had lounged against them for two hours."

John winked at her. "And, you know I saw you squirming your lovely backside deep into that pink floral bag. What I wouldn't give to see that lady's face if she had seen you!"

The Clarks were a delightful young couple. And Kay presented herself with confidence; smart and just sassy enough Eliza hoped to get her through the tough days that lie ahead.

The car sent by the Center turned the corner into the driveway of the 1,200-acre campus built by the Warm Springs Foundation. A quiet rural town, known for its country inns and Victorian-styled mansions, the site had transformed into the country's preeminent treatment center for poliomyelitis victims. At the top of a quad, Eliza caught sight of Georgia Hall. The U-shaped building with its white pillared entrance was the obvious hub of activity.

Inside, John rapped on the glass barrier at the front office. A young woman paused her typing and slid it aside two inches.

"I assume this is Kay?" Her eyes narrowed as she looked straight at Kay's placid, caramel colored face.

"I am Mrs. John Clark," she said.

"You're in Hilliard Cottage. Your appointment with the director of physical therapy, Miss Cleveland, is at three o'clock. You can unpack and rest. Your man can deliver your suitcases and then walk back to the train."

With Kay and John too stunned to respond, Eliza stepped in closer to the woman's desk. "I'm Dr. Edwards. I'm attending to Mrs. Clark while she's here. And this gentleman is Mr. Clark. If you would kindly point us in the right direction, he'll see Mrs. Clark to her cottage and then will be back with her for the appointment and dinner. His train isn't until this evening. I'm sure you can call a car for him."

The secretary jerked her head and nodded towards Eliza. "Fine, fine, but they'll take their dinner in the cottage. There's a phone in Miss Cleveland's office. Here's a campus map and a list of men who might drive him." She slipped a folded map and scrap of paper through the window.

As she waved them off, she paused, "Wait, did you say you're Dr. Edwards? There must be a mistake. The doctors' apartments are out of the question. And the nurses and physical therapists' rooms are filled." She lowered her chin and muttered, "I expected problems with this arrival, although you're not the one I expected."

"Excuse me?" Eliza demanded.

The woman ignored Eliza's inquiry. "Let me ring for the campus bus, then I'll deal with figuring out where you'll stay." She slid the glass divider shut with a snap.

To Kay and John, Eliza said, "Hmm. The genteel Southern hospitality everyone talks about skipped this one. Kay, you should lie down for a bit."

"Yes, Doctor Ma'am," Kay grinned and added, "Welcome to Georgia. Home of pecans, peaches, and petty peons."

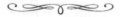

Eliza wandered into the dining room, eager to see where she'd heard patients sat alongside the President for annual Thanksgiving dinners. Seated at the head of a long banquet table, he carved turkeys, to the delight of the children seated around him who affectionately called him "Rosey". He didn't correct them. What a shame Kay's December due date would send her and Eliza home before Thanksgiving. Imagine! Meeting the President and Mrs. Roosevelt over a plate of turkey legs and mashed potatoes. That would be a story to tell her grandchildren someday.

A large stone fireplace gave the large room a rustic feel, despite the marble mantel above it and the engraved plaque hanging next to it. The plaque listed the names of donors who had raised more than $100,000 to build the Hall three years ago, marking it as a place for patients to *leave with bodies improved, but also with strengthened characters, a determination to rise when they fall, and to carry on despite all handicaps; a spirit of cheerfulness, of self-reliance and confidence which is an inspiration to all mankind.* Those afflicted with polio were girls and boys, teens, and young adults on the cusp of life. Their struggle struck them down. Warm Springs sought to raise them up. Eliza's hands may have age spots and the creep of wrinkles from loose skin, but they were still confident and strong. The words on the plaque filled Eliza with a new sense of purpose. She would eagerly learn, without fear, new ways to practice her trade.

Four teenaged girls sat at a square table near the dining room's entrance. Wide aisles between tables provided clear paths for push-boys to wheel patients in for their meals three times a day and afternoon recreation time. The girls' high cane-backed wheelchairs tucked in tight to the table's edge. A draped tablecloth covered their limp, atrophied legs. Giggling and slapping their cards down, they looked like any other animated foursome found at an afternoon bridge game. As Eliza passed them on her way to the dining room's coffee service in the back corner, one girl with a spray of sandy curls tied back by two red satin ribbons tossed her head, declaring, "Priscilla, did you tuck that ace down your dress? It's a wonder Mac didn't find it last night."

Three sets of eyes sparkled before they all laughed. The titter and teasing heartened Eliza. At home, the girls' peers would have shunned them, fearful that the polio virus would jump and strike them down, too. In the embrace of Warm Springs, paralyzed limbs no longer isolated them. Here they found companions and friends. It was normal to be different.

After pouring herself a cup of strong, black coffee, Eliza paused to peek over the shoulder of the girl with the sandy curls. "You'll want to play two hearts," Eliza whispered in the girl's ear.

The girl stiffened in her chair. Her shoulders hunched as if she was trying to ward off Eliza's nearness. Walking away, Eliza heard the muffled remarks.

"I heard she's the lady who arrived with the Negro."

"Whoever heard of a colored having her own nurse, and a White lady to boot? What's wrong with her?"

"Let's hope Miss Cleveland doesn't put them in our cottage."

The girl, Priscilla, said, "She wouldn't dare. I'll call my parents as fast as Mac can push me to the phone carrel. My mother will be fit to be tied if she hears there's a colored in my cottage."

Eliza realized now that the patients and staff who hailed from rural Georgia towns would make sure there was no bed available for her, the woman who tended to the colored woman. For Miss Cleveland's purposes, if she placed Eliza in Hilliard Cottage with Kay, she would dispel any rumors that the Foundation had built a cabin just for Negro polio victims, as Eleanor Roosevelt had suggested. Construction of such a cabin would not be desirable in Georgia, the Foundation had told Mrs. Roosevelt. The Foundation, and Eliza, would do their best to avoid any racial unrest within the small community and its small-mindedness.

CHAPTER SIX

August 1936

Ⅰn the month that Eliza had been at Warm Springs, she quickly
settled into a routine. Mornings began early with two-hour
sessions in the pools at six-thirty, before any other patients
arrived from breakfast. Upon learning of how long Kay would be
in the hot springs-fed pool, Eliza voiced her concerns. The
maintenance man, however, assured her that the temperature
remained at a constant eighty-eight degrees, well below the one
hundred mark which may be unsafe for a pregnant woman. Eliza
bit her tongue when she heard him add as an aside, "And the
constant water flow works well to flush out any impurities a
patient may leave." He would know the polio patients wouldn't
transmit any contagions by the time they arrived at Warm Springs.
Eliza knew the man meant any impurities a Black woman may
leave.

At first, the private sessions to keep Kay apart from the other
patients irked Eliza, until she realized the benefits, despite the
blatant display of segregation. With one-on-one therapy with Miss
Cleveland, Kay could focus on the slow and consistent efforts she
needed to strengthen her legs. She avoided the glaring stares and
behind the hand remarks about her dark skin mingling in the same
waters as the other patients. Eliza also welcomed the solitude to
hide her own body. Clad in the standard, black Lastex swimsuit

which stressed every bulge and roll, Eliza looked more like a woman in her fifth month of pregnancy than did the fit and trim Kay. A bump the size of a small cantaloupe pushed against the confines of Kay's suit.

After accompanying Kay to a fitting for her custom leg braces, Eliza waited in the pool building, next to the workshop. A group of twelve women toweled off after a pool session. The "physios", as Eliza learned the recent graduates of Peabody College liked to be called, reminded Eliza of her classmates at Woman's Med. Their eyes shone with an eager determination to put their study into practice. Each one had answered Roosevelt's call for pioneers. Through tireless hours, they taught children and adults how to stand and walk with their dignity and self-esteem restored. Snippets of their conversations drifted toward her.

A tall brunette, her face glowing with satisfaction from the morning exertions, said, "I have the most darling little girl. She clung tight around my neck as I lowered her into the pool, saying, 'Why Miss, I love floating! It's ever so much better than what Momma tried to help me feel good.' Do you know what the poor mother had done? Covered the sweet one in dew-laden peach leaves and tied cloth-wrapped sliced onions to the bottom of her feet."

"Your patient sounds adorable. The teenage boy I have is a handful," said another. "You'd think he would be grateful after a year in an iron lung. I'm not sure he'll ever move beyond that horror. His rage simmers just beneath the surface every minute. He tenses his muscles while I try to soothe him, making the flexibility exercises doubly difficult. One of his friends told me that when he was in the hospital, a nurse had said to him, 'Stop crying or I'll turn it off.' The collar of the lung had rubbed his neck raw down to the bone. It still hasn't healed completely. I've got my work cut out with him to earn his trust."

The brunette, tossing her wet hair to and fro for air drying, noticed Eliza on the pool chaise. "Excuse, ma'am? What time do they serve lunch? They told us at orientation yesterday, but they threw so much information at us, we forgot the most important."

The woman next to her said, "Please tell me it's soon. I'm starving!"

"You're in luck," Eliza said. "They keep a strict schedule here. Twelve noon on the button up at Georgia Hall. I saw you all working in the pool this morning. I'm sure you're ravenous."

"Thanks so much, Missus..." the first girl said.

"Dr. Edwards," replied Eliza.

The group turned in unison, their eyes wide and mouths parted in a row of O's.

"Surprised?" Eliza said with a soft smile.

The brunette stammered. "I'm so sorry. I just assumed you worked in the office. I mean, you're not wearing a white coat like the other doctors, and you're not..."

"A man? No need to apologize. I know we're still as rare as snowfall in Georgia on a July day." Eliza winked. "Especially down here in the South. Most of the medical schools which admit women are up in Philadelphia, Boston, and New York."

The second woman piped in, "I think it's wonderful! I wish we had women doctors in Tennessee. I'd love to hear more. Do you work exclusively with polio patients? Are you looking more at treatments, causes, or preventative measures? Can you join us for lunch? Is that allowed? Doctors and physios? Oh, by the way, I'm Trudy."

The rest of the women followed Trudy's lead and introduced themselves. Eliza did the same as she explained her role at Warm Springs and her one-on-one work with Kay.

"Wait, you live in Hilliard Cottage?" said Trudy.

"Yes. It's a trek to the dining hall, but after living in a city my whole life, I find the air refreshing. Well, except on the days when it's thick enough to drink. How do you bear it?"

The woman who had introduced herself as Louise said, "Ma'am, we know where Hilliard Cottage is. It's just, well, you're living with the Negro woman? You're caring for her?"

Eliza narrowed her eyes. "Yes. Mrs. Clark is a lovely woman. She's my patient. Of course, I'm caring for her." Eliza had been drawn to these young women, thinking that they were like her and her classmates, professionals committed to caring for their patients. Yet, they were no different than the girls at the bridge game or the secretary in the reception office.

"You all work with the polios, the cripples which society has shunned. How is my tending to Mrs. Clark any different? We've been called to care for others." She leveled her eyes at Trudy and Louise. "Paralyzed limbs and skin color make no difference."

Riled by Louise's petty peon comment, as Kay would have called it, Eliza stooped to pick up her bag. "Well Mrs. Clark's appointment should be wrapping up and she'll need me to push her to the cottage. Good day, ladies."

Trudy and Louise lowered their heads and slipped their bare feet into sandals. A third girl placed her hand on Eliza's arm. "Dr. Edwards, can you join me this evening after dinner? I'd love to talk to you some more about how you're managing Mrs. Clark's therapy sessions and the complications with her pregnancy."

Eliza allowed herself a quiet smile. "Thank you. Vera, was it? I'd be happy to if you might help me? Miss Cleveland expects me to take over Mrs. Clark's pool sessions soon. I'm really at a loss. I've taken copious notes, but I'm afraid I'm going to hurt Kay more than I help her. Could I pick your brains a bit?"

"Yes, we can help," Trudy interjected. "Imagine that. Us the teachers, and you the student."

"At my age, no less," Eliza said.

Eliza's meeting with the twelve physios became part of her daily routine. Pool time with Kay in the morning. Breakfast at Georgia Hall, emptied after the rest of the patients attended their morning therapy sessions. Rest time. Kay's afternoon flexibility and walking exercises. Lunch and dinner at the cottage. Review sessions in the evening when they compared notes on their patients' progress and roadblocks. The physios listened as Eliza asked for clarifications on how to manipulate Kay's legs while minimizing the pain. For maximum effect, they demonstrated each method, asking Eliza to stand in as the patient, and then the therapist. In turn, Eliza shared with them her cases in Philadelphia and leading mother-baby wellness classes at the settlement houses, and finally, her thrill of running a practice with Olga.

"I am forever grateful for those years. We gained a modest level of respect throughout Boston, from our patients, their husbands, and even Massachusetts General. It only took six months to convince them to grant us admitting rights. We achieved as much as one could expect from a women's practice," Eliza told them one night in late August as they gathered in a corner of Georgia Hall for their evening session.

"Of course, I also wore my mother hat during those years. Trudy, you were right. Boys are a handful! They never tell you what they're thinking or feeling."

Eliza sighed. In the past six weeks she'd been in Warm Springs, she'd received one short note from Teddy and no news from Will. "Then again, maybe I wasn't approachable. I can't think how many times I feigned interest in Will's endless play-by-play recaps of Boston Red Sox games. Teddy drove me crazy with his constant pleas to visit the garage down the street so he could watch the mechanics fix an engine."

Louise interrupted. "I can't blame you. My guy, Joe, only reads the sports pages. But, really, Dr. Edwards, you're probably a great mother. And I bet your boys are proud of you, even if they don't say it."

"I suppose they are. And don't get me wrong; they're wonderful young men. I'm proud of them, too. So, who would like to be introduced to two kind, smart, hard-working, eligible bachelors. And, I'd say they're quite handsome, too."

Eliza pointed around the circle. "Trudy? Vera? Nancy...?"

Each day, with Eliza supporting Kay's back, Kay lengthened her body, pushing the soles of her feet against the smooth tiles of the pool. After their sessions, Kay shared how, with each press, she felt her hamstrings relax as the soothing warm water massaged her thighs. When she spoke of how the excruciating pains which continually shot through her legs and up her spine dissolved into the bliss of the water, Eliza teared up. This dear young woman swam toward strength and serenity. She would need both for motherhood.

They took their breakfast late in the empty dining room, followed by a brief rest at the cottage. Not allowed in the main gymnasium, Kay's exercises moved outside to the shade of the giant oaks and pines dotting the postage stamp-sized backyard area. At the request of and with payment from Kay's father, workers installed a narrow, twenty-foot wooden ramp, bracketed by parallel bars set to a comfortable height for Kay's hands to grasp. Her jellylike body jerked forward in a repetitive pattern: grip the bar, throw her body forward, drag, fling, and scuffle each foot ahead in a lurching step-by-step advance.

By the seventh week, Kay managed ten successive steps without holding the bars. Eliza watched from a chair set beneath the pine canopy, a fan in her hand. Kay called out, "I did it! Did you see?"

"Brava! Brava!" Eliza clapped.

Kay picked up the crutches at the end of the ramp and headed toward the chair next to Eliza, who sang out the words from one of her favorite poems from her school days, *Invictus*, by William Ernest Henley. She may have been off-key, but her sentiment rang true.

It matters not how strait the gate, how charged with
punishments the scroll,
I am the master of my Fate,
I am the Captain of my Soul.

"You are a marvel, Kay. I'm so proud of you. You are Invictus."

CHAPTER SEVEN

L aughter spilled from the dining room. Lunchtime at Georgia Hall brought the residents together as they dug into protein-packed meals, set on tables covered in starched white linen. Eliza eyed the heaping portions of a bacon, bean, and tomato casserole on blue porcelain plates. Smoky, savory scents from the bacon mixed with earthy, sweet tomatoes tingled Eliza's nose and taste buds. She peeked inside the brown bag in her hand. Two squares of wax-paper wrapped sandwiches and an apple. She hoped she would find a scoop of egg or ham salad with chunks of chopped celery between the white bread.

Before exiting the Hall, Eliza emptied the bag onto a side table near the reception area. For too many lunches, she and Kay had been served different meals than the rest of the patients, like yesterday's slipshod concoction of corn, cooked with local Vidalia onions, and thickened tomato sauce. She peeled back the paper and removed a slice of buttered bread. Today's slop revealed layers of cottage cheese, mayonnaise, and shredded carrots topped with pickles. Her jaw clenched. She crunched the bag into a ball. *Enough*, she thought. Kay deserved a plate of bacon, beans and tomatoes as much as any other resident. Perhaps more so. She worked as hard as any of them with her exercises and therapy sessions. She also had to nourish a growing child.

Kitchen staff paused from their tasks when Eliza pushed through a set of swinging doors. She held up the crumpled paper bag.

"I'd like to speak to whomever is in charge here," she said.

An older, plump woman lifted her head from concentrating on sizzling green tomato slices in a large frying pan. A long, mousy brown braid wound its way at the nape of her neck, held in place by netting. She lowered the flame under the pan.

"We do not allow visitors in the kitchen," she said.

Eliza squared her shoulders and strode over to her. "I am not a visitor. I'm Dr. Edwards, the doctor caring for Mrs. Clark. The one who gets sent these intolerable and unacceptable meals." She thrust the bag toward the cook.

"Who told you to prepare less appealing, less nutritious meals for Mrs. Clark? It doesn't matter. I'm here to tell you it ends today. If not, this afternoon's out-going mail will include a letter to Mrs. Roosevelt. She will be most interested in learning that the only Negro patient here receives a different menu."

The woman's stunned face slacked. She mumbled to a line cook, who pulled two plates from the rack and ladled out extra-large servings of the casserole. A fork speared four cooked tomatoes. She added them to the side of the plates and covered them with wax paper. The cook handed the plates to Eliza. "I just do as I'm told, Ma'am. But I'll report your request. No one wants Mrs. Roosevelt marching in here."

Eliza nodded in satisfaction. If you wanted something done, best to leave it to a woman. Even if it meant dropping the name of the First Lady. She sniffed at the tomatoes as she exited. Ah, a special treat. Twice, over the past eight weeks, she had dined at the restaurant downtown, where she acquired a taste for the tangy and sweet rounds of fried green tomatoes. She had asked the server how they made them crispy on the outside and gooey on the inside. The Warm Springs native extracted a promise from Eliza not to divulge their Southern secret. "Cut the slices into thick slabs, then dip them in a beaten egg. Dredge them through a mixture of cornmeal, salt, and cayenne pepper. May take two or three swipes to fully coat them. Then *always* fry 'em in bacon grease. None of that lard stuff off the grocer's shelf."

Kay thanked Eliza ten different times for addressing the meal situation, as she smacked her lips with the last bite of tomato. After their pleasurable lunch, Eliza took Kay's pulse and listened for the baby's heartbeat. Assured all was well, she removed Kay's clunky leg braces and settled her in for a nap. The southern swelter continued, sending Eliza to Georgia Hall's large common room. The Hall had benefited from the work of the Tennessee Valley Authority, which brought more affordable electricity to rural areas and sent electric fans whirring nonstop.

The demands of her schedule had taken her away from *Gone with the Wind*. She was desperate to return to the story and escape into Scarlett and Rhett's fiery and tantalizing tête-à-tête. Eliza chose a tufted chair and ottoman close to a window in case any breeze visited for a breath of fresh air in the stale room. As she turned to her bookmarked page, the receptionist waved to her from the doorway.

"Mizzus Edwards."

Why, pray tell, couldn't the woman remember to call her Dr. Edwards? She raised her hand, signaling her acknowledgement, despite her annoyance.

"Yes, Miss Goodman. Do you need me?" Eliza said.

"No, it's just you had a phone call. I sent a boy down to the cottage, but he didn't find you. I couldn't keep the line on hold. That's quite expensive."

Eliza winced. She'd received letters from Olga and Aunt Florence, her classmate, Charlotte Fairbanks, and even a couple from Bess, and one more from Teddy alerting her of their passage through the Panama Canal. But no phone calls.

"Who was it?"

"Your son. Bill?"

A sense of dread rose from her stomach to her chest to a catch in her throat. Will. She had had no news from him.

"Will," she answered. "The gentleman must have said his name was Will. May I use Miss Cleveland's phone to return the call? I'd appreciate the privacy. We have an ill family member. I fear there may be terrible news. And I'll place it collect."

Miss Goodman cocked her head. "That's really not done. Miss Cleveland isn't the tidiest of ladies. There are patient folders and documents everywhere. I need a good half an hour to organize her chaos."

"I'm a doctor, Miss Goodman. Surely, you've heard of doctor-patient confidentiality. I would never read or reveal any information within those files."

"Fine," she scoffed. "I'll get the key. You'll need to be quick. Miss Cleveland has a four o'clock appointment and she'll be back from the pools shortly."

Inside, Eliza scanned the desk for the phone. Miss Goodman hadn't joked about the mess. Beneath a splayed newspaper and progress reports, Eliza unearthed the chunky black Bakelite phone.

Will's secretary, Phyllis, accepted the collect charges. "Mr. Shaw's office."

"Phyllis. Is he in? I'm returning his call."

"Oh, Dr. Edwards. Hello. How is Georgia? It must be dreadfully hot. We've had a spell of it…"

"Phyllis, can you put me through, dear?" Eliza interrupted before Phyllis could ask about what she'd eaten for lunch. The casual, meandering conversation at least implied that Harrison had not passed, which had been Eliza's first thought. While a bit daft at times, in Eliza's opinion, Phyllis had proper manners and would have expressed her condolences, even over an ex-husband, before she prattled on about the weather.

On the other end, Will's voice faltered. "Mother?"

His one word sent Eliza reeling. Distress in his voice traveled a thousand miles, picking up speed as its sound waves pulsed through wires strung from pole to pole, inching toward her. Her strong, confident, larger-than-life, rambunctious boy needed his mother. Eliza leaned against the desk, bracing herself. A manilla folder fell to the floor.

"Will, I'm here. What is it?"

"Thanks for calling right back. Can you talk? Are you alone?"

Eliza closed her eyes. "Yes. Is it your father?"

"No. I saw Dad over the weekend. He's okay. Helen set up an easel for him on the deck. When he can manage, he paints twice a day."

Isn't that just ducky, thought Eliza. She flung aside the image of the newlyweds on a porch swing overlooking the harbor, their thighs lightly touching, his arm draped over Helen's shoulders.

"Oh, dear, is it Teddy? His letter last week said they'd made an uneventful trip through the Canal. Is he sick?"

"As far as I know, he's as right as rain. Swabbing the decks and all that nonsense."

The rest of her family raced through her mind. "Albie? Freddy? Bessie? Florence? Olga? Will, what's wrong?" she demanded, her voice rising an octave with each name. Sweat formed on her brow. Tremors coursed through her body.

"They're all fine. This isn't easy for me. It's um…it's ah, about a woman. I met her at a party the night of Teddy's graduation."

A new love interest shouldn't cause distress. The handful of times when Will had mentioned a girl to her, he'd blushed and mumbled her name. His hesitation and discomfort now stirred a mother's intuition. A maternity doctor's senses. Eliza silently ticked off the weeks from June 5 to today. Nine weeks. Two missed menses. From his light brown hair to his wit and charm, her son emulated his father. Now, it appeared Will's indiscretion had dropped to the ground like the apple fell next to its tree. Eliza rubbed her forehead, wiping the beads of sweat, and massaging the corner of her temple.

"She's pregnant," Eliza said.

Silence from Boston.

"Will. Are you there? Is this woman in Maryland pregnant?"

A choked breath came through the line. "Yes. I'm sorry. The party went wild. Servicemen letting loose. Women looking to send them off with their own special thank you and salute."

His words tumbled out now without reserve. "I got caught up in the frenzy. One of Teddy's friends brought a dozen handles of pure grain alcohol. He started pouring a splash, then three fingers, into everyone's drink. This woman stumbled into me. Thinking I was one of the cadets, she pushed me toward the men's room. Before I could gather my wits, she was unbuttoning my shirt, then my pants..."

"Stop. I don't need the details. Will, I don't care how drunk you, or this woman, were. It's no excuse. You were completely irresponsible."

Fury stormed through her veins. Heat rose to her face. The throbbing at her temple pulsed like the moments she squeezed the bulb of a blood pressure cuff, building toward a crescendo.

She continued, "If the baby is indeed yours, I hope you took the responsible step and told her you'll marry her."

"I did." Another dead moment of silence.

"And?" asked Eliza.

"She told me that she wasn't looking for a marriage proposal. She doesn't want to get married, let alone to a man who isn't a naval officer, who lives in Boston and works as a low-level manager of a wool company. She insists it's mine, but she has no intention of keeping it. She demanded one hundred dollars from me so she can end the pregnancy. She wants to get rid of my child."

Eliza's stomach churned. The acid from the green tomatoes mixed with the beans. Dropping her hand holding the phone to her side, Eliza turned from the desk and vomited into the black metal waste can. A dribble from her chin missed the inside of the basket and stuck to the rim. A sharp rap drew her from an abyss of debilitation.

"Mizzus, er, Dr. Edwards," Miss Goodman called through the door. "You must wrap up your phone call. Miss Cleveland will be back shortly."

Eliza's arms and legs went limp. "Yes, Miss Goodman. Just a moment," she said over her shoulder, pressing the receiver harder against her ear.

On the other end of the line, Will whispered, "Mother, I'm so sorry. Did you retch?

Eliza wiped her chin with the back of her hand. "I'm fine. Continue," she said.

"I didn't know what to do. I can't bother Dad in his state. And Uncle Albie and Uncle Freddy, well, I'm not sure how they'd react. I can ask for an advance on my wages, but I can't tell them why. I don't want them to think I'm completely irresponsible or they'll never promote me. I saw how angry they got when Dad's drinking got out of control. But the child…"

The stench wafted up from the basket. Another rap on the door sounded. Eliza stared at the folder she had knocked from the desk. The contents on the floor looked like jigsaw pieces. A photo stapled to an intake sheet revealed a young woman with long black hair and a Mediterranean tint to her complexion. Her soft eyes pleaded with the camera lens.

Times like this called for an inner resolve to put aside selfish yearning and blind obedience, close one's eyes, and yield to the choices of another. If the woman Will had met would take steps to break a law and sin in the eyes of others, she alone would bear the burden of suffering.

"Will," Eliza said, "I need to go. I'll call you tomorrow morning. But tonight, I want you to ask yourself a question. Could you cede your body, like a woman does, to an unwanted child for nine months?"

She hung up the phone, picked up the wastebasket, opened the office door, and walked past Miss Goodman. Her son found himself in an ungodly, perfect mess. Eliza needed the night to consider other questions. This unnamed woman carried her grandchild.

Passing six other cottages situated in a semicircle, Eliza shuffled down the dirt path to Hilliard Cottage, set alone at the lane's end. Her head hung heavy with a weight she hadn't shouldered since losing her mother. One of her final pieces of motherly advice for Eliza, spoken with wisdom and imbued with love, surfaced from Eliza's heart. *You have Will and Teddy. They are your life.* You do not abandon your life. You raise it up and care for it through every triumph and misstep.

CHAPTER EIGHT

O n the front porch, Eliza found Kay in a rocker, arisen from her nap. She'd strapped her leg braces on and walked unassisted from the bedroom. Refreshed and chipper, she held a letter in her hand, waving it at Eliza. "From John!"

Kay beamed like a young bride and mother-to-be, full of love and hope despite the grip of a crippling disease. Eliza had been right. The notion of *Invictus* suited Kay. Yet not every woman could thank the gods for surrounding them with strength and support. Others fell in defeat to their conquerors. Those women stood alone in back alleys, clutching a hundred dollars in their fists. They proclaimed mastering their Fate and captaining their Soul and Body the only way they knew how. Many would cry out haunting words like those Eliza had heard from a young woman in Philadelphia. The Italian girl, Sharon D'Amato, had told Eliza how she had lain upon a kitchen table while an abortionist "took a long rubber tubing from a drawer and pushed it up into... She left it there and sent me home." Eliza had dealt with the aftermath, watching as Sharon's body bled and her life slipped away. Eliza could not allow another woman in Baltimore to utter the same words and face the same fate. If she had made a choice, and according to Will, she clearly had, then Eliza would see that a trained professional safely performed the procedure. She may be unable to save an unwanted, unborn child, but she could save its mother.

"How wonderful," she said to Kay, collapsing into the rocking chair. "What's the news? Any progress with the painting project? Didn't you choose yellow for the nursery?"

"Doctor Ma'am," Kay said, using the endearing term she'd adopted for Eliza, and Eliza never asked her to amend. Whenever Kay addressed her, Eliza thought of sweet Salvatore Silvestri, the baby who'd won her heart at the West Philadelphia Hospital during her first year of residency. He had called her *Doctor Ma'am* until his seventeenth birthday.

"Doctor Ma'am," Kay said again, carrying Eliza back to the present. "What's wrong? There's more on your mind than color choices for a nursery."

Eliza couldn't discuss an unwanted pregnancy with a woman who held a cherished life in her womb. Kay's rehabilitation at Warm Springs stemmed from her desire and determination to give her baby a strong mother. She ignored the whispered comments and every effort to keep her segregated from the patient community. All the exercise, pain, and exhaustion were worth it if it meant she'd be able to walk to her baby's crib, put him to her breast, and soothe him like any other mother.

"Nothing to worry about. I got too engrossed in my book this afternoon. Silly, isn't it, that I'm so concerned about fictional characters?"

Eliza nodded at Kay's letter. "So, please tell me. Did John find the bunny stencils and did your mother pick out the fabric for the quilt she wants to make?"

Up the lane, amidst the cluster of cottages, puffs of dirt clouds rose from the Georgia red clay. The cooler, early evening with daylight past seven o'clock brought out the chariot races. Relay teams formed of push-boys and their assigned patients. In front of Spencer Cottage, a young girl of eight held a dinner napkin over her head as she balanced on wobbly legs, her braces locked in place. She dropped her arm and cried, "Go!"

Four wheelchairs sprang forward. As Eliza drew nearer to the improvised racetrack, she noticed the girl with the impish smile from the bridge game. The boy pushing her bent down to whisper in her ear. His easy smile broadened as she tossed her head of sandy curls and reached up to grab his hand on the chair's handles. Eliza waited for the race results. The other three chairs couldn't catch the leader. He outpaced them all, powered by more than strong legs. Young love blossomed in the most unexpected places.

Happy to know that the favored couple would bask in their victory for a while longer, Eliza quickened her step. While Kay completed her final sets of exercises, Eliza had pondered over what she would say to Will in the morning. The only person whom she trusted adhered to a strict routine of a cigarette and vodka at seven-thirty, wash-up by eight and in bed by eight-fifteen to review her research notes. Olga had explained to Eliza during their college days, "I go to sleep with equations and formulas fresh in my brain." Tonight, Eliza needed her old friend. The best time to catch her was as she lit her cigarette on the dot of seven-thirty.

By this hour, the five other doctors would have retired to the recreation room in Georgia Hall or stepped out for a smoke and drink downtown at the Baldwin House Tavern. They left their offices behind the pool building empty, save for the woman who cleaned at night. Eliza would use the phone in the front office, assured of privacy. The cleaning woman spoke little English.

Eliza approached the pools, smelling the scent of a lit match as the sulfur from the springs mixed through a gentle flow from pipes. She checked her watch. Seven-twenty. With ten minutes to spare, she lowered her body to the pool edge. She dipped her hand in the water and dragged her fingers through the warm liquid. Back and forth. Ripples from the rhythmic movement spiraled away from her. She watched them expand in concentric circles until they dissipated like the edges of a cirrus cloud. In a moment, reality disappeared. A brief clutch at the image of a grandchild would fade when Eliza located a willing physician.

Checking her watch again, she let herself into the doctors' office with the key they had begrudgingly given her. Olga answered the phone in her sister's New York apartment on the second ring. "Hello, Novikov residence."

Eliza settled on the edge of the desk, cradling the receiver between her chin and shoulder. Her right hand poised her pen over a small notepad. "Olga. I'm so glad to have caught you. How are you?"

"Eliza, my friend," Olga said. "What a pleasant surprise. A call from the woods of Georgia? I didn't realize they have phone lines there. You're not in the Little White House, are you? Using FDR's private quarters?"

"Ha. Not likely. You'd be amazed, though, at all the modern conveniences we have here. No tin cans strung between trees for communication. There's even a radio in the main hall and indoor plumbing in every cottage."

"That's good. I can't imagine you trekking to an outhouse in your silk dressing gown carrying a roll of tissue and a switch to ward off critters."

Olga Povitsky, from the first day of classes at Woman's Med, brought a smile to Eliza's face and a chuckle to her throat.

"Olga," her voice caught. "I'd best get to the point. Wait, is anyone home with you? Anyone else on the line?"

She waited while Olga clicked through the line. Hearing no other open line, she said, "Taniya and the family are out. The line is clear. What is it my friend?" The concern in her voice reached through and pulled Eliza in.

"I need your help. By chance, do you have an alumnae directory? I hope to find a sympathetic sister in the Baltimore area.

Someone who looks the other way in the face of the law or knows someone trusted to perform procedures in a safe manner."

Eliza heard Olga pull a long drag on the cigarette and a deep swallow of vodka as she considered Eliza's request.

"I can check. I assume you need these services soon? No time to spare?" Olga said.

"Yes. And Olga," Eliza paused. Olga had become as attached to her sons as any blood-related aunt. "It's Will's. He did offer to marry her, but she refused, and made her choice. The least I can do is make sure a professional takes care of her."

"I understand. Let me run through the directory. I can make discreet calls from my office. Can you accept a call around lunchtime tomorrow?"

"Thank you. Yes. You can call the Main Office. I'll wait in the lobby. Honestly, what would I do without you?"

"That's a fair question. The few times I left you on your own, you fell in love with the wrong man. Twice! Now don't go falling for a suave Southern gent, fooled by a syrupy drawl and rugged good looks. A third time isn't always a charm. Try to get some rest. I'll be in touch tomorrow."

Eliza placed the receiver into the phone cradle. *Rest.* The mere concept lurked in the recesses of Eliza's psyche. *Olga, my friend, show me a time when a woman truly rests.*

CHAPTER NINE

November 1936

Ascattering of brittle leaves crunched under Eliza's feet. Behind the cottage, a copse of mighty oaks stood bare. The slight autumn breeze set the gray branches swaying. Late fall in Georgia, while not as harsh as New England, still nipped noses and pulled sweaters from cedar chests. In the distance, a scurry of squirrels searched for acorns beneath the blanket of dead leaves, fallen pieces of bark, and snapped twigs. Eliza tightened the belt of her wool coat against the swirl of crisp air. "I hear you, Happy Jack," she called. "You are a wise one. Save a little every day, and for the future put away."

She knew each of Thornton Burgess's woodland characters from his children's books, beginning with *Mother West Wind*, which she had given to her precious favorite patient, Salvatore Silvestri. She had read to him from a new book every year on his birthday. When she became a mother and snuggled with Will and Teddy for bedtime reading adventures, she made sure her sons enjoyed the book series, too.

She spread her arms, gesturing toward the Pine Mountains, as if to beckon the woodland creatures to life. If only she could harvest and savor the renewed sense of purpose she had found in Warm Springs. The smallness and stillness consumed her. A person could lose herself in a spot like this with few distractions but the purpose at hand. Or find herself. Over the past four and a half months, with each step Kay took, Eliza matched her in walking ahead to days filled with meaning. Beyond the three-hundred dollars Congressman Morrison paid her to take Kay's blood pressure and fundal height measurements, she had learned new skills and an admiration for the arduous, physical work of the patients and their therapists.

The cottage door thudded close behind her. Footsteps neared, one set sure and steady, the other heavy and halting. She gazed one last time to the mountain range in the distance. In front of them, tall Georgia pines stood firm in a sentry line at the edge of campus. Their needles clung to the branches, green with everlasting life. Fresh pine lingered in the air. Eliza inhaled, pulling the invigorating scent deep into her lungs. The majesty of the outdoors had inhabited her bones. After a lifetime of city living, the woods calmed her. Unchanged for centuries, they endured and taught her the same. Whatever lay ahead after she left Georgia, she'd recall all that she had found. From learning new skills, to making new friends in Kay and the delightful group of physios. From trusting her mothering and doctoring instincts to guide others, to developing a taste for fried green tomatoes. Her time in Warm Springs had found a forever place in her heart.

John Clark interrupted her reverie. "The car's here, Eliza."

She turned to find John and Kay standing at the end of the cottage path. Kay linked one arm through John's and clutched the handle of her arm brace with her other hand. Her blue maternity dress swelled over her ballooning belly, her coat unbuttoned, unable to stretch across the expanse. Eliza joined them, partially encircling Kay's waist. The threesome walked to the idling car.

At the Atlanta train station, Eliza said goodbye to the Clarks. Before Eliza could call out her reminders for Kay to write with weekly updates, John rushed his waddling wife along to make their connection. Eliza knew how much Kay looked forward to spending Thanksgiving in Chicago with her family and a full inspection of the yellow painted nursery with bunnies hopping along a wainscoting's top edge, and a new quilt lying across a waiting bassinet.

Eliza settled into her seat on the north-bound train and picked up her book. Twenty-three small town stops dotted a line across Georgia. Time to get back to Scarlett's conversation with Ashley, her long forbidden love. Ashley has told Scarlett that she shouldn't be surprised at how her life has changed from what she had hoped for once upon a time as a young, naïve, Southern belle. *How true, Ashley, how true*, Eliza thought. We must not expect our lives will follow straight and narrow paths.

But what awaited her at the other end of these train tracks? The thought of the encroaching winter in Boston troubled her. Frozen ponds, barren tree limbs, and a rudderless existence. Her usefulness in Warm Springs had teased her into affirming she wasn't ready for retirement. People like Congressman Morrison, Kay and John Clark, and Miss Cleveland had validated her. Who in Boston could do the same? Dr. Miles at the Peter Bent Brigham Hospital hadn't. Olga had left her. Her patients had slinked into soup lines and male physicians' offices. Her sons lived their own lives. She let the book drop onto her lap. Embracing herself, she slid her hands up and down her upper arms. How would she find her way in those cold, empty streets of Boston?

The train shuddered and chugged forward. A blast of smoke spewed out behind its cars as it pulled away from the depot.

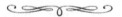

Seventeen hours later, Eliza felt a tap on her shoulder, rousing her from her third nap of the trip. "Is this seat taken?"

Eliza stirred, opening her eyes to see the station sign for Wilmington, Delaware. A woman peered at Eliza from behind thin, rimless wire glasses. Beneath her black cloche hat, trimmed with a band of mink fur, her snowy white hair strayed from a

Victorian styled bun. Eliza moved her doctor's bag from the seat next to her to the floor.

Eliza gestured to the cleared spot.

"Your companion won't mind?"

Puzzled, Eliza replied, "Companion? Oh, no. No one's sitting here."

She followed the woman's eye to the bag.

"Ah, a common mistake. The bag is mine. Dr. Eliza Edwards." Eliza extended her hand. The woman grasped it and shook it with familiarity.

"A common one indeed, which I, too, am well aware of." She hefted a medical bag up to Eliza's line of sight. "Dr. Esther Lovejoy, with the American Women's Hospitals."

"Oh, Dr. Lovejoy. What a pleasure to meet you! Yes, please, sit."

What an honor and stroke of good luck! she thought. After stewing about leaving Kay and Warm Springs, a past president of the American Medical Women's Association and current director of the American Women's Hospital, stood next to her. Eliza had read *Angels and Amazons: A Hundred Years of American Women*, three years ago. In it, the author had called the AWH's service a *Cullinan*—a gem among gems in recognition of the group's achievements overseas after the Great War. Perhaps Dr. Lovejoy would have some brilliant ideas for Eliza's future.

The older woman placed her medical bag on her lap. Its black leather, scraped and gouged, told stories of history and travel. Eliza wondered if Dr. Lovejoy's multi-stamped passport was tucked inside. Did the small booklet document all her trips to Greece, Turkey, Serbia, Armenia, and Russia, where the AWH had tended to the displaced and disillusioned after the war?

"I'm surprised to see you here, in Delaware of all places," said Eliza.

Dr. Lovejoy removed her hat and gave her head a slight shake as if to clear her mind. "Oh, no. I boarded back in Greenville,

South Carolina. I'd finally had enough of an intolerable seat mate. A man, droning on about the disgrace of the Hoovervilles and hobo camps we've passed. Worrying about how many men may jump the train for a free ride. As if they have many choices. For land's sakes, they're trying to get to a spot where they can find work."

Aren't we all, thought Eliza. At least the idea of train-hopping hadn't crossed her mind, yet.

"Greenville? Why, that spot's smaller than Delaware. Do you have family in the area?"

A snort of laughter spilled from Dr. Lovejoy. "Claysons in South Carolina? Certainly not. I'm from Oregon by way of logging camps in Washington State. No, I've been touring the Southern Highlands, primarily Greenville, where we've set up a new health center and mobile unit. The needs in these rural, mountain communities are as dire as the war-ravaged areas of Europe. It's time to take care of our own."

Eliza nodded in agreement. *Indeed, it is.*

Dr. Lovejoy pulled a thin notebook from her bag. "I'd love to chat further, Dr. Edwards, but I must finish reviewing some reports before New York. Perhaps another time? If you're ever in the city, do call. I always enjoy hearing what our Angels and Amazons are up to across the country." She winked at Eliza.

"I'm not sure anyone can call me an Angel or an Amazon, but I would love to call on you and learn more about your work," said Eliza.

CHAPTER TEN

November 1936
New York, NY

S ubmission to The Journal of Immunology
Abstract: *Diphtheria Toxoid. Preparation and Dosage.*
Olga Povitzky, M.D., Erla Jackson, M.D., Minnie Eisner,
M.D.
New York City Department of Public Health

Under the old nomenclature the term "toxoid" meant a slightly toxic diphtheria toxin which was used instead of toxin-antitoxin in some cases for immunization against diphtheria.

Detoxification shall be so complete that five human doses given subcutaneously in each of ten guinea pigs weighing 300 grams will cause no signs of diphtheria poisoning, including paralysis at any time during a period of thirty days.

The minimum antigenic requirements are put down as follows: The original toxin from which the toxoid is made shall have an L + dose of not more than 0.20 cc. or an M.L.D. of not more than 0.0025 cc.

Eliza's eyes glazed under a cloud of confusion. The neatly typed page shook with her hands' tremble. She set it upon Olga's desk, careful to avoid the overflowing ashtray.

"Is it succinct?" Olga asked. "The Journal outlines explicit guidelines for publication: identify the problem, summarize your objectives, identify methods used, and report research findings."

Eliza drew the back of her hand to her forehead. "I daresay you're trying to give me the night-scaring dreams. With one simple piece of paper, you hurled me into my long ago, never-ending battle against Organic Chemistry. I may have passed the classes, in large part thanks to your tutoring, but I certainly haven't retained the lessons like you have. I think the need for ten guinea pigs may be the only part I understood. Poor little pets."

"Well, frankly, my dear, I don't give a damn what you think about guinea pigs."

The two women burst into laughter, finding comfort in their ability to step into each other's lives and pick up their friendship without missing a beat.

"Please tell me, though, how many poor little guinea pigs succumbed to the toxin? I hate to imagine their cute little twitching noses, with their big, soft eyes, expecting a scratch behind their ears, only to have you plunge a syringe into their backside."

Olga waved her off. "Focus on the end results. Think of the number of human lives we'll save, not the guinea pigs we lose."

"I shall," Eliza said, her cheeks warming. "I may not follow all the intricacies, but I realize its importance in your study. Diphtheria, influenza, measles, pneumonia, rubella, polio. They damage and take too many lives. Place burdens upon so many."

She rose from her lean against the desk's edge and wrapped her arm around Olga's waist. "I'm proud of you, my friend. We'll raise a glass after dinner tonight, to you, Erla, and Minnie. That's the most rewarding part of your abstract. Three women's names at the top, where they belong, front and center, and in bold print."

Packing up her briefcase, Olga suggested they dine at one of the few restaurants which allowed unescorted women. En route to Hamilton Heights where Olga lived with her sister, they could stop at Schrafft's on 107th Street on the city's west side. Its menu offered reasonable prices and a variety of items.

Once seated, Eliza perused the menu. The creamed chicken on toast with string beans on the side for ninety cents meant she could splurge for a slice of chocolate layer cake, topped with a scoop of vanilla ice cream and a dollop of whipped cream. *To hell with a diet.* After five and a half months at Warm Springs, where she often tossed her lunch in the trash and walked miles every day, she had lost a few pounds. Her shirtwaists felt a tad looser. Olga reveled in finding a plate reminiscent of her childhood and ordered potato pancakes with new peas and old-fashioned coleslaw awash in mayonnaise and vinegar. Around them, women on their way home from work filled the tables. With Roosevelt's re-election, WPA programs continued to expand, adding more jobs across occupations. Restaurants like Schrafft's benefitted from slowly filling change purses and wallets.

"I have to say Olga, New York agrees with you," Eliza said as the waiter left. "I'm so happy to see you engrossed in your work. You belong in a laboratory. I guess my loss is the Health Department's gain."

Olga beamed as she tapped a cigarette out of a blue enameled case. "I am lucky to have Erla and Minnie on my team. Their younger eyes catch subtle variants while I direct the next steps we might consider. My experience and their fresh ideas—it's a winning combination."

She lit the cigarette and drew on it, exhaling slowly.

"That's exactly how I felt with the physios at Warm Springs. My goodness, but they were young! Most had barely reached twenty. I learned so much from them. One gal, Vera, expressed great interest in my maternity work. She might apply to medical school, especially after I told her about Woman's Med. They had never heard of it, coming from Tennessee."

"You're a model alumna, Eliza. How about returning to Philadelphia? Give Dean Tracy a call. Ask her about a position in Admissions."

By November 1936, Woman's Med remained on an unapproved list for membership in the Association of American Medical Colleges. Fundraising efforts to reduce mortgage debt included a "brick sale," asking supporters, one-on-one, to sponsor a brick for a new East Falls building. Meanwhile, philanthropists like John D. Rockefeller wrote checks for millions to endow Yale, Johns Hopkins, and other primarily male-only medical schools.

Eliza placed her napkin in her lap. "I'm not all that keen on returning to Boston with no prospects, but I can't go to Philadelphia. At least in Boston there's Florence, Will, and my brothers. The only people I know in Philadelphia are six feet under at Laurel Hill Cemetery. Besides, the college must be having a difficult time recruiting students to a school on the brink of collapse. But I appreciate the suggestion. Getting through the holidays and settling in with Florence should keep me busy until the end of the year. After that? I have no idea what I'll do."

"Mmmm…" Eliza sighed as she slid the first bite of cake over her tongue. It was dense, dark, and sweet. "Does anything come close to chocolate to soothe a soul?"

"Dah, yes," said Olga. "Red wine to wash it down. This restaurant needs to realize their revenues would increase if the ladies could order a glass or two from a bar. Women enjoy the comforts of a good pour, too."

Eliza nodded. "Does Taniya have any at home? I'll wrap up the other half of my cake. We can split it back at the house."

"I'm sure we can ferret a bottle out if we ask her to join us for a nightcap," Olga said. "But before we go, while we still have some privacy, did you hear anything else from Baltimore?"

Eliza leaned in closer over the table. "Only what I told you in my letter, that Barbara Yates asked that I not share her name with anyone else. I still don't know if she performed the procedure or referred the woman to someone else. Regardless, I'm assured she received proper care if a Woman's Med sister handled her. Will hasn't heard from her since he gave her Barbara's information, and the money. I only hope he can move on from the incident. He was quite upset."

"As were you," Olga said.

"Yes, I was." In the days after her call from Will, she had thought often of the days she had held him as a baby, feeling a weight of responsibility and boundless love. How that image of him had blurred into what a child of his might look like, with the same glint of mischievousness. With a light sigh, she dabbed her napkin to her lips.

"Oh, Eliza. Our Will is young. Plenty of time ahead before we call you *Babushka*."

CHAPTER ELEVEN

February 1937
Boston, Massachusetts

A pile of empty corrugated boxes and crumpled newspaper awaited Will to carry them to the alley trash bins. After the whirlwind of the holidays, Eliza had finally unpacked in her new home. Today, she finished the last carton, removing an Oriental jewelry box. The inlaid black walnut pictured tiny figures in a rickshaw and cherry trees made from mother-of-pearl. The pearly flakes reflected the lamp's light. Eliza ran her hand over the smooth, lacquered top. Nestled inside, a string of pearls and a pair of earrings.

A rustle from Florence's bedroom and a slam of the closet door told Eliza that her formidable aunt had arisen from her afternoon rest. *Here we go*, thought Eliza as she peeked out the front windows. A swirl of gray clouds hovered in the sky. Icy snow pelted against the glass with a sharp *ping-ping-ping*. Florence appeared in the living room doorway. With a brown knit hat pulled down tight over her ears and her bulky, wool coat buttoned to the top, she ambled up to Eliza, her rubber boots slapping against the hardwood floor.

"Aunt Florence," Eliza said. "Have you looked outside? You're not going anywhere in this weather."

Florence glared at Eliza as she pulled on her gloves. "Of course, I am. Story hour at the West End is at three. A few snowflakes won't stop boys from skidding down the street, nor cause the director at a settlement house to change their schedule. They're expecting me. Frank and Joe are hunting for a sinister surgeon in *A Figure in Hiding*. With race cars and a hydrofoil boat tossed in, none of us can wait until Monday to discover if they can save more victims from the shady surgeon's fraudulent practices."

"Those Hardy boys. They have quite the adventures. A story about a surgeon sounds interesting," she said. "I'll walk with you. Let me grab my coat and leave a note for Will."

If you couldn't stop Florence, you might as well join her.

The afternoon snow squall abated for Eliza's and Florence's return home. Stopping at the corner market, Eliza picked up the ingredients for Will's favorite dinner: six boned chicken breasts and two cans of Campbell's Cream of Mushroom Soup. She always baked enough to have extra servings to send home with him. God love her son. In his own studio apartment for nearly two years, and he still hadn't cracked open the cookbook she'd given him. At least he could re-heat a chicken dish on his hot plate. She called over her shoulder to Florence who was thumbing through the latest issue of *LIFE*. "Do we need another bottle of sherry?"

Florence turned another page of the magazine.

"Aunt Florence? Sherry. Do we need more?" Eliza said louder, hesitant to lift her voice much higher inside the store.

"Hmm. What? Sherry?" Florence asked. "Yes, if you're making Boozey Chicken, you'd better grab another bottle. I think there's only a swallow left, certainly not enough for the amount you use, drowning those poor chicks in a lake of liquor."

"I forgot my change purse," said Florence as Eliza got in line at the register. "Do you have an extra dime?" She held up the magazine.

Eliza nodded, although the idea why Florence wanted an issue which featured a lone steer in front of a snowy ranch background escaped her.

"You're interested in livestock now? Don't tell me you want to move out west and become a rancher. You know people are fleeing the Plains states in droves, heading to California, leaving their wind-stripped, dust-covered farms."

Florence slapped the air in front of her with a flick of her wrist. "Beyond me why they led with a story about *Winter in Wyoming*. Inside, there's an article I want to read about that German. Herman Göring visiting Italy can only spell trouble. And there's a full spread of photos, showing the floods in Tennessee and Kentucky. As if those poor souls in Appalachia haven't endured enough. I wonder if Bess is there. The photos were taken by that photographer, Jack Hansen. Doesn't Bess sometimes collaborate with him?"

Jack Hansen. So that was the name of Bess's beau. Eliza hadn't heard from her niece since her short visit home at Christmas, but knew her next assignment would take her to Appalachia. *Oh, she collaborates with him, all right. More like, copulates*, Eliza almost uttered. "Yes, I think that's his name. Maybe Bess will have an article in next week's issue. I'll try to remember to look for it." *But first, I'd better write to Bess, reminding her she might need more spermicide by now*, she thought.

The banjo clock chimed seven. In the kitchen, Florence stacked their dinner dishes in the sink, while Eliza covered a sherry-doused chicken dinner plate in tin foil. She knew Will worked half a day on Friday. Where was he on a frigid February night? Perhaps one of his friends had rustled up tickets to the Boston Bruins. If the Bruins played, Will would be preoccupied with grabbing his spot on a wooden plank in a cold hockey rink and forgetting to call his mother.

There was a rap on the front door, muffled by the dense wood and howling wind, which began again as soon as they had sat to eat. Eliza placed the plate on a rack in the refrigerator and firmly latched the handle down. The knock sounded louder and more urgent. "I'm coming," she called.

Opening the door, she found Will, his black fedora pulled tight, earflaps flipped down, and his maroon striped wool scarf wound twice around his neck. He briskly rubbed his gloved hands together. Eliza gestured to him to come in as he stamped his boots free of snow. His red-rimmed eyes stared into her. The winter gusts hadn't reddened them. He swallowed hard, his Adam's apple rising and falling as the lump of sadness burst from his lips. "He's gone, Mom. Helen called this morning. Dad's gone."

Eliza opened her arms. Will stepped in. She laid her cheek against the rough wool of his tweed overcoat and held him. It didn't matter that he had to bend down eight inches to reach his mother's embrace. She put aside her sixteen-year separation from Harrison and the insufferable years before the separation. A hole was taking hold in her son's heart, one which had started last summer as a pinprick, when a woman in Baltimore aborted his child. Now, it would grow like a tumor and linger for the rest of his life. *A presence without purpose, except to remind and regret.* And even though every filament of her soul ached to comfort her boy, telling him Harrison's pain was over, it didn't matter. She could never fill that void nor cut away the tumor.

You are too much like him, she thought. She pulled forth the memory of his twinkling eyes when he needed to charm her. Running off to join stick-ball games the same way Harrison headed to tennis courts, never being able to sit still for long. This son, who resembled his father in so many ways, would suffer. *I should have done more for Harrison. I don't care if Will is twenty-*

four. He's going to need me. I'll be damned if I let him find solace in a bottle.

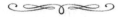

Laurel Hill. Mosswood. Why did city planners name cemeteries after living elements in the natural world? Did they portend a sense of hope that life would continue? Or that names of peaceful settings would soothe a visitor's grief? Eliza let her mind wander with nonsensical questions as she gazed out from atop the knoll. Withered grass blades lay flat, trampled by boots. A bank of rhododendrons huddled in a mass of dead leaves curled tight on brown branches, awaiting spring buds. Glimpses of a Cape Cod harbor filtered between the short heights of scrub pines and oaks. Steel-colored waves lapped the shore, then returned to the depths.

Eight thousand miles away, sea water splashed against the hull of the *USS Mississippi* as it plied the Pacific Ocean near Guam. On board, Eliza imagined Ensign Edward Shaw, her Teddy, lying in a hammock strung between pipes, staring at the ceiling inches from his head. The thought of Teddy bobbing in the middle of an ocean on a ship filled with men, inflamed her mothering anguish. She longed to reach her arms across the miles to hold her youngest in his moments of solitary sorrow.

As the minister read the closing from Ecclesiastes 3:1-8, Eliza shifted her attention back to the open grave awaiting Harrison's polished walnut coffin. "*… a time to search and a time to give up, a time to keep and a time to throw away, a time to tear and a time to mend, a time to be silent and a time to speak, a time to love and a time to hate…*". The minister, or whomever had selected the readings for the service, chose well. The words of duality had defined Eliza's life with Harrison. The moment had arrived to toss aside despair and quell the anguish of a broken marriage. A time to mend loomed on the horizon, as silent yet persistent as the incoming tide pushing its way further up the beach.

The group of a dozen men standing at the graveside broke apart. She had met Congressman Morrison, Kay's father, at the church. Their quick conversation brought Eliza a moment of bliss when she learned how well Kay was managing with her new baby. Eliza drew comfort in knowing that her work with the new mother had made a difference. Congressman Gifford, Harrison's employer for the last seventeen years, offered his arm to the widow. Helen Warner Shaw, dressed from head to toe in black, from her sensible boots to the tight-fitting cloche complete with a black lace veil which hung down to the tip of her nose, leaned heavily on the Congressman's arm. Will, leaving Eliza's side, strode over to the pair and offered his arm to Helen. Gifford and Will balanced Helen like Libra's scales.

Behind them, Eliza tucked her chin down against the chilling February air. In a hushed whisper, she spoke to the spray of white snapdragons laying across the coffin. "You had promised to love and honor me. I suppose you did for a brief time. I hope you did. Learning that you wanted Helen with you in the end though, that truth destroyed me. I cannot forgive you, just yet. I will, however, be civil to Helen, for the boys' sake."

Alone, she trailed the men to the cars waiting at the edge of the cemetery.

CHAPTER TWELVE

March 1937

S imple, paltry figures filled the boxes of Eliza's 1936 federal tax return form. A single numeral three and two ovals the size of *Humpty Dumpty* teetered on the black line where she filled in *Annual Wages and Income*. Even with the help of all the king's horses and all the king's men, she doubted she could put her fractured life back together again. From her four months in Warm Springs, she could claim three hundred dollars in income, plus free room and board. A squeaky metal-framed bed and cottage cheese sandwiches during her first weeks carried little value. The only payment worth its weight in gold was her time with Kay.

She picked up the letter from Chicago which had arrived in the morning mail.

Dear Doctor Ma'am,

A quick note to report that Johnny is sleeping through the night! My goodness, I feel like a new woman. I know you told me not to get too comfortable, that just when you think you've gotten them on a schedule, they throw a change-up at you. Four nights in a row, however, has given us a nice long stretch of extra hours. I'm also following your advice to nap when he does. My doctor, while he's capable enough, has never shared those personal gems with me. So, thank you!

With love and appreciation, Kay

P.S. Two-month check-up results: 24 inches and 12 pounds, 8 ounces. I think he's going to be taller than his Daddy!

From the moment Eliza had declined the use of chloroform for her first personal experience with childbirth, she had willingly shared her mothering advice. *How kind of Kay to mention that she is heeding my advice.*

As Eliza slipped the note back into the card, she tidied up the rest of the week's mail spread across the kitchen table. These letters carried far less cheery news with their mocking words. *Regrettably, we received a large volume of applications...Though your experience is impressive, we have selected a candidate whose qualifications are better suited...In these economic times, we must reserve any open positions for candidates who can commit to the role for a long-term...*

Eliza allowed herself a sigh which bounced against the wall and returned to her ears with a hard smack. She tilted her head to the ceiling. A hairline crack in the paint around the light fixture appeared larger than her examination two days ago when she had stared at the ceiling, lost in a reverie of nothingness. She rose to place Kay's letter in the box of correspondence that she stored on a shelf in the front closet.

Next to the box, a fine layer of dust coated her medical bag. She took it down and brushed aside the specks. Her thumb pressed the latch, releasing the wide strap over the top from its metal confines. The tools of her life's work lay inside, each item sterilized and wrapped, awaiting her hands to put them to use. Bottles of ether and morphine lay swaddled in flannel like babes in a nursery. The bottles' dark blue and brown glass veiled the pain-erasing liquids. Eliza was fully aware of the effects of both. Ether was milder and less addictive. Ingestion in vapor form provided a safer method with fewer gastric side effects than a swig of the liquid.

She checked the clock. A salad fork would be in Florence's hand as she and her friends began a first course at a Museum of

Fine Arts luncheon. Eliza could finish her taxes in the afternoon, ready to mail them by tomorrow's deadline. Why in God's name did the Internal Revenue Service demand a due date of March 15? Hadn't any of them read Shakespeare's *Julius Caesar*? Across the country, American citizens didn't need any reminder to beware the ides of March. Enough despair permeated their lives. Eliza's empty life. If only she could escape, even for a couple of hours. To float away, her mind cleared of aimless and meaningless days.

One time, she thought. *One afternoon to float away, unburdened of worry.* With the jar of ether and a mesh mask in her hand, she headed to her bedroom.

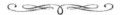

...two hundred and ninety-eight, two hundred and ninety-nine, three hundred. Cottage by the River was the tenth puzzle Eliza had completed in the past month. She placed the wooden piece into the empty spot. Then, with a sweep of her arm, she cleared the idyllic scene from the desktop. The thatched English cottage with its blooming flower garden broke apart, landing on the Oriental rug. Several stubborn pieces remained interlocked, while others settled into the corner of the living room. Eliza rose from her desk chair, stepping on the scattered pieces as she made her way to the front closet to retrieve the puzzle's box.

Today, Aunt Florence had plans to visit Eliza's sister-in-law for the afternoon and would stay for dinner. Eliza grabbed her medical bag. In her bedroom, on top of a floral chenille bedspread, she drifted into a haze of nothingness.

Floating, the air embraces. Tingling. Singling. Alone. Bemoan. Hide away. Go away. Find me, sweet friend.

Two weeks later, a distant ringing in her ears raised Eliza from her bed. *Brringgg, brringg.* The telephone vibrated with the force of a jackhammer breaking through a cement sidewalk. She pressed her palms against her face and drew them down, pulling against the loose skin of her cheeks and neck to clear the cobwebs from her mind. Looking at her watch, she groaned. Four-thirty PM. Almost three hours this time. Over the past month, whenever a rejection letter arrived in her mailbox, she increased the number of drips of ether onto the cloth. Her legs wobbled as she rose from the bed. *Brrringg, brrringg.* "I'm coming," she called to the phone as her senses awoke and she realized Aunt Florence wasn't home from story hour.

In a raspy voice, she answered, "Edwards Pearson residence."

An accent from Vermont's Green Mountains announced herself. "Eliza. It's Charlotte."

Dr. Charlotte Fairbanks had graduated with Eliza and Olga from Woman's Med. After her residency at a women's prison in Philadelphia, she opened a private practice in her native Vermont. Residents of the rural towns traveled far and wide, seeking her acumen with a surgical knife. Eliza had recognized Charlotte's talents, too. When Eliza had diagnosed her mother's breast cancer, she wanted Charlotte's steady hand and careful approach to assessing a patients' needs to perform the mastectomy. Although the surgery couldn't save Eliza's mother, Charlotte helped ease the endless pain for a few weeks. Those extra days brought comfort to Eliza.

"Why, Charlotte. How lovely to hear from you! How's the North Country? Do you still have snow?"

"Honestly, I haven't noticed. I guess there's a snowbank or two around. I wanted to let you know I'm coming to Boston. The American Women's Hospital contacted me. They dug my name out from their old records. They're in dire need of a surgeon."

At the height of the Great War, in 1918, Charlotte had traveled with a group of sixty other women to France. Denied by the United States Army to serve with its medical corps, instead the doctors, nurses, a dentist, and other staff, all women, arrived in France as volunteers, committed to providing medical and emergency relief for French civilians and refugees. Upon the Armistice and in recognition of her work, the French government awarded a gold *Medaille Militarie* of gratitude and honorary citizenship to chief surgeon, Charlotte Fairbanks, and other members of the AWH.

"Why, that's wonderful, Charlotte," said Eliza. Needed, she thought. Eliza twisted the phone cord in her hands. An esteemed medical association needed sixty-six-year-old Charlotte. Her qualifications as a talented surgeon remained in high demand.

"Did I tell you I met Dr. Lovejoy, on my way home from Georgia?" she continued. "Her last seat mate mistook her for a doddering grandmother. She had a good laugh on him. What a force she is! She had just toured the facilities in Greenville, South Carolina. How old do you think she is? Dr. Lovejoy's stamina for all that traveling is amazing."

"Dr. Lovejoy is two years older than I," Charlotte said. "I expect she has no plans to slow down, nor should she. With all that's going on in Spain and rumblings from Italy and Germany, I fear dark days lie ahead. War-stricken areas may again put out the plea for our services. Many of us will answer to join our sisters over there."

"Is that where you're heading? Leaving from Boston to go to Spain?"

"No. What else did Dr. Lovejoy mention about their work in Appalachia?"

"Not much. But the idea of their health centers intrigued me. At the library, I found a smattering of articles in some South Carolina newspapers. An article in the Spartanburg paper quoted the County Department of Health as reporting that the AWH-sponsored nutrition classes which teach the importance of healthier diets has stemmed the spread of pellagra and cut deaths by more than one-half."

"Yes, progress has been made, but years of vitamin deficiency and tobacco use by the women have produced an above average incidence of cleft lips and palates. They've also identified multiple children requiring tonsillectomies and adenoidectomies."

Eliza had seen some of the photos in the newspaper articles of the rural families, living in squalor. Six or more malnourished children standing next to rail-thin parents. To think that in addition to the scourge of pellagra, they also suffered from deformities and illnesses which required surgeries tugged at Eliza's heart.

"I'm guessing that Dr. Lovejoy wants the best the AWH can offer to those families. She wants you to perform the surgeries?"

"Yes. I'm heading to Tennessee. I may be lined up with appointments from morning to night for at least a week."

"That's so kind of you, Charlotte." Eliza's fingers ran up and down the twisted phone cord, beginning to wonder about the point of Charlotte's call. Sharing news of the trip didn't warrant the expense of a long-distance phone call by the frugal Vermonter.

"Eliza, I can't do this alone. I could use an assistant. Someone I know and trust."

The phone cord unwound itself as Eliza dropped it.

"That's quite a request, Charlotte."

While an operating theatre still provoked waves of nausea and beads of sweat to form on her brow, over the years Eliza had assisted with hysterectomies and ovariotomies. Under Charlotte's tutelage, she could re-learn surgical procedures. Like the physical therapy exercises she had learned to help Kay. *New skills*, she thought. Perhaps it would be enough for her to highlight in the next round of application letters.

"May I get back to you by tomorrow?" said Eliza.

"At the latest. I'll need to find someone else if you're not interested. We'll talk tomorrow."

After the call, Eliza settled into a kitchen chair to ponder Charlotte's request. On the table, Florence had left the latest issue of *Harper's Magazine* open to an article, *Eager to Learn*, by Bess Edwards with photographs by Jack Hansen. Black and white photographs of children seated at school desks in Appalachia filled a page. Bare feet peeked out from pant legs too short and dresses too long. Uneven cropped hair framed their shining faces, fresh from a morning scrubbing to wash away dirt, grime, and coal dust, brought home by fathers who worked in the nearby mines. The fortunate fathers, Eliza surmised. She counted forty-four children. Eliza estimated they were between the ages of six and fourteen. The children's attention focused on the teacher standing at a well-worn chalkboard. In her hand, she held a nub of chalk as she wrote out lessons for each grade level. Alongside the photograph, Bess had penned a pleading description. *Look into their eyes. A hunger lurks, created by not just scanty meals of fat-back bacon and cornbread, but from meager servings of textbooks, supplies, and teachers. They want to learn. Kentucky's future, the country's future, lies in the dreams of these children.* Not one child with a cleft lip smiled at Jack's camera. Those children languished at home, barely able to lift a crumb of cornbread to their lips. Charlotte could help them.

Charlotte said she'd be there for one week. Eliza had endured a whole summer in Georgia's heat. Surely, a May week in Tennessee would pale in comparison.

Four weeks later, she snapped shut the brass lock on her medical bag. She hesitated. Inside, wrapped in white cotton, the jar of ether held less than a finger of liquid, as Harrison would have called the measure. She needed to meet Charlotte at South Station in less than an hour. She couldn't call in a refill, pick it up from the druggist, and make the ten o'clock train departure. *I'll have to figure out a way to manage without it until we reach Tennessee.*

With a week's worth of surgeries scheduled and Charlotte's careful attention to detail, there would be ample jars of ether and morphine. Charlotte wouldn't notice if Eliza sneaked a few drops from a different jar each time.

Aunt Florence rapped her cane on the floor behind her. "Will's outside with the car. He's put your suitcase in. You best get going. He'll catch the dickens for double parking at this time of morning. These Bostonians really should have widened the streets beyond the width of a cow path. Puritan frugality be damned."

Picking up her bag and tapping her straw hat down on the top of her head, Eliza slipped her free arm around Aunt Florence's thick waist. As she pulled her close, she inhaled the lingering fragrance of Pond's face cream. Florence never failed to smear a generous scoop of Pond's across her face and neck every night, letting the rich, dense cream seep in until she washed it away in the morning. She swore to its results. Eliza had to agree. For a woman in her late seventies, Aunt Florence had the firm, clear skin of a twenty-year-old. Tucked into the bottom of her suitcase, Eliza had placed a small, white porcelain jar with a teal cover into the case's pleated pocket. If she could look younger, maybe she would feel younger, regain her confidence, and think of a new future, rather than dwell on a disappointing present.

PART TWO

CHAPTER THIRTEEN

May 1937
En route to Jellico, Tennessee

The tremor began in her lower leg. Eliza placed her sweaty palms on the top of her thighs, pressing hard to send a command to still the jittery bounce. Beyond the shroud descending over her brain, a voice droned. Her pulse quickened as her eyes fluttered to the senseless words coming from the seat next to her.

"Dirt roads... mud... pack animals... shoes... netting... competent..."

A clap of hands stirred Eliza from the cobwebs weaving circles around her head.

"Eliza," said Charlotte. "Did you hear me?"

"For God's sakes, Charlotte. What are you going on about?" Eliza spit her words toward her seatmate.

Charlotte's jaw dropped. The couple sitting across the aisle from the two doctors turned their heads, as if startled by the tone spoken by the refined-looking woman in the pale green linen suit. With a sharp grab of Eliza's forearm, Charlotte lowered her voice as she narrowed her eyes. "What is wrong with you?"

From the depths of her stupor, Charlotte's tone pulled Eliza into a stronger sense of presence. She collected her medical bag and yanked the handkerchief from inside her sleeve, patting the drips of sweat beading on her forehead. "I'm not feeling myself. This train is so stuffy. Excuse me while I go to the lavatory."

The train lurched to a stop. Eliza faltered in the aisle as the train swayed. Her bag slipped. The hard bounce on the floor knocked the bag to its side. She had unclasped the latch when she picked it up, anxious to withdraw the instruments as soon as she locked herself in the restroom. A near-empty jar of ether rolled out and hit against the toe of Charlotte's brown shoe. The mesh mask, with folded squares of sterile cotton tucked into the cone area, slid under the seat.

Charlotte looked from the bag's contents to Eliza. She shook her head and reached for Eliza's hand. Eliza shuddered as her eyes welled. She turned away from the esteemed surgeon, whose confidence and conviction had carried her across the ocean to battlefields. A woman who had persevered during wartime and who had come to Eliza's side to help her mother. A doctor who had never stumbled.

"Splash water on your face and get a breath of air," said Charlotte.

Eliza bent to gather up the items of her guilt.

"Leave them," Charlotte said. "If you take that bag with you, you can keep going, right to the exit door, and disembark at the next station, even if it's Newark. I won't tolerate weakness in any form."

Eliza swallowed the knot in her throat. She relinquished the bag to Charlotte's waiting hand. Like the parallel bars Kay had used in Warm Springs, Eliza grasped the tops of the seats to steady her sway down the aisle. She hoped a splash of water could summon the inner resolve she'd need to continue to Tennessee.

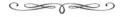

Twenty-two hours later, the Southern Railways train approached their destination. With Charlotte gripping her fingers throughout the rest of the trip, Eliza's nerves settled as her desire for the ether quieted. Charlotte used the time to distract Eliza with details of the AWH in the Southern Highlands.

Dr. Lillian South, a 1904 graduate of Woman's Med, led the AWH's expansion to Jellico on the Kentucky-Tennessee border. From hookworm to rabies to leprosy, during Dr. South's treatment of the children in the area, she had identified the overabundance of cleft palates and lips. Although three years behind Charlotte at Woman's Med, every alumnus knew of Dr. Fairbanks' reputation and skill with a knife, including Lillian South.

Lillian greeted the fatigued travelers from the porch of the AWH health center, a small, whitewashed, wooden structure. "Welcome. We are so appreciative you've come to our humble town."

Brunette waves framing her face tapered to a loose chignon. Her dark floral print dress boasted a wide white cotton cuff on her upper left arm embroidered with AWH in large, black lettering. A strand of pearls mimicked the drape of the dress's neckline. She reached beyond Charlotte's offered hand and embraced first Charlotte, then Eliza. "Come meet one of our young lads. Bless his soul. He's the last one for vaccinations against typhoid this week."

A tow-headed boy of about eight peeked behind Lillian. She held up her index finger in a mock scold. "Timmy, let me see you inch your fingers back down to the marbles in your pocket. Remember what I told you? No pulling off the nice little Band-Aid," she said, tip-tapping her fingers down his arm. "We need that wonderful juice I injected to hop and skip through your body to keep you from getting sick."

Timmy nodded and rushed past her, slamming the screen door behind him. Eliza watched him scamper over to where a carbon-copy, larger version of the boy stood at the end of the dirt driveway. The man's overall straps slipped from his drooped, bony shoulders. The frayed hems of his pants hung loose against thin ankles. Timmy slid his frail hand into his father's weathered, pale one.

"Don't forget, Mr. Newcombe," Lillian called to the pair. "Rosie Mae's appointment is at three o'clock." She waved toward Charlotte and Eliza. "Dr. Fairbanks is the doctor I spoke about with you. She'll be tending to Rosie. And, lucky for us, she's brought Dr. Edwards to assist. Gentle, capable hands will take good care of our Rosie Ray of Sunshine. Timmy, keep those fingers away from your arm. Your momma wants to see you chasing Bowser down by the creek, not lying in bed like your sister."

Despite her weariness, Eliza perked up, listening to Lillian intone simple instructions. Lillian typified the Woman's Med training to practice medicine with a sense of science and sympathy. Her obvious care and commitment to these families ran deep.

Lillian's face darkened as they all watched four bare feet shuffle off toward the tree line and the rise of the mountains. "We had a rough time with the spring floods. Typhoid cases surged as high as the rivers. We tried to vaccinate as many as physically possible with a limited supply. Swollen streams cut off most of the mountain families, like the Newcombes. They lost their dear four-year-old daughter to the fever."

She opened the door and gestured Charlotte and Eliza to enter, "I'm concerned about the mother. Pregnant with her sixth and not much over twenty-five-years-old herself. A wee bit of a thing whose grief consumes her. I'm grateful that the father finally brought Timmy in today. What I really need, though, is someone to check on the mother. Elk Creek swallowed the closest midwife's house. She's moved down to Habersham. By mule, she might as well be in Knoxville."

As the pair disappeared into the dense thicket, Eliza realized that although she stood on soil which may have been united under the Rebel cause, Jellico, Tennessee and Warm Springs, Georgia stood worlds apart. With its telephones and radios, well-stocked dining halls, rehabilitative waters, and full complement of trained staff, Warm Springs hid the truth. While polio patients faced a dire health struggle, they arrived in Warm Springs with hope, encouraged by words on a plaque *to carry on despite all handicaps*. The challenges facing the families of Jellico and the surrounding area paralyzed their lives from birth to death. Where did they find their inspiration to rise when they fell?

CHAPTER FOURTEEN

The next morning, the sound of bacon sizzling woke Eliza from an exhausted slumber. Before Lillian had left the health center for her home in Williamsburg, Kentucky, fourteen miles north of Jellico, she had outfitted two narrow cots with starched white sheets and green Army-issued blankets. Weak daybreak stole in past the gauzy curtains. Eliza stretched her arms and swiveled her head to extend her kinked neck muscles. She had tried to plump the pillow last night, but to no avail. You can't plump corn husks.

She donned a plain navy shirtwaist and brushed her hair into a bun. When they arrived yesterday, Eliza had noticed a two-burner stove top and sink which doubled for instrument sterilization and as their kitchenette. Charlotte stood at the stove flipping pancakes in a well-seasoned cast iron pan. Coffee boiled in a glass percolator. Dark and strong. *Come to me, my comfortable companion*, thought Eliza. Coffee had been one of her best friends since medical school days. A tin plate of crisp bacon strips and a bottle of Vermont Maid syrup awaited the doctors on a rough-hewn table. You could take Charlotte out of state, but you couldn't banish a native Vermonter's inbred habits of early to bed, early to rise, and a penchant for local maple syrup.

Eliza reached for two cups perched on a wooden shelf above the sink. "Good morning, Charlotte," she said, laying them down on the counter. She lifted the pot from the burner. "Thank you for making breakfast."

"You're welcome, but I admit, I had self-preservation on my mind. I'm starving, and from your snoring, I knew there was no hope you'd be up on my schedule. We'll make a plan right now. I'm on breakfast detail. You can take dinner."

"Agreed." Eliza clinked her cup against Charlotte's. "But I fear my dinners won't come close to this spread, nor did I think of packing any important sustenance, like maple syrup."

Charlotte eyed her with pursed lips. "No, but you packed a jar of ether and a mask. Surely you knew Dr. South would provide all necessary surgical supplies. Eliza, we must address this. I have no tolerance for someone without her full faculties. These children are depending on us for safe and quick procedures."

Eliza felt the heat rising in her cheeks while the coffee cooled in the tin cup. She stared into the inky black liquid, unable to lift her head. "I'm so ashamed, Charlotte. There is no excuse, only my promise that the items in my bag will remain there."

For the next week, a job awaited her. She had a reason to be present. Charlotte had requested her assistance. Children with damaged lips and palates deserved the best treatment. Eliza must bury her need for the ether in her medical bag.

"I appreciate that you've had a rough year," said Charlotte. "But I'm here with you, for you. I'll help you keep that promise." She closed her hand over Eliza's and squeezed.

"Now. Shall we move on to today's agenda?"

Eliza wiped the corner of her eye, pulling a drip into the crevices of her crow's feet, and nodded.

"First, we'll walk through a practice procedure to ensure we're in perfect alignment. When I ask for a scalpel, I want it placed directly in my left hand. Immediately. I'll time the steps."

Flashbacks of operating theaters from their school days grounded Eliza. No matter what, no one dared to faint during one of Dr. Fairbanks' surgeries. Facial procedures could be especially gruesome. Even more trying, here in Jellico, the procedures involved young children, most of them under five years old. Mind-numbing fear would accompany those children. They and their parents would need assurance from confident doctors that success lay on the other side.

"Next, we need to prepare the operating area. I'm sure Lillian has seen that it's been cleaned, but I prefer to know it's been done to my standards. I'll take care of sterilizing the instruments. You can scrub the table. It wouldn't hurt to boil an extra set of gowns and caps as back-up and for this afternoon's appointments.

Eliza groaned. The need for housekeeper duties had not occurred to her, nor that they would fall to her responsibility. To think that a year ago she had managed a private practice as Dr. Eliza Edwards in the city of Boston. Today, she would tie an apron around her waist and a kerchief around her head to kneel upon the floor like a scullery maid.

Charlotte hadn't ceased her litany of the day's line-up. "At nine o'clock, we expect our first surgery. Jeremiah MacDonald is twenty-seven-months old. He's a palate patient. From Lillian's notes, I expect the repair should take us two hours, but I won't know for sure until I examine him myself. God willing, the parents have heeded her instructions to not feed him anything this morning. You will sit with him and the parents as he comes around. We'll need to plan on a home visit tomorrow and then send the healthmobile on their daily rounds for post-operative checks for the rest of the week."

Charlotte continued with the rest of the schedule, having committed to memory the details of each patient, from the surgery required to their age and family situation. Eliza picked up the breakfast dishes and headed to the sink. Her maid duties began now.

The morning wore on in silence. Table scrubbed. Gowns and caps washed. Instruments sterilized. The wall clock's hands ticked into place at ten-thirty. Eliza didn't dare to peek at Charlotte.

Next to her on the porch's wooden bench, Eliza wasn't sure if the heat seeping into the air between them came from the advance of the sun higher into the sky, or Charlotte's fury over the no-show patients.

Rather than face Charlotte's frown, Eliza surveyed the Center's front yard. The grounds bloomed with vines of white flowers on the verge of transforming into plump, red bells of sweetness. Pale pink dogwood petals swayed in the breeze, clinging to their branches. Irregular patches of sky blurred between birch tree limbs into shades of blue and gray. Below, lush ferns encircled the narrow trunks like greenery around Advent candles. The natural beauty of the woodlands settled Eliza. They offered a far more pleasing sight than Charlotte's pressed lips and drawn scowl.

A rustle arose from a corner of the woods' edge. A plaid cotton sleeve pushed aside a briar, allowing a woman with a child on her hip to emerge. The child's extended belly from malnutrition poked out from a ragged undershirt which partially covered his torso. His limbs, as thin as the dogwood tree's twigs, hung loose against his mother's body. The MacDonalds had arrived. Ninety minutes late and unaware of the disgruntled surgeon waiting for them.

"It's about time," Charlotte huffed to Eliza from the porch. "Confirm that the child is ready and tell the parents to wait outside." She disappeared into the front room to scrub in and reassemble her instruments.

Eliza waved to the approaching group. The father tipped the brim of his black felt hat. Mrs. MacDonald, with Jeremiah squirming on her hip, bent her head down to speak to a young girl tugging at the hem of her flour-sack dress. As they grew nearer, Eliza heard the mother shushing both children. "Look, there's a nice nurse waiting for us. See her smiling? She's happy we're here. She's gonna help the doctor take real good care of our 'Miah."

The sage words that John Clark had shared with her in Warm Springs reminded Eliza she should take up the battle of misconceived perceptions at another time. For now, she needed to focus on preparing Jeremiah for the steady, gloved hands of Dr. Fairbanks. With a corrected palate, he would grow quickly into a robust three-year-old, scooping up handfuls of the wild strawberries and cramming them into his mouth with painless ease as he called out to his sister to join him. His sister would clap her hands in glee that he could clearly enunciate his words.

Eliza opened her arms as she welcomed the family. "Good morning, Mr. MacDonald? Mrs. MacDonald? And this must be our brave soldier, Master Jeremiah. How are you today, young man?"

Jeremiah burrowed his shaking head into his mother's shoulder, kicking his legs against her thighs. His father peeled him from his mother's grip and said, "I'll bring him in. I want to meet the fancy man who Dr. South has brought down from New England. Wanna make sure he's not too wet behind the ears. My wife is a puddle just thinking about this." He nodded toward the woman standing with empty arms and vacant eyes, wringing her hands in silence.

"Miah's awfully small, as you can see. Not a lot of fight in him. Hasn't been able to suckle right since he was a pup. Still can't get much down 'cepting some corn mush."

A white-gowned figure appeared at the screen door. Eliza froze. If Mr. MacDonald had concerns about the doctor's age, Lord knows what he would think about her gender.

"Dr. Edwards," Charlotte said. "Bring the child in. We're drastically behind schedule."

Mr. MacDonald turned on his heel toward Eliza. "Are you the doctor??" he sputtered. His eyes ran up and down her body, pausing on her chest. Even with sagging breasts, no one could mistake that she was a woman. He reached to take Miah back.

"No. I mean, yes. I am Dr. Edwards, but I am not a surgeon. I'll be assisting Dr. Fairbanks." She tilted her head toward the doorway.

"Hell will freeze, and gold coins will rain from the sky before some woman uses my son to practice for next month's quilting bee, let alone a doddering old hag like her." He snatched Jeremiah from Eliza's arms with such force, the child dropped to the ground. At the tone of his father's voice, Jeremiah began to wail and fling clumps of dirt at the source of his father's distress. He scampered on his hands and knees back to his mother, lifting his bony arms in a plea. Eliza bent to brush the dirt from her stockinged legs.

"Mr. MacDonald, let me assure you, Dr. Fairbanks is as skilled as any man. Her eyes are sharp and her hand, steady. She graduated at the top of our class from medical school. After working within the Pennsylvania prison system, treating men and women, she answered the call of the American Women's Hospital. Perhaps you had a father or uncle who served in France? She was there. The Army allowed her to stitch up our soldiers."

At the doorway, Charlotte stood stoic, allowing Eliza the right to defend her abilities, and that of all women doctors.

"When my mother required a delicate surgery," Eliza continued, "I ignored the Harvard trained men at my doorstep and insisted that Dr. Fairbanks tend to her. If my sons had needed the procedure Jeremiah requires, I would have sent for her again. You won't find a more dedicated, capable, and knowledgeable surgeon. Neither her gender nor her age affects her abilities. If the United States Army, Dr. South, and I trust her, you should, too. Jeremiah is in the best of hands. Please. Bring him inside."

A soft voice spoke up. "Henry. How long have we waited for someone to come to our wretched spot? I can't bear to see my baby scarred and unable to eat any longer. I'm his mother. I trust them. Let them do it. Let him speak. Let him smile. Let my baby live."

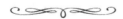

The height of the afternoon sun shone through the Center's front windows, competing with the glow of the shadeless floor lamp positioned next to the make-shift operating table. As Charlotte stepped back from the table, Eliza's fingertips brushed across

Miah's forehead and down over his eyelids. The wisps of his brown hair stuck to his temples. His relaxed breaths came as tiny puffs from his open mouth. A neat row of even sutures on the roof of his mouth boasted the steady and nimble fingers of Dr. Fairbanks.

"What a brave boy," Eliza whispered. And to herself, she thought, *well done, Dr. Edwards*. Charlotte was pleased. She'd even nodded her assent to allow Eliza to administer the ether in its rightful spot, over the mouth and nose of a surgical patient. Trust had been restored between doctor and assistant.

In a smooth, careful motion, Eliza eased her hands under Miah's bare back. Keeping him flat to prevent aspiration from any remaining trickle of blood from the suture areas, she carried Miah to the cot. She lowered him onto the starched white sheet, listening to Charlotte run through instructions with his parents.

"Wash your hands, under your fingernails, and up your arms at the sink. Use the brush for a good scrubbing. It would be best if your daughter waits outside. It's critical that we minimize the risk of exposing him to any germs. He's extremely vulnerable, but I expect he'll make a full recovery if you maintain the highest degree of cleanliness around him. Dr. South prepared a small bag for you to take home. Sterilized undershirts, extra soap, and some Blaud's iron pills to help with the blood loss. Crush the pills and mix them with water."

"Praise God," said Mrs. MacDonald with a catch in her throat. "Thank you ever so much." A heavy silence filled the room until Eliza heard Mr. MacDonald say the words she hoped would follow.

"Yes. Thank you, Dr. Fairbanks."

The sink faucet ran steadily for ten minutes as Mr. and Mrs. MacDonald scrubbed their skin raw, ignoring the pain in favor of their son's well-being. Eliza stood from kneeling next to the cot as they entered the room. "It was a complete success. Miah took the ether without a fuss. He should wake up soon. Stay with him through the afternoon to keep him still. He'll be groggy even after he wakes."

She placed a stack of sterilized rags into Mrs. MacDonald's hands. "Don't be alarmed if he drools a good amount and if there's some blood mixed in."

Mrs. MacDonald's frail body quivered.

"The blood is completely normal after a surgery. Do not wipe the inside of his mouth. Just let nature take its course," Eliza finished.

She handed a sheet of notepaper to Mr. MacDonald. "Here are some other instructions. Lots of water to keep the stitches clean and hydrated. Tomorrow, you can start him on a few spoonfuls of mush and gradually move on to soft fruits and vegetables. By the end of the week, add small pieces of meat. We'll send a nurse from the healthmobile out for checks every day for the next week. If he develops a fever, bring him back here immediately."

Mr. McDonald folded the sheet and tucked it into his back pocket without a glance. Eliza could have written the instructions in Arabic for all he knew. A knock came upon the door. "Dr. Edwards. The surgical area needs cleaning."

Eliza placed her hand on Mrs. MacDonald's shoulder. "Thank you for letting us take care of your Jeremiah," she said. "And don't worry, the nurse can review all the instructions again with you when you're home and settled and can focus better."

CHAPTER FIFTEEN

" *If you go out in the woods today, you're sure of a big surprise. If you go out in the woods today, you'd better go in disguise...*"

A singsong voice sounded across the yard, reaching Eliza as she sat on the health center's porch. Charlotte busied herself with sterilizing her equipment, preparing for the next scheduled surgery, three-year-old Rosie Mae Newcombe and her cleft lip. If the lines of *The Teddy Bear's Picnic* came from Mrs. Newcombe, Eliza expected a more pleasant first encounter than Mr. MacDonald's hostility. Silently, Eliza joined in as the song grew nearer. She had often hummed the tune to Will and Teddy.

"*For every bear that ever there was, will gather there together because, today's the day the teddy bears have their picnic.*"

As if on cue, a girl of three and a young woman in her late teens appeared. The girl dragged a ragtag cloth bundle that someone had tried to form into a bear shape without much success. True to the nickname that Dr. South had coined, Rosie Mae beamed like tiny rays of sun from her crooked smile and dancing green eyes. Billowing blonde locks framed her face. She held the older girl's hand in a tight grip as she gazed up at her with adoration. The woman, whom Eliza guessed to be seventeen or eighteen, resembled a wildflower with her delicate features. Beneath an outward beauty, an inner strength shone through to weather the pressure of an unexpected spring storm. A tumbling mass of rich brown curls hung over her shoulders, swaying in time to the swing of her arm holding onto to Rosie. With her free hand, she waved to Eliza.

"We're here, the fine and adorable Miss Rosie Mae Newcombe." She nodded toward the cloth bundle, "And Master Ted. Ready for the teddy bear picnic this afternoon, a perfect time for tea and jam." She winked at Eliza, hinting to play along with the ruse.

"Why, yes indeed," said Eliza. "The picnic will begin shortly, but we're not quite ready. I need to pull biscuits from the oven, and someone to mix the lemon tea. Could you help me, Miss...?"

"Grace Wilson. I'm an expert lemon tea mixer. Right, Rosie Ray? Now, you sit here on the stoop. I'll come get you as soon as everything's ready." She settled Rosie onto the step with the bear balanced in her lap before following Eliza inside.

"Thank you, Ma'am," she said under her breath to Eliza. "My brother-in-law didn't think Rosie would understand what's going on, so I thought a distraction would keep her calm. You know, pretend she's going on a fun adventure, not a scary surgery where a stranger cuts apart and re-sews her lip."

An astute plan dreamed up by a sympathetic doctor in the making, thought Eliza. "You're Rosie's aunt, then?" asked Eliza. "Her father, your brother-in-law. Where is he? Or your sister, Rosie's mother? We can't perform the procedure without them present."

From her skirt pocket, Grace withdrew a folded sheet of paper. "I came to the evaluation appointment. I understand the procedure, maybe better than her parents. I have her father's signature here on the form." She handed the paper to Eliza, marked with a *T N* on the bottom line.

"Please. My sister, well, she's gone down the gulley."

Eliza scrunched her face in puzzlement. "Where did she go?"

Grace chuckled. "Oh, no Ma'am. She didn't get anywhere. She's gone down the gulley—you know, blue? Sad, down in the dumps. Ever since they lost the baby. She won't leave the house. My brother-in-law, Tom, heard there's a crew in Burke Hollow for the new road coming through. He had to go and get a few dollars in his pocket. They're real bad off, like most folks around here. I tend to the kids all the time when Thomas finds work."

In her hand, she held a small composition notebook and a pencil used down to its nib.

"I promise to take notes to review with Rosie's momma and poppa."

Grace's deep blue eyes, heavy with a sudden rush of unshed tears, pleaded with Eliza. "I'll do whatever you say to make sure all goes right for our Rosie Ray of Sunshine. Please."

"It's not my place to decide," said Eliza. "I'm Dr. Edwards. I'm not the attending surgeon, I'm here only to assist. I'll need to confer with Dr. Fairbanks. She stepped out to use the privy. Please, wait outside with Rosie. I'll let you know when we've discussed the situation."

She heard Charlotte re-enter through the back door. Knowing that Dr. Fairbanks wouldn't sidestep protocols, Eliza explained they would have to trust Dr. South, that she had indeed witnessed Mr. Newcombe's signature on the consent form. "The aunt seems to be a capable and concerned caregiver. I think we need to proceed," Eliza said.

Charlotte placed the sterilized scalpel back down on the tray after a second inspection. "What about the post-op? The father signed the form with his initials. Can the parents even read instructions? How do we know this girl can?"

"She's prepared. Brought a notebook and even her own pencil."

"Since I'm not looking to return anytime soon, and certainly not waiting for a father to finish a job he needs, we might as well proceed."

Eliza called the girls in, suggesting Rosie might want to take a short nap before the picnic. Already drowsy by three o'clock, she clutched the bear to her chest as Grace laid her down on the cot. With a mother's touch, Grace stroked aside Rosie's blonde curls, crooning in a close whisper, *"Lullaby and good night, to my Rosie's delight. Those green eyes close them tight. Heavenly angels kiss you light. Hush-a-bye my sweet girl. Rest your head, hold my hand. Grace is near, so sleep on, I'll keep you from any fear."*

"What a lovely rendition, Grace," said Eliza, bending to scoop the sleeping child into her arms. "You've thought of everything to make this surgery as stress-free as possible for your niece. You are a gift to her."

Grace beamed at the encouragement from the doctor. "I love all my nieces and nephews. Really, all the children around here. They are God's gift to us. Most of 'em are so fragile. The hunger took many these past years. The ones it didn't take are still weak. Makes them easy prey for typhoid and all the other diseases. It breaks my heart. When I see a bunch of kiddos, it's like looking out at a flower garden that needs tending all the time to keep them blooming year after year. I know how much joy they bring to everyone."

Eliza removed Rosie's cotton dress and washed her face, chest, and arms when Grace placed her hand over Eliza's. "May I watch the surgery?"

Charlotte, who had finished scrubbing up at the sink, raised her eyebrows above her wire-rimmed glasses in Eliza's direction. In a flash, Eliza saw herself, Charlotte, and their classmates walking into an operating room to observe a facial surgery during medical school. Charlotte had advised the group then of how grucsome the surgery could be and that they should pinch each other to make sure no one fainted. Swooning women belonged on the pages of tiresome fairy tales, not on an operating room floor. And, with male students in attendance, they didn't need to cement the men's perception that women didn't belong in the operating room. Eliza chuckled to herself, recalling the three men prone on the floor, with their classmates fussing over them like a brood of hens. Not a single rooster crowed at that surgery, while the "hen medics," as the women were often called, stood in silent solidarity with pinch marks up and down their arms.

"Are you sure you could stand it?" Eliza asked. "One hundred percent of our attention will be on Rosie. We can't tend to you should you faint."

"Faint? Why would I faint?" Grace tossed her head, sending her hair swirling in the air. "When I was but ten years old, I saw an axe slip from my pappy's hand and tear open his shin. He spilled out a mugful of blood; axe must've hit an artery. I cleaned and bandaged it with a tourniquet until we got it stitched. I helped old Mrs. Carmichael, the midwife, before she moved away, with two deliveries last winter. I watched one of the Baker boys shove pebbles up his nose so far, we needed a blacksmith's horseshoe pick to pull them out. Every day since she was born, I've seen nothing but a beautiful smile on my Rosie Mae's face where most see a deformity to be a scared of or to make fun of. No, ma'am. You don't need to worry about me fainting. You just take care of my Rosie."

With experiences which could rival a first-year medical student, Charlotte gestured toward the sink. "Scrub in, Miss Wilson. You may observe, and if the opportunity arises, you can assist Dr. Edwards with simple tasks if we ask you to do so. I'll look for another gown and cap for you."

"Thank you, Doctor," Grace said. "I'll stay out of the way and learn with the guidance of our Lord, *who is my strength and my shield; my heart trusts in him, and he helps me.*"

"Psalms 28:7. Also from Psalms, *May he give you the desire of your heart and make all your plans succeed,*" said Eliza, handing Grace the bar of soap and brush. "Best get to scrubbing in. Dr. Fairbanks runs a tight ship. We need to start while Rosie is napping. She'll take the ether easier that way."

Pulling her hair back into a quick knot, Grace's assured smile filled the room with confidence. A young woman from the foothills of the Cumberland Mountains donned the clothing that Charlotte handed to her. The gown and cap fit her perfectly.

CHAPTER SIXTEEN

The rain pelted against the health center's corrugated tin roof, increasing to thunderous bangs. By early evening, Elk Creek's late spring trickle surged to a roar, overflowing its banks, and turning the dirt paths and roads to sludge. Charlotte declared that Grace and Rosie Mae would remain at the center after the surgery. A trek on foot across the turbulent waters of the creek and through the slick mud back to the Newcombes' cabin would be treacherous. Instead, they fashioned a crib from a large storage drawer for Rosie while Eliza heaped extra blankets and sheets into a bedroll on the floor next to it for Grace.

In the morning, Eliza found Grace at the cooktop, barefoot and with her faded red gingham dress belted at her waist. "I'm sorry, Dr. Edwards," said Grace. "Did I wake you?"

"Not at all. Between the rain drumming on the roof and worrying about Rosie, I haven't slept. How is she?"

"Still asleep. She stirred a few times during the night. I checked the gauze like you showed me and changed it once. I don't think she scratched it in her sleep. That's good, right?"

"Very good, yes."

Eliza tiptoed over to the drawer. Gazing down, she marveled at the innocence and peace she always found on the face of a sleeping child. Furrowed brows relaxed. Breaths eased into light puffs of exhale, *ppff, ppff*. Eyelids bared grim reminders of a harsh and troubled life. Rosie slept on her back; the thin sheet covering her tossed aside in a mangle at her feet. Her balled fists lay on either side of her head like a marathoner's raise of her arms in victory crossing the finish line. The square pad above her lip covered the sutures. The scar would fade over time, leaving the child with a sunny smile to match her nickname of Rosie Ray of Sunshine.

Grace sidled over to Eliza, "Can I take her home this morning? I know her momma wants her back quick. Ever since she lost the little one, she's afeared to let any of the kids out of her sight. Until she sees the good work you did, and that the kids who got the shot don't catch the typhoid, she doesn't trust doctors the way I do. I want her to know that Rosie's gonna be as right as rain."

"I don't see why not. But Dr. Fairbanks needs to evaluate her condition and make the final decision."

"Of course. Maybe you could come with me? I'm sure if Ruth meets you, she'll understand your kindness and will know that you would never hurt Rosie."

"Dr. South mentioned she's expecting another baby, and that she hasn't seen a doctor yet?"

"Number six is in the oven. I hope this one helps her get over losing Doris. It won't be a replacement. You can never replace a child. But if it fills a corner of the hole in her heart, then maybe she'll find her way out of the gulley."

"Our schedule is clear this morning," said Eliza. "I'd be happy to come with you."

A narrow, twisting footpath wove deeper into the woods. Outcropping ledges of granite, decaying tree trunks, and dense briars littered the edges of the well-trodden path. Clouds remaining from the evening's storm hung low over the

Cumberlands, dripping a mist into the air the higher Eliza, Grace, and Rosie climbed. In a sudden burst, a blaze of sunlight flooded the hillside, warming Eliza's cheeks and drying the sweat which dripped from her brow to her chin. Ahead of her, Grace led the way with Rosie balanced on her hip. Grace showed no signs of slowing, nor exertion after their two-mile walk. Her unaltered stride up the hill seemed to devour the ground. Every fifteen minutes, she'd pause and glance back. Eliza, teetering with every step, trudged forward, trying to keep up and feeling the years between them deepen into a chasm. She faced an uphill battle against the mountain and all that Grace possessed. Vitality versus fragility. Familiarity versus strangeness. Youth versus age.

Eliza wiped her forehead with another swipe of her handkerchief, now so damp that its purpose had disappeared. From the recesses of the laurel thicket, a crunch startled her. 'Coon? Snake? Fox? Porcupine? Skunk? Which foreign creature from the pages of a Thornton Burgess book, yet far less friendly, would bound from the woods and bite her ankle? A city girl from birth had no right to roam a forest, guided or unguided.

As the path widened, they came upon a clearing encircled by a ring of birch trees. The white bark of the trees framed the area like a white picket fence. Beneath one tree, a spray of purple, yellow, pink, and blue wildflowers rested on a small dirt mound. Eliza watched Rosie break free from Grace's clutch as they approached the area. Grace stopped, letting Rosie proceed alone to the grave. Rosie, in her three-year-old voice, lowered her head and spoke to the hillock, "Hi Dorie. Momma left you flowers today. They're lots of pretty colors. I's misses you."

Grace arrived by her side. "They are beautiful flowers, Rosie. Can you tell Dorie the colors?"

She reached her hand to the stalks, picking them up one by one. "Dis one is yallah, dis one is boo. Ooo, pretty pink. See dis one Gracie? What color is dis one?" She thrust the purple thistle toward Grace. "Ouch! Dis one bit me."

The thorny stem dropped to the dirt. Grace snatched at Rosie's hand before the girl could pop it in her mouth to nurse the pricker.

"Give me your finger, sweetness. It's dirty. Remember what the doctor said? We need to keep your lip cut clean. Let me check for the pricker."

Grace extracted a handkerchief from her skirt pocket, wiped the dirt from Rosie's index finger, and examined it for any puncture. "All okay!" she declared as she picked Rosie up and settled her on her hip.

Past the birches and after another five minutes, Grace called over her shoulder. "We're almost there. See? Up ahead?" Grace slid Rosie to the ground as she pointed to a small hollow.

Squinting through the mist, a formation took shape. Nestled amid poplar trees lush with fresh growth, a low log cabin with a slanting roof came into view. A porch ran along the length of its front. Eliza recognized young Timmy Newcombe lounging on the top step, leaning his elbows back upon the porch's rough-hewn planked floor. Arranged like Russian nesting dolls, two other Newcombe children sat on each step below him. Three pairs of silent, green eyes watched their approach. On the lowest stoop, another boy of about six years pushed a stick in the dirt, making uneven arcs. The sweep of the stick also kept three pecking chickens from coming too close to his bare toes. The youngest child, a girl, squirmed between Timmy's knees. He had his legs vise-clamped against her bony shoulders. Bare-chested, only a sagging cloth diaper covered her.

In front of her, Eliza heard Grace sniff and tsk. "Lookee here, Timmy. Alice got a soiled nappy. Why you letting her sit there in that mess? Ain't not her fault. How'd you like to be sitting in a pile of sheeet? You think you gonna be the man of the house whilst your pappy gone off to work? Then be the man and clean her up."

A different Grace than the one Eliza had met yesterday left the footpath and stomped up the steps. On her way, she tweaked Timmy's ear as she placed the hand of the girl with the sagging diaper into Timmy's and shooed them both toward the cabin's open doorway. Eighteen hours ago, Grace quoted the Bible. Choosing the right words and tone to fit an audience displayed an intellect which you couldn't teach.

The boy on the bottom step looked up from his dirt art. "Whaz that there on Rosie's lip? Lookin' like she growed a funny white 'stache like grumpy ol' man Foster. She gonna grow some whiskers on her chin, too?"

Upon hearing the taunt in her brother's voice and seeing him point the stick at her face, Rosie let loose the wail of a fisher cat, loud and agonized. She leaned into Eliza and buried her head in the soft cotton of Eliza's skirt.

Eliza bent to caress Rosie's back. She whispered into the girl's ear, pushing aside the blonde wisps. "Hush now. That silly brother of yours is just jealous that he's not wearing a badge of courage. That's what you have, Rosie dear. A little bandage over your cut to keep it clean so it will heal up quick. When we remove it, don't let him take it for himself. It's yours. You earned that badge."

Emboldened by Eliza's wise words, Rosie scampered toward the steps. The chickens scurried out of her path. As she passed her brother, she slapped the side of his head. "You da old man. And lazy. You got no badges." She disappeared through the doorway, calling ahead, "Momma, Momma, looks what I got."

The boy pointed his stick at Eliza. "Hey lady. I wants a badge. Not fair just Rosie get one."

"Well, Mr.—what's your name, dear?"

"I am Harold Newcombe," he said, puffing out his sunken chest.

"Mr. Harold, those chickens scare the dickens out of me. If you keep them away from me, that would be a brave deed deserving of a badge of courage. Can you do that?" She winked at the boy, opened her bag, and extracted a gauze square and roll of white tape as proof she had the tools to fashion a badge.

Through the cabin door, Eliza stepped into a scene like those she had read in Laura Ingalls Wilder's *Little House* series, depicting life in the woods over sixty years ago. A rock fireplace, chinked with light gray mud, dominated the side wall of the large room. Its open hearth served as the cabin's primary heating source. Next to it, a wood box held a few pieces of kindling. In the corner, a heap of blankets atop a straw tick mattress on a low rope bed frame declared the space as the children's sleeping quarters. From the looks of it, Eliza figured the three oldest children shared the single bed. The two boys with their heads at the top of the bed and Rosie with her head at the footboard edge; six legs entwined like the briar bushes' twiggy thicket. The youngest one in the diaper must still sleep with her parents.

Flour sacks torn and stitched into uneven lengths hung at the two paned windows, lining the cabin's front wall, and blocking any daylight which might shine through the grime-streaked glass. Positioned between them, a black cast iron cookstove resembled the cold and unused lumps of coal sitting inside its drawer space. A pewter oil lamp emitted a low glow from the middle of a long table covered with a red checkered oilcloth. Next to the table, an ice box's door had been left unlatched and open. Eliza could see two earthenware crocks inside. She feared the contents would spoil if a block of ice didn't appear soon.

A rocker and ladder-backed chair, both with rush seats, faced the fireplace. Beneath them, a braided rag rug lay over the earth-packed floor, its colors faded to dull browns and reds. A woman with hollow eyes rocked, staring into the charred remains of a long-dead fire. Only the mouse-brown color of her hair told her age. Otherwise, Eliza assumed that Grace's grandmother sat in the chair. Grace knelt before the woman. She tucked greasy strands of hair behind the woman's ears and murmured in her sing-song cadence.

"Ruth, your Rosie Ray of Sunshine is here. My, she was a brave girl. And so good. Stayed nice and still while the doctors took care of her. Rosie, hon, give your momma a smile."

Rosie twisted a lock of her blonde hair around her index finger. She looked up at her mother's vacant stare. Grace nodded, urging Rosie to spread a smile across her face like an upside-down rainbow. Her radiance washed away darkness and brought hope for a new day. Eliza felt Grace's plea that a ray of sunshine from Rosie could wash away her mother's darkness. Rosie responded to her aunt's encouraging nudge. She fingered the square above her lip. "See Momma? I's got a badge of porridge."

She took Eliza's hand. "Here, Momma. The doctery lady come, too. She's a nice doctery lady. Says I'm way braver than silly Hadold."

At the mention of an intruder into her sphere of despair, Mrs. Newcombe twisted around to find Eliza standing a foot behind her. She hissed toward Grace, "What's she doing here? You said you'd take care of Rosie afterwards. I don't want anyone here seeing me like this." Her ashen cheeks flushed. "The house. The kids. Oh, Grace. Now, what have you done?"

Eliza stepped forward, alerted to the fear and fury in Mrs. Newcomb's voice. To many mountain people, a person in authority, someone like a doctor, meant one thing. They wielded the power to make decisions and changes. If they found an incapacitated mother and father who left for weeks on end to find work, they could seize the children and place them in foster homes and orphanages.

"Good afternoon, Mrs. Newcombe." Eliza said. "I'm Dr. Edwards with the American Women's Hospital. I assure you, I'm not here in any capacity except to see Rosie settled and review some of her follow-up care with you. If Grace can stay for a few days, that would be a tremendous help to you; she's very capable and devoted to what's best for Rosie."

Mrs. Newcombe buried her face in the heels of her hands and burst into tears. Between sobs, she spoke toward the fireplace, muffled behind her cupped hands. "I'm devoted. I love my kids. All of 'em. I love my Doris. I loved her. I tried to take care of her. I did." She doubled over the bump in her belly and stroked it like the top of a kitten's head. Her shoulders heaved as grief claimed her frail body.

Grace rubbed her sister's back. "Oh, Ruthie. We know you did."

Inching around to the front of the rocker, Eliza knelt before the broken woman. "Shh, dear. I'm sure you looked after your little one as well as any mother. It's not your fault. Typhoid is a terrible disease. Many lose their lives to it. Healthy children and adults. No one knows why it takes some and not others. There's little that anyone can do once it takes a tight grip." Eliza reached for Ruth's hands, pulling them down from her face, revealing the tear tracks upon her cheeks.

"But you, you've helped your other children," continued Eliza. "You sent them for vaccination shots. You made sure Rosie's cleft was corrected. You are caring for your children. You're doing a remarkable job."

Timmy and the youngest one, wearing a fresh diaper, appeared from the back bedroom. Harold, finished with warding off chickens, joined them. Eliza beckoned the three children over to stand next to Rosie.

"Mrs. Newcombe, look," said Eliza. "These four need you. Your next baby will need you, too. But you can't care for them unless you take care of yourself first."

CHAPTER SEVENTEEN

True to her declaration to Ruth, Eliza focused on Rosie's follow-up care to give Ruth a single purpose. One child at a time. One day at a time. If Ruth managed a few tasks each day, Eliza hoped she would climb out of her grief gulley.

By noon, Eliza finished her last demonstration of how to change Rosie's bandage. Using the extra scraps, she fashioned another small square for her protector from the attack chickens. She showed it to him, saying, "And here you are, Mr. Harold. If you clear those chickens out of my way to leave, I have your badge of courage ready. Where would you like to wear it? On your lip like Rosie, or shall I pin it here, over your strong and worthy heart?" She tapped the loose overalls strap draped over his chest.

Harold giggled, running outside to pick up his stick and began shooing the hens back toward the coop.

"All clear for me to head out," Eliza said.

On the porch, Grace said, "Are you sure you can manage walking back alone? The kids need lunch, and I should put Rosie and Alice down for naps. Unless you want to join us, and then Timmy or I could walk you back?" From the hesitation in Grace's voice, Eliza understood the scant meal fixings wouldn't adequately feed four children and three adults. Grace was kind to offer, but Eliza would rather the meager foodstuffs she saw in the icebox go to the children and their pregnant mother.

"Although it would have been wise to drop some breadcrumbs like Hansel and Gretel, I think I can find my way. I don't recall many forks in the path. And, if I promise not to take Mr. Frost's less traveled one, I should be fine," said Eliza.

A puzzled look crossed over Grace's face. "Who? We don't have a Mr. Frost around these parts."

Eager to expand Grace's interest in literature, Eliza said, "Robert Frost is a poet from New England. He wrote a famous poem about the choices we make in life, using forest paths to illustrate his idea. It closes with the lines, *Two roads diverged in a wood, and I—I took the one less traveled by, And that has made all the difference.*"

Grace rested her chin on her fist as she looked out to the pathway leading away from the house. "Hmmm. If the pack horse librarians come by again, I'll ask if they have any of Mr. Frost's books. We never read Yankee poets in school."

From the moment Eliza had met Grace, she had wondered about the young woman's education. Children from mountain families often stopped their schooling by the sixth grade when they were old enough to work.

"How far did you go in school, Grace?" asked Eliza.

"I earned the only high school diploma handed out in the last two years. Teacher suggested I head down to Knoxville for the University or up to Williamsburg for Cumberland College. I guess teaching follows a well-known road. Right? But even if I had the money, I'm not sure teaching's where my true heart lies."

Eliza recalled the months before she started Woman's Med. She, too, had had questions about where her true desires lay. A fortunate encounter with a student at Woman's Med, Anandibai Joshi, had inspired Eliza to consider a path into the world of medicine. At the bottom of her medical bag, folded neatly into thirds inside a yellowed envelope, Eliza carried a copy of Anandibai's application letter written over forty years ago. As she reached for the bag, she said to Grace, "And to be true to oneself, you must not only follow, but throw your entire soul into realizing those desires. I'd like to share a few words of wisdom from a woman who helped unlock my desire."

With the treasured page in her hand, Eliza read the final lines aloud, "*My soul is moved to help the many who cannot help themselves.* Grace, perhaps your love of children stems from knowing how helpless they are. Maybe you are meant to help them by becoming a pediatrician, a children's doctor. The only way children in this area will grow up to see the better days you want for them is by receiving the proper medical care which they desperately need and from someone they trust."

"But..." Grace started.

"I understand. The money. I'll consult with Dr. Fairbanks and Dr. South and discuss ideas about how you could finance your undergraduate work as a first step. Come by before I leave on Saturday. Hopefully, we'll have a plan for you."

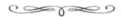

Eliza checked her wristwatch. Fifteen minutes had passed since she had left the Newcombes' cabin. A sensible woman would have hurried along to limit her time in the woods alone. Did bears live in these woods? Wolves? Mountain lions? Animals could smell fear. With every step she took, panic rose within her veins, oozing out of her pores to alert the hungry beasts which may lie in the thickets. A snapped twig, if she misplaced her step, would further signal her presence.

The path ran parallel to the edges of the creek. After yesterday's storm, it had tamed to a light gurgle, keeping the waters below its banks. Up ahead, she saw the path divert away from the guiding creek into the denser wooden section, which would take her back to the health center. She felt exposed, like open prey which exhausted her more than the trek. She needed to rest and collect her wits, tamping down her trepidation.

A boulder jutted out from the creek banks, leveled off with a flat top as high as Eliza's waist. She paused to immerse herself in the beauty of the natural world, pushing aside images of hulking bears like boulders and mountain lions with teeth as sharp as any wood axe. Delicate drops of lady slippers grew scattered amid the trunks of dogwoods, horse chestnuts, and poplars. A leafy canopy created a latticed arbor to shield from the sun's blinding heat. Birdsong filled the air with tweets, chirps, and titters. Flits of a tufted titmouse and yellow-rumped warbler startled Eliza as they descended upon a cluster of plump huckleberry bushes.

As she watched the birds peck at the berries, she hopped up onto the natural seat the rock provided. Tranquility washed over her. Uncertainty, upheaval, and loss had consumed her over the past year. Today's trip to the Newcombes' cabin formed an idea in her mind. These mountain families deserved more than an occasional healthmobile visit. Eliza needed a purpose. A new life compass, fashioned in the mountains of Tennessee, could point her away from despair and darkness. She would put her idle hands to work and plug her empty heart.

Lost in her thoughts, she didn't see nor hear the tall, barrel-chested man with a fishing pole balanced over his shoulder until he was next to the rock.

"You forgot your pole," he said in a pleasing baritone voice.

"Excuse me?" said Eliza with a small gasp, pulling her stare from the creek's ripples.

"Most folks sit in that spot for one reason. 'Tis the best place to cast into the downstream current. Many a trout have taken their final breaths on this here rock."

Flustered and unsure if the man was asking her to relinquish the prime fishing spot, Eliza slid off the granite seat. Her shoes hit the dirt and kept on sliding until she found herself plopped onto the ground. Her dress shimmed up above her knees. With a quick tug, she pulled at the hem and stood. The man offered his hand to help her rise as a tight-lipped smile stole across his weathered, chiseled face. Creases of crow's feet, years in the making, deepened like quotation marks around his steel gray-blue eyes. Eliza accepted his calloused hand for a moment to regain her upright balance. She let go of his hand and smoothed her dress. With his freed hand, he brushed back his wavy salt and pepper hair from his high, square forehead. A goatee, whiter at his chin than the faded blonde red above his lip, grew in a thick stubble around his mouth. The rest of his hair fell in waves to his chin line.

She gestured to the cleared spot on the rock. "Ready for your fish, sir."

"Sir?" he said. "I haven't been called that in a hog's lifetime. Been called pappy, Pops, hey you, geezer. My wife used a few choice names. But only my momma called me by my given one—Chester. Most folks call me Chet. Chet Wilson. Pleased to meet you, ma'am."

"Wilson? Are you related to Grace Wilson?"

His thin-lipped smile broke into a full-faced grin. His eyes twinkled with adoration. "Gracie is my granddaughter."

"You must be a very proud grandfather. She is a remarkable young woman. I met her when she brought Rosie in for her surgery. I'm Dr. Edwards with the American Women's Hospital. I've just left them after we got Rosie settled at home." She extended her hand back to his rough one for a proper introduction, as she had been taught.

He let out a low whistle. "A lady doctor. You don't say. I'd heard there were some in these parts giving the shots and all but didn't know they was doing much more than nursing duties. If that ain't the bees' knees. How do you do, Dr. Edwards?" he said with a slight bow.

Eliza pondered whether he meant his bow to be facetious or sincere. Lord knows she had met enough men throughout her career who found her doctor title off-putting, unbelievable, or downright abhorrent. After glancing at his honest smile, however, she decided he intended a show of respect, and maybe a touch of wonder. The extra minute he held their handshake beyond a polite length of time made her consider him with a touch of wonder, too.

"You haven't heard of the healthmobile with the American Women's Hospital?"

"No, ma'am. Me and the family have gotten along fine these years. Midwife Carmichael knows her way around an herbal remedy for just about anything that ails ya. She's been the one that has caught many a babe, if not most all of 'em, for as long as I can remember."

"Dr. South mentioned her. But did she recently move? Lost her house in the spring flood? I wonder who'll be tending to your granddaughter, Ruth, when her time comes? I'm concerned with her mental state and that she may need extra help for the delivery."

"Aw, we'll figure it out. The girl may be down the gulley now, but we'll pull her through. We always do with our own."

Eliza studied the strong bear of a man standing before her. His large, gentle arms could coax his granddaughter from her despair. She imagined him standing next to Ruth's birthing bed, holding her hand with as much love and concern as any woman.

"I expect you will, Mr. Wilson," Eliza smiled at him. "Now, I mustn't keep you from your fishing. What's the expression? Catch them when they're running?"

"Before the best ones get away," he chuckled. "You'll be able to find your way back?"

"I can manage. I would appreciate, however, if you can assure me no wild beasts lurk ahead."

"Nah. You'll be fine. Just stay clear of the wild turkeys. They can be meaner than a stuck pig. Flap your arms and they'll think you're one 'em. Pleased to meet you, Dr. Edwards." He tipped his head and picked up his fishing pole.

"Thank you for the advice, Mr. Wilson. Very nice to meet you, too."

Eliza brushed the front of her dress. With her medical bag bouncing against her hip, she set off with clear images in her head. She, a city girl her whole life, flapping her arms like a wild turkey. And Chester Wilson. Chet. Caring grandfather. Able fisherman of the Cumberland Mountains. A man who had a wife. A friend to the lost.

What was it Olga had said to her over the phone when she was in Warm Springs? *The few times I left you on your own, you fell in love with the wrong man. Twice! Now don't go falling for a suave Southern gent, fooled by a syrupy drawl and rugged good looks.*

CHAPTER EIGHTEEN

By Friday afternoon, Charlotte pulled through the last stitch, neat and taut, on the final patient of the week. Nine fledgling lives forever changed. The doctors had tended to the parents, too. They had stitched hope into hearts as enduring as the cross-stitched *Count Your Blessings* samplers, which hung on many of the families' cabin walls.

Eliza gathered the sleeping child from the operating table. She gestured to the mother through the window to join her as she took him into the back room for his waking from the ether. Eliza had administered every drop of the ether in the clinic's supply cabinet and from the near-empty bottles in her bag to the young patients. Each child had melted into a pain-free slumber while Charlotte operated. The gas had been used for its intended purpose. With their busy schedule throughout the week, Eliza had fallen into her cot each night, exhausted, yet fulfilled, without the aid of a mesh mask over her face.

After settling the child and his mother together, Eliza returned to help Charlotte clean the area. "Congratulations, Charlotte. Another fine operation. We've served these children and families in ways we may never fully appreciate." She untied her gown and pushed the cap off her head. "I, too, am grateful to you. You can't know how much this trip means to me. What I've learned. What I've given up...I don't mean a sacrifice. I mean my..."

"I know, Eliza," said Charlotte. "You kept your promise. Just see to it you continue to keep it back in Boston. You had only used the ether, correct?"

Eliza nodded.

"Well, that's a blessing. Morphine would have presented a more serious situation. If you keep yourself busy and your mind focused on the work we did here, you shouldn't have a problem overcoming the urge."

The slam of a car door in the health center's circular drive interrupted their discussion. A mingle of cheery voices lifted and blended into a lighthearted cadence to welcome the week's end. Charlotte nodded toward the doorway. "That'll be the mobile. Make sure they know that we've depleted their stock of adhesive tape, gauze, antiseptic cream, peroxide, and hypodermic needles. They could use at least three more sets of sheets, and this gown has seen enough washings to fall apart the next time it hits the boiling vat."

On the road from Tennessee to Florida, a small, but mighty group of women—doctors, dentists, nurses, and nutrition workers—made up the AWH's mobile health unit. Their Chevrolet Coupe towed a trailer outfitted with built-in cabinets to store supplies, as well as a two-burner gas stove for heating and sterilizing instruments. Four women spilled from the black coupe, with equal parts exhaustion and elation written across their faces. Eliza greeted them from the porch. "Welcome back! Whew, you all look done in. Come in. I threw together my son's favorite chicken dish for us. I hope no one minds if I used up the sherry."

A young woman wearing a nurse's cap tilted her head to the side, saying, "It's been a week. I don't know about the rest of you, but I'll trust you Dr. Edwards that there's enough sherry in the chicken pot to soothe my frazzled nerves."

"My son calls it my *Boozey Chicken*. It should do the trick," said Eliza.

Gathered at the makeshift dining table, Eliza and Charlotte listened to the team recap their week's tally. All surgical patients who required post-op checks showed no signs of infection. Their parents had followed the instructions Eliza had reviewed with them. Fifty-eight Cumberland Mountain area residents had received typhoid and smallpox vaccinations. Four families agreed to sit through a discussion about meal planning and the benefits of a more robust diet, including fruits and vegetables. Two families refused, stating that the green leafy vegetation the nutrition worker suggested should be left to the cows and mules. That stuff wasn't fit for human consumption. The dentist had extracted seven decayed teeth; three of them from one obstinate man who complained he had nothing left with which to "chaw his tabaccy". A ten-year-old boy showed symptoms of either strep throat or made him a candidate for a tonsillectomy. Charlotte groaned at the hint that she may need to stay on for another surgery. Five children, all in the same family, presented evidence of hookworm.

The doctor of the group added her notes. "Will one of you ask Dr. South to order more albendazole for the hookworm cases? I expect more flare-ups over the summer months."

She shifted her gaze to Eliza. "The results of too many days stuck inside this winter with unemployed men appear to be taking shape. I'd say we have at least six pregnant women on the route. With Midwife Carmichael's move, I fear for their well-being. Dr. South cannot expect me to sit awaiting a call. Nor do I have much more training than from my intern rotation fifteen years ago."

Eliza doled out another serving of chicken to the young nurse as she ticked off numbers in her head. Ruth Newcombe, plus six others that were known of, would need maternity services. Grace could assist Ruth, but what of the others? The lives of seven women and seven babies, maybe more, were at risk.

After the AWH team departed for their boarding house, Charlotte headed to the bedroom to pack, leaving Eliza with the dinner dishes. *She really does expect me to play second fiddle,* thought Eliza as she plunged her hands into the sink filled with hot, sudsy water. The burn echoed the heat in her throat. As she drew the dishrag across each earthenware plate, experiences from the past year swirled in her head. Her four and a half months in Warm Springs with Kay had provided a short-term stint of work, yielding a pitiful three hundred dollars in income. Back in Boston, when on the rare occasion, Aunt Florence had invited Eliza to join her long-time friends for a museum outing or lecture, Eliza sat silent, an outsider, listening to inside jokes and gossip. Eliza's last letter from Teddy reported they would depart San Diego next week. Will's weekly dinner visits for one of his mother's home-cooked meals had become more sporadic. Eliza suspected a woman occupied a seat at a restaurant across from her son, apparently offering him something more enticing than a chicken soaked in sherry and chewy gingersnaps. She should be relieved. At least Will wasn't dwelling on the episode in Baltimore or his father's death. Here in Jellico, Eliza handed off surgical duties to the expert Dr. Fairbanks. What awaited her in Boston? A barren appointment calendar, a list of more hospitals without a position for a fifty-eight-year-old woman doctor, and a promise she needed to keep in the face of temptation. Her medical license still allowed her to order supplies, like jars of ether.

Enough, she thought. She snapped the dish towel with a hard flick of her wrist. *Dr. Edwards,* she said to herself and the line of plates in the drying rack, *idle hands are the devil's workshop. It's time to hone your craft in your own workshop.* If a position couldn't be found, she'd make one. Right here in the foothills of Tennessee.

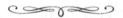

Saturday morning arrived with Charlotte up at daybreak. Her steel surgical instruments clinked as she rolled them into a felt pocketed wrap and tucked them inside the open suitcase sitting on her cot. Eliza rose from the one next to her. She swung her arms high and then down to reach her fingertips to her toes. The elongated stretch of her back tingled her nerves. The energy pulse quickened her heartbeat. She smiled, turning over the plan in her mind that she had developed overnight.

"Did you pack last night, Eliza?" said Charlotte. "The car is due at eight to get us out of this God-forsaken place."

Eliza brushed back the muslin curtain hanging at the single window. She gazed at the early sun gilding the tops of the green mountains in the distance. Powder puff clouds softened into a bluebell sky. Swaths of mist dispersed as the sun's rays hit them. She imagined other women inside the cabins nestled in the woods, rising from a rope bed to poke embers into flames. Life stirred and called for blessings to fortify oneself against the challenges of another day in Appalachia.

"I am not packed," Eliza said.

"Well, shake a leg. I, for one, have had my fill of sleeping on a cot, dirty and uncouth children milling about, uneducated parents with no teeth, and arguing with them about why I should operate on their children. Honestly, this past week has been nearly as difficult as wartime in France. It's time I got home to Vermont, where I can inhale without swallowing a mouthful of no-see-ums mixed with a pint of humidity."

"I'm sorry to hear this week has been a burden for you. I guess my opinion of this spot is quite different. In fact, I don't want to leave."

Charlotte pressed down the suitcase top and snapped the brass tuck locks into place. "Have you started using the ether again? Having delusional thoughts? Your home, like mine, is in a civilized world. It's called New England."

"I'm considering that there's a place for me here," stated Eliza. She let the curtain drop and faced Charlotte full-on. "When Lillian arrives, I'm going to propose we build a Maternity Shelter like the ones AWH built in Spartanburg and Greenville. As you've seen, there's a desperate need. And I desperately need to be useful somewhere. Here is as good as any place."

She glimpsed gray wisps swirling into the sky from a stone chimney in the distance. A new path awaited if she yielded to her footsteps marking the way.

CHAPTER NINETEEN

July 1937

*C*alls –
~~Florence, Will, Olga.~~
    Letters
Dean Tracy – '37 graduates for possible positions.
Dr. Lovejoy – guidelines for proposal.
Bessie – pitch story idea, photos needed.
Teddy – your mother has not gone mad.
Which agencies most likely to fund? County / state / federal
Congressman Morrisson – what committees does he sit on? Ask
    Kay.
Items/Budget/Donations/Funding: equipment, beds, supplies, pay
    scales, phone.
Local hospitals for items they may discard.
Sewing circles – uniforms, mother nightgowns, layettes
Red Cross – linens
Edwards Wool – formal letter to Albie and Fred for blankets.
Junior League – Sally for Philadelphia chapter, Mamie for Boston,
    others???
Girls' Friendly Society – draft letter, quote their motto, "Help us
    all to bear one another's burdens."
Meals – dairy farm, bakery, produce – garden for the Center?

Referrals and admitting privileges – need to secure for complicated
  cases.
For Grace: list of medical texts for Will to ship down, Bessie's
  closet cast-offs.

Eliza tapped the sheets against the counter, which served as a makeshift desk. Over the week following Charlotte's departure, Eliza and Lillian discussed ways to enroll Grace at Cumberland College. Lillian agreed that the young woman showed the intellect and desire to continue her education. She would provide Grace with room and board in exchange for assisting at Lillian's Williamsburg clinic. With Grace's secondary school credentials in hand and recommendations from her teacher and Dr. South, along with the College's well-endowed funding, Grace would easily qualify for a full tuition scholarship.

Once plans for Grace were settled, Eliza turned to how they might build a Maternity Shelter in Jellico. She had been pleased with Lillian's reaction. But now, as the idea grew in scope and her list filled multiple pages, anxiety elbowed its way into her psyche. Eliza had never managed such an undertaking. When she began her practice in Boston, Olga had sat at the desk across from her. This project would demand skills in bargaining, budget planning, hiring and supervising staff, and other areas she had not thought of yet. Her long-ago classes in Organic Chemistry explored the structure of chemical compounds, not the building blocks of a business's financial plan.

"Doc Edwards! Dr. Edwards, are you there?" A high-pitched yell called her name, becoming louder as the voice came closer. Eliza dropped the papers on the counter and rushed to the door. Timmy Newcombe emerged from the wooded path. In his hand he held the end of a frayed rope. The other end of the rope looped around the neck of a sway-backed mule. Its ribs pushed against the brown horsehair of its belly. Timmy tugged the animal forward, calling again. "It's Momma! Gracie says she needs ya. Oh, Doc Edwards, please, can you come?"

The beast stopped in its tracks, laid back its black ears, and brayed a mournful guttural opinion of its roped situation. Eliza stumbled through the screen door, startled by the scene and the noise.

"Ah, hush up, you dang thang," Timmy said as he swatted the rope in the mule's face.

"Timmy. Don't do that. You'll only upset it more. What is it? What's wrong with your momma?" said Eliza.

"Grace says the baby's coming too soon. She don't know what to do. She's afeared. Sent me to get you."

Eliza raced back inside. She scrawled a message on her notepad to the healthmobile team, who were due to return by the afternoon. *At Newcombes, past the creek. Mother in pre-term labor. E.E.*

From the chair next to the door, she picked up her medical bag, then turned to the cabinets. In a frantic rush, she jammed two extra folded sheets into a pillowcase. She hoped she wouldn't need them. But once a baby decided its time had come, it was near impossible to stop. Eliza feared Ruth's mental state would swallow her whole if she lost this baby, too. She banged the swinging porch door open with her hip, the linen bundle under one arm and her bag dangling from her tight grip in her other hand.

"You go on ahead, Timmy. Let them know I'm coming as fast as I can," said Eliza.

Timmy jerked the mule's rope. Its head bobbed down with the tug. "That's whys I got ol' Ollie. Pops said if I poke enough, he'll trot and I can run alongside. You need a hoist up?" Timmy interlaced his fingers into his version of a mounting block.

Eliza suppressed a bray of her own. Were they all a bit crazy? Chet suggesting she ride a mule? And Timmy, thinking that his small, frail fingers could withstand the heft of her matronly figure? Thick woods and a running creek lay ahead over a two-mile trek. How long had it taken the last trip when she went with Grace to bring Rosie home? Forty-five minutes? Scattered rocks required careful foot placement to avoid a turned ankle. High creek waters involved stopping to take off shoes and then putting them back on. She would waste precious time while Ruth's contractions built, attended by her seventeen-year-old sister and anxious grandfather. Grace and Chet couldn't be expected to handle a potentially life-threatening situation for both Ruth and the baby. How much faster could a mule walk, or trot?

"Hold these," she said, thrusting the linens into Timmy's arms and dropping her bag to the ground. As she'd seen done in the days of her childhood when horses still clopped down the streets of Philadelphia, she positioned her hands on the mule's back and hoisted her body up until she was draped across it like a saddle bag. Her hair fell loose from its bun and covered her face. Swiping at the strands with one hand, with her other, she reached to clutch the beast's black mane. She swung her right leg over its back. She wobbled. Her dress and slip rose. The rough horsehair scratched around her girdle's garter clips against her bare thighs. The daughter of an English wool merchant and a Philadelphian society woman thought to herself, *Dear Lord, if my mother could see me now*. With one hand, she grabbed a hank of mane.

"Timmy, hand me my bag," she said, gesturing for him to place it in the crook of her arm.

Her stockinged legs hung down against the mule's ribs. She tapped the heels of her sensible black-tie shoes into Ollie's sides.

"Ok, let's go. But please. Don't poke Ollie. I'm not made for a Wild West bronco show."

After twenty minutes of trotting along, Eliza and Ollie entered a clearing in front of the Newcombes' cabin. Timmy jogged next to them. From inside, Eliza heard Ruth's begging words sob. "There's another one comin', Grace. How do we stop 'em?"

Chet burst through the door. Eliza looked down at the balled-up navy day dress and white lace slip at her waist. Her thick, exposed calves trembled. There would be no graceful way to dismount from Ollie. Chet reached up his arms and grabbed her torso. As if she were a sack of potatoes, he swung her off the mule and planted her on the ground. After jostling through the woods, she welcomed the packed dirt beneath her feet. She motioned for Chet to relieve Timmy of the bundle of linens. Together, they hurried up the porch steps.

In the front room, Rosie, Alice, and Harold huddled in a mangle of limbs, whimpering in unison. Grace stood next to Ruth's bed, her fingers splayed across her cheeks and her eyes red. Eliza saw the fear in the girl's face despite her desperate attempt to hide it from her sister. Ruth thrashed on the bed. The bed clothes had been tossed on the floor in a heap. Eliza had delivered many home births over the course of her practice, but never in a spot as disorderly and with as many distractions as the Newcombes' cabin. She set to righting the scene from its chaos.

To Chet, she said, "Have Timmy take the other children outside. They're upsetting Ruth. Is the fireplace going? Can you get some water boiling? I don't know how many times Timmy dropped the sheets on our way. We'll need to re-sterilize at least one set to be sure. My instruments may need to be sterilized, too."

Grace placed her hand on Eliza's shoulder. "What should I do?"

"Can you give me an assessment?" asked Eliza. "Do you know how many months along she is? When did the contractions start? Have you timed how long between each contraction? Have her waters broken? Does she show any signs of fever? Any evidence of a bloody or mucus discharge?"

"Um. Um." Grace's voice quivered. Despair claimed her soft features.

Eliza calmed her approach. "It's all right, Grace. I'm sorry. Let's take them one at a time." Eliza opened her bag and pulled out two headscarves. She handed one to Grace. "When I saw Ruth last week, I estimated she might be about seven months. But I don't know her body. With the others, did she ever get so large she had difficulty walking?"

"Oh, no. Not at all. She barely ever needed a hatching jacket. Wore most of her same clothes. If she hadn't told me, I would hardly of known another kid was coming," said Grace. The color returned to her cheeks, rising with confidence that she could provide details about the patient.

"That helps. Maybe it's a situation where she's scared after losing Doris. In her mind, she isn't ready. She wants to delay the arrival, so she thinks it's early. The baby may be full-term. Or close enough that she'll be okay. What else can you tell me?"

Grace slipped into a careful recap of the afternoon. She had been at Chet's house when Timmy arrived with the news that his momma had taken to her bed and sent him to fetch her.

Ruth admitted to her that the contractions had come in sporadic, uneven spurts since the morning. Her waters had not broken, and she showed no signs of fever, blood, or other discharge. The discomfort, however, had increased into the afternoon hours.

"Excellent," said Eliza. "I have a better understanding of what we're facing. I need to examine Ruth now. Do you want to help your grandfather, or come with me?"

"I'll be right there. Gotta grab a few things."

Eliza watched Grace exit the cabin. She heard snippets of instructions to the children outside. *Chickens. Crows. Woodpile, no, not you Rosie, let Timmy. Rosie cut some...out back by Granny's grave. Coke bottle. Harold, check the garbage pit.* None of the items would be packed into a physician's tote of tools. Perplexed, Eliza grew more curious what things would be found outside and how Grace's list figured into the collection. The mention of the chickens put Eliza on heightened alert. She hoped Grace didn't intend to make soup, beginning with beheading a chicken just steps away from where Eliza stood.

She pushed aside the green canvas drape, which divided the bedroom from the main room. Ruth opened her eyes to find Eliza sitting on the three-legged stool next to her. In a weak voice, already exhausted before the forcing pains of the middle stage of labor began, Ruth spoke to Eliza. "Ma'am. It's no good. I don't deserve this one. It shouldn't be coming. I should a gotten some wormwood and taken care of it."

Eliza realized that despite a government ban on wormwood, midwives and mountain medicine healers kept their bags filled with a steady supply grown in their backwoods, hidden gardens. When distilled, wormwood turned into absinthe, a potent liquor favored by many during Prohibition. But its most common use was steeped into a tea and drunk by desperate women.

"Hush now, Ruth. I'm here to help you. Together, we're going to guide this little blessing into the arms of her loving mother. You do deserve her."

A commotion in the front room pulled Eliza from the stool before she could begin her exam. Chaos had returned. Chet had strung the boiled sheets from a beam across the midsection of the room for them to drip dry. He kept shooing the three younger children away from the clean sheets while Rosie waved a black crow's feather in the air above Alice's and Harold's heads. They jumped up and down, shrieking as they tried to grab the feather from Rosie's tight grip. As she jumped, Alice dropped a clump of scraggly greens surrounding densely packed lavender florets. Timmy dragged an axe behind him, presumably from the woodpile Grace had mentioned. In the center of them, Grace drew a butcher's knife back and forth across a gray sharpening stone. A macabre scene straight out of a horror picture show played across the floor.

Five long hours later, Eliza commanded Ruth to summon every ounce of her remaining energy to deliver her child. Ruth exploded with a bellow which reverberated against the mountain walls. The newest Newcombe slipped into Eliza's waiting hands. They hadn't needed to resort to the crow's feather, which Grace insisted they keep at the ready. When Grace explained the midwife's trick of feathering, Eliza had shaken her head in amazement. Old wives', or rather midwives', tales lived on in the Cumberland Mountains. In fact, Eliza had said no to most of Grace's suggestions. They would not heat Rosie's crow feather to smoldering and hold it under Ruth's nose for the smoke to make her cough and sneeze and push out the baby. Eliza had also forbidden Grace from placing the butcher knife beneath Ruth's pillow and the axe under the bed to help cut her pain. To not dismiss Grace's superstitions in entirety, Eliza took the empty Coke bottle from Harold. If Ruth needed help in expelling the afterbirth, Eliza would relent and let Ruth blow into the bottle once it had been cleaned and sterilized. And, she had to admit, the soothing, floral sweetness wafting through the air after Grace had dropped the lavender stems into a pot of boiling water seemed to relax Ruth, and Eliza, as they readied for the final stages of labor.

Next to Eliza, Grace stared down at her motionless niece in the doctor's hands. She whispered, "Is she…"

Eliza placed the baby on her white smocked lap. With her gloved index finger, she wiped the insides of the baby's mouth. She motioned to Grace to return her attention to Ruth and hold her hand. Under her breath she murmured to the still child, "Don't you dare. Your mother needs you."

With quick, vigorous circles, Eliza rubbed the baby's back. "Come on, little one, come on. Tell your mother you're here.

Scream so the whole mountainside knows a strong little girl has arrived. Make your mark. Use your voice."

A tear formed in the corner of Eliza's eye. It dripped down her cheek onto the child's head. A shudder ran through its small body, slick with blood and amniotic fluids. She flailed her arms, opened her mouth, and wailed.

"Thatta girl," Eliza said. "You tell them."

CHAPTER TWENTY

October 1937

The first hints of fall reached the mountains. Streams of gold speckled against the white-barked birch trees like a scene of angels dancing. Dogwood leaves turned every shade of red, from maroon to orange to purple. Like an old friend, a new season opened her arms to Eliza. On a warm morning, she walked back to the health center after checking on three-month-old Elisabeth Newcombe's ear infection. The paths had become familiar over the past three months. She no longer feared the crunches rustling from the underbrush. Her worry about slipping on wet rocks as she crossed the low-running creek disappeared once she packed away her Enna Jettick pumps in exchange for a pair of low-heeled brown oxfords. Priced at seventy-nine cents from the Sears Roebuck catalog, they were worth every penny for the peace of mind they provided.

Progress on building a Maternity Shelter crawled in starts and stops like an eight-month-old baby. The AWH had approved her plan but turning an idea into reality fell upon Eliza. Small donations trickled in from Junior League chapters. Eliza earmarked those dollars for staff wages, a nominal stipend for herself and for Grace, whom Eliza had hired to work the weekends that she came home from Cumberland College. Grace's mid-term report had pleased Eliza. *She'll be ready for Woman's Med before we know it.*

Large expenses of lumber, electricity, plumbing—Eliza desperately wanted an indoor shower installed—furnishings, equipment, and labor—together they tallied up to a staggering amount. The maternity care desert, as Eliza had described the situation, needed more donations with zeroes attached and broader exposure.

Today, she awaited the arrival of her niece, Bess, and Bess's associate, Jack Hansen, the photographer. Bessie had agreed with Eliza. The plight of generations of women and children in Appalachia should reach more eyes and ears, namely the men in Washington who decided on New Deal spending. Bess would frame a story around the alarmingly high maternal death rates in the rural areas. Lack of prenatal care, births unattended by a professionally trained physician, and evidence of physical disabilities and communicable diseases among some midwives, all contributed to the high rates. Since Dr. Hilla Sheriff opened the first Shelter in Greenville five years ago, only one maternal death had been reported, that of a twenty-eight-year-old woman who had borne six children in seven years. She had walked herself to the Shelter in active labor. She died from heart complications, unrelated to her maternity care.

As Eliza approached the center, she heard a mingle of voices in the driveway area. One woman's voice dropped her R's saying, "Where shall we pahk? My ahnt said the healthmobile comes heah on Wednesdays to re-stock."

Lillian South replied, "You must be Miss Edwards. Welcome! If you could pull around back, that would be fine."

Bessie! Eliza quickened her pace.

"There's my girl!" called out Eliza as Bess bounced out of the car, slamming the door behind her.

Aunt and niece enfolded into a familial hug until Bess pushed back. "Well, look at you Auntie E! Hale, hearty and as red in the cheeks as the apples ready to be plucked from the trees we passed on our way in."

Eliza tapped her cheeks. The warmth had risen with longing to see the first member of her family in nearly five months, especially her darling niece.

Bessie continued her assessment while the driver of the car unlatched the car's trunk. "And what's this?" She pointed to Eliza's feet. "Sensible walking shoes? What have you done with my city proper aunt?"

She ran a pointed finger in the air up along Eliza's stockinged legs, past the hem of her blue and cream print dress, the white coat that hung to her knee, and ending with a stab in the air at the teal, felt cloche on Eliza's head. "I'm happy to see some things haven't changed."

Eliza laughed. "One must adapt to one's environment with baby steps lest things get turned topsy-turvy into chaos."

Bessie edged closer, narrowing her eyes onto an armband on Eliza's upper left arm. "And I absolutely adore this!"

Eliza wore the AWH armband that Dr. South had given her with as much pride as the badge of courage she had fashioned out of a gauze square for Harold Newcombe.

A deep voice behind the women interrupted their whimsical catch-up. "Chaos? What's going on out here? Are the doctors running a still? Putting their chemistry classes to good use?"

Bess slapped the man's shoulder, "Oh, Jack. You clearly don't know my aunt." She stepped aside to make introductions, "Aunt Eliza, Jack Hansen. Jack, my Aunt Eliza, Dr. Edwards."

"How do you do, Mr. Hansen? I've heard much about your work from my niece and seen several of your spreads in *LIFE* and *Harper's*. You are a talented photographer."

"Pleased to meet you Dr. Edwards, I hear you're a talented doctor. It's a fine mission you've undertaken down here."

Well-mannered, Eliza thought. And good-looking. Blonde and blue-eyed, Jack Hansen appeared of Nordic descent. Large frame like a Viking. A glint of adventure in his eye, muscular arms, and an ability for easy conversation. *We'll see, my Bess. But so far, I can see why you'd fall for him.*

The trio settled on the center's porch for plates of pound cake and glasses of apple cider. Preferring to catch up on family news when she and Bess were alone, Eliza suggested they review the visits she had scheduled. Most of the families had declined Eliza's request for interviews. Eliza appreciated that they were prideful people and unwilling to allow strangers to witness their abject poverty.

"As of now, three families have agreed to interviews," said Eliza, flipping her notepad open to a list of names. "I've told you about the Newcombes. Ruth was my first maternity patient. She understands the different levels of modern care she didn't have with a midwife. She has three daughters, Rosie Mae, Alice, and the baby I delivered, Elisabeth. She wants more for them. And, for the one she lost, Doris."

Bess tapped Jack's bare forearm. He had rolled up his sleeves, as the October afternoon in Tennessee lingered into the mid-seventies. "We should start outlining the shots. Aunt Eliza, you mentioned the little one who died of typhoid. Will Mrs. Newcombe let us photograph the gravesite? The solitary marker in the wooded clearing with the fresh flowers that she leaves sounds endearing. We could address not only the Maternity Shelter in the article, but the good work the AWH provides with the vaccination clinics."

"We can ask. I can't make any promises. Ruth Newcombe is fragile and volatile. I'm still monitoring her. She's not out of the woods by any means. The next ones we'll visit are the Bakers. I convinced them by saying they'd receive a photograph of the children, all fourteen of them. Can you do that, Mr. Hansen? Can you develop and make the prints in town before you leave?"

Jack, startled by Eliza's pronouncement of a family with fourteen children, let out a low whistle. "Good God. I hope you've considered a few clinics for these women on family planning as part of your services."

Eliza bit her tongue as she drew a sharp intake of breath. What arrogance, she thought. He must know that Eliza had helped Bess secure birth control. Why was it always the woman's job? Maybe if a husband in Appalachia who wore coveralls and walked barefoot would shoulder a greater responsibility in his marriage, there wouldn't be families with fourteen children. Maybe if a man from the city who sported suits and carried a camera would stock up on condoms from a drug store before heading to the mountains, then maybe a single woman wouldn't fret every twenty-eight days whether their lives would be turned upside down.

With a glare directed at the man in the porch chair with a casual slouch, slicked back blonde hair, and gold wedding band on his left hand, she said, "Yes. We discuss family planning with the women and the men. Cartons of prophylactics are already on my list of requested supplies."

Bess held her aunt's gaze. "And the third family?" she asked, diverting the direction of the conversation to the assignment on the table.

"The Sloanes," said Eliza. "I'm still on the fence with them. I'm unsure they understand my request. I want to make sure we follow the ethical procedures of informed consent to the interviews. Both the parents seem slow. From my initial assessment, at least two of the children may also be well below average in their developmental state. People don't move from or into this rural area. I fear there have been some first-cousin marriages within the family. Maybe even some incest."

Out of the corner of her eye, Eliza caught Bessie's wince and Jack's snicker.

"The Shelter's training classes will consider the best way to approach the delicate topic of genetics."

She allowed a small shoulder shrug. "What's done is done. But moving forward, I want to teach about the dangers of inherited diseases and conditions which can be exacerbated by a constricted gene pool. To gain these families' trust, we must speak to them honestly but with a level of tact and compassion, too."

"We're pretty far from Boston, aren't we?" Bess asked. "Where over three quarters of a million people mingle and marry."

"Exactly. There are plenty of eligible partners in Boston. One needn't even look outside the city," Eliza said, shooting another look at Jack. "We've a long day tomorrow. Jack, why don't you get checked in downtown? Bess, I have the extra cot in my room made up for you."

Jack rose from the porch rocker. Eliza noted his full height must be over six feet. His athletic build told her he must have played at least one sport in college. Perhaps he and Bess shared a love of tennis, among other activities, she thought. Jack drained the cider and handed the glass to Eliza, saying, "The boarding house rooms are surely more comfortable than a folding cot. Bess, your bags are still in the car. Let's head out for dinner before serving times end."

"No, Jack," said Bessie. "Aunt Eliza and I have a lot to catch up on. You go on. I'll see you in the morning. Coffee will be ready and waiting. If you could swing by the general store, though, and grab me a hairbrush, that would be swell. I can't believe I forgot mine back in Richmond. Thanks, hon."

Eliza's fierce grip on the empty glass eased. Despite the familiarity between them, Eliza found it satisfying that Bess spoke up and didn't cave to Jack's demands. She had always known what she wanted. *Don't change now, Miss Bess Edwards.*

CHAPTER TWENTY-ONE

"**N**ext!" Bess called out to the cluster of Baker children. Bess and Jack had discussed various tableaus for each portrait. They began from youngest to oldest, knowing the little ones wouldn't have the patience to wait their turn. The baby sat naked except for her nappy on the dirt floor inside a cramped lean-to. Bessie placed a wooden spoon in her hand to bang on an upside-down pot to keep a smile on her face. A set of twins held hands, facing each other with matched gap-toothed grins. Four children stood outside the cabin, clustered like the pile of rocks behind them, which served as a tilting foundation for the cabin. A girl of ten tossed feed to two scrawny chickens at her bare feet.

The sleeves of a threadbare tweed jacket stopped three inches above the wrists of an eight-year-old boy. His crossed eyes stared directly at Jack. His younger brother begged to have the black, tan, and white hound with drooping ears next to him. Another boy posed by the woodpile. In his arms, he cradled a stack of kindling. Each stick was thicker than his arms.

An older teenaged girl stepped forward at Bess's request. Her downcast eyes hid behind thick lenses. She fidgeted in constant motion, pushing the glasses up her nose and scanning the fringes of the woods. When the group had arrived at the Bakers', the mother had nudged the girl toward Eliza. "Lookie at my Leonie.

She can see ya, now. Ever so grateful you and Doc South got the eye doctor down here."

Eliza made a note to tell Bess about the ophthalmologist's visit she had arranged. Beyond the maternity cases, Eliza felt strongly that they should schedule regular visits from specialists. The Shelter staff could screen families to identify when enough cases warranted a visit by a surgeon, ophthalmologist, dermatologist, or any other specialty. Psychiatric cases presented a different challenge. They couldn't wait weeks or a month for a psychiatrist to visit. All staff would require training in detecting and delineating acute psychopathic disorders from pellagra, feeble-mindedness, epileptics, alcohol and syphilis-induced psychoses, as well as situational depression. An understanding of the causes meant the difference between summoning a sheriff or sending someone home with a family member armed with supervision instructions until a psychiatrist arrived.

"Leonie," said Eliza as she approached the girl. "Your rag curls are so stylish, just like Shirley Temple."

A quizzical look spread over Leonie's face. "Shirley who?" she asked.

Once again, Eliza had misspoken. She constantly forgot how much these families lacked: electricity, telephones, running water, and indoor plumbing. It was 1937 in Appalachia. A black and white photograph was a novelty; watching a movie in a theater with velvet seats and a curly-topped girl singing about the *Good Ship Lollipop* on a giant screen might stun these families into a silent stupor.

Bessie clapped her hands. "All right, Leonie, can we step around back? I saw a tree with a thick trunk. The bark is almost black and contrasts with your light dress and blonde hair."

Leonie froze for a brief moment, her eyes downcast. Wordless, and as if summoning her legs into action, she ran into the cabin. "Did I say something wrong?" Bess asked.

"Oh, leave her be," said Mrs. Baker. "I don't know what gets into that girl sometimes. How 'bout me and my man next? See over there?" She pointed toward a stand of pine trees. A blanket of fallen needles lay scattered around the trunks. "That's the spot we got this whole passel started. Eighteen years ago, when I was 'bout Leonie's age. Figured we should build the cabin right where the first seed got planted." She smirked and winked at Bess.

Jack dropped his forehead into the heel of his hand while Bess chuckled. "That's a fine idea, Mrs. Baker. But let's keep that story your secret. There's no need to share it in a magazine article."

Bessie sent Jack to set up a dark room in town, allowing her to stay over a second night with Eliza. After a dinner of skillet steaks, carrots, and new potatoes, they lingered on the porch. The crisp mountain air teased their bare arms. Eliza brought out a quilt decorated with a red and pink geometric pattern. One of Eliza's patients had presented it to her as a thank you payment. Eliza sat down on the rough-hewn bench next to Bess and draped it over their shoulders.

"Just like old times," said Bess. She giggled and snuggled in closer to Eliza. "Auntie E, can you read me a book?"

"Oh shoot, I meant to ask Florence to have Will box up the Thornton Burgess books and ship them down. The kids here will adore them. How about you read to me for a change? I'd love to hear your notes for the article. Any thoughts off the top of your head?"

"I want to open with hard-hitting examples of the need and the solutions. Frame up how the AWH has already helped. Like Charlotte's surgeries and then go into the Baker girl with the glasses. I think Jack got some good shots of Ruth and baby Elisabeth. If the gravesite one comes out well, that would be a great juxtaposition and opening. Something like, *The Lost and Found Lives of Appalachia.*"

"I like it. Succinct, yet powerful and direct. Do you need a subtitle? I'd love to see AWH noted right away."

Bess tapped her pencil against her notebook cover. Eliza watched as the gears turned. Her niece had grown into a fine young woman. Quick-witted, observant, sympathetic.

"How's this? *Contributions from the American Women's Hospitals Help Rural Communities Survive and Thrive.*"

"Excellent. I only wish we could show some of those contributions, like before pictures of Rosie Mae. And now, her ray of sunshine smiling with hope. If Jack captured the sunlight hitting her hair, that would be perfect."

"He's a real artist, Aunt Eliza. I'm sure he did. Too bad we didn't get one of Leonie. We could have shot her with and without the glasses for a before and after story. What do you think of that running inside business? Seemed like she was spooked when I suggested she stand next to the tree."

"No idea, but Mrs. Baker didn't seem concerned. I'll ask Grace if she knows anything. They must be close to the same age."

With fourteen children to tend to, Eliza doubted that Mrs. Baker noticed subtle changes in her kids' behavior. Most often, however, Eliza had learned those types of small cues disguised larger, troubling issues. She feared Leonie had experienced some sort of trauma associated with the tree. If anyone in the area might tease information from her, it would be Grace. Family or friend, Grace Wilson offered a ready ear to listen and a strong shoulder for support. Hopefully, she had lent her ear and shoulder to Leonie Baker.

An engine hum purred over the crickets' song of the early evening. The car came to a stop fifty yards from where Eliza and Bess sat. Dim headlights flicked on and off in quick succession. Once, twice, three times. Bess lifted the quilt from her shoulders and folded it over Eliza's chest.

"That's my cue," said Bess.

"Your what?"

"Jack. I suggested a little drive tonight. It's still warm and there are so many lovely private spots around here. We should be able to find one like Mr. and Mrs. Baker's." She winked at Eliza.

Eliza couldn't suppress an old lady tsk.

"Don't worry." Bess opened her purse and pulled out a wooden box that fit in her palm. The grooves for the slide-top lid looked well-used. "I've got it right here."

At least there would be no Hansen seeds planted tonight, thought Eliza.

"That's a relief, but really, Bess. How much longer are you going to let yourself be strung along?"

"Did it ever occur to you that I'm stringing him along? I'm perfectly happy with the arrangement. We have good times together and I don't worry that I'll have a passel of kids like Mrs. Baker, keeping me tied to one spot. I come and go as the story takes me. It's a freedom few women take advantage of. You should try it sometime, Auntie E. Think of yourself and your needs." Bess bent over with a quick peck on Eliza's cheek before she dashed off the porch and down the lighted drive to Jack.

The next morning, Jack slammed the trunk closed and opened the passenger door. "All set. Let's get going, Bess. I don't like the looks of those clouds. Better we hit paved roads sooner than later. The mud around here must be dreadful. It was nice to meet you, Dr. Edwards. I'll send along a few more prints once we're back in civilization."

"Thank you, Mr. Hansen. I'd like to frame some for the Shelter's walls," said Eliza.

Bess hugged her aunt one more time before she hopped into the car. Rolling down the window, she leaned out, saying,

"Christmas bells will ring you home to Boston before we know it. And with Teddy on leave, we'll have a rip snorting good time." She kissed her fingertips and flicked her hand toward Eliza.

"Please give me a quick call to let me know you've made it safely to New York."

"I'll make sure she does, Dr. Edwards."

Eliza watched as Bess ran her fingers through his thick hair. The engine revved as Jack put the car in gear and turned down the drive, away from forecasts of mud-filled roads, babies buried in wooded clearings, suggestions of incest, families with fourteen children, and the woman who eagerly embraced them all like her family.

CHAPTER TWENTY-TWO

November 1937

Eliza welcomed quiet days to organize the files she had compiled on every mountain family in a ten-mile radius. Across from her at the kitchen table, Grace, home for her Thanksgiving break, pulled her rich brown curls back and wound an elastic band around the locks. Despite the late nights Eliza surmised she kept for studying, Grace's fresh face carried the same radiance she brought with her for every visit to the mountain health center and a chat with Eliza.

"So, tell me, with your first semester almost done, how are you managing?" asked Eliza.

Grace gripped the coffee mug with her delicate hands and drained the remaining drops with a gulp. "It's...been a whirlwind. Classes, work with Dr. South, studying, meeting new people. It's a lot to take in. But I'd be fibbin' if I didn't say that I'm loving every minute, even my Latin class. Thank you for suggesting I take that one right away."

"I'm happy to hear that. The Latin will come in handy when you read medical texts. My extra copies that my son shipped down arrived. Don't let me forget to give them to you before I leave for Christmas in case you want some pleasure reading over your break." Eliza winked as she said *pleasure*, knowing full well that not all medical texts were interesting, especially the ones for Organic Chemistry.

"Thank you. I will. I just need to get through finals." Grace picked up the draft of Bess's article and a stack of Jack's photos which Eliza had left on the table.

"I'm sorry I missed meeting your niece. But I'd say she and the photographer did a great job capturing the lives of the families round here."

"I think so, too. There's one story, however, that they failed to include." Eliza turned their conversation to the mysterious behavior of Leonie Baker. She shared Leonie's initial excitement over having her picture taken, wearing her new glasses. "But the minute Bess motioned to a large hickory tree and requested Leonie stand in front of it, she looked terrified and fled inside. Isn't that odd?" said Eliza.

Grace dropped Bessie's article and watched as it fell to the floor. The rosy color faded from her cheeks. Her extra pause before picking up the paper rattled Eliza. She waited. Grace seemed to consider how she would answer Eliza's question.

Without lifting her eyes, Grace said, "Dr. Edwards, has anyone been around since I've been up at Williamsburg? Someone you haven't met before?"

"Well, yes, now that you speak of it, I saw a young man heading toward your grandfather's place on Tuesday morning. I didn't speak to him, just saw him from a distance. He had an uneven gait which looked like his natural walk, not one from an injury. I wondered if he might have had polio. He walked like some of the Warm Springs patients. He had long, greasy hair. I don't recall anyone else who keeps his hair so long, or who walks like that."

With a slight shake of her head, Grace muttered more to herself than Eliza. "Why didn't Pops say he was back?"

"Who, Grace? Who's back from where?" Eliza placed her hand on Grace's trembling arm.

"My brother, Ian. We thought he had left us for good. He's bad news, Dr. Edwards."

"Why's that?"

Grace lifted her face. "He hurts people." She wiped the back of her hand across her brow and swallowed hard before telling Eliza about her brother. Twenty-years-old, a polio victim, jobless and angry at the world, Ian had decided three months ago that marrying Leonie Baker would put him in favor with Leonie's father, a foreman at the Elk Valley lumber mill. If a job opened, Ian figured he'd give it to a son-in-law. Ian didn't plan on his reputation as a mean and ugly drunk preceding him. When he visited the Bakers to ask for Leonie's hand, they showed him to the door with a quick refusal and a directive to never come around again asking to marry any of their daughters. He disappeared the next day. Pops heard he had moved further up the mountain and had bunked down with a crew running moonshine. Apparently, he drank as much as he delivered to homesteads on the other side of the mountain.

"He must have come looking for Leonie," Grace continued. "I'm afraid he hurt her. Whatever he may have done to her, he did near or against that hickory tree. Probably figured if he got her pregnant, her father would demand he marry her."

Eliza gasped. "How could you know such a thing? Why would the tree be involved?"

"Last summer, he tried the same with me. Backed me up against a big tree."

Eliza rose and reached her arms around Grace, pulling her tight. "Oh, Gracie. I'm so sorry. Did he...?"

"I'm stronger than Leonie. You saw her. She's a little waif. I got away. Leonie probably didn't."

"That must have been terrifying. An attack like that constitutes assault, even without a rape. Did you consider pressing charges? And Leonie. The poor girl. She's been traumatized. I doubt she's told her mother, or anyone."

"No. He's my brother, and he didn't get too far with me. But Leonie. Don't think she'll tell anyone. Most girls around here can't wait to catch a man to get out of their parents' house and have babies, even if that catch isn't as good as someone like Ruthie's Tom, or my Pops. Leonie's different. Her terrible eyesight always made her like a little mole, slinking away from people. Scared of her own shadow."

"I understand, but she needs to be evaluated. Not only for a pregnancy, but she could have been exposed to a venereal disease. She'll need treatment immediately. Syphilis can produce long-term devastating effects, including her ability to have healthy children someday. With her poor eyesight, there can be further complications if the disease invades her eye and further impairs her vision."

Eliza hadn't planned a lecture about venereal disease over coffee. However, with men on the campus at Cumberland College, college freshmen like Grace, needed to understand the risks. She could hardly expect a grandfather to discuss such matters with his granddaughters. Eliza could only imagine how Chet had dealt with Ruth's and Grace's start of their menses. He may also be unaware of Ian's volatile and dangerous behavior around women. Someone, a medical professional, may need to sit Chet Wilson down for a lecture, too.

"Can you convince Leonie to allow me to examine her?"

"I can try," said Grace.

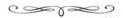

After Sunday services at a chapel in the woods, Grace motioned to Eliza to join her on the long narrow bench which served as a pew. In barely a whisper, Grace said. "I spoke to Leonie before services. In the name of being a good Christian, I told her I wanted her to trust me. I promised I wouldn't say anything to her momma."

Eliza smoothed her skirt and folded her hands in her lap. She'd prayed enough this morning. Another short prayer for the health of Leonie Baker wouldn't hurt. She nodded to Grace to continue.

"Once she started, the whole story bubbled out of her. I was right. A couple of months ago, Ian watched her head to the privy in the back of their cabin in the early morning. She had nothing on but her scrap of a nightdress. Ian jumped out of the bushes and pushed her against the tree."

Grace hugged her elbows tight and clutched the edge of her cardigan, pushing a button through its hole and back out again. "I'm not sure I should say all this in God's house."

"God's house is a place to feel safe. It's okay. Pops has raised you to be a respectful young woman. This type of situation is delicate to discuss. But, if you mean to be a doctor, you must learn to separate the personal from the clinical and focus on the facts. I won't judge you for what you're about to say. Keep that in mind. This is to help Leonie."

Grace bit her lip. "He put his hand under her nightie. Then, he...with his fingers. You know. Right? He put them..."

Eliza unfolded her hands and took Grace's in her own. She rubbed her thumb over the back of Grace's hand.

"Poor little mouse," said Grace. "Leonie said she couldn't scream with Ian's other hand over her mouth. She just stood there. Was she in shock?"

"Yes, Grace. I expect she was. She tried to step out of herself. It's called dissociation. She refused to believe that what Ian was doing to her was real. She's probably still denying it happened. Dirty fingers are, of course, a concern. But if she hasn't developed any signs of a bacterial infection by now, she should be all right on that front."

Eliza looked straight into Grace's eyes ready to deliver her direct question. "More importantly, did Ian penetrate her with his penis? Syphilis is transmitted only through bodily fluids. Do you understand what I'm describing?"

"Yes, ma'am. There are plenty of farm animals around. We know how those pups and piglets appear a few months later."

"And was there? Penetration?"

With a weary sigh, Grace said, "No. Leonie said in her sixteen years she's never been so happy to have thirteen brothers and sisters. The possum stew must not have sat right with most of them. Just as Ian was unbuttoning his pants, the twins came flying out the door, hand in hand, running toward the privy. Ian heard them and took off. One pesky little brother is bad enough, two is double trouble."

Eliza squeezed Grace's hand. "Thank God. I'd still like to speak with Leonie. But for now, she should be okay, at least physically."

"Please don't. Leonie made me swear I wouldn't tell anyone. She's afraid her father will blame her for enticing Ian. Now that you know she's okay, you need to leave it be. Leonie knows to be more aware and said she won't ever go anywhere alone as long as Ian's around."

"I understand Leonie's fears. Too often, men make women believe that they're the cause of an assault. It's wrong to assign fault to a woman. I won't say anything, but your brother—I'm concerned he'll try again, if not with Leonie, with someone else."

Grace pushed back from the table and rose, "Preacher may have read from Luke 23 this morning, but I can't forgive Ian for what he's done. He knows exactly what he's doing. I guess I better figure out a way to tell Pops. He'll know what to do. Boys, he can handle."

Yes, thought Eliza. *Leave the girls to me.*

CHAPTER TWENTY-THREE

November 26, 1937

*D*ear Olga,

At the ripe old age of fifty-eight, I've survived my first Thanksgiving without my mother's cranberry chutney on a table. My blues disappeared the minute I stepped into the Newcombes' cabin. Chet, Grace's grandfather with whom she lives, bagged the freshest turkey I've ever tasted right outside their backdoor. He carved it with a hand as steady and deft as Charlotte's. Ruth whipped up a delectable cornbread stuffing. The chicken broth kept it extra moist. She tossed in some apple chunks and hickory nut meat for an unusual crunch and tang. Straight from their garden, we enjoyed steamed collard greens and onions. The addition of leafy vegetables to the mountain families' diet has made a marked difference in the incidence of pellagra. I had to move the prong on my dress belt to another hole after not one, but two! slices of pumpkin pie. The extra effort which goes into preparing these meals makes each mouthful even sweeter. Grace had cut the pumpkin into chunks, steamed them to a soft mush, then rotated turns with Timmy, using a wire masher and hand-cranked eggbeater to puree the chunks and mix in cream and cinnamon. Don't forget, there's still no electricity in most homes down here, which means you can't just plug in a KitchenAid!

The week before Thanksgiving, Bessie sent me a clipping of her article, which ran in the Richmond newspaper. Not a major paper, but it's a start for our campaign. Dr. Lovejoy shared she has earmarked $2,500 for the Shelter in the AWH's 1938 budget. The Knoxville Hospital has set aside six bedframes and mattresses for us, and Woman's Med is sending us linens. Congressman Morrison has written a funding request for several AWH operations. It will be heard by the Labor, Health, and Human Services Appropriations Committee after Congress's Christmas recess. If the approvals come by January and weather permitting, Mr. Baker thinks he'll have the building complete by March. Say a prayer for us!

I plan on heading home on December 19. There's one maternity case, however, which gives me pause. She's due in January but her last delivery was breech and at each exam she presents with the wrong position for this point in the pregnancy. She may be better off in Knoxville for the rest of her time instead of me managing this one by myself out here in the woods. Or worse, have her go early and the only one around with any training is young Grace.

I can't stop in New York, but will try for an overnight on my way back around January 5. Teddy arrives on December 20!!!! It's been the longest eighteen months of my life with him gone. I need to make sure Will borrowed the extra cot from Albie. Knowing him, he may have seen to the cot, but I doubt he's thought about sheets, blankets, and a pillow. It will be nice for the boys to spend time together. Bessie hinted that Will's young lady friend is also expected to join us for Christmas Eve dinner. I'm not sure who's more nervous about the meeting, me or the woman who has set her sights on my son.

In your last letter you said you had hit a wall on your latest project. Please send me an update. Struggles continue here without adequate supplies for vaccines. With winter setting in, the healthmobile team has warned me that we may face difficult days ahead. *We need more of your excellent research work to hit the mainstream, including the back corners here in Appalachia. These families deserve as much help as the immigrants of our cities. Out of sight shouldn't mean out of mind.*

With much love to my dearest, Eliza

December 6, 1937
Dear Eliza,
Thank you for your newsy letter of the 26th. Your Thanksgiving sounds nearly as primitive as the first one. Did you pluck the turkey's feathers and stick a few in your hair like a regular heathen? Or maybe you ground the maize for cornbread? No. Perhaps you gathered the nuts while the man, this Chet, did the hunting? First names, are we? Hmm… I need more details than his turkey hunting abilities. What other special skills does this mountain man possess?

I'll catch you up on my research when you stop in January. Suffice it to say that I've switched my attention from chemical reactions to the ideal environments needed to stimulate those reactions. The beakers we use are too clunky. I have contracted a glass blower from Corning to work on my designs for a different culture bottle. He should deliver a few prototypes by the time of your visit. These designs are my creations. They may not give me a lopsided grin, a warm hug nor inquire about my health, but I also don't worry about who they may marry or what dangerous waters their ship may enter. Best of all, I didn't have to endure the dirty diaper or trying teenage years with them. My children stand tall and silent, ready to serve me and my work. Pause here to laugh at my wit.

Send my warmest Christmas greetings along to Florence, Albie, Freddy, their families, and, of course, Bess. Give our boys a hug from their Aunt Olga and tell them to raise a glass of vodka

in my name. See if they can pronounce it correctly - za lyuBOF'!
To love!

    Your truly and ever friend and sister,
    Olga

CHAPTER TWENTY-FOUR

December 1937

No, *no, no!* thought Eliza. The flakes grew larger and fell quicker. A Tennessee mountain winter was making an unusually early arrival. Outside, icy white sparkles swirled into eddies around the cabin yard. Fowl of all sorts, winged and footed, sought refuge in the corners of briar patches and chicken coops. Under the porch, a hound dog curled into a ball, its nose buried beneath its tail. A cow lowered its head and plodded toward the lean-to shelter attached to the back of the cabin.

Inside, a new mother rested. Her newborn son suckled at her breast, hungry to begin his life. His smack against the nipple told Eliza that he had latched on without difficulty. She had checked the afterbirth to ensure no fragments had remained in the uterus to cause post-partum complications. The umbilical cord had been cut, securely tied off, and the area was well swabbed. She had administered the two drops of silver nitrate into the baby's eyes. The father was told to keep his wife comfortable with a fire going and warm chicken broth for the first twelve hours. The healthmobile team had dispersed yesterday for the Christmas holiday back to their respective homes, north, south, east, and west. If the woman experienced any excessive bleeding, her husband should go to the center to use the phone and call Dr.

South's office in Williamsburg. Eliza's train departed from Jellico at one o'clock that afternoon. Boston awaited. Teddy's boat had docked two days ahead of schedule. Eliza had every intention of being comfortably settled in a train seat by five after one. She couldn't wait a single minute longer to get home.

Throughout the woman's ten-hour labor, Eliza had paced over to the window, watching the clouds color from a pussy willow fluff to dark, hard granite. With the final pushing stage, Eliza urged the woman on before total exhaustion took hold of all of them: mother, child, and doctor. With weary eyes, she watched the morning's dawn darken instead of brightening as the hours rose toward noon. Eliza needed to make it back to the center before the snowstorm intensified. She knew this section of the woods well after six months. The path wove less than a mile from front porch to front porch. Her stamina had increased as much as her knowledge of the area. On a clear day, she could cover the distance in less than twenty minutes, even in a heavy coat and boots and carrying her bag. A tired body, however, may not.

Eliza draped a scarf over her head and wound it around her neck, tucking it inside the top of her woolen coat. She tiptoed out the door. The latch clicked behind her. A blast of needles stabbed her cheeks and nose with pin pricks. *Twenty minutes, that's all.* Less time than it takes to cook grits. *Keep your head down and count.* The path would lead her to the train ticket waiting on the counter. *Just one step. One more. Sixty-seven, sixty-eight, sixty-nine.* The wind sliced through her coat, lifting the ends of the scarf to flap into her face. She brushed them down. Her hands burned with the cold. Shards turned to flakes and back to shards. The path became a glassy snake, slithering into the woods.

Looping her bag handles over her arm, she thrust her gloveless hands into her pockets. The bag filled with her instruments banged against her hip. Its heft may leave a bruise. She would deal with that pain later. Ahead of her, a white screen filtered through the tree trunks along the path's edge. Eliza looked back toward the cabin. It had disappeared from her view. She must have walked at least a quarter mile. Compared to her normal gait, her pace slowed. A flicker of fear ignited a picture of panic.

Her breath matched her quickening pulse. Ice crystals rimmed her eyelashes. The heavy flakes blurred her vision. In the distance, a dark mass formed. Another creature seeking shelter? The silent, moving hulk approached her as it emerged from the bend in the path.

Ready to face down a furry animal foe, she began swinging her bag in the motions that Chet had told her to do if she encountered a wild turkey. With her focus on the creature, she missed the rock half-buried in the snowfall. Her heel caught as her ankle twisted like the slow turn of a weathervane. All signs pointed toward calamity. She slipped and stumbled forward. As she flung her arms out to break her fall, the bag flew out of her hand. Her head grazed a corner of the stone while her right knee slammed into the frozen dirt. The thin, sheer silk-stocking tore open. "Dad-blasted!" she screamed to the wind, the snow, the mountain, the creature.

A damn fool she was. Still wearing dresses and stockings in the middle of the woods instead of pants and a wool sweater like any intelligent, native person to the area. Her head throbbed. The jagged edge of the rock had cut deep into her knee cap. Rich red blood burst forth, streaming in rivulets down her leg. She cupped her hand against the wound to staunch the flow. Her bag, landing several feet away, contained gauze, tape, and an iodine bottle. With her other hand, she alternated in rubbing the shooting pain coursing through her head and ankle. Like a toddler who had yet to stand and take her first steps, she scooted on her rear along the path.

The snow continued to fall, collecting in the folds of Eliza's coat. She panted through the pain in her ankle and head. Her exhalation formed steam puffs in front of her face. The snow mound circling her foot turned pink, then red. Exhaustion from the night spent in the cabin captured her weakened body. More crystals fell from the sky like glistening stars. She tried to stand, reaching for a tree trunk to steady her sway. Her head wobbled as she peered down the path. The strain made her dizzy. The beast's approach quickened. With a sob caught in her throat, her legs buckled, succumbing to the grip of pain, exhaustion, and despair. Before the world went black, she heard a muffled noise. Upright on two legs, the beast called her name. "Eliza?"

Pungent odors of boiled onions, mixed with a greasy gamey scent, lifted Eliza from her stupor. A weight pressed down on her chest. She opened her eyes to find a pile of colored patchwork quilts tucked around her like a warm hug. A crackle from a log breaking and falling against stone told her a fire roared nearby. With a push against the blue-ticked mattress, she raised her body to rest on her elbows. She stretched her left leg, flexing her ankle. The bottom of her bare foot rubbed against a flannel covered metal bed warmer pan; the coals inside had lost their heat. As she attempted the same with her right leg, a dull ache traveled up her ankle to her knee. She slipped her hand down, finding a patch over the knee wound as if it had been treated by a trained hand. Grace must have found her and taken her back to Chet's cabin. Yet, in her delirium, Eliza didn't remember seeing Grace, nor walking to the cabin with a twisted ankle.

A fog clouded her vision. A man tended a fire fifteen feet away from her. He stirred a wooden spoon in a cauldron hanging from a spit over the flames. In a cracked rasp, she said, "Chet, thank you for letting Grace bring me in."

"I ain't Chet," said a deep voice. "Grace ain't here neither. Chet went to meet her train, but the storm blew in and delayed her. He saw you lying on the path on his way back. He brung you here." A younger version of Chet jabbed at the fire's embers with a poker.

She rose to a sitting position, pulling the quilts up tighter over her chest. A gust of cold air flew into the room as the heavy door banged against the inside wall. Chet entered the cabin, kicking the door closed behind him. He looked toward the bed where Eliza sat, her hair loose around her shoulders and her eyes wide with inquiry.

"You're awake," he said. She felt his gaze linger over her. Her mind ran to her bare leg above her thigh. Her silk stocking, even with a slight tear at her knee, would have provided a shield from another's hand. The shield, however, was gone. Her legs were bare. Someone had removed her stockings. Grace was still at school in Williamsburg. Eliza scanned her hunched shoulders, reassured to find the black tweed of her jacket covering them.

"Good thing I found you. This storm came outta nowhere. Must be having a Northerner down here. Did you think we needed a traditional New England Christmas and sent us some snow?"

Christmas! Eliza dropped the quilts and moved to swing her legs over the side of the bed. Waves sloshed through her head. Her body swayed. "Chet," she said. "What time is it?"

Chet moved closer to the bed. He dropped his gloves to the floor and gently nudged her against the headboard. "Whoa, there. You took a good conk on your head. Don't be getting up just yet. It's near abouts supper time. We've got a stew going. You might as well stay and eat. And that ankle needs more rest."

His warm hands pressed on her shoulders. She had started back to the health center just after noontime; she'd been out for nearly six hours. A train with one unoccupied seat would be halfway to Washington, chugging ahead to its destination at Boston's South Station. Her hopes of being home by this time tomorrow night, embraced by her family, vanished like the smoke curling up the stone chimney.

"I can't stay. I need to make some phone calls. My sons are expecting me on tomorrow's train. And, well, um, Grace isn't here. It's just you and…?"

"I reckon the power's off. Phone lines are probably down, too. It's no bother for you to stay. Plenty of stew. I'll put a pallet for myself by the fire to keep it going. Ian will be fine in the barn. He's spent many a night out there by his choice or mine."

"Ian?" Eliza asked.

"Yeah," said the man with the fire poker. "Grace, didn't say nothin' about me? She sure has gone on all 'bout you, Miz Edwards. No thanks to you, she got that idea of going to college. Spending money she ain't got, takin' charity like that. She belongs right here, taking care of her family. That sister of ourn, Ruthie, needs her. And what about Pops here? He has the nerve to offer you this stew. You think it's any good? It probably tastes like horse shit. Men don't know how to cook. That's a woman's job, not running off to read a bunch of books and put other stupid ideas in her head, like becoming a doctor."

"That's enough, Ian. No need for your disrespect. Doc Edwards been helping lots of folks around here, including our Ruthie. Get some more firewood. It's gonna be a long, cold night."

Thankful for Chet stepping in, Eliza withheld any retort to set straight Ian's views of a woman's role. Grace had earned her well-deserved scholarship. With Grace's instructions, Ruth's older children had learned how to watch over the younger ones to help their mother. And further, Eliza fumed to herself, men should learn how to cook. Independence, not co-dependence between the sexes, was the key to successful relationships. Eliza tamped down those thoughts before they spewed forth from her tongue. Some people's ignorance wasn't worth your breath or time. Ian's belligerence and drunken outbursts may be a larger issue that would require Eliza's intervention at some point. There was no need to antagonize him at their first meeting.

Eliza had slept soundly through the night under the worn quilts, heaped over her like a pile of sleeping pups. She slid her hand down to her ankle. The throbbing had subsided and the ache in her head had waned to a slow drumbeat. Heat and a welcoming aroma beckoned her to arise and meet the day as coffee brewed on the top of a cast-iron pot belly stove. At the foot of the bed, she found a pair of woolen trousers and a familiar, blue-checked flannel shirt. Chet had left her some of Grace's clothes. She changed into them quickly, stooping to cuff the pant legs. Grace had a good four inches on her, but the shirt fit snug across her matronly bosom.

From outside, she heard the sputter of a car coming to a stop. Eliza went to the door and cracked it open an inch. The Bakers' Model-T idled in front of the cabin. Eliza had seen the beat-up car parked at several homes. It was more a communal car than the Bakers. If you brought it back with the same amount of gas as when you took it, and without another dent in its tired fenders, it would be available to any mountain family who needed transportation to the town. With her bag and clothes tucked under her arm, she stepped outside as Chet and Ian came around the side of the car.

"Good morning," she said, wary of Ian's downcast eyes and awkward gait toward her.

He grunted a "morning" greeting to her feet and went inside.

Chet tipped his hat to her. "Morning, Eliza. I must say, blue brings out your eyes. You should wear it more often."

"The color blue, or flannel?" she said with a twinkle creeping into her eyes.

"Both. But we really don't have time to sit and discuss spring fashions. Grace will be on the ten o'clock and you should be able to change your ticket for the ten-thirty. I'll swing you back by the center to grab your things. We should make it on time if this jalopy cooperates."

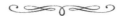

Forty minutes later, after their short detour to pick up Eliza's packed luggage, they pulled up to the train station. A warmth surpassing the winter chill spread through Eliza's body. She reached out her hand to find Chet's. "You're truly a special man, Chet Wilson," her voice barely above a whisper.

Silence lingered between them. Eliza felt her palm turn clammy in his clasp. Despite the roar of a train on a southbound track, the world seemed to slow down. Chet leaned into her, his lips meeting hers in a kiss, as sweet as a melting caramel.

She closed her eyes, feeling her tensed shoulders drop. How could such a simple act—a mere brush of lips to lips, summon forth longings buried so deep and for so long that she had forgotten how delicious the feeling could be?

With his forehead pressed against hers, Chet said, "I'm not sure I should have brought you here."

"To the train? But I need to get home to Boston. My boys. For Christmas. I'm so thankful you did."

"Of course. It's just that, if you leave, are you sure you're coming back?"

Eliza squeezed his hand and looked into his eyes. "Of course, I'm coming back. I'm nowhere near done with the project here. We have only just started."

CHAPTER TWENTY-FIVE

December 1937
Boston, Massachusetts

"Then what happened, Aunt Eliza?" asked Mary, Eliza's youngest great-niece, as she squirmed in Eliza's lap.

Eliza had arrived home three days later than planned but still in time for Christmas Eve festivities at her brother Fred's house. Seeing a dinner table set with her mother's spring green china with its coral pink scalloped edges always brought a pang of loss and tender memories to Eliza. Tonight, she brushed aside sadder thoughts. This generation of her family gathered at the table, savoring a bountiful spread. Baked ham, glazed with brown sugar and pineapple rings stuck with cloves. Potatoes au gratin drowned in a cheesy sauce. Waxy buttered green beans complemented red cranberry chutney on the side of the plate to accent Christmas hues across the table. Plates of plum pudding and mugs of warm cider gathered the family around a blazing hearth to finish their meal.

After dinner, before the adults headed to midnight services, Eliza regaled the group by recounting how she had twisted her ankle. For the children's benefit, she transformed the tale into a heroine's adventure rather than a pitiful damsel in distress.

"The wind was nipping at my nose," she said, playfully tweaking Mary's nose. "I'd better hurry and find shelter soon. Ahead of me on the snowy path, I saw a creature. It was big. It was dark. It was scary."

"Oooo," Mary leaned in closer to Eliza's chest. "What did you do?"

"I raised my arms," Eliza lifted her arms. "And flapped them up and down. With my black overcoat on, I looked like a giant crow. I even cawed. Caw! Caw!"

Laughter pealed throughout the large living room. High-pitched squeals from the children mingled with the sonorous guffaws of her sons and Florence's tittering. Will's lady friend, Anne Walters, joined in with a light laugh. There may not be a more rewarding sound on earth than four generations of loved ones delighting in each other's company. Eliza had maneuvered to claim a large, overstuffed chair directly across from the settee where Will and Teddy sat. She appreciated Anne hadn't claimed the spot next to Will. *She understands he needs to spend time close to his brother. I like that*, Eliza thought. And, for Eliza, she needn't turn her head from one to the other. She could look straight at them, taking in their relaxed slouch into the plush cushions. Will, with his arm resting over Teddy's shoulders, assumed not only an elder brother's duties but also stepped into a father's role. His confidence and maturity spilled from his deep-set hazel eyes. To his right, Teddy, in his Navy-issued blue serge slacks, smiled and winked at Eliza when she tweaked Mary's nose. He hadn't forgotten her tender touch when she would tap his nose with a secret only the two of them would ever know.

How she wished she could freeze this scene and tuck it away with others she had collected over the past twenty-four years. The day she came upon the boys nestled together with Will reading to Teddy, guiding Teddy's finger over the words to help him learn. The weeks Will had missed school, laid up with a broken leg, and Teddy had raced home every day with Will's schoolwork and asking if he was better yet. The night she overheard them whispering about Teddy escorting a girl to a dance and how he tried to steal a kiss on her doorstep, and she'd slapped him. And Will admonishing him and advising, "You need a private spot for those kisses, not when her father might peer through the curtain". Each cherished memory could never be photographed. These pictures were far more precious. She had raised boys who cared for each other on a deep level. They were brothers and friends. A photographer would never capture those moments on film, nor should they ever be shared with anyone else but her. Best of all, she could carry them wherever she went. She snapped the image of them tonight and tucked it away to bring with her back to Jellico.

The week flowed into family dinners, card games, and a special night out at the Boston Symphony with maestro Arthur Fiedler conducting a selection of classical and popular holiday favorites. Yet, as much as she relished her family time, a yearning for her other family planted itself in her heart. She missed the sun rising over the mountains. She wondered how Grace had fared with her finals. If Chet had bagged another turkey, or if they had slaughtered the Newcombes' hog. Simple scenes could create the most complex emotions.

On the fourth of January, Eliza and Will huddled together on the piers of the Charlestown Navy Yard. Will encircled Eliza's waist to steady her trembling body. She summoned a forced smile across her face as she waved a weak goodbye to the figure with a duffle bag over his shoulder walking away from them. Teddy turned once and brought his cupped fingers to his hat in a salute. Eliza choked back a sob and leaned deeper into Will's cashmere coat. The black veil on her blue hat, although placed on the brim as a fashionable accent, hid her mourning eyes.

"He'll be fine, Mom. Look at him. He can't wait to get back on board. He loves the Navy and the purpose it gives him," said Will, patting Eliza's arm.

Eliza gripped his hand. "I know he loves it. That's the problem. The *Mississippi's* orders are for the Pacific. After the events last month in Nanking, how can we continue to stay passive against Japan?"

"Roosevelt has enough to deal with. Until we get more Americans back on payrolls and off bread lines, he'll keep our nose out of international business. He's kept quiet over Germany's blatant military build-ups. If he thinks that sanctions against Japan are enough, I guess the Sphinx thinks he's doing the right thing. Not that we should take our eye off either of them."

"I hope you're right, for Teddy's sake and all of us," said Eliza.

When she was in Appalachia, patient care and plans for the Shelter distracted her from the worries of home and family. With those distractions halted, worry reared its ugly head. Like a writhing serpent, it gathered strength and fed upon her anxieties. It would not be sated until it constricted the very breath from her lungs.

After Will dropped her off at home, Eliza retreated to her room. She paused by Florence's door, listening for a soft snore, an assurance of well-being. On her bed, Eliza left her suitcase half-packed. She patted the two pairs of wool trousers, folded into thirds, and placed them on top of the long johns Bess had convinced her to purchase to wear underneath pants. If she found herself outside in the middle of a snowstorm again, at least she would be dressed appropriately, Bess had joked. In the back pocket of her suitcase, Eliza tucked three boxes of L'Oreal hair dye in the shade of auburn that had taken her several tries to find the right match.

That morning, Eliza had filled her medical bag with additional supplies which the health center couldn't easily secure, including a new jar of ether. She had dribbled the brown liquid onto a cloth for four maternity patients. Eliza had kept the promise she made in front of Charlotte. In the Cumberlands, like she had in the Pine Mountains of Warm Springs, she found a new resolve and purpose. She didn't want to escape. She wanted to live every moment with a presence of mind. The clean air wrestled the serpent of worry into submission.

As Eliza took an extra cardigan sweater from her bureau, Florence appeared in the doorway of her room. "I'm sorry, Florence, did I wake you?" asked Eliza.

"Certainly not. I wasn't asleep, just resting my eyes."

Eliza smirked, recalling the line she had used many nights when Olga found her asleep over a spread of open textbooks. Florence picked up a gray shirtwaist Eliza had flung onto the bed. Dangling it in the air like a soiled napkin, she said, "This one is rather dour for your dinner at the Forbes'. Harrison will have a fit."

Twenty years ago, Eliza and Harrison had attended many elegant dinner parties at Beacon Hill's most prominent addresses. For each soirée, Eliza had chosen her most stylish gown to fit in with the crowd Harrison wanted to impress. Florence's references and mentioning Harrison in the present tense sent Eliza reeling. She wondered if another affliction had set in beyond the arthritis in Florence's seventy-eight-year-old joints. Tremors and pains in a body could be a challenge for physical activity. Jumbles within the mind presented a whole different challenge. And worry.

In a soothing lilt, Eliza said, "No Forbes dinner party tonight, Aunt Florence. Just packing for my trip."

Florence huffed. "The Forbes? Why would you be going there? There's no need for you to parade along with Harrison's charade of your marriage. He's dead, my dear, and your marriage was deceased long before he was."

"Yes, but..." Eliza stopped. Better to let the faulty recall pass without further commentary. *She's fine*, Eliza thought. Florence had awoken from a rest. Foggy remnants from sleep explained a single slip-up. Eliza had murky moments herself when she woke.

Florence clapped her hands. "What time does your train leave? I've adored having you home, but you've got a lot of work ahead of you." She gestured to the pile of clothing on the bed. "Let me help. What else do you need for Warm Springs?"

"Jellico, Aunt Florence. Remember? I'm starting the Maternity Shelter in Jellico. I was in Warm Springs last year."

"Oh yes, silly me. With Dr. Lillian South. You're amazing, dear. Those families are fortunate to have you. Here, let me fold some."

Eliza handed a pile of stockings, socks, and slips to her aunt. *Sit yourself back down, Mr. Serpent of Worry. Fearless Florence is fine. Absolutely fine.*

CHAPTER TWENTY-SIX

Spring 1938
Jellico, Tennessee

Eliza stood by a bed, her face etched with weariness. Her head shook slowly from side to side, chin down. On the bed, a young woman, a girl really, thought Eliza, at fifteen, clutched the sheets in a tight fist. Next to Eliza, the girl's mother wiped her daughter's brow. The dark room, save for a kerosene lamp which the mother held above Eliza's shoulder, quieted as the girl's sobs ebbed into whimpers.

"I'm sorry, dear. But we need another push." Eliza's hands, gloved and steady, awaited the afterbirth of the stillborn child. The moment Eliza began her examination an hour ago, she knew. Life had left the little one, now lying on a sheet of newspaper, before he left his mother's womb.

Chinks in the log wall ushered in wisps of cool, damp air. Eliza wrapped the placenta in another sheet of crumpled newspaper. From her bag, she withdrew a cotton diaper. Picking the child up from the newspaper on the table, she placed him on the diaper. His entire body fit on the square. She folded the corners up and tucked the edges around him, pulling the last corner over his gray face, his eyes closed, the veins on his lids, dark and motionless.

She gestured to the mother to open the girl's arms. With a soft murmur, she bent closer to the girl. "I'm so sorry. It's not your fault. He was too early and too small. Do you want to see him?"

The girl shook her head. "Momma, take it away."

The mother took the bundle, leaving her daughter's side as she nodded to Eliza. "It's for the best. Look at her. She's not fit for a young 'un. One less mouth to feed around here isn't a bad thing."

Eliza had delivered joy to many throughout her career. Nearly every child she had held, first in her hands and then placed at a mother's breast, had been welcomed with tears of happiness and wonderment. Here in rural Appalachia, where despair clung to the walls of tilted lean-tos and drafty cabins, hope fell into shafts as deep as the empty, boarded up nearby mines. A tiny infant would join that lost hope when his grandmother dug a hole next to an outcropping of rocks aside a swollen creek.

"Please bring her to see me in a couple of days. I'm here for you both," Eliza said to the mother. "She'll need to be checked for any lingering infections." *And, her mental state*, Eliza thought. Grief, like hope, was too often buried in the foothills of these mountains where it could fester and erupt like an underground spring.

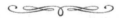

That afternoon, Eliza lay on her cot. Fatigue invaded her bones and mind, yet sleep evaded her. The image of the stillborn lying on the newspaper in the cold, dark cabin haunted her thoughts. The headlines beneath its tiny skull blurred. Eliza formed new ones in her mind with a renewed determination. *Free Maternity Services Available to All. Eliza P. Edwards, M.D., formerly of Boston, announces the opening of the first American Women's Hospital Maternity Shelter in the Jellico area. Women throughout the region are invited to visit for the care they need which will help*

them deliver healthy children. Clean beds will be available for
safer and more comfortable deliveries…

A whistling tune came through the front open window. Eliza
wiped the imaginary headlines from her thoughts and rose from
the cot.

Through the screen door, Chet called, "Eliza? You there? I
picked up the mail."

Since returning from her Christmas visit, Chet had begun
postal service deliveries on Tuesdays and Fridays. With a quick
peek in the small mirror over a washbasin in the corner, Eliza
shrugged at the dark circles under her eyes. A whole bottle of
pancake make-up couldn't conceal the rings. Instead, she pinched
her cheeks as she had read Scarlett O'Hara had done when she
went to visit Rhett in prison.

She opened the door, noticing a spray of pale pink apple
blossoms on twiggy branches dangling from Chet's hand.

"I heard you were out at the Trumbull's this morning. Heard
about the girl. The baby…" his voice trailed off as he presented
the sweet-smelling blooms. "Thought you may need a bit of
cheering up."

A natural glow of gratitude replaced the pinch of her cheeks.
"Yes, poor thing had no chance. Most folks generally think of the
mother and her family when there's a loss like this. Few consider
the doctor who stands by, helpless, and delivers not only a
stillborn, but the tragic news, too. You are very kind to think of
me, Chet."

"I was the one standing by, feeling helpless, when Grace lost
her mother. The midwife didn't have her wits about her when she
saw a leg coming out first."

He paused. Eliza knew how those births ended. A stubborn
breech position compromised the infant's life and could take the
will to fight and breath out of the mother.

"I'm sorry to hear that, Chet. I knew Grace had lost her
mother, but I didn't want to pry."

"Turned our family upside down. My no-good son, Grace's father, high-tailed it out of here that night. Guess he couldn't figure out how to take care of three kids after digging a hole for their mother. Me and my wife took them in."

Eliza traced the delicate petals of the blossoms. "And Grace's and Ruth's adoration of you shows their gratitude."

His open heart drew Eliza in. She reached up and brushed a hint of a trickle at the corner of his eye.

CHAPTER TWENTY-SEVEN

Fall 1938

Blue-black ink smudges dotted the desktop like dead flies. The mechanical click of the typewriter keys against the roller rang in Eliza's ears. The sound teased a false sense of accomplishment. She ripped the sheet from the roller and sent it to its fate in the wastebasket. The hunt-and-peck method, using her two index fingers, slowed her down. When she attempted a quicker pace, her errors increased. A losing battle ensued, speed versus accuracy.

From the pile of paper, she inserted three pages into the typewriter: paper, carbon, paper. With a heavy sigh, she began again. Hunt-peck for "D", hunt-peck for "e". Her fingers slammed each key with a silent command. *Don't make a mistake, don't make a mistake.*

She checked off five names in her ledger. Each appeal included a flicker of faith for the future. Her formal proposal to the AWH outlined the need for ten thousand dollars for building and start-up costs. The tedium of waiting for replies for the final two thousand dollars weighed on Eliza. She may fail in her grandiose plan to build a Maternity Shelter. She would slink back to Boston, leaving behind a note asking for forgiveness from the women of Jellico.

She heard the screen door catch on its latch. Her gloom lifted when she saw Chet stride toward her with a cluster of Queen Anne's lace skirting a center of lavender wild geraniums in one hand and envelopes in the other. Each week since apple blossoms had bloomed, Chet arrived with a different bunch of wildflowers along with the mail. Eliza filled empty milk bottles with his bursts of color, from the pop of contrasts in the yellow and black-eyed Susans to vibrant purple coneflowers. Their friendship had unfolded like the petals of each bouquet.

"Anything look promising?" she asked.

"One," he said, depositing the short stack on the table next to the Underwood and placing the envelope in her hand. A defined bulge outlined the contents—thicker than the common replies of *no funds currently available, otherwise committed, our best wishes that you find.* Eliza slid her finger under the back flap and opened it.

"Bless their hearts. The Girls' Friendly Society in Knoxville held a dance for us." Eliza waved a fan of twenty one-dollar bills in the air. She stepped into Chet's arms and kissed his cheek. He cupped her chin in his hand and lowered his lips to hers. They melted into a delicate dance of their own, finding each other in comfort and closeness. Gentle, warm, subtle. When spring had awakened, Eliza had roused her own desires. A need, buried by self-denial, awoke.

Outside, a gaggle of giggles and chatty conversations approached. Chet dropped his hands to his sides. "Your class awaits."

Upon hearing that the knitting mill in town would re-open for fifteen shifts a week, Ruth had shared the good news with Eliza. Jobs had returned to Jellico. Canned vegetables, yeasty bread loaves, meat from a grocer instead of a shot squirrel or possum, even a treat of an orange shipped from Florida, could grace pantry shelves and ice boxes. Growing feet would slip into new, well-fitting shoes. A warm coat could button to the top of a child's neck. A horizon of hope dawned on the valley.

Although thrilled by the news, Eliza thought of the children. With many husbands away on WPA projects, dead, or disinterested, who would watch the children while the women worked? She reminded Ruth that Grace was at college and Timmy was but nine-years-old.

"Timmy'll do okay with the kids. Alice is out of her nappies," said Ruth. "I can leave Elisabeth with old Mrs. Jackson."

Remembering the scene when she first met the Newcombe children, with Timmy sitting on the stoop and Alice lolling in a soiled diaper, Eliza proposed an idea for a Mothers' Helper class. Every child whom their mothers expected to watch younger siblings would learn about basic hygiene. She would show them how to scrub their hands with lye and water after each trip to the outhouse and before lunch. Demonstrations would be given on changing a diaper, wrapping it up, and putting it in a bucket to await the return of their mother for proper cleaning. They would learn how to flush cuts with warm water and to wrap them with a simple, clean rag. Most importantly, she would impress on them the seriousness of their job. Toddlers needed to be watched every minute. Their mothers were entrusting them with their siblings' lives.

She slid her AWH armband up and over her sleeve, adjusting it for the letters to proclaim her position. Ruth Newcombe, Mrs. Baker and five other women rustled their children on to rows of split logs. Eliza thought of her first day at Woman's Med. Nerves, anticipation, and worries had plagued her until she listened to the Anatomy lecture by Dr. Patrick Callahan. He had put the class at ease by opening with a joke. Eliza would do the same.

Dragging a ladder-backed chair from the porch, she settled on it in front of the group and began. "Why is grass dangerous?" she asked.

Silence, until Rosie Mae shot up her arm. "I's know! 'Cuz eating it gives you the runs."

Not the punchline Eliza planned, *because they're full of blades,* but it provided her first teaching moment. "Very good, Rosie, you're correct. One of the first things Mothers' Helpers need to learn is to make sure the littles don't put things in their mouths they shouldn't, like grass, or stones, or twigs..."

"Or poop!" cried out one of the Baker boys.

"Especially poop," said Eliza. She couldn't leave these families and slink back to Boston, she thought. They needed her plan to succeed as much as she did. Their simple lives and honesty teemed and echoed against the mountains, plugging empty holes and hearts with their love for one another.

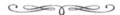

Chet had left with Ruth after class. The cow that the AWH had secured for her had turned ornery. She had kicked when Ruth tried to milk it that morning. Could Chet swing by and soothe the beast? "Pops, everyone knows you've got the magic touch," she had said. Eliza silently agreed. With a tip of his hat and a boyish grin toward Eliza, he plopped Rosie onto his shoulders and picked up Alice. His magic touch with Eliza would have to wait for another day.

Inside, she opened the ivory envelope she'd left on top of the stack of mail by the typewriter.

October 2, 1938
Dear Aunt Eliza,
All is well here as Boston continues its clean-up from the hurricane. Jack and I were fortunate that our story on the paper mills took us to the northern interior part of Maine. The mills remain closed and silent. I'm happy to hear the knitting mill down

there has some shifts available. I'm not sure how those families in Maine will survive another winter.

I've given more thought to your request for ideas of who else to approach with your appeal. I'm afraid I'm at a loss, too. Unless. Unless you shoot for the stars. I learned from the best. When faced with a challenge, or a 'fear fence' as you called it, back up a few paces, then run forward with all your might and hurdle that fence. Ignore the naysayers about women's abilities. Grab onto your dream and don't let go. Become a doctor. Become a journalist. Make it happen.

So, soar high. Since Congressman Morrison struck out with his request to the Appropriations Committee, go over his head. Write a letter to Labor Secretary Perkins. Woman to woman. Make your appeal that she considers your Maternity Shelter as not only a medical care facility, but a means to provide jobs in the area. You've identified five Health Aides positions, plus the cleaner and cook, along with Grace as a part-time assistant. That's seven jobs.

Of course! thought Eliza. Surely, Frances Perkins would support her proposal. Eliza recalled reading a full profile on Perkins after FDR named her as the first woman Cabinet member. Prior to her work with then Governor Roosevelt, Perkins had founded the Maternity Center Association in New York City after learning the disgraceful fact that the highest rates of infant mortality among developed countries lay within the borders of the United States. Eliza continued to see what else Bess suggested.

Here's a recent quote I read by Perkins that you could parlay into a convincing appeal: 'There is always a large horizon...There is much to be done...I am not going to be doing it! It is up to you to contribute some small part to a program of human betterment.' You are playing more than a small part in contributing to human betterment. Put my old Underwood to good use. Good Luck!

Now, for other news. I've called on Florence every day since I got back. I think she finds me tiresome. Yesterday, she snipped at me, "Tell that aunt of yours I'm fine. I don't need babysitting."

To spare my knuckles from another encounter with her cane, I'll leave her to my Mother and Aunt Mamie to keep an eye on her.

As for your boy, Will. He's more than fine. I intruded on his dinner at Durgin Park with Miss Walters on Saturday. He played a good sport and asked the waiter to add a chair to their cozy table for two. She really is lovely.

I'm off to meet a few of the Cliffie girls and catch the new movie, You Can't Take It With You. *Reviews say it's hysterical. And who wouldn't want to spend a couple of hours looking at Jimmy Stewart on the big screen? Who knew his down-to-earth, laid-back, every-man would also be my type? That easy smile and smooth talk can make this girl swoon as much as the rugged good looks of a certain photographer. Yes, I'm still seeing Jack, albeit not as frequently. He's been sent out west to visit some of the migrant camps, that is if he can elbow his way in on some of Dorothea Lange's assignments from the Farm Security Administration.*

XOXO,

Bess

Wise words from her wordsmith niece. She added Frances Perkins' name to her ledger and smirked at the thought of Jack being sent to California, hopefully for a good long assignment. Surely Bess could find herself a laid-back, every-man with an easy smile—an unmarried one.

The next letter displayed the familiar New York City postmark and Department of Public Health return address. She counted on letters from Olga to lighten her mood. Her witty friend never failed her.

October 5, 1938

Dear Eliza,

Thank you for the call to check on us after the devastating hurricane. I expect Taniya mentioned I had volunteered to assist with the overflow of injuries. Many people were caught outside and unaware of the danger of falling trees and debris.

In response to your earlier letter, I'm sorry to hear you're struggling to secure the final funds. Our Department of Public Health limps along as well. I'm in desperate need of more equipment to test my culture bottle designs, but my pleas fall on deaf ears. I imagine the Tennessee state and county offices face the same. Too much demand on too few dollars. As a result, I have investigated some private foundations here in NY. While my project does not meet their criteria, I think your Shelter does.

I recently met Doctor Eleanor Anderson Campbell (Boston University Medical, 1916). She serves as the director of the Judson Health Center on the Lower West Side. She also oversees her mother's philanthropic trust, the Milbank Memorial Fund. Their mission reads in part: "Seeks to care for the sick, the young, the aged and disabled; to minister to the needs of the poor." In a letter to her, make note that the Jellico Maternity Shelter will serve the rural populations of Appalachia with the same level of care as the immigrant populations of New York.

Eliza bit her lip, recalling that Dr. Sheriff in South Carolina had tapped the Milbank Fund. She hoped her request would be considered with equal merit.

Please keep me updated on your progress. What news of the boys? An engagement announcement yet from Will? Teddy's whereabouts? I pray he's still in the Pacific. The turmoil in Europe concerns me. With no disrespect to your English father, but I don't trust that Brit Chamberlain. His statement about "Peace for our time" is not only naïve, but dangerous thinking.

I'll leave you to get back to work. Write some more letters. Deliver some more babies. Ride a mule. Take a walk in the woods. Maybe with a certain mountain man???

Yours truly and ever friend and sister,
Olga

"Oh, Olga, if you only knew," Eliza said to the milk bottle vase of purple geraniums. As she ran her fingertips up and down over the bottle's thick glass, she thought, *Why did I deny myself for all those years?* Her relationship with Chet had caught her by surprise. His gentle kiss. His small and thoughtful gestures, from bringing flowers to quelling her fears about mules and chickens. The way he could hold her hand like a teenager, his palms sweaty as they stood silent together staring at the majesty of his mountains. A sigh of pleasure settled her.

Her thoughts returned to the suggestions of Secretary Perkins and Dr. Campbell. In times of need, Eliza appreciated the constants in her life. The women in her circle of family and friends never abandoned her. Their interest in each other's work and lives remained true. Success would come from other women. Tomorrow, reinvigorated, she would pull out the Underwood and begin another hunt-and-peck session.

CHAPTER TWENTY-EIGHT

Spring 1939

Pounding metal against metal disturbed the quiet morning. *Bang, bang, bang.* Hammer face against nail head resounded up and down the lengths of the freshly cut wood planks. Eliza's dream was forming before her eyes. The workers, Chet and Ian, Tom Newcombe, and Mr. Baker from the lumber mill, had worked from sunup to sundown to install the sides and interior framing of the new Maternity Shelter. Eliza turned up the flame under the glass percolator. The warmth and kick of a well-deserved cup of strong caffeine would re-energize them until lunchtime. Twenty minutes later, as the men lingered at a makeshift table of a plywood sheet over two sawhorses inside the Shelter, Eliza heard a familiar voice outside say, "Who's got the box of twelve-pennies?"

With a hammer tucked into a frayed piece of rope cinched at the waist of blue denim overalls, Grace rounded the corner of an unfinished wall. Her hands went to retie a red kerchief into a tight knot on top of her head.

"Grace," exclaimed Eliza, surprised to find the young woman outfitted and ready to join the construction crew.

"Good morning, Dr. Edwards. Have you seen Pops? I think he's got all the nail boxes."

Grace never ceased to amaze Eliza. With an ability to focus on the task at hand and a determination to see it through to completion, Eliza held no doubts that Grace would become a pediatrician.

"Inside. They're having a cup of coffee."

"We should get this wall finished before those clouds decide to dump. Better tell him to finish up."

Before Eliza could head inside with Grace's request, Ian pushed his way through the door.

"You gotta be kiddin'," he said. "Girl, if you're gonna come home from that college, at least stay out of the way. Us men need the work. I ain't sharing my wages with youse. 'Sides, you'll just go git yourself or someone else hurt, swinging that hammer. It ain't a rug beater."

"Ah Ian, hush up. Hammering a nail t'aint no different than swinging an axe to split a log or chop a chicken's neck. I've done both. Many times. Not that you'd know, the way you disappear to hole up there in the mountain sipping the devil's juice."

His face red with rage, Ian stomped toward Grace, bumping Eliza on his way. Grace planted her feet and glared at him. Under her breath, Eliza heard Grace say, "Come on, you fool."

Inches from Grace, Ian raised his clenched fists. His biceps flexed and quivered beneath his flannel shirt. He snorted and kicked the toe of his boot into the dirt like a bull taunted by her red kerchief. He drew his right arm back and lunged, his fist seeking Grace's chin. "I do as I damn please, you little bi…"

Grace heaved the hammer above her head with both hands. Eliza cried out, "Don't!" at the same moment Grace found her target.

Crack.

Ian howled with a guttural scream. He fell to the ground, grabbing his right humerus. Grace dropped the hammer and knelt at his side. "I ain't sorry, Ian. I'm only sorry you've turned mean and ugly. Next time you try to come at me, or Leonie Baker, or any woman—if I find out, I'll be aiming a lot lower than your upper arm."

She turned to Eliza, who stood with her mouth agape in awe and admiration. Eliza had witnessed a young woman handling a situation the only way she knew how, on her terms with confidence and acumen.

Hearing Ian's yowl, Chet and the other men appeared at the door. Chet stormed over to his writhing grandson. "Boy. I've told you too many times. You've gotta figure out how to lock up that devil inside you. I can't say I blame Gracie for what she's done. She beat me to it."

He lowered his shoulder to help the groaning man stand. Ian glowered at the collection of his family and neighbors who had witnessed his defeat at the hands of his younger sister.

Grace tossed her head and looked past him to Eliza. "Dr. Edwards, may I assist you with setting the break?"

The final funding arrived in early April from the Elizabeth Milbank Anderson Memorial Fund. After consulting with Dr. South, Eliza opened an account at Jellico's new savings and loan. They felt secure in their choice to deposit the $3,000 donation with new federal guarantees in place. The funds would cover them through the end of the year. Then, the AWH would add Jellico as a permanent location and budget item.

With her grandfather's pen, a gift from her aunts when she started medical school, Eliza wrote each announcement with an elite flourish.

Eliza P. Edwards, M.D., and Lillian South, M.D., of the American Women's Hospital, request the honor of your attendance at the opening of the Jellico Maternity Shelter, Jellico, Tennessee on Mother's Day, Sunday, May 8, 1939.

Through the generous donations of many, our countrywomen of this corner of Appalachia will now receive the true medical aid they need.

Your support is greatly appreciated.

Her index finger lingered over the line about the countrywomen of Appalachia. "I hope you don't mind I borrowed your words, Anandibai," Eliza said to the empty room. "I know you will bear witness and give me the strength and humanity to provide care for these mothers. I will not fail them, or you."

She licked the three-cent stamp and patted Honest Abe's face onto the last envelope. Three of the envelopes would make their way to New York City, addressed to: Dr. Olga Povitsky, New York Department of Public Health, Dr. Esther Lovejoy, American Women's Hospitals, and Dr. Eleanor Anderson Campbell, Judson Health Center. One would travel to Vermont to the office of Dr. Charlotte Fairbanks. Two more would head to Boston for Miss Florence Pearson and Miss Bess Edwards. Eliza beamed, thinking of the moment she would share one of her greatest achievements. Doctors, mentors, journalists, teachers. Friends. Family. Sisters of the heart.

By this time next month, infants would fill the Maternity Shelter with rosy cheeks to match the pink and white mountain laurel blooming outside the window. Eliza placed a clutch of the branches in a milk bottle. Their breezy, fresh scent would welcome the visitors to Appalachia with a touch of homegrown flora. She had foregone lessons in flower arranging that most of her childhood friends had taken. The only arrangements she made were the placement of slides under microscopes. With a gentle nudge, she shifted a bottle from a table edge and plucked one faded bloom from its stem.

"Perfect," said a deep voice behind her. Chet stood in the doorway; his arms were filled with another bundle of mountain laurel. He had trimmed his bushy beard into a neat, close crop and slicked back his hair, clearing his forehead which accentuated his piercing gray eyes. His black suit jacket, which looked like it had been sitting in the recesses of a closet for over twenty years, fit snugly. Back then, it had hung loose on a younger man's body.

"Oh, Chet. Thank you, but I'm out of milk bottles," said Eliza.

He dropped the bundle to the floor and snapped off two thin branches. First, he walked to the corner where Eliza had positioned a small desk for her administrative duties. On the wall abutting the desk, she had hung her diploma from Woman's Med. Chet tucked the end of the branch behind a corner of a black lacquered frame.

"The city meets the country. They balance each other, don't you think? It's really something what you've done here, Eliza. You've persevered just like these flowers through a cold, raw spring to blossom even on the grayest of days." He turned to Eliza, proffering the second branch to her. "No milk bottles, but I reckon you've got plenty of diaper pins. How about a corsage? You look like you're near ready to burst, just like these flowers."

As his cheeks rose into a blush, matching the petals in his hand, he cleared his throat.

"I don't mean nothing about your figure. Um. What I mean is, your smile, your glow."

Eliza, her hands on her hips, twirled in a small circle. A faint odor of the last coat of shellac on the wooden floor beneath her feet teased her nostrils. She threw her arms wide. "It's happening. It's really happening. We've done it, Chet."

"You've done it, Eliza. You, the remarkable doctor from Boston who didn't give up on us."

A cascade of emotions flooded her. She stepped toward him with unspoken words on her lips. Her fingers threaded through his hair as he tilted his lips to her. In their embrace, the world faded. Only the warmth of each other's touch and their hearts melding into silent communion held them within the moment.

"Thank you," she said.

CHAPTER TWENTY-NINE

December 1939

Eliza guided Grace's fingers to the spot where a firm ball formed beneath the skin. "Ok," Eliza said. "Keep one end here on the fundus."

Moving down toward the pubis, Eliza allowed Grace to find the pubic bone. She nodded her head as Grace stretched the measuring tape taut from one point to the other. "Number of centimeters?" Eliza asked.

"Twenty-two," replied Grace.

"Excellent. Mrs. Conley, this measurement puts you at twenty-two weeks, four and a half months pregnant. Do you think that's close? You would have conceived around the first week of July and missed your menses by early August."

Mrs. Conley pushed herself up from lying on the exam table. "Sounds 'bout right. Remember the Fourth? Hotter than a steam bath on a Saturday night. Jake was sweating all over me. Ugh. Figures that was the one night he wasn't his normal three-minute man!"

Grace blushed four shades of red and looked away. Eliza grinned. How many intimate details of marital relations had she heard over the past thirty-five years? She could write a book. Although she wouldn't dare put her own name on the cover. No need to stir her mother from eternal rest.

"Thank you for confirming," Eliza said. "Grace. Please note on Mrs. Conley's chart. Estimated conception is July 7. That should put us around April 7, 1940, for a due date. I wonder when Easter falls next year? Wouldn't that be lovely? Baby chicks, baby bunnies, and a new baby bundle for you! We're almost finished. Lie back again please, we need a blood sample and a few smears for the lab. Grace, I'll let you take the blood for the Wasserman."

Eliza always used formal names for these blood tests. Better to let a patient ponder the mystery than evoke a worry about what the test results for syphilis may bring.

After they sent Mrs. Conley off with instructions for maintaining a healthy diet and watching for any symptoms which may cause concern, Eliza and Grace sat for a break of crackers and blackberry jam. The late fall sun spilled through the windows, hitting the white-washed walls with an amber glow. Grace nibbled at the crystals on top of a saltine. With a swish of milk to wash down the crumbs, she cleared her throat. "Um, Dr. Edwards. Do all patients speak so openly, like Mrs. Conley? I'm not sure I'm comfortable hearing details about her, um, husband's performance."

Eliza pushed back in her chair. Ah, the naiveté of a young medical student, exposed to sexual relations only as found within textbook pages. She wondered how the professors at medical schools which now admitted women presented those chapters in Gray's Anatomy to co-educational classes. Eliza and her friends had squirmed like river eels in their seats when Patrick Callahan reviewed those sections with an all-female audience.

"I wouldn't call Mrs. Conley the exception, nor the norm. Many women, like most men, enjoy boasting about their sexual activities, even comparing notes with their friends," said Eliza. She looked to make sure Grace hadn't turned beet red again. Thankfully no, although Eliza caught a suppressed giggle.

"That's the lesson you should take from Mrs. Conley's comments. She's comfortable speaking with us, like a friend. I think it's highly doubtful she would have mentioned anything about her husband to a male doctor. By sharing her personal experience, she demonstrated she trusts us. This will help her, and us as her attending medical professionals, throughout her pregnancy. A woman knows her body better than anyone. You never want a patient to withhold information about what they're feeling. Those instances can lead to difficulties down the road for the mother and child. Too many suffer simply because women don't trust a male doctor to understand their complaints."

Eliza felt that small teachable moments often held more sway in developing a doctor than a chapter review in a textbook. She would jot down others she wanted to impart to Grace before she headed off to medical school, in case she ended up at the University of Tennessee where men filled every professor position.

A week later, Eliza opened the appointment book. She had booked back-to-back appointments for the women with prenatal and post-delivery check-ups to clear her schedule for the following two weeks. And, thanks to some higher power or lower libidos in late February, no patients had an expected due date for the end of December. Eliza could travel home for Christmas, secure in knowing that the Health Aides, healthmobile team, and Grace could handle any emergencies which may arise.

Grace peered over Eliza's shoulder. "Really?" she exclaimed. "Mrs. Baker in at 11 o'clock for a Pre1? Dr. Edwards, there's no question that she qualifies for a pessary. Don't we have an ethical obligation at this point to inform her of the life-threatening risks she's facing with another pregnancy?"

"You're absolutely right, Grace," said Eliza. "I'm concerned as well. When she brought the little ones in for vaccines, I noted her extreme fatigue. I'll speak to her today. She may also be our first candidate for the mandatory pre- and post-delivery stays I'd like to institute to monitor special cases. The discussion of birth control, however, needs to extend beyond Mrs. Baker. We should incorporate it into the new mother classes, let them know they now have the freedom and control to decide when and how many children they want. Check your history books, Grace. I bet you won't find mention of the insidious Comstock Laws which shackled us women until three years ago."

Grace tugged at her sleeve; her eyes wandering over the bookshelf where Eliza stored her reference books. Eliza saw the wheels turning again in the bright young woman's mind. She hadn't been surprised to learn that Grace was sailing through college classes on pace to finish her degree in three years instead of four.

"North Carolina has incorporated birth control as part of their state-wide public health services," Grace said. "Perhaps I can find a name down there and write to ask for some of their materials. I could outline a curriculum over my vacation. It would give me something to do since we don't have any scheduled appointments."

"Excellent. I appreciate your ideas, Grace. You're two steps ahead of me many days."

The radiance which spread across Grace's face touched Eliza's heart. In a Shelter built to care for mothers and children, two women stood facing each other. A mother without a daughter; a daughter without a mother. A bond had formed without any help from an umbilical cord. One had made the other proud.

"Thank you. I'll start tomorrow." Grace returned to the calendar, running her finger down the list, and moving forward two days.

"What's this on Thursday? The 6-0? Have you developed a new appointment code?"

"What? Oh, that? It's nothing. You can erase it."

An erasure of that number would be a kind, smart gesture on Grace's part. If only sliding a pink rubber end of a pencil across a page could erase 6-0. Eliza dreaded her sixtieth birthday as much as finding the second row of crow's feet, which had formed at the corners of her eyes. Why had she jotted the numbers? She didn't want to remind herself, let alone have anyone else find out her true age.

"I know you better than that. If you made a note in the appointment book, it must be important," said Grace.

Clever girl. Was Eliza's meticulous attention to detail that apparent? Time to parlay and deke away from the conversation.

"Did you say 6-0? The numbers must have smudged. It's 5-0, for my birthday. Just a silly doodle."

"Your birthday! You never told us! Wow—so fun! We'll have a party." Grace twirled with a sparkle in her eyes.

"Absolutely not. I don't need a party and don't you tell anyone my age, Miss Wilson. Not that fifty is old, you understand."

"No, of course it isn't! Pops is sixty-five and proud of it. You wouldn't know it, the way he horses around with the kids and splits a cord of wood without breaking a sweat."

No, you wouldn't, thought Eliza.

CHAPTER THIRTY

Eliza wished Will congratulations in the cheeriest telephone voice she could muster and then slammed down the receiver after she knew that he had hung up first. Neither of her boys would be home for Christmas! Teddy's ship had docked in San Diego for leave, but he wasn't granted enough time to travel round-trip to Boston. And now news from Will. He had asked Anne Walters to marry him. A June wedding was in the works. *Happy Birthday, Mom! Isn't that one of the best presents I've ever given you? Better than the packet of baseball cards when I was ten?* he had said. She could see him beaming on the other end of the phone, flush in love. He ended the call by sneaking in the news that he and Anne would spend Christmas with her family in Connecticut. *And Mom, can you send Anne your recipe for Boozey Chicken? She wants to make it for all of us over the holiday.* His request sliced her as if she were halving the chicken breasts into two pieces, one for him and one for her.

Her fingers ran over the glass of a picture frame on her desk. In the studio photograph, Teddy stood next to a seated Will. Dressed in gray pinstriped Sunday suits, pressed sharp with crisply knotted ties tucked inside the buttoned front flaps of vests, they looked like young, leading men of Hollywood. Despite the sixteen- and fourteen-year-old men staring out with serious countenances, they would always be her children—the babies she had waited for so long to hold in her arms. Now, Will would take a major step firmly into adulthood. *Congratulations, my dear. She seems like a sweet girl and if she makes you happy, that's most important.*

With a heavy heart, she planted herself in the desk chair, picking up her pen to write an Ovariian prescription for Mrs. Brody's mother-gone symptoms. One should savor small victories. She had finally convinced Mrs. Brody to stop applying goose fat poultices to her vagina and drinking three extra glasses of milk daily, thinking she was re-stimulating her mammary glands. When Eliza shared the relief that she had found from the Ovariian to minimize her hot flashes and night sweats, Mrs. Brody relented. As to its effect on vaginal dryness, however, Eliza drew the line in opting not to discuss how a divorcee tended to those needs. Some secrets should remain between the sheets of a woman alone with her body or with a local widower.

In need of a distraction, Eliza turned on the second-hand tabletop radio Lillian South had donated to the Shelter. *The Chase and Sanborn Show* with Edgar Bergen and his sidekick, ventriloquist dummy, Charlie McCarthy, never failed to bring smiles and guffaws to millions of listeners who continued to face dark days. She'd heard advertisements that tonight's special guest featured Maureen O'Hara, the fresh new face with RKO studios straight from Dublin. A crooning Irish lilt always had the power to soothe and distract Eliza from dwelling thoughts. She swiveled in the chair and pulled a small, tufted ottoman out from under the desk. Kicking off her shoes, she leaned back and propped her heels on the stool.

Forty minutes into the show, a rap sounded against the door. Nearly nine o'clock on a Sunday night meant an emergency. In no mood to bundle into her winter coat, wrap a muffler around her throat, and head out into the woods in someone's old jalopy, or worse, on their nag or mule, she sighed and called out a weary, "Come in."

The swipe of heavy boots rustled against the hard bristles of the porch mat. The door pushed open. Chet walked in, carrying a newspaper-wrapped square object in his gloved hands.

"Happy Birthday, Eliza."

Oh, Grace. She thought she could rely upon the young woman to keep her secret. But apparently, Grace spilled the beans the moment she got home last week. As if he had read her mind, Chet said, "Now don't be blaming Grace. She told me in strictest confidence. I didn't tell anyone else. But no one should be alone on her birthday, lest of all on a big one."

Before she could button up the cardigan she wore over the baggy day dress, he deposited the square into her lap. Puzzled, she looked up at him. "I hope this is the extra box of talcum powder I asked Grace to add to our wish list," she said, half joking, half serious. The Shelter could always use more supplies.

"Sorry to disappoint," Chet winked at her, lifting his chin, and gesturing for her to open the package.

She peeled back the double layer of pages. Her fingers found a smooth, firm surface. The paper fell to the floor, revealing a twelve-inch square wooden box. A reddish hue streaked through the oak wood grain, giving the sides a fiery presence. A cover fit snugly into grooves along the top edges. Centered in the cover, blonde ash triangles meshed into an inlaid star design. Every inch had been sanded, including rounded corners and edges.

A lump formed in Eliza's throat. Her hand glided across the top, feeling the work and care which had gone into creating the gift. Her fingertips tingled. His hands had spent hours thinking of her while measuring, cutting, and sanding pieces of wood into the hand-crafted piece of art, which sat in her lap. She swiped at a tear, daring to emerge from the corner of her eye.

"Something to hold all your letters—the ones with the good news, which funded this mighty fine Shelter," said Chet.

Eliza pushed aside the array of papers on the desk and gently positioned the box in front of the radio. "Chet, thank you so much. It's beautiful. It may be one of the most thoughtful gifts I've received in my...sixty years. Yes, sixty. There, I admit it. I may have fibbed to Grace."

In three steps, she moved to embrace him. He opened his arms. She laid her cheek against his chest. Beneath his worn flannel shirt, his heart pulsed with strong, even beats. His breaths in and out steadied her own. She fit against his body like a shadow cast by a noon-day sun.

He murmured into the top of her head, brushing aside a few loose silver strands. "I know. I did the math when you first arrived here and mentioned your sons' ages. I figured you didn't have them when you were in medical school, or even just after you finished."

"No. I waited a rather long time for them," Eliza sighed.

"There's no need to hide your age. I don't care how old you are. In fact, sixty makes me feel less like I'm robbing the cradle, as they say." He pulled her tighter.

On the radio, mellow undertones from clarinets muted soulful saxophones. Their bodies swayed in sync. Eliza relaxed into the musical rhythm of Glenn Miller's *Moonlight Serenade*, matching her heartbeat to Chet's. Muscle memory took over as he steered her in a slow, skating glide through the cramped floor space of the reception room. The light, even tones built toward a crescendo. Chet dropped his hand from the small of her back as he raised his other hand, clutching hers. She twirled under his raised arm and returned to the found spot alongside his body.

Her throat clamped. Her eyes softened and fluttered open to catch Chet's full-face grin staring down at her. "Where's Grace tonight?" she asked.

"She's over at Ruth's. 'Lisabet has the bark again. They'll take turns tonight holding her over the steam bath like you taught them."

"Poor thing. The minute the weather turns, the croup grabs her. She'll outgrow it soon enough and at least it's not contagious, so Ruth needn't worry about the other kids."

Today, Eliza turned sixty. She had received a beautiful, thoughtful gift. One more would complete her day.

"You're right. No one should be alone on her birthday," she said. She slipped her hand into his again and tugged him gently toward the bedroom.

CHAPTER THIRTY-ONE

May 1940

"**C**ome with me."

Eliza rolled onto her back, sliding into the crevice formed between the two single beds pushed together. Above her, the ceiling fan blades rotated in a methodical wobble, *click, click, click*. The mid-May morning dawned like a hot flash, as prickly and sweaty as Eliza remembered when she had them ten years ago. Her bare skin stuck to the white cotton sheet. She rose to a sitting position, propping herself against the bed's cool, metal headboard. Chet remained on his side facing her, just as he did on every spare night she found in the Shelter's calendar since December. Eliza joked he knew the due dates of her patients better than she did. The week before and the ten days following due dates, women filled the beds. On those nights, Eliza slept alone in her narrow bed in the back bedroom while a health aide took one of the empty maternity beds to stay close to the patient and newborn for overnight observation.

Chet pushed himself up onto an elbow. The gray mat of his chest hair glistened with perspiration. With his free hand, he brushed her loose hair from her forehead. "We've had this discussion, Eliza. I'd look like a damn fool sitting in my threadbare suit and scuffed-through-to-the-toes boots in that fancy church pew. The mother of the groom next to me in her elegant, satin gown, with pearls draped around her neck and clipped to her ears. Your family will think you've lost your mind, taking up with a hillbilly like me. I bet a sweet potato pie that your brothers would figure out how to use a shotgun on me with the same accuracy as a Hatfield staring down a McCoy. Maybe your sons, too. 'Specially the Navy man."

"I don't have a recipe for sweet potato pie to take you up on that bet. And I don't expect either of my brothers have handled a gun in their lives. When and if they needed any dirty business attended to, they had connections to the Italians in the North End of Boston. Albie did offer to rustle one up when I wanted Harrison out of my life."

"In that case, I've got no hankering to meet up with an Eye-talian, either."

Eliza reached over to pat his cheek. *Leave it be, Eliza,* she thought. He's right. Chet belongs in this spot, in this mountain valley. On the nights that the Shelter was empty, she wanted him in the chair next to her, listening to the radio and waltzing her around a six-foot square dance floor. When the music ended, they started a melody of their own in the makeshift double bed. Tender rhythms based on experience moved them into a slow, fulfilling orbit of oneness. After, when he held her close, she would fall asleep in his arms, amazed, and thankful she had found a man who could satisfy her with simple pleasure.

"All right, we'll leave you off the wedding guest list, but you can bet that sweet potato pie that I'm coming to Grace's graduation."

"She'd be devastated if you didn't," he said.

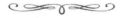

On the stoop of her home at Smith Court in Boston, Eliza fumbled to open the clasp of the black beaded evening bag. Her fingertips rummaged among the wadded, damp handkerchief, change purse, and pill box three-quarters emptied of its aspirin tablets, until she felt the jagged edge of the single key. She pulled out the key and inserted it into the door. Her other hand gripped the hem of Florence's dusty rose crocheted lace capelet.

"Here we are, Florence," said Eliza as she guided her aunt through the doorway. She waved over her shoulder to her brother, Albie, waiting in his car. He tooted the horn and sped off to his house four blocks away.

In the dimly lit front room, Eliza watched Florence amble toward her bedroom, her cane *tap-tap-tapping* ahead of her. "Good night," she called, "Sleep in tomorrow; it's been an exhausting day. I probably won't be up before nine myself."

No response came from Florence, only the shuffle of feet and creak of bedsprings as she lowered herself upon the summer coverlet. A fist of emotions that had been stuck in Eliza's throat ever since Anne walked down the church aisle that morning exploded with the might of a roaring avalanche. Eliza crumpled in a heap on the floor. Silent sobs found their voice as tears streamed down her cheeks, both in an unabated release.

Over the course of the ceremony, reception, and five-hour drive back from Connecticut, Eliza diverted her attention from situations developing around her. She had danced with her handsome sons—Will, the jubilant, dashing groom in his black tails and Teddy, the serious, dignified lieutenant in his dress whites. She had told stories about her patients, the healthmobile team, and Dr. South. Described the beauty of the majestic mountains, lush green valley, and rippling creeks, along with the critters who hid in the brambles. Touted the accomplishments of her protégé, Grace Wilson, earning her college degree in three years and headed to Woman's Med on a full scholarship in the fall.

In a puddle on the floor, she sat and reflected on the changes life had hurled at her. A woman had claimed Will's life with two words uttered in front of an altar. Anne would select the new suit and ties Will needed with his promotion to contracts manager. She would prepare Boozey Chicken for Will's upcoming birthday. Eliza was thankful; however, that the chicken dish would be cooked in a Boston apartment, not Connecticut. The young couple had no reason to move now that the Edwards Wool Company had resumed full operation as orders rolled in from the United Kingdom to outfit its armed services.

Another war in Europe brought more business and greater worries. Teddy had received a new assignment with the *USS Mississippi*. After four years as part of the Pacific Fleet, they crossed through the Panama Canal and pointed north to join Roosevelt's Neutrality Patrols. Censors and reporters couldn't quell American's fears that the battleships, although they may be publicly denoted to escort American and British ships through trade routes, also patrolled the East Coast to report on German U-boat activity. Whether they had orders to shoot on sight, only men like Lieutenant Shaw and his ranking officers knew.

Nearly as sinister as submerged vessels laden with stealth torpedoes, another evil announced itself during the reception. Eliza's beloved aunt was unwell. Did blame also fall on Eliza? Over the past eighteen months, she had relied on intermittent reports from Will, Bessie, her brothers, and her sisters-in-law as to Florence's well-being. Either they had omitted information or failed to detect the nuanced instances of *dementia praecox*.

Olga had alerted her. On her way back from the lavatory, she caught a glimpse of Florence's rose capelet through an open door of a different banquet room. Seated at a table whose occupants had headed to the dance floor, Florence showed no sign of realizing that she had wandered into a room filled with strangers. As she reached for a half-filled crystal wineglass at the place setting, Olga moved into the room. She asked Florence to accompany her to the restroom as a ploy to steer her back to the Shaw-Walters banquet room. Through a whisper behind her hand to Eliza, Olga detailed where she found Florence.

"I'm afraid your suspicions are correct," Olga said. "Not even the sounds of polka music tipped her off she was in the wrong room. She shouldn't be left alone. She could wander off to someplace far more dangerous than a Polish wedding reception."

As Eliza joined the others in tossing handfuls of rice at the newlyweds in Will's mint green, top-down Buick Roadmaster, she kept a watchful eye on Florence. Twenty-five years ago, a headstrong three-year-old Will would slip away from Eliza's firm grip of his hand to sprint through the Boston Garden or wade into a pond, chasing the ducks. Would strong-willed Florence be next? Holding tight to an eighty-year-old's hand or threatening to send her to bed without dessert would be impossible and impractical.

Sticky, strangling threads caught Eliza tight as she fought to escape from new worries. They blurred her vision and clouded her mind as she tried to imagine holding Florence's hand when she lived nearly a thousand miles away in Jellico, Tennessee.

CHAPTER THIRTY-TWO

June 1940
Boston, Massachusetts

Two days after the unnerving episode with Florence at Will's wedding, Eliza cajoled Bessie into spending an evening with her great-aunt while Eliza arranged a family sit-down. Over the course of an hour, Eliza admonished her brothers and sisters-in-law for failing to notice Florence's decline.

"Why are you making such a fuss?" asked her oldest brother, Albie.

"She's Fearless Florence," said Fred. "She's always been eccentric. You're over-reacting."

"It was an exhausting day for all of us," Fred's wife, Bea, added. "And she is eighty."

Eliza twisted in her chair to face Bea head-on. "You don't need to tell me how old my aunt is. I grew up sharing a room with her as if she were my older sister. There are exactly twenty years between us. I turned sixty in December."

Since the barbs were flying, she may as well remind them that they had missed her birthday. *Out of sight, out of mind* couldn't be a truer statement of loss.

"Eliza," said Albie's wife, Mamie. "A moment of confusion doesn't warrant a lock-down. Being in a strange place and a change in her routine put her out of sorts. I've seen it happen with my parents. Once they're in the comforts and familiarity of their home, they're fine."

From the entryway of Albie and Mamie's house, the grandfather clock chimed five. Each reverberating gong of the hammer carried Eliza back another decade to her childhood, where the clock stood in her grandparents' home on Race Street. Every evening upon the eight o'clock hour, Florence would take young Eliza by the hand and lead her upstairs. Together they'd read Eliza's favorites: Jules Verne's collection of far-away destinations and Lewis Carroll's *The Adventures of Alice in Wonderland*. As she closed the book and tucked the covers around Eliza, Florence would lean down and whisper a quote from Alice. "'I know who I WAS when I got up this morning, but I think I must have been changed several times since then.' How about you, Lizzy? How did you change today?" Then she would tap her index finger against the tip of Eliza's nose. Their secret good night.

Eliza rubbed her nose and let her fingertips linger over her lips. She knew who she WAS. The roles of mother, doctor, sister, founder of the AWH's Maternity Shelter in Jellico, and niece, filled her with pride and satisfaction. But who was Florence? The former artist and teacher had lost her vibrancy and zest the day arthritis claimed her paintbrushes and ability to express herself. Apart from her story time reading hours at the settlement house and the dwindling outings with a rapidly declining circle of friends, Florence had withdrawn into a simple existence. When Eliza had left for Tennessee, Florence slipped a few more pegs into spiraling change. A solitary life devoid of meaning stalked her like the shadowy figures who slunk through Boston's back alleys, ready to pounce and grab the riches of a fulfilled life.

Mamie's last remark settled over the room, cloaking it in silence. Eliza stood. She positioned herself in front of the group like a schoolteacher addressing a third-grade class. She clasped her shaking hands and said, "I wish this episode was an isolated moment, Mamie. I really do. But what I found at the house tells me differently."

One by one, she ticked off evidence of an addled mind. Bamboo paintbrushes in the toothbrush holder. Unopened canned vegetables stacked into towers on a refrigerator shelf. Half pints of cream placed in the pantry, emitting a curdled, sour odor from beneath the door. Scrawled notes tucked under pillows and into book pages.

She continued, "These are not innocent lapses in judgment. She's overwhelmed with simple decision making. This morning, she needed my help to pick out clothes to wear. When I opened her top dresser drawer, I found soiled undergarments. I don't think she's sent her laundry out for the last couple of weeks."

Bea and Mamie shook their heads in disbelief. Albie and Fred's stoic faces paled.

"If she's unable to manage her laundry, what else is she ignoring? Paying the bills? Personal hygiene is one thing. Personal safety is a whole other concern. What if she forgets to light the gas burner? What if she takes a wrong turn going to the market? God help us all, if she sheds her dress and takes a dip in a Public Garden pond to cool off this summer.

Worries of what ifs clamored for attention, raced through her mind, gained speed, and stole her breath. Like a Shakespearean tragedy, scene after scene developed before her eyes until the crescendo of the final act. Fearless Florence, the heroine of her own story, would tumble.

Eliza grabbed the edge of the mantle behind her. "Once a week for Sunday dinner isn't enough. One of you needs to take her."

"Whoa, now Eliza," said Albie as he jumped to his feet. "You can't just waltz in here, making ridiculous demands on us. Mamie's busy checking on her parents twice a week and has church guild duties."

Fred joined in. "Bea has her hands full with the grandkids. Nor do we have extra room since they moved in." He pointed his finger at her. "How about you, Eliza? Will's married. Teddy's where? The Atlantic or the Pacific? You're the one without real responsibilities. Where are you in this picture? Scampering back to the mountains to take care of charity cases? Have you ever heard that charity begins at home?"

Throughout the prior night, Eliza had lain awake debating solutions to Florence's situation, including the one Fred proffered. She was the one without family responsibilities and with practical medical experience. But, the Shelter, her Shelter, had one doctor on staff, Dr. Eliza Edwards. Funding from the AWH would cease without a licensed medical professional on staff. A door, which opened to any who pushed against its wrought iron hinges, would close. Once again, mountain families would be forgotten. An entire community's well-being hung in the balance.

Eliza waved Fred off, pursing her lips into a thin line as she clenched her fists. She couldn't, she wouldn't, let the past fourteen months turn into a tease. "I have responsibilities there, Fred. You haven't seen the dire straits these families face. Women who live in squalor in dirt-floor cabins. No electricity or running water. Dying on childbirth beds made of rope and corn husks, covered with filthy sheets. Struggling to raise their children past the age of five. My Maternity Shelter serves a tremendous need. We're saving lives. Many lives. Among people who have no one else. They may mean nothing to you. But for me, these people, this Shelter, have given me hope that our country has a future."

Like children sneaking out of a classroom after a teacher's scolding, her sisters-in-law excused themselves. Alone with her brothers, Eliza tried a different tack.

"I know it's difficult for you to understand, but building and running the Shelter has saved one other life," she said.

Fred raised his eyebrows as Albie crossed his legs at the ankles, slouching into his chair. "Whose all-important life, Eliza? Who is the mountain martyr who makes you forsake caring for your own aunt? Ignoring her needs," asked Albie, raising his voice in agitation with the last two words.

Head lowered; Eliza studied the intricate weave of the Oriental carpet beneath her feet. The lush, rich hues of browns, reds, and greens melded together as her eyes filled. The lines of the geometric patterns in the carpet blurred. The colors swirled and transformed into thousands of brittle leaves, which covered the paths through the Cumberlands every October. Paths which led her to a place where she reclaimed her life, in purpose and with love. Beyond her work at the Shelter, what about Chet? How could she leave behind her desire, as selfish as it may be?

She lifted her tired eyes to look upon the men who had always supported her, whether it was her decision to attend medical school or to end her marriage. She needed them now more than ever to understand the salvation she found in Jellico. And how she had packed away a jar of ether to a medicine cabinet for patient use only.

"Mine," she said.

The next morning, sitting in her kitchen, Eliza ran her fingertip over the ceramic saltshaker shaped like a rooster. She thought of her first encounter with chickens at the Newcombes' cabin. The abject fear of a farm creature seemed inconsequential compared to the fears she faced now. The situation with Florence was much more terrifying than a pecking chicken. She had spent last night tossing in her bed, trapped in an unresolved situation. Neither of her brothers could take Florence, even if she agreed to move. When Eliza proposed hiring a ladies' companion to live with their aunt, Albie spewed his gin and tonic halfway across the room with his laughter.

Eliza's return train ticket lay under a cut glass sugar bowl. Dated Monday, July 1, 1940, her planned week home in Boston would end in two days. Time ran short. Decisions had to be made. Behind her, the door swung open with a soft whoosh and a scrape against the floor. A scented talcum powder preceded Florence into the room. The flowery, fresh aroma swept away Eliza's dark cloud. Florence had washed and dressed herself—the makings for a good day. Eliza felt a doughy hand squeeze her shoulder.

"Coffee ready, Lizzy?" asked Florence.

Distracted in her musings, Eliza had forgotten to lower the flame under the glass percolator. The coffee boiled at a low rumble. She jumped from the kitchen chair and rushed to turn off the burner.

"May be a tad stronger than you like. Let me get the cream," Eliza said as she poured two cups.

"Bah," Florence waved a napkin and placed it in her lap. "In fact, hold the cream and the sugar. A nice strong cup will invigorate these old bones and wake up a tired brain. We'll be able to face today's storms of life. Didn't that Irish bloke—your Patrick—used to say something like that?"

Yesterday, Florence couldn't remember the name of Fred's grandson. Today, she pulled forth parts of an Irish saying Patrick would quote with their after-dinner coffee, one she hadn't heard since Patrick had left. Eliza considered the words. Storms of life. Coffee. Patrick uttered many Irish sayings, dropping a pearl of wisdom, or sarcasm, as the situation demanded.

"*Through the storms of life may the only thing brewing be your coffee,*" she said after a few moments of reflection, attempting a sing-song Gaelic lilt as she spoke the phrase.

"That's it! Dr. Patrick Callahan. He was always quick with his quips, wasn't he? And a real looker. Those blue eyes. And my, those broad shoulders! Such a treat when he'd take off his jacket and we'd get a nice look-see at him in his shirtsleeves." She let out a loud sigh and winked at Eliza.

"Why, Aunt Florence, you never mentioned your...um, admiration for Patrick."

"Admiration? My girl, call it like you see it. Longing. Desire. Lust. Don't forget. Patrick, being ten years older than you meant he was ten years younger than me. It could've been possible if you shared that tomato with me. What I would've given to take a bite out of that ripe, red, juicy piece."

Fearless Florence had returned. Eliza beamed. Even if Florence's statements took a turn into the crass and uncomfortable, knowing that she spoke from a sound mind brought Eliza comfort. She could endure moments of unease over worrisome ramblings of nonsense.

"Pity the drink got him. You made the right decision to send him away to Washington. Better that way than the boys growing up with his irresponsible antics, setting a poor example."

Florence picked up her coffee and headed to the front room in search of the morning newspaper. Eliza started to call after her, "Florence, Patrick wasn't an alcoholic. You're thinking of Harrison." Realizing she was out of earshot and her mind once again muddled, Eliza stopped. From her reading about dementia, she had learned that confronting and contradicting the patient would cause more agitation.

Instead, she thought of the picture Florence painted with her words about the tomato, the handsome, quick-witted, well-proportioned anatomical figure of Dr. Patrick Callahan. Eliza hadn't sent him away. That was the man she had married, Harrison Shaw. Patrick had left her at an altar twenty-eight years ago, just weeks before they were to stand before God, family, and friends to commit themselves to one another. The minister had never uttered the phrase, "What therefore God hath joined together, let not man put asunder." Yet, Patrick had done just that. He had torn apart their union and shredded it to pieces as easily as he had ripped open her heart. Out of a sense of filial duty, he had returned to Ireland to visit his dying mother. He followed his destiny to a place and people that needed him. A place where he felt divine intervention had kept him when he missed sailing on the *Titanic*.

Aware of the duty facing her and the sacrifice she needed to make, Eliza pulled a small notebook from her purse. She peeked to check that Florence had the pages of *The Boston Globe* spread across her lap. Headlines about the Republican convention with the unlikely emergence of Wendell Wilkie for the ticket and articles detailing the Nazis' incessant bombings over Britain and a new build-up of forces in North Africa would keep her occupied. Eliza picked up the phone receiver. On the train ride home from Warm Springs, a kind woman had suggested she call upon her if she were ever in New York. In the throes of the situation with Florence, Eliza didn't have the luxury of time to travel to New York.

She dialed a number. Upon hearing an answer come through, she squared her shoulders and asked, "Dr. Eliza Edwards calling on behalf of the AWH's Jellico Maternity Shelter. I need to speak with Dr. Lovejoy. Is she available?"

CHAPTER THIRTY-THREE

July 1940
Jellico, Tennessee

Behind the Shelter, neat rows of vines and stems reached upward, their lush foliage providing shade for smaller plants below. Eliza plucked two firm green tomatoes from a cluster of three on a sturdy stalk. She lifted them to her nose, inhaling their earthy perfume. Before she left Jellico, she promised herself that she'd cook up a batch of fried green tomatoes for lunch. On her recipe card from Warm Springs, she had underlined the word *always* fry in bacon grease. One thing they never lacked in Appalachia was bacon grease.

Beyond a row of lettuce and another of spinach, Chet bent over a narrow dirt path. With a jackknife in one hand, he sliced a length of twine from a ball at his feet. As he looped the string around the green bean shoot and the slender twig stuck into the soft earth, he called over to Eliza, "We'll need some extra hands to harvest all this come September."

But they won't be my hands, thought Eliza. She had returned two days ago, knowing she had fourteen days to uproot her life from the sanctuary that had nourished her mind, body, and soul. Her to-do list of preparations covered two pages in her notebook, from preparing patient files for the arrival of her replacement on July 10 to checking on the measles case over at the Bakers' house.

The task, however, which she couldn't bear to add to her list remained untended. For the past twenty-four hours, she had allowed cowardice and denial a victory they didn't deserve.

On the other side of a split-rail fence, Ollie swatted his tail, flicking flies toward the garden's rows. Eliza sidled over to him. His soft nose nuzzled against her white coat, searching for the dried apple slices she kept in her pocket, ready for a hungry child. The gentle beast of burden had become her friend. She stroked his long, silky ears, marveling at how they perked forward at the sound of Chet's voice and lay back against his head when he sensed Ian approaching. Thankfully, those occurrences had ceased when Ian disappeared into the mountains again, his arm in a sling and a lost look in his eyes.

"Chet," Eliza began, her voice shaky as she summoned the words she needed to say, "I'm afraid I won't be here for the harvest."

He raised his head from the hoeing he had started after finishing with the bean poles. "Another wedding? Did your Navy man find a nurse on base? Or Bess? Did she finally convince Jack to leave his wife?"

A lump in her throat halted her reply. She grasped Ollie's black mane, its hair coarse and uneven. She tried to lighten the tension building in the air. "Ha, ha. No, no wedding bells. Although you know how I long to hear them for Teddy and yes, I wish Bessie would give Jack an ultimatum. But I fear they may both be lost causes."

She looked past Ollie to the Maternity Shelter where it stood on a solid slab foundation, its one-year-old white clapboards still bright and unblemished from the weather. Best to blurt it out. Bite the bullet. Be brave. She squared her shoulders and turned toward Chet again.

"It's my Aunt Florence. She's failing. It's not safe for her to live alone and my brothers are unable to care for her. I'm moving back to Boston."

Chet dropped the hoe with a soft thud. A puff of dirt rose from the dried, caked earth. In four strides he was by her side. "Not visiting? Moving? That means, permanently?"

Her chin quivered. "Yes. Dementia is a slow, wicked disease. There's no telling how long she'll be with us."

He picked up her hand and enfolded it in his. "Bring her here. You know they say clean mountain air can be a cure-all."

"If only it were that easy. Unfortunately, any disruptions to a patient's routine only further agitates them. I want her final days to be as comfortable as possible, which is why I need to go there."

Despite the sweat seeping through his thin cotton shirt on a Tennessee summer day, she rested her face against his chest. His scent drew her closer. She longed to crawl inside him and burrow deep away from the tug of responsibility. His hand stroked the back of her head.

"I'll miss you, Eliza. There's no doubt about that. But I understand. My son leaving his kids was despicable. Family is too precious of a gift we are given."

"I know that, too. But it doesn't necessarily make it any easier to say good-bye to my family here."

"No, it doesn't."

Amidst the vibrant patches of the vegetables at their feet, Eliza and Chet clung to each other in a tight embrace. Their time to etch each detail of one another into their memories diminished as the sun rose higher into the sky.

The words on the prescription pad would bring comfort to the Baker twins and their mother. *Oatmeal paste for the rash. Plenty of water to avoid dehydration—milk is fine, too. Foods rich in Vitamin A: spinach, sweet potato, carrots, and liver (they may not like it, but it's the best thing for them!). The contagious period should be over by next Tuesday—day five—wait until then before*

you allow them out of the barn. Minor ear infections may develop. Watch for signs of pneumonia (high fever, prolonged cough). You must not go near them. Severe complications with the pregnancy if you contract measles. Leonie can manage. Eliza P. Edwards, M.D., July 14, 1940

Eliza tore the sheet from the pad and set it aside. The treatment plan may be the final prescription she wrote and validated with her signature loops of an M and the slightly slanted straight edge of a D, finished with a flourish after Eliza Edwards. The pad held another thirty slips. Eliza fanned them between her fingers. Like the unwritten chapters in a half-finished book, the blank pages mocked her. Unpacking it in Boston might bring her more grief. She watched the pad's descent into the wastebasket at her feet.

She laid the pen down on the desk. William Pearson, Eliza's grandfather, had used the pen with a deep inkwell over ninety years ago, writing defense arguments which won cases for runaway slaves tried under the Fugitive Slave Act. Thanks to his work, Black men received their right to step outside a courtroom. At the same time that he had tried cases in Philadelphia's courts, William Pearson penned the incorporation documents which founded the Female Medical College of Pennsylvania. Freed from barriers erected by nearly every other medical school in the world, women developed ways to combine a sense of sympathy and science for a more evolved approach to practicing medicine.

Over the forty-three years of use by Eliza, the pen's ink reservoir had run dry many times. From study notes—with pleas to herself in the margins to memorize the formulas until she could recite them like a child's nursery rhyme—to class examinations in Obstetrics, written in a firm and confident hand. From patient records to prescriptions. From seeking advice from Fearless Florence in Boston to newsy letters to Olga during the years she had returned home to Russia, to crisp, terse replies to her mother's inquiries about Patrick's intentions, to funding requests for the Maternity Shelter, her grandfather's pen had been an implement of change. Eliza rolled the pen between her fingers. With each rotation, statements of personal and professional histories beckoned her thoughts to the lessons she had learned from her grandfather. Every person deserved the right to answer their calling. She would pack the pen carefully into her medical bag and bring it home. There would be others after her whose eager hands would need to grasp its firm barrel to pen their freed thoughts and desires.

Also on the desk, a pile of fourteen cream envelopes lay stacked and tied with a red grosgrain ribbon. Each envelope bore a three-cent stamp in the upper right corner and an address scripted in the middle:

Eliza P. Edwards, M.D.
Five Smith Court
Boston, Massachusetts

"I promise," said Grace, drawing her forearm across her damp eyes.

Eliza took Grace's hand and turned it over, unfolding her slender fingers. She placed the stack of envelopes in Grace's open palm. "I trust you will," Eliza said. "But I also know how much time you'll spend in class and studying. They will make getting a note off to me a tad easier. And they're a good reminder that I want a weekly report on how you're managing. There's one for every week between September and December, although I've allowed for one week off to prepare for mid-term examinations."

Grace fell into Eliza's open arms. Eliza had held Will and Teddy when they were young in tender embraces, inhaling their childhood sweetness. Once they entered their adolescent years, however, hugs disappeared as fast as a gallon of milk from her refrigerator. Unspoken words hung in the air, ready to be snatched and savored. Those moments came easily to Eliza when she'd settle into an embrace with her mother, one of her aunts, or Olga.

With Grace, she held a daughter, one who longed for a mother's touch.

"I can't thank you enough, Dr. Edwards, for all you've done for me," Grace said. "Before you came, I would have probably ended up like Ruthie and just about every other mountain girl—not that there's anything wrong with Ruthie's life, loving those kids as best she can. But I've always wanted more; I just couldn't think what that more could be. I never dreamed I could be a doctor, let alone go to a city—a real city like Philadelphia. Meeting other women from around world. To be truthful, I'm scared witless. I hope I can make you proud."

"Grace, have you read *Little Women* by Louisa May Alcott?"

"Yes, of course! I loved Jo, Meg, Amy, and dear, sweet Beth."

"Well, besides her novels, Miss Alcott wrote essays, often to support the suffrage movement. My Aunt Florence, the one I'm going home to take care of, worked tirelessly as a suffragist. When I was about your age, she shared some of Miss Alcott's writings with me. One of my favorites is this: *We all have our own life to pursue, our own kind of dream to be weaving, and we all have the power to make wishes come true, as long as we keep believing.* Keep weaving your dreams, Grace, and never stop believing in yourself. I won't. That's all I ask of you. Now, before I turn into a complete blubbering fool, can you review all the patient files again? Let me know if I missed anything."

A dimple cut into Grace's cheek. "I'll pore through them like I pick nits out of Rosie Mae's hair."

Eliza shuddered with a whole-body tremor. Eliza would not miss a few things she met in Jellico. Nits and chickens topped the list.

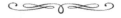

Outside, an engine sputtered to a stop in the dusty drive of the Shelter. Eliza peered through the screen door to find the Bakers' jalopy and Chet emerging from the driver's side door.

"You're early," she said as Chet rounded the front of the truck.

"No point in sitting 'round the house looking at Grace's mopey face. I'd rather steal some extra moments with you."

He stepped through the doorway and pulled her close, murmuring in her ear, "I'll tuck them into a safe spot. When I'm down by the fishing hole where I first met you, your face will flicker back at me in the stream's ripples. Floatin' there for a moment to remember you before you trickle away with the running water."

His arms locked behind her back. She lifted her trembling hand to his cheek, bare and smooth with his winter beard shaved clean. She curled in her lower lip and bit down hard. The pressure stung, increasing its ache to match the pains shooting through her heart. A metallic tang lingered on her tongue as a drop of blood dribbled from her lip.

"I shall remember you every time *Moonlight Serenade* plays on the radio," she said. She encircled her arms around his neck and tilted her head up to him. A slow, furious kiss held them together in a sway until a rumble echoed in the mountains.

He released her and stepped back; his eyes wandering to the bedroom door. "Best not tempt this old geezer with one last memory-making moment."

With a playful slap to his chest, Eliza said, "Mr. Wilson, you're hardly an old geezer. Not with the moves you've shown me."

"You mean, like this?" He grabbed her again, pulled her in and flung her into a spin, then lowered her into a dip. She laughed as she raised one foot off the floor in a graceful swoon worthy of any twenty-two-year-old leading lady on the silver screen.

"Yes, that."

PART THREE

CHAPTER THIRTY-FOUR

July 1940
Boston, Massachusetts

Eliza rifled through her undergarments and stockings in her top bureau drawer. Nothing. She slammed it shut. On top of the bureau, a picture frame and cut-glass jewelry dish jiggled and rattled. Eliza opened the next drawer down of the dark cherry bureau. Freshly pressed cotton blouses in two neat piles toppled over as she pushed them aside into rumpled heaps. The next two drawers also failed to produce the object of her hunt. With a clenched jaw, she turned to the upended suitcase on her bed. She rummaged through the satin pleated pockets lining the inside edges and each crevice. Save for a wad of lint and two loose bobby pins, she withdrew empty hands. She had already removed every item in her medical bag and carefully repacked it to no avail. The wooden box had disappeared somewhere between Jellico and Boston.

God damn it, she thought. With complete certainty, she recalled wrapping Chet's gift with an extra flannel cloth and placing it in her suitcase, layered and cushioned by two wool skirts. She hadn't opened the case until she returned to Boston yesterday. She clearly saw herself moving aside the photo of Will and Teddy on her nightstand and placing the box next to the picture frame. Was she losing her mind, like Florence? Would the doctor become the patient? She sat on the bed, her toe tapping against the wooden floor like a hammer pounding a nail, driving deeper into a wall of despair.

"What in God's name is all the racket?" Florence pushed open the bedroom door. "Sounds like the devil's den—as if he was banging his way up from Hades."

Eliza looked up from her toe-tapping foot. Florence wore a paint-splattered navy skirt, long to her ankles like the ones she wore when she had led art classes at the turn of the century. Wisps of white hair fell loose on her shoulders. Tangles knotted in clumps like the ends of corn tassels.

"I'm sorry, Aunt Florence," said Eliza. "I can't seem to find something I thought I brought home."

She intended to keep the box forever on her nightstand. Every morning she could run her fingers over the top and let them linger in a moment of memory. She didn't want to forget Chet. He had come to her as a friend and stayed in her heart as a lover. His gift of the wooden box extended beyond sanded edges and an inlaid star design.

A thick, wool, cabled sweater ended below Florence's expansive hips. Beneath the unbuttoned gray cardigan, her brassiere flapped against her doughy skin. Eliza suspected, once again, Florence had not fastened the hooks and eyes. She eyed the cardigan and brassiere and sighed deeply. Heat had rolled up from the south, descended, and stalled within small pockets between buildings. The air grew stagnant. Bodies which dared to venture outside dripped with sweat. Eliza would need to convince Florence to change her clothes and accept help with the hooks and eyes. She had planned an outing for them, visiting the Isabella Stewart Gardner Museum. The Museum's courtyard settled Florence with its tranquility and lush, green plantings. She became animated, chatting with Eliza about masterpieces and her days at the Pennsylvania Academy of the Fine Arts. Unbothered by the heat wave and repetition, Eliza would take her aunt to the museum every day of the week if it meant the return of her beloved Fearless Florence.

"How about the Gardner, today?" she asked. "I'd love to hear more about your interpretation of Titian's *The Rape of Europa*."

Florence's eyes flickered, replacing an empty glaze. "That would be nice. Thank you, dear."

As she headed toward the living room, Eliza cupped Florence's elbow and steered her back to the bedroom. "Let's find something else for you to wear. How about your paisley cotton? That print is so vibrant. Wouldn't that be more comfortable?"

Inside Florence's room, the sun shone through the window. It passed through the filaments of a lacy tie-backed curtain and bounced against the sheen of blonde ash triangles meshed into an inlaid star design on the cover of a lacquered wooden box. The holder of Jellico memories sat on a pie-crust bedside table.

"Florence. You took my box? You can't just walk into my room and take personal items." Eliza moved to reclaim the box.

Her aunt's eyes narrowed. The flicker disappeared, replaced by a hard-edged glare. "It's mine, Laura. Mama gave it to me. She let me pick it out at the crafts stall. You wanted that silly rag doll—stupid, ugly thing with black yarn hair. *Blech*, the way you sucked on those braids was disgusting."

In a flash, Florence's mind had retreated to childhood visits, shopping at the Amish craftsmen's stalls at the New Market with her mother and sisters, including Eliza's mother, Laura. A sharp sting on her wrist stopped Eliza's hand. Eliza cried out, stunned by the brutal force of Florence's slap. She bumped into the table, sending the box to the floor. Its cover popped off, spewing the contents across the floor. Eliza's correspondence for the Shelter. Her AWH armband which she had proudly slid up her arm over her white coat every morning. The dried and pressed mountain laurel Chet had given her to decorate for the Shelter's opening. She had kept the blooms, recalling how Chet had told her, "Their perseverance to thrive in any climate, even the rocky crags of the Cumberlands, remind me of you. You didn't give up on us."

Next to her, Florence stood with an open, reddened palm hovering in the air, ready to strike again. "What is all that mess? Who put those things in my box? Where are my paints?"

A sob of anguish escaped from Florence's throat.

Don't argue with her. Don't upset her. She's not to blame for her behavior. *She's not Florence.* An irrational being lives within her brain. Guidance for caring for a dementia patient leaped from the articles Eliza had read before her arrival home and in her new position as caregiver. She softened her expression and gently pushed Florence's hand down to her side. "It's okay, Florence. Why don't you lie down for a bit? I'll clean this up and will look for your brushes and paint pots."

Eliza pulled back the cotton quilted bedspread and eased Florence down to rest her head on the pillow. A light snore came quickly. The moment passed. Eliza took the box. Florence wouldn't remember the episode when she awoke.

CHAPTER THIRTY-FIVE

September 1940

Two months later, Eliza sat on a bench in the Boston Public Garden, thankful for a couple of hours off from Florence-duty. Determined to organize a schedule, she asked her sisters-in-law to help watch Florence. *Really, was it so much to ask?* One morning and one afternoon a week for Eliza to find time for herself? During those hours, she'd escape to the outdoors, searching for a spot to commune with the natural world which had given her peace in the foothills of the Cumberland Mountains.

On this mid-September afternoon, she drank in the glory of the gardens. The maples clung to their green leaves, unwilling to relinquish them to dead autumn browns. Fall asters in magenta pink and periwinkle blue sprouted from the beds like stars of life; their vibrancy suspending the impeding cold, gray, winter months which lay ahead. A cluster of the asters would have looked inviting displayed in a milk bottle. She wondered if Chet still delivered the mail to the Shelter every week, lingering for a chat, or something more, with the doctor who had replaced her.

The city was relatively quiet. School had resumed, drawing children into classrooms. Office workers finished their lunches and retreated to the confines of the Statler building and State House, workplaces within walking distance of the Public Garden. Eliza opened her medical bag on the bench next to her. Emptied of most of her tools, save her stethoscope, notepad, and pen, she used it as her preferred tote. While not its intended purpose, by keeping it close, like another appendage of her body, she carried her ties to a past life wherever she went. During her early days as a young intern at West Philadelphia Hospital, she had clutched the handle in a vise-grip, hoping passersby would acknowledge her as a doctor. It had knocked against brick walls and clapboard shingles when she entered homes to visit patients. It had ridden on train seats to Warm Springs and Jellico and back again.

From the open bag, she withdrew a stack of letters. She relished reading news in the quiet shade from her dearest ones before heading home and the unpredictable woes of life which awaited. The top letter held a return address of Solomons Island, Maryland. Eliza pulled the single typed page out of the envelope.

September 2, 1940
Dear Mom,
We're at the training base again after escorting a cargo ship to Iceland. Now, we're sitting in drydock, hanging around, doing nothing. There is a nice officer's club here, a movie theater, and the chance to catch up with our mail, but what the men really may need is a mental ward. I fear they may slowly go mad, forgetting what we learned at sea and not having the opportunity to put it into practice. We hear what's going on in England and France and get close enough to sniff the smoke-filled air, but our orders return us back here to Little Creek and Big Boredom.
Love,
Teddy

Eliza sent a prayer of thanks skyward beyond the canopy of elm trees. Better to be bored in the shoals of Maryland than dodging bombs from above and torpedoes from below in the open Atlantic. Her son, and the lads on the ships with him, needed to appreciate the grace of an uneventful, safe routine in their daily lives. Or did that wish exist only in a mother's mind?

Under the letter from Teddy, she picked out a pre-addressed, stamped envelope postmarked from Philadelphia.

September 10, 1940
Dear Dr. Edwards,
You were right. The pile of envelopes you gave me are a reminder and a time-saver. My first weekly update reports that all is well here at Woman's Med. I secured a room in the dormitory. My roommate is a wonderful Japanese gal from Nevada, Toshiko Nakamura. I expect we'll both have our noses buried in our studies for long nights ahead. We have six! women professors, including the one you called Rabid Rabi, Dr. Rabinowitsch, for Bacteriology. She's as spry as you described her from forty years ago, though she must be close to seventy. The city is loud, crowded, and smelly, which makes me miss even more the fresh air of my mountains, the kids, Ruthie, and Pops. But soon my days will be jammed with no time to pine for home. I shan't dwell on what I've left behind. As I packed for school, Pops saw my envelopes. He asked that I send on his "hello" to you and hopes that you're managing okay with your aunt. I think you've probably figured out by now that he's a proud man. He'd never let on that Timmy can read and write better than he can.
With my sincere thanks and deepest gratitude for all you have given me,
Grace

Eliza pressed the letter to her chest. *Oh Chet. I don't care that you can't send me a newsy letter. It's enough to know you're still thinking of me.*

Eliza made a note on the back of the envelope from Olga, the next one in her pile. *Ask Olga for a clothes pin for Grace. Ha ha.* She chuckled. Oh, what light mirth she'd send to Grace: a clothes pin with secret instructions on how Olga and Eliza would pinch their noses on lab days with Rabid Rabi when they had to slide the most odiferous specimens under their microscopes.

Olga's letter carried more updates about her research.

... But the best news by far comes from the U.S. Patent Office. They acknowledged receipt of my submission for consideration. In case you're interested at all in this revolutionary advancement, here are the specifications: The 2-liter size holds large quantities to prepare toxins, grow molds and general tissue culture work. The unique rectangular shape allows stacking of the bottles to reduce incubator space. The thick Pyrex glass can withstand heating temperatures to 142 degrees...

As Eliza turned the page over, a twitch began in her cheek. While she admired the intricacies of Olga's reporting, she couldn't help but feel a pang of envy. Lab work demanded twelve-hour days. Olga kept herself occupied and keenly focused on interesting challenges which would benefit medical research. Of recent note, her team had perfected the diphtheria vaccine, making its widespread adoption a standard procedure across the country. Eliza spent many of her days playing Old Maid card games with Florence.

The tic stopped as a teardrop trickled down her cheek when she read Olga's final words.

P.S. Sending you the strength to carry on and hope that you realize, somewhere, deep inside, though unspoken, Florence knows you are there for her. She loves you. She appreciates you.
  Your ever-loving friend and sister,
  Olga

"I'm trying," Eliza said to the breeze rippling through the elm leaves.

She picked up an unopened letter from the pile postmarked from Chicago. Every time she heard from Kay Clark; Eliza reveled in learning how she kept up with her physical therapy exercises to stay strong. The polio may have weakened her leg permanently, but it had not weakened Kay's resolve. The last news from Kay was a Christmas card ten months ago. Eliza couldn't blame her for a slip in correspondence. She remembered well the busy days with two under the age of four. Kay's second baby must be almost a year by now. She noted on Kay's envelope: *Pick up a copy of* Pat the Bunny *for the Clark children.*

September 14, 1940
Dear Eliza,
My apologies. Letter writing has fallen by the wayside, along with shopping excursions on Michigan Avenue and listening to jazz at the Green Mill—my pre-motherhood guilty pleasures! Of course, I wouldn't trade my precious dears for all the shopping bags or bathtub gin in Chicago. I'm sure you can relate to these busy days and won't mind that this note is brief and to the point. Has the news from Minneapolis traveled to Boston about Sister Elizabeth Kenny? Newly arrived from Australia and trained during the War with the Army Nursing Service there, she has brought with her new treatment ideas for polio patients. The verdict remains unclear as to its efficacy, but I think it can't hurt to try it and track any changes over a determined period. While I'm not a scientist, I recall enough of my high school classes to know the larger the sample size, the more valid the results—good or bad. The process involves packing the patient's joints and afflicted areas in wool, heated first in a tub of steaming hot water, removed with tongs, and run through a wringer twice before placing the wool on the patient. The wool is replaced hourly for the first twenty-four hours, then every two hours for a twelve-hour period during the daytime. After removing the wool packs, the patient's muscles are stretched. The assumption is the hot wool

re-awakens impulses in the nerves and immediately makes the bones more pliable than being constricted in plaster or braces.

I call this new 'Kenny Method' to your attention, hoping your family's wool company could provide scrap materials to as many hospitals and treatment centers across the country as possible. Until we have a vaccination to protect my children, and all children around the world from this debilitating disease, we must experiment and explore all means to alleviate the suffering of those when they are first afflicted. I enclose a list of locations which currently, to my knowledge, have the highest caseloads.

God bless you and yours,

Kay

She dropped the letter onto her lap and clapped her hands together once, shaking them with quick forward thrusts in triumph. *God bless you, Kay Clark! You are brilliant!* thought Eliza. Kay had given her a worthy task. She could contact hospitals. Once she determined their desire and need for wool, she would organize shipments. Florence could help with the simple task of packing boxes. Most of all, she would fill empty hours in her day. Her job as a caregiver seemed to have dissolved into babysitter and sentry guard. She packed the letters into her medical bag.

With a firm step upon the walkway, she marched toward the wrought-iron gates at the edge of the Public Garden. On her left, she passed one of the Garden's oldest and most famous statues. She paused in front of it, her eyes tracking upward along the shunted shafts of polished red marble to the figures carved in white granite at the top. A seated man, representing a Good Samaritan, held a cloth in his left hand above the face of another man drooping across the Samaritan's knee. Installed in 1868 at a spot just blocks away from Massachusetts General Hospital, the Ether Monument commemorated the first use of ether in medicine. Each side of the base featured a bas-relief framed by a carved arch with an inscription beneath in a flat square. Eliza ran her hand over the words, clearing grains of dirt and pieces of moss. The phrase paralleled the scene above it, that of a figure intended to depict an angel of mercy. From Revelation 21:4 *Neither shall there be any more pain.* The words mirrored the guiding principle every medical professional held true. Ether was meant to provide relief from physical pain. Mental anguish, as Eliza had learned, could only be relieved by a strong will and compassion from others, like Charlotte standing by her, believing in her to put away her jar of ether and mask.

And, while wet wool may not achieve the platitudes and widespread use of ether, if it wiped away the grimaces and choked sobs of patients suffering in silence, like the ones Eliza saw at Warm Springs, the method could be worthy of its own recognition someday.

Eliza pushed the wrought-iron gate open, her medical bag swinging from the crook of her arm. As she turned onto Arlington Street and headed toward Smith Court, she hummed the opening bars from Glenn Miller's latest chart-topper. Continuing down the street, she snapped her fingers along to the tune of *In the Mood.*

CHAPTER THIRTY-SIX

February 1941

Eliza splayed her fingers across the extended bare abdomen. She molded her hands around the body beneath Anne's pale, taut skin. Spidery blue veins pushed like creeping ivy against the tissue, separating Eliza's touch from her grandchild. At seven months along, Anne carried the fetus high where it crammed against her diaphragm. Today's complaint emanated from the pressure and Anne's insistence that she couldn't catch her breath.

"If my oxygen is compromised, will it stunt the baby's growth? Harm his brain like when my uncle had his stroke?" Anne asked as she lay on Eliza's couch and makeshift examination table.

Eliza straightened up from bending over the couch. She winced, sending her hand to the ache in her lower back. With a quick circular rub against the knot, she dismissed the nagging throb.

"All perfectly normal," said Eliza. "The body adjusts on its own. Your lungs know you're breathing for two. In fact, I think walking home would do you good. The fresh air and exercise will strengthen your muscles to prepare for the harder work to come. With the warmer weather, you should walk every day. But first, stay for lunch. Then, I can take Florence and walk halfway with you. It'll be good for all three of us. I, for one, have been cooped up too long."

She leaned in closer to Anne, swiping aside the blonde waves from the brow of the girl who had become like a daughter to her. She lightly tweaked one of the curls and let it fall back into shape. "Further, I might go mad if I don't get out soon," she said with a wink.

Anne stood and slipped her billowing maternity dress over her head. It settled over her bump like a fitted hairnet. "I'll walk home but can't stay for lunch. I expect the painters for the nursery this afternoon. I want to tidy up a bit before they arrive."

With a shrug of her shoulders, Eliza wouldn't argue with her daughter-in-law. She knew Will planned on tackling the paint job himself. Anne used the hired painters as an excuse. Watching Florence eat lunch could turn anyone's stomach, let alone a pregnant woman who had suffered severe bouts of morning sickness for five months. Each day that passed in recent weeks, Florence showed less interest in mealtimes. She would take two mouthfuls of whatever Eliza placed in front of her and then drop her fork or spoon down with a clatter. As she chewed a piece of toast or slurped a swallow of soup, morsels would dribble from the corners of her mouth. By bedtime, Eliza collected a pile of napkins that she had tied around Florence's neck at each meal and left them in the bathroom sink to soak in Borax along with pairs of soiled underwear.

"Of course," said Eliza. "We need that darling room ready and waiting. Before you leave though, let me check if the mail arrived. I asked Ruth Newcombe to send up some lavender from her back garden in Jellico. Place the sprigs in a bowl and pour boiling water over them when you're sitting down for a rest. The fresh, clean, sweet scent really does wonders for relaxing the mind. And Anne, please make sure you…"

Eliza caught herself. She wouldn't fall into the cliché of a meddling mother-in-law. Yet, the doctor inside her desperately wanted to tell Anne to eat more.

Two weeks later, Eliza sat on her living room floor surrounded by a dozen open corrugated boxes. Next to her on the couch, Florence counted out pieces of wool strips as she stacked them in a pile. "One, two, three, four, five, six, seven." Florence halted. A vacant stare crossed over her face as the banjo wall clock chimed three. She closed her empty eyes and sniffled.

"What comes next?" she asked, her voice low and pleading.

For the past six months since Eliza started her *Operation Wool Strips*, Florence had managed the simple task of separating the strips into piles of ten which Eliza bound with elastic bands and packed into boxes. The clock's sound-off of three chimes must have interrupted Florence's count. Eliza sighed. She hoped she could blame the clock.

"Eight," she said. "Maybe you should start over?"

Florence tossed the strips to the floor, kicking them toward the cross-legged Eliza. "NO." She scratched her forearms with a furious stroke before heading to her bedroom.

From the kitchen, the phone rang, interrupting Eliza's anxious gaze down the hallway. She jumped to answer it with the fifth ring. Frantic sobs came in gulps through the receiver.

Trying to quell her frustration, Eliza asked, "Anne. What is it now?"

"I'm in labor! I'm alone here. I don't think I can make it to the hospital. Please. You must come immediately. Ohhhhh... owwww..."

"I'm coming." Too early, thought Eliza. Thirty-four weeks. Anne required the services and equipment at a hospital for a premature birth. The image of the tiny, gray form on a newspaper in a Jellico cabin flashed before her eyes. She depressed the switch hook with two firm pulses. With swift instructions, she asked the operator to send an ambulance to 29 Bowdoin Street. She rushed to her bedroom to grab a shawl from her closet. A soft snore came from Florence's room. *She's settled. I'll call Mamie or Bea to come over as soon as I get to Anne's.* She threw the shawl around her shoulders and grabbed her medical bag from the front closet. Without looking back, she burst out the front door and set off to Will and Anne's house, four and a half blocks away.

The bite in the early March air stung her cheeks as she headed up Joy Street at a quick two-step pace. By the time she turned the corner onto Myrtle where the street plateaued, she stooped and bent over, her palms resting on top of her knees. She panted, in and out, in and out. She'd grown soft since her days in Tennessee, when she would walk two miles to visit a patient. A group of children skipping home from school rushed past her, leapfrogging over her medical bag she had dropped on the sidewalk. She shook her head and straightened. Never one to jog in her life, she grabbed the handles, inhaled through her nose, and pressed onward for the flatter three blocks. Another child in a hurry awaited her trained hands.

Eliza arrived at number 29 ten minutes later. A siren wailed from the direction of Cambridge Street. Thankful that Anne had left the door unlocked, she found her inside the second-floor apartment, sitting in a wingback chair with her feet propped on a matching footrest. She didn't look up when Eliza barged in.

"Anne," Eliza said, gasping with each word to catch her breath. "Has anything happened? Did your water break? When was the last contraction? Have you timed them?"

A silent Anne focused her eyes downward to the folded hands in her lap. "No. I mean, I haven't had another one since I called you."

"How long did the contraction last? More or less than a minute?" asked Eliza as she opened her bag and withdrew the well-worn stethoscope. She unclasped Anne's wristwatch and laid it on the coffee table. Eliza preferred the reliability of her own watch to time Anne's pulse. Steady and normal.

"I'd say relatively brief. I guess it lasted less than a minute."

"It? You only had the one?" The sound of the ambulance screeching to a halt outside the apartment interrupted Eliza's questions. "Oh, Anne, my dear. You are having Braxton Hicks contractions. You're not in labor. I told you about them three weeks ago and to be prepared in case they started. We've got a false alarm here. I called an ambulance out on a wild goose chase."

Eliza snapped her bag close with a jerk. She'd have to speak with the ambulance driver and hope she could placate him with the tale of a nervous, expectant mother. Despite hopes of deflecting the blame on Anne, Eliza knew her name would appear on the report for the call. She groaned, realizing she had used her full name. Dr. Eliza Edwards had bothered the Massachusetts General Hospital with an unnecessary run. The administration would flag her and match it to the request she had filed a month ago to reinstate her admitting privileges. She had yet to receive a reply.

After speaking with the ambulance driver outside, Eliza started up the steps to Will and Anne's apartment. The driver pulled away from the curb and headed up Bowdoin Street. At the intersection, a teenaged boy appeared, gesticulating for the ambulance to stop.

"Over here," he yelled, pointing down Derne Street toward Myrtle. "An old lady fell. She banged up her head."

The siren blasted. The red light on the roof blinked and rotated like the whir of a KitchenAid mixer as the ambulance zoomed off in the direction the boy pointed. Eliza's eyes followed the taillights up the street before it turned the corner. *An old lady*, the boy yelled. On Myrtle Street, a half block from Eliza's home.

Eliza's hand flew to her pounding chest. She hadn't called one of her sisters-in-law yet. Eliza had left Florence alone. Would Florence have woken and wandered outside with her sentry guard gone? Was the old lady who had fallen on Myrtle Street her aunt? Bewildered and calling *Lizzy. Help me, Lizzy.*

CHAPTER THIRTY-SEVEN

A surge of adrenaline propelled Eliza's weary muscles into a run. At the corner of Joy and Myrtle, the ambulance driver, teenaged boy, and an older woman clustered around a figure seated on the top granite step of a garden-level apartment. Wisps of corn-silk white hair fluttered over her shoulders covered by a bulky gray wool cabled cardigan.

As she approached, Eliza heard the standing woman say, "All right, dear. Let this nice man look at your head."

Eliza pushed the woman aside. "Don't. I'll take care of her. I'm her niece. And a doctor."

The woman spun around to face Eliza. Her pursed lips hissed, "Then you should know better than to allow a woman in her condition to wander the streets alone. Poor thing has had a dreadful fright. She doesn't know her address. Just kept saying Race Street. There's no Race Street on Beacon Hill. Good thing I saw her stumble, and this boy heard the siren and offered to flag it down."

Seated with nothing but a thin cotton skirt between her and the cold stone, Florence swayed, her arms crisscrossed tight around her waist. The sway faded into a bob as she bent forward and back, moaning. A jagged gash the length of Eliza's thumb oozed blood from Florence's forehead. A half inch lower and her temple area would have taken a direct hit against the granite.

The ambulance driver put up his hand to stop Eliza. "Hold on. What do you mean, you're a doctor? Once I've been called to a medical scene, I'm in charge. I need to clean this wound and assess if she needs stitches. You can go get my bag from the ambulance."

"I will do no such thing. My name is Dr. Eliza Edwards. My aunt, Florence Pearson, and I live at Five Smith Court. I have far superior training to you and have no intention of standing here debating who will tend to her. You're wasting time. Get the bag," said Eliza.

Shocked into silence, the driver slunk away to the ambulance. Florence bent over, rubbing her lower leg under a heavy wool stocking. Eliza saw a swell blooming above and below the ankle. She walked down the two steps to face her straight on. "Florence. I'm here. It's Eliza. Lizzy."

She placed her index finger under Florence's chin and tilted up her head. Florence grasped Eliza's hand. "Don't touch me. My head hurts. Laura, my leg hurts. Where's Mama?"

Wonderful, thought Eliza. Florence had failed to confirm Eliza's credentials and their family connection in front of the bystander. As Eliza watched the woman walk away, she feared judgmental opinions went with her, spreading up and down Beacon Hill like a seeping ooze of sewage from a pipe. *Some woman who claims to be a doctor can't even care for her senile elderly aunt.*

Eliza pressed a dime into the teenaged boy's hand and asked him to run back to Anne's to explain the reason for Eliza's hasty departure. As he trotted off, she took the bag from the driver and rummaged for gauze and an antiseptic. After a quick cleaning and temporary bandaging, she thanked the driver for his help.

"I still need to write up an incident report," he said. "You'll have to sign it as the attending medical personnel. I'm going to catch a boatload of guff from my boss. Do you have anything to prove your license is valid?"

Eliza patted her empty dress pockets. Her medical bag lay open on the floor next to Anne's chair, back on Bowdoin Street. Her license and one remaining prescription pad, both covered in a thin layer of dust, sat in her top bureau drawer.

"Please, take my word for it. If it helps, tell your supervisor that I can stop by tomorrow with my license as confirmation. Although, I hope you will explain to him the unusual circumstance that I was tending to my daughter-in-law's pregnancy issues." She gestured for his pen and signed the report.

Thankful to see him leave, Eliza turned her attention back to her aunt. With a promise of an ice pack for her ankle and a tumbler of brandy, she lured Florence home. Each halting step of their walk felt like they were heading toward an inevitable point of no return.

The next day, with Florence set up in the living room, paging through the most recent issue of *LIFE* magazine, Eliza busied herself in the kitchen. Index cards fell in a haphazard pile around the red tin recipe box on the table. Eliza fanned the cards out in an arc. Over the years, she had used them in multiple ways. From study cards during medical school to jotted patient notes. To recipes smudged by greasy fingers and the scrawl of a child play-acting as a pastry chef with flour covered hands. The harried shorthand of a mother and doctor in Boston learning how the secret wonder of condensed soup made any dinner tastier and easier to prepare. The refined hand of an almost-debutante from Philadelphia discovering delectable treats in the rural South in the form of bacon-grease fried green tomatoes and cornbread stuffing, complete with apple chunks and hickory nuts.

She turned over each card, searching for a blank side to write a name. The next forty-two days required an organizational plan worthy of any corporate boardroom. Yesterday's scare, both

Anne's false labor and Florence's wandering, woke Eliza to the reality of the moment. She'd need someone who lived near enough to dash over as Eliza darted out. During the weeks that Bess had out-of-town assignments, Eliza had contacted Boston University to request references for nursing students who roomed near Beacon Hill.

One by one, she taped a card into squares of a makeshift calendar she had hung on her bedroom wall. Stepping back, she surveyed the chart as complex as the periodic table she had pinned next to her bed during medical school. Dang. She'd put a MAMIE card in on a Sunday when she claimed altar guild duties. And one of BEA's cards covered a Tuesday. Bea had been emphatic that she wouldn't miss her Tuesday bridge group. On a Wednesday to Thursday stretch, she had placed a STUDENT card. No one should have forty-eight hours in a row of being on call for Florence duty heaved onto them.

Eliza's hands flew to the sides of her head. She pressed hard against her ears as a "Gggrrrr…" escaped from her throat. She ripped the errant cards off the wall. These puzzle pieces proved to be more challenging than the three hundred pieces stowed in a box on the front closet shelf.

With the cards dangling from her hand, she sat on her bed facing the puzzle. Her fingers twitched, itching to take the cards awaiting an assigned space and rip them in half. If only she could rip herself into two pieces or figure out a way to clone herself. She allowed herself a soft chuckle, envisioning a lab. Olga's research hours would be more productive if she improved upon the work being done on cloning. If Dr. Povitsky developed a way for women to clone themselves whenever the call came to be in two places at once, women around the world would genuflect before her, toss rose petals at her feet, and hail Olga Povitsky, M.D. as a savior of female sanity.

Eliza re-arranged three more cards, re-taped another four, and *Voila*! One problem solved. She smoothed her hand over the box circled in red. Wednesday, April 9, 1941. *All right, you little grandchild of mine. Please wait a few more weeks. But we are ready.* Eliza needed the extra time. She hadn't received an acceptance from any Boston hospital yet to reinstate her admitting privileges.

CHAPTER THIRTY-EIGHT

April 1941

"I'm sorry, Dr. Miles. But I must ask that you reconsider my request."

Eliza found herself in the same seat that she had sat in five years ago. The same hospital administrator who had offered her a nursing position now held the welfare of her daughter-in-law and grandchild in his hands. Anne had bestowed the kindest compliment upon Eliza when she requested the services of Dr. Edwards. After eight and a half months of monitoring every pound gained, consulting on symptoms to watch for, and sharing in the joy of the impending arrival, Eliza would not abandon Anne now.

The administrator sat stone-faced across the desk from Eliza. He pushed his glasses back up his nose and left his index finger in place to hold the frame between his eyes. "I cannot present this to the Board, let alone for a woman who has not held a formal position in over five years. Mountain midwifery hardly qualifies your skills compared to the superior ones our physicians possess. You see, it's more of a liability situation."

Eliza gripped the armrests of the chair, directing her fury to burn the wood beneath the leather pads. At the top corner of Dr. Miles' desk, the cover photo on the latest issue of *TIME* magazine informed its readers of the Nazis' march across the Balkans. Eliza had read the inside story. Campaigns of the spring and coming summer would intensify. A world on edge watched and waited. For Americans, the question continued to loom. Not if, but when, would they come to the aid of their Allies, sending soldiers, equipment, and medics?

"Dr. Miles," said Eliza, her tone turning from a plea to a statement. "At this time, I do not have plans to reopen my practice. The AMA renewed my license. Their endorsement warrants your consideration. Further, if anything, I enhanced my skills in Jellico by managing a staff of six and supervising the care of over one hundred maternity cases. While I am asking for a one-time exception for this patient, I believe you may soon find yourself in need of my full capabilities. In fact, you're going to need the services of many women in the medical field. We've been sidelined for too many years."

She watched as he sat up straighter in his chair. "My son serves on the *USS Mississippi* as a lieutenant in the United States Navy, patrolling the Atlantic Ocean. Each morning, I offer thanks he is not involved in a conflict. But every week that passes with news of another city in Europe falling and the rise of the Axis powers, not to mention the threats from Japan, I fear our ships will carry troops across those waters. And, when they do, just like in 1917, we'll send millions. Who do you think will keep this country going on the home front when those troops vacate countless jobs in all forms of professions?"

Eliza paused. Her question lingered in the stale air hanging between her and Dr. Miles.

"We will," she said, tapping her chest with two fingers. "It will be up to the women to answer the call, just as Mrs. Roosevelt asked us to do during the deepest throes of our recent economic depression. She said that 'the success of our nation in meeting the great crises in our country was very largely due to the women in those trying times.'"

The mention of Eleanor Roosevelt added credence to any conversation. Over the years, Eliza had made a mental note of many of the First Lady's quotes to reference in relevant conversations. This one was not wasted on Dr. Miles as she watched the crinkle around his eyes soften.

"When this next crisis tears us apart, who will deliver the babies when even maternity doctors are called to serve as medics and surgeons? The women trained to the highest degree with the same level of ability as any man on your staff. Dr. Miles, I suggest you prime your Board now with the idea of women doctors walking the halls of your hospital wards."

She pushed her request form forward across the desk.

He picked up his pen, looked at the *TIME* magazine cover with the Nazi general standing on a hill surveying a line of tanks below him and signed the form.

Eliza P. Edwards, M.D. is hereby acknowledged and accepted as a licensed, AMA approved physician with full rights to admit her patient, Mrs. William Shaw, and to supervise her maternity care throughout her stay at the Peter Bent Brigham Hospital, Boston, Massachusetts.

Joseph S. Miles, M.D., April 2, 1941

For the past four nights, Eliza had lain in bed; her ears perked, straining to hear a ring. During the day, she'd answer the phone with a curt, *Edwards' residence*, assess the reason for the call and quickly disconnect with some semblance of decorum. Anne could call at any time. Eliza needed the line open and ready.

This morning, her eyelids heavy, she smeared orange marmalade across slices of toast. Her hand continued past the toast's edge, dropping a sticky dollop on the kitchen counter. As she wiped the counter clean, a weak call came from the back hall.

"Ow, owwww."

Florence had not risen from her bed in three days. Dehydration set in as she refused to eat or drink. Throughout the day, Eliza pressed wet cloths to her aunt's cracked lips, hoping to moisten her tongue and dribble water droplets down her parched throat. Eliza followed the cry of pain down the hallway, the plate of toast in her hand. If Florence wouldn't nibble a corner, Eliza would. She needed all the sustenance she could find to soldier through the coming days.

She pulled the wooden chair with a caned seat next to Florence's bed. Florence's left leg jerked with small tics. Eliza's hand ran gently over the toothpick leg, feeling the knot of the muscle cramp. She kneaded it in rhythmic circles. The furrow in Florence's brow softened. Her mouth fell open, releasing a rank, decaying odor. Eliza gagged and turned away. Her eyes awash with tears, she sat on the chair next to the bed.

"I'm here, Aunt Florence," said Eliza.

The dried parchment skin covering Florence's eyes fluttered. Her beloved aunt remained motionless. A pile of books stacked eight inches high on the nightstand had given Eliza a task over the past weeks. She read to her aunt in the same way Florence had read to her as a girl, tucked into their shared bedroom, listening to stories of faraway places. Eliza ran her finger down the books' spines. From the bottom, she chose a slim, brown leather-bound book. The hour had passed for tales of adventure. Today was a time for reflection. She opened the pages and read to herself until she reached the passage.

"*When you love you should not say 'God is in my heart,' but rather, 'I am in the heart of God.' And think not you can direct the course of love, for love, if it finds you worthy, directs your course.*"

She entwined her fingers into Florence's. "Aunt Florence, your love directed my course and set me on my path. Without your wise words, I never would have thought of attending medical school. You lifted me and gave me confidence."

The next few passages from *The Prophet* further expounded upon Kahlil Gibran's thoughts about *Love*. Eliza read the final lines of the passage aloud, hoping they would soothe Florence toward heavenly gates. "*...let these be your desires...To return home at eventide with gratitude; And then to sleep with a prayer for the beloved in your heart and a song of praise upon your lips.*"

"You are forever in my heart," Eliza said to her aunt as a shallow breath escaped over Florence's cracked lips. She skimmed her lips over Florence's cheek and for the last time, touched the tip of her aunt's nose with her finger. "I love you."

On Tuesday, April 8, 1941, with Eliza alternating between holding her daughter-in-law's hand and checking dilation measurements of Anne's cervix, at 7:42 in the morning, Flora Ellen Shaw slipped into the hands of her waiting grandmother. After she checked the infant's vitals, placed the silver nitrate drops in her blue eyes, and handed her to the nurse to bathe and swaddle into the hospital-issued blanket, Eliza spoke to Anne in her ether-induced slumber, "Well done, my girl. And thank you, her name is perfect. Aunt Florence would be honored."

In the bassinet, Flora wriggled and mewled. Eliza bent over her, whispering to the miracle wrapped in pink, "Shhh, sweet angel. Nana's here."

Lifting her eyes heavenward, she sent another message of thanks. "Aunt Florence, I am here with my granddaughter, Flora Ellen. She's beautiful. Thank you for this gift."

Deep in her heart, Eliza had reconciled with Florence's death. Florence had given Eliza one last gift, possibly the last conscious decision she made. In dying, Florence had freed Eliza from sentry duty. Eliza could devote her time, attention, and love to the next generation of the Pearson-Edwards-Shaw family. Before Anne announced her pregnancy, Eliza had thought she would return to Jellico when the inevitable happened and Florence passed. Back to her Shelter. Back to Chet where she had found solace and a redefined sense of belonging. But with Flora's birth, those connections dissipated into distant dreams. She would stay in Boston. Another family member needed her. There were books to read and toes to count. Gingersnaps to bake and walks in the park. She had a granddaughter. The title of Nana may be as cherished as Mom and Doctor.

CHAPTER THIRTY-NINE

December 1941

The stomp of feet hitting stairs sounded throughout the building. Each footfall grew louder and more urgent as they neared Will and Anne's apartment. Eliza pulled eight-month-old Flora tighter against her chest and placed her foot out to stop the rocking chair. Whoever had raced up the stairs approached with purpose on a quiet Sunday afternoon. Outside the door, Eliza heard the fumbling of keys, metal scratching against the inside of the lock. Will burst through the doorway. His cheeks, reddened from the exertion of running up two flights, failed to mask an ashen pallor underneath. His hazel eyes darted across the room, coming to a halt at his peaceful daughter sleeping in Eliza's arms.

"Will, dear God. What is it?" said Eliza in a hushed voice. "Don't wake her, she's just gone down."

"Take her to the nursery. I've got to turn on the radio, Mom. They interrupted the movie with an announcement. An all-out attack by the Japanese on Pearl Harbor."

Eliza gasped. The Pacific Fleet of the U.S. Navy was based at Pearl Harbor. Teddy's battleship was commissioned with the Pacific Fleet, regardless of its more recent assignments, to patrol the Atlantic. Her face went white as she squeezed the satin-trimmed edges of Flora's blanket. Every vein in her arms tightened. A strap of tension rose through her shoulders and into her neck.

Anne tip-toed in, catching up with Will after their hasty departure from the movie theater. She gently pried Flora from Eliza and disappeared into the nursery. With his arm around Eliza's shoulders, Will guided his mother to the chair next to the radio.

Words spit from Eliza's mouth. "Where is he? Do you know? I haven't had a letter since before Thanksgiving."

The room rotated as her breaths quickened. Terror seized control of every movement as if she no longer belonged to the body sitting in a wing-backed chair. Her mind floated over the Pacific waters as her lips murmured, "Please. Please."

Will spun the radio dials. Static stuttered until he hit upon a news report. The announcer's grave voice penetrated the room "...a Japanese attack upon all naval activities on Pearl Harbor. It would naturally mean war. There is no doubt from the temper of Congress that such a declaration will be granted. Just now comes word from the President's office that a second air attack has been reported on army and naval bases in Manila. We will update you as more information becomes available."

Across the land, a collective wail turned toward the skies where the attack had rained down bombs onto the innocent and unsuspecting. With the United States caught in the middle, the East and the West teemed with troops marching forward on an unbridled quest for power. Complete annihilation teetered off the shores of America. The drivers of Italian tanks, captains of German U-boats and pilots of Japanese Zero planes proved their determination to follow the orders of fanatical madmen. Eliza's son, in a U.S. naval officer's uniform, would face the fury. If he was still alive.

Eliza struck the wooden case holding the tubes and dials which emitted the news broadcast. The sting against her open-faced palm and the loud thwack woke her numbed senses. On returning home, half-carried by Will, she commanded her ears to listen; to hear a mention of the USS *Mississippi*. Instead, the same report repeated in an endless loop. *Pearl Harbor. Naval activities. War. Details are not available.*

"You break that radio, and we'll never get the updates," said Olga.

"What is taking so long? We deserve to know what's going on out there." Eliza twisted the knob again in a desperate search for answers. Olga placed her hand on Eliza's, stemming the frantic turns.

"Let me. It's almost time for Mrs. Roosevelt's show. Where is the NBC station up here?"

Eliza released her strangle-hold on the radio dial and ceded to Olga's steady hand and sensible plan. The First Lady broadcast her news show, *Over Our Coffee Cups*, on Sunday evening, covering topics as far-ranging as her opposition to planned cuts of New Deal programs to industrial accidents and their effects on wartime production. Tonight, Eliza hoped the female voice of Washington would provide a few more details than had been released thus far.

"1030. WBZ is our Boston station," said Eliza, minimally impressed she could recall a minute detail in her panicked state. "Oh, Olga. I still can't believe how the glory of the Fates brought you back to me. I couldn't bear to sit here alone, nor could I sit at Will's any longer. When I look at his face, all I see is his worry and an older version of Teddy."

"As I've told you before, I'm like a bad penny. You can't get rid of me."

In June, Olga had shown up on Eliza's doorstep, valises in hand and thick, black frame eyeglasses perched upon her nose. The dark rings circling her eyes made her look like a furtive raccoon rather than the playful otter Eliza had always considered her friend in animal form. After decades of gluing her eyes to a microscope, Olga's sight had failed. She made mistakes in her observations. She broke slides. The director of the lab had suggested she step aside in favor of younger, stronger eyes found in recent graduate students. Olga agreed. She wouldn't risk having her calculations lead to inaccurate or misleading results. Unable to accept retirement, however, she argued for and won a position to write opinions on the research and consult about notable findings. The Department concurred, approving her move to Boston, where she hired Eliza to type her reports, providing Eliza with a small income as well. To have Olga share a desk and home with her again, Eliza had readily opened her door and welcomed her friend, holding an overstuffed valise filled with cigarette smoke stitched into every seam of her clothing and a half empty vodka bottle.

"Shh. She's on," said Olga, turning up the volume on the radio.

"And now, here's the Pan-American Coffee Bureau's Sunday evening news reviewer and newsmaker, to give us her usual interesting observations of the world we live in, Mrs. Franklin D. Roosevelt."

"Good evening, ladies and gentlemen. I'm speaking to you tonight at a very serious moment in our history...I should like to say just a word to the women in the country tonight. I have a boy at sea on a destroyer. For all I know, he may be on his way to the Pacific..."

Eliza had forgotten Franklin Jr., the same age as Teddy, also served in the Navy. And Mrs. Roosevelt, the woman who, for all intents and purposes, shared the Oval Office with her husband, didn't know her son's location. With an immediate connection to the personal and maternal side of the First Lady, Eliza leaned closer to the radio.

"...Many of you, all over this country, have boys in the services who will now be called upon to go into action. You cannot escape anxiety, you cannot escape the clutch of fear at your heart, and yet I hope that the certainty of what we have to meet will make you rise above these fears...Whatever is asked of us, I'm sure we can accomplish it. We are the free and unconquerable people of the United States of America."

Olga switched off the radio. "There you have it. Direct from one of the wisest women in the world. Eliza, you are as strong a woman as Mrs. Roosevelt. If she refuses to let anxiety and fear conquer her, so can you. We will believe Teddy is not in Pearl Harbor. He's safe. And no matter what his next orders may be, and possibly if they call Will too, we will rise above our fears. We cannot allow it to beat us, or we'll lose the fight before it begins."

Another shot of panic coursed through Eliza's heart. By tomorrow morning, recruiting stations across the country would overflow with men ready to enlist. Men whose fathers had instilled in them a sense of duty to their country, just as Will's father had in 1918. Eliza would be powerless to stop her oldest son, the one who sought adventures at every turn, from joining those lines at the Federal Building. And what of those he left behind? Anne, struggling with the demands as a new mother, could crumble. Flora would need her grandmother now more than ever. Eliza cleared the image of both her sons in uniform, standing on a naval destroyer, staring down the red eye of an incoming bomber.

"You're right, Olga. We'll get through this. For as long as it takes. The alternative is unspeakable."

Eliza loosened the belt of her bathrobe. A familiar snore echoed from the back bedroom. Olga had always been able to fall asleep quicker than Eliza, even on nights before school examinations. At nine o'clock, she had retired, telling Eliza to do the same. As Eliza reached for the pull chain on the floor lamp, a rap sounded at the front door. Will would have called through the door. Her brothers would do the same. A stranger stood on her stoop with news Eliza had been dreading. She was sure of it. She pushed aside the curtain at the narrow window next to the door. A young male figure with the distinctive Western Union cap on his head lifted his hand to rap again. If she opened the door, the words on the slip in his hand would become real.

"Olga," she screamed. She couldn't receive the envelope without the arms of a loved one to catch her fall.

The delivery boy announced himself. "Ma'am? Western Union for Dr. Edwards. I need you to sign for a telegram."

She stepped back from the window as Olga came to her side, barefoot and bleary-eyed. Olga heaved open the door, signed, and took the small yellow envelope. She looked to Eliza for confirmation to proceed. Eliza nodded, her eyes brimming with tears as she awaited the brief lines from the Secretary of the Navy.

A burst of elation filled Olga's face as she read aloud, "I cannot divulge location. It is not Pearl Harbor. Letter to follow. Love, Ted." Lieutenant Edward Shaw, U.S.N. Time stamp: 1941 Dec 7 6:35 PM.

Eliza tilted her head to the heavens. "Thank you. Thank you."

Olga encircled her. Her worn maroon terrycloth bathrobe brushed against Eliza's cheek as the two women sobbed with joy and relief.

CHAPTER FORTY

April 1942

Afurther a single, brief letter in February, Eliza excitedly waved another one from Lt. Shaw in the air, announcing to Olga, "News from Teddy!!"

Olga looked up from the notes spread across the desk and laid her cigarette into the ash tray. "Go on, then, let's hear it."

Despite her desire to rip the page from the envelope, she slid the letter opener under the back flap and pried it open. She fingered the new brooch on her dress collar, a gift from Bess for Easter. A red enamel circle with a silver eagle and blue anchor embossed into sterling included the words *Ships for Victory* in a banner across the eagle's breast. Breathless, she began.

> *March 10, 1942*
>
> *Dear Mom (and Olga—I hope you're sharing my letters with her and everyone else),*
>
> *All goes well out here in the South Pacific, even if we've had no mail since the 2nd of February. We have been fortunate with no sickness and no casualties! Sure, we gripe and grumble, but really about nothing serious, thank goodness; but it gives us something to do! After being held up for about two weeks, due to some storms that were hula-hulaing around us, mail finally got*

through. Forgive my handwriting. It's off today because we are firing rockets and the ship trembles somewhat.

Eliza shook her head. "Can you imagine? He's sitting there in his bunk, as if he were slung across his bed at the Academy, writing a letter while above they're shooting rockets?"

"Sadly, I expect they're used to it by now," said Olga. "Continue."

Within our mail, newspapers and magazines caught up with us, too. It's strange to be in the middle of making of history, and yet, not know as much as you people at home. One article I read has disturbed me greatly. It's quite disgraceful. Not only have they begun to relocate Japanese Americans to internment camps, but in Mt. Hood, Oregon, they have stricken the names of Neisi-Japs from the town's honor roll—talk about bigotry in the "good old days of witch burning". Certainly, a person who was loyal to the United States and served in the armed forces, creditably, regardless of color of skin, should be treated better than that.

Please keep writing. Your letters will catch up with us someday, and when they do, I'll savor every minute detail about your work with the Red Cross training classes, spring in Boston, and how the Red Sox do this season—has the Army snagged our star, Ted Williams, yet?

Love,
Ted

Olga picked up her cigarette and pulled on it hard for a long drag. She blew the smoke into the air above her head. "You've raised a fine young man, Eliza. Out there on a ship where every minute, they're hunting down Japanese to save the world from its maniacal emperor. And he comments on the treatment of Japs here in the States."

A radiant smile illuminated Eliza's face. At her grandfather's knee, she had learned the important lesson of coming to the aid of the others, regardless of the color of their skin, as he had done in winning the freedom of runaway slaves. In some unconscious way, unable to pinpoint the exact moment, Eliza had instilled rules of civility and a sense of empathy in her sons.

"Thank you, Olga. I am proud of him. I just hope every letter brings news of no casualties or illnesses. Then, I can sleep a wink better each night."

She placed the letter back in the envelope and took the rest of the mail to her bedroom. She preferred reading Grace's weekly report in private, in case she included any news from Chet.

April 8, 1942
Dear Dr. Edwards,
Mid-terms went well and my attention now turns to finals in a few more weeks. I wish I could say Toshiko fared as well. Just before exams she received the most dreadful news. Her family has been sent to the Minidoka Internment Camp in Idaho. The poor thing, rightfully so, is beside herself with worry about them. She was so distracted that she performed miserably. I'm trying to keep her spirits up and help her buckle down for finals, but I fear I'm not much help. I'll keep trying.

I didn't get home for Easter. Pops told Ruthie that he should have enough saved for my train ticket for summer break since taking a supervisor job at the knitting mill. They're on full shifts, and overtime, too. Lots of folks are happy about that. I hope you had a pleasant Easter with your new little granddaughter. She sounds darling.

With gratitude,
Grace

As rockets fired in the South Pacific and tanks rolled across Europe, Eliza felt a foreboding darkness descending. The ravages of war had reached out its tentacles, grabbing at those on the home front. Rationing had exploded, making the idea of candied yams for Easter dinner a frivolous, faraway thought. Families were being torn apart, sent to the vast wastelands of Idaho and suited up, ready to report for duty. Eliza feared it was only a matter of time before her family was one of those ripped apart.

CHAPTER FORTY-ONE

May 1942

Life gives. Life takes. At different moments, the giving outweighs the taking. At other times, like today, the taking grabs with greedy hands. Eliza reflected upon those imbalances as she folded a tiny pink sleeve against the back of a smocked dress, breathing in the motes of baby powder nestled in tight pleats. She picked up a pair of white socks trimmed with lace and turned them into a ball, recalling one-year-old Flora's squeal whenever Eliza caressed each toe to *This Little Piggy*.

From the open window, she heard Will slam the trunk door down. She had an hour left before Will would drive Anne and Flora to Connecticut. Upon Will's enlistment, Anne had announced she'd prefer to be home with her parents to await a telegram from the Secretary of War. Will had called her melodramatic but acquiesced. Eliza couldn't fight that battle. The comfort of the familiar, with her own mother at her side, not a mother-in-law, would be best for Anne. Will would travel on to New York after leaving his family in Connecticut, joining the over fifty thousand other enlistees scheduled to ship out in May.

Flora sat on a pink blanket on the floor. Eliza had positioned a stuffed white rabbit with a blue bow at its neck and a Raggedy Ann doll in front of her to keep her occupied. The baby fingered the bunny's floppy ears before sticking them into her mouth to suck on the fur. Bending down, Eliza retrieved a picture book with a deep green cover from an open wooden crate in the middle of the floor. She had already reminded Anne that she should read to Flora every day.

"Okay my darling," Eliza said, picking up Flora and settling her on her lap as she sat in the rocker. "One last book. Let's see what adventures Mrs. Mallard and her brood of ducklings are up to."

She turned the pages of *Make Way for Ducklings*, bringing the story to life with sing-song quacks. At the end, the ducklings settled into sleep on their little island in the middle of the pond.

"Did you know that when your daddy was a little boy, he would race into this very same Public Garden pond, flap his arms and quack just like Jack, Kack, Lack, Mack, Nack, Ouack, Pack, and Quack? Your daddy was a mischievous little boy. He loved adventures."

Flora looked up at her, "Da-da, da-da."

"Yes, da-da. It sounds like he's finished packing the car." Eliza choked down a wad of sorrow. She could hardly call the Army Air Corps an adventure: Will kneeling in the cramped tail end of a plane, his finger on the trigger of a rapid-fire machine gun, aiming for German aircraft circling in the surrounding skies. A death wish would be more appropriate. He would make it too easy to be taken from their lives. As easy as placing Eliza's only grandchild in a basket and driving her away to Connecticut.

She closed the book and placed it back on top of the stack in the crate. In an easy swoop, she gathered up Flora, the stuffed rabbit and doll. Flora giggled at her grandmother's tender touch.

"You be the best little girl for Mommy, my sweetest. Nana will think of you every single day. I love you, darling." She tapped the end of Flora's nose and kissed the top of her head.

Flora reached up her chubby finger to Eliza's nose. "Na-na."

Outside, Will gripped the steering wheel of his black Packard. His eagle-eyes, now trained to pick out specks in the sky, glistened. Eliza motioned for Will to reach behind and crank down the back window. She leaned through it, her bosom weighing heavily against the rounded edge of the glass to reach Flora one last time in her basket on the seat. She stroked the wisps of her granddaughter's strawberry blonde hair, grown just long enough to hold a red bow above her left eye. Eliza longed to reach through Will's open window, smooth down his cowlick, and kiss the thinning spot on the top of his head. Instead, she encircled his upper arm, feeling the bulge of muscle, primed and ready for action. "Please, take care of yourself. I'll be thinking of you and Teddy every day. I love you, darling."

Next to him, Anne sniffled, averting her eyes from the mother and son farewell. Will placed his hand over Eliza's. "I love you, too, Mom. I know you're worried. But the sooner we get over there and knock off Hitler and Mussolini and then turn around and help Ted and the boys with the Emperor, the sooner we'll all be home. Americans have the will and might to fight for democracy. We won't stop now."

As the car pulled away from the curb, Olga, who had arrived for the farewell, said, "He's right. The sooner we get into this mess, the sooner we'll be out. Time to get back to work."

She draped her arm around Eliza's shoulders and steered her toward home. A list of appeal letters awaited. Women doctors, with training and experience equal to any man, wanted to serve in their country's defense. Their first battle, however, wouldn't play out in field hospitals across Europe or in jungle tents on Pacific Ocean islands. After making pleas to no avail to President Roosevelt, the Secretary and the Surgeon-General of the Navy and the Army, the American Medical Women's Association (AMWA) turned their efforts toward Congress. They needed to counter the War Department's interpretation which claimed that women were not people.

Two forward-thinking Representatives in Congress had taken up their cause. Emanuel Celler and John Sparkman would seek to amend Public Law 252. In part, the Law stated that temporary appointments as officers in the United States Army may be made from among qualified persons. The War Department, however, had ruled that where the word "person" appears, they intended "person" meant "man". As far as the interpretation was concerned, a woman was not a person. Representatives Celler and Sparkman pointed to Victorian-era thinking, suggesting that the words *came out of holes of an old-moth-eaten parlor sofa*. Their impeding Bill would argue that a woman is a "person" and that wherever the words "person" was used, it should be changed to "man and woman".

But they needed help. Members of the AMWA rallied, armed with ammunition that if the armed services projected a shortage of 42,000 physicians by year's end, rather than enact a forced draft, shouldn't they consider the eight thousand women skilled in bone surgery, radiology, anesthesiology, and other specialties?

As they rounded the corner to Smith Court, Eliza noticed Bess's blue bicycle leaning against the front railing. Bess, in a pair of high-waisted, wide-legged green trousers with a short-sleeved yellow print top knotted at her waist, sat on the steps. She waved when she saw Eliza and Olga approach.

"Olga, I told you not to let her drag out the goodbyes," said Bess with a wink.

Olga shot back, "Hmmph. Did you really think anyone could have stopped her from gobbling up a few more baby kisses?"

Eliza summoned a light smirk across her lips. "Sorry, Bess. You know a new little girl has squirmed her way into my heart. You had to go and grow up on me, didn't you? Just like my boys."

"I know, I know. Flora is a cutie. But I've only got an hour. I'm on deadline myself. If you want my help, let's get crackin'."

Eliza unlocked the door for the three women to enter. With Bess's persuasive journalism skills guiding them, Eliza hoped she and Olga could craft letters which conveyed the importance of Congress's consideration. After all, if a woman could strap on work belts and drill rivets into the sides of a bomber, couldn't equally strong women with the appropriate talents face the strain and fatigue of military medical tasks?

Forty-five minutes later, Bess swiveled her wrist, checking the time. Olga intertwined her fingers and stretched her arms out straight. Eliza ceased her hen-pecking on the typewriter keys.

"How'd you do?" asked Bess. "Let me hear them before I leave."

Eliza and Olga addressed their letters to Dr. Emily Barringer, who would appear in front of Congress armed with petitions. Their requests called for justice and fair-mindedness that women doctors receive full commissions, entitling them to rank, pay, care if they were wounded, and pension rights.

Olga started. "*As a native Russian, I am proud that Soviet Union, and its allies in Great Britain, do not bow to the misplaced belief that a woman doctor would embarrass soldiers. But I find no honor in the continued and outmoded prejudices held by the United States. We can no longer overlook the vast reservoir of professional skills available among our M.D.s—which stands for MEDICAL Doctors, not MALE Doctors,*" said Olga, her voice sliding into a childhood Russian dialect as she stressed *Voman* doctor.

"Oh, I love that ending, Olga!" Bess said. She turned to Eliza. "You're up, Auntie E. Let's see if you can beat the Russian."

Eliza pulled the sheet of paper from the typewriter roll and stood. *"I write to you in honor of Dr. Charlotte Fairbanks, who died last year, after a long and successful career as a surgeon. She treated thousands through her private practice in Vermont and traveled with the American Women's Hospitals to the Appalachian mountains in 1937 to create better lives for children afflicted with cleft lips and palates. She began her service with AWH during the Great War. The AWH funded the expedition and paid for their supplies to aid French civilians and eventually US troops. The French awarded Dr. Fairbanks a Medal of French Gratitude and an honorary French citizenship. The US Army Medical Reserves never commissioned Dr. Fairbanks and her peers into its ranks, nor provided associated pay or retirement benefits. She was one of our country's highest skilled surgeons. If your son's face should be shredded by shrapnel or his internal organs perforated with slits, wouldn't you want a professional like Dr. Fairbanks, regardless of her gender, working on him? Shouldn't she have received her due of recognition and compensation from her country?"*

"Excellent. Make it personal. Lean on their fears." Bess rose from the couch and bent to tie a string above her ankle to save her wide trouser leg from catching in the bicycle chain. "My work is done here. I'm heading over to Congresswoman Rogers' office now to finish our interview. Her work in securing some benefits for the women serving in the WAVES and WAACs gives us a jump start. If she hammers home the message she shared yesterday, I don't see how they can avoid changing the protocols."

Eliza beamed at the mention of Congresswoman Rogers. Less than a decade after she earned the right to vote, Eliza had cast her ballot to send Edith Nourse Rogers to Washington as the sixth female representative in the entire country. "What was her message?" asked Eliza.

"She's smart, that's for sure," said Bessie. "She intends to focus on the general, overwhelming need and to reiterate that women are not looking to interfere with or force their way into the rank and file of the Army or Navy. They only want to serve where they are needed during this current crisis of wartime."

"One step at a time. Dah. That's the ticket." Olga picked up her letter, took Eliza's, and handed them to Bessie. "You make sure the Congresswoman knows, we will come deliver our statements in person, if she wants us. There's nothing like a swarm of women to wake those dolts up from their slumber of ignorance."

CHAPTER FORTY-TWO

November 1942

The pile of wool strips overflowed from the wicker basket like the arms of a giant octopus. Eliza tucked three of them back into the heap. She hadn't had time in the past week to send any shipments to the polio hospitals that were using Sister Kenny's hot wool treatments. As she tossed them into the basket, knots at the end of each strip formed a vision in her mind. She retrieved them from the pile and pulled out three more. Three feet. Six feet. She may have enough. An image of a little boy in a Philadelphia hospital flashed from her memories. The boy had told her how his mother would tie him to a chair to prevent him from running out of the house. Eliza had thought at the time that the mother was either inhumane or a genius in her resourceful way to keep a mischievous child safe.

Octopus arms made of wool strips could wrap around a well-built young man's body eight times. She could weave them through the back of the chair slats and secure the ends with a square knot he had taught her how to tie. Would that hold him home? Protect him from torpedoes hurtling through open seas and torrents of bullets raining down from the sky?

From the kitchen, a whistling tune filled the air with light-hearted joy. Eliza didn't recognize the melody from any of the radio's popular playlists. More likely, it was a sea shanty which crews enjoyed. Teddy knew that, in his mother's house, he'd better not sing aloud the accompanying raunchy lyrics found in most shanties. Eliza picked up the notes and hummed along with him. She would do just about anything to stay in sync with him for the next forty-eight hours before he shipped out after his first leave in two years.

With his shirt sleeves rolled up above his elbows and a dish towel hanging over his shoulder, Ted joined Eliza in the living room. "All done. Thanks again, Mom. Dinner was swell."

"I would hardly call meatloaf the pinnacle of fine dining, but I guess we should be thankful we have the meat. For now. I expect they'll be adding to the ration list soon."

"Really, Mom. It was great. A taste of home. That's all I needed." Ted stretched his long, ropey arms toward the ceiling. "Now, I hope you don't mind, but I made plans to meet up with Commander Cole and his wife, Shirley, tonight; she's bringing her sister. He promises the sister is not only a real looker but has a fun sense of humor. They want to go dancing and there's a headliner at the Cocoanut Grove, who will put us all in stitches. We could use a few more laughs before we board that new destroyer on Monday."

Eliza felt the glow in her cheeks fade fast. With Olga in New York for Thanksgiving, Eliza had hoped for another night alone with Ted, enjoying a round of rummy, listening to the radio, and sipping a glass, sherry for her and whisky for him. But how could she deny him one night after the last eight they had spent together? A young, single naval officer deserved an evening out on the town with a date on his arm, searching for other strands of normalcy before he headed back to war.

She stifled a sigh. "Of course. That sounds like loads of fun. Didn't you say the wife is expecting? I hope she can get out on the dance floor, so you don't have to share your date."

"I think another couple of months. Commander Cole, Rob, has tried every which way to Sunday to have his leave extended until the baby arrives, but neither the US Navy nor the Emperor of Japan plan schedules around a baby due in Boston."

"Ask her if she'd like me to call on her. These final weeks are so trying."

"Aye-aye, ma'am," said Ted with a wink and a feigned salute. He planted a peck on her cheek and left to change back into his uniform, a hard and fast rule for an officer when out in public.

Eliza called after him, "I'll leave the extra key on the table by the door. I'm guessing you'll be out well past the old lady's bedtime."

In her bedroom, she went to her bureau, pulling out a clean flannel nightgown for the chillier November night. After Will had shipped out in May, she added two matching frames with photos of each son in his service uniform to the bureau top. Her nightly ritual soothed her mind. She ran her finger down Will's cheek in the photo and swiped up, ending on the tip of his nose. "Wherever you are, my boy, remain strong, stay safe. We are with you, and you are with us. Come home soon with victory on your lips and in your heart."

She lifted her finger to repeat her touch and prayer on Teddy's photo and stopped. This son was in the room next to her, whistling another tune as he splashed water on his face. The fresh scent of menthol from his shaving cream seeped through the door, cracked open an inch. He was home. A night of fanciful fun, music, and the company of a pretty girl awaited. He was safe.

She finished her nightly routine by applying a dab of Pond's face cream to her neck, smoothing it with upward strokes from her clavicle to her chin. Pulling back the covers of her bedspread, she slipped under the blanket. Half of her heart would sleep well tonight.

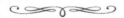

A siren wailed and tires spun against pavement. Eliza often slept through the sound of ambulances heading up Joy Street to the bustling downtown area on the other side of Beacon Hill. They were all-too-common occurrences when one lived near Mass General Hospital. Another screech followed the first from a second ambulance. Eliza shook herself to a full wake at the sound of a third ambulance. She grabbed her bathrobe and hurried to the living room. The extra key was gone from the table. She checked the banjo clock. Five to eleven. A red light flickered in a circular strobe through her front windows, casting a fiery glow against the walls. With one hand clutching the edges of her robe to her throat, she opened the front door to peer out. Another ambulance flew by. Four taxis speeding at the same pace as the emergency vehicles followed. A multi-car accident or an explosion of some sort, she guessed. What were the chances another molasses tank could explode like the one in 1919?

The chilly November air thickened with gray plumes against the night sky. Eliza lifted her head to sniff. An acrid scent lingered over the streets and in the alleys. The smoke would be thicker, closer to the source, covering the sidewalks that Teddy would take home. She dismissed a stirring of worry. He had more emergency training than most who might walk the same sidewalks tonight. He would know to cover his face or take a circuitous route away from the scene of an unknown tragedy. Still. She wouldn't sleep until she saw him saunter through the door after an entertaining evening, a grin on his face and a pep in his step. A copy of Beryl Markham's *West with the Night* lay face-down, spread eagled at Chapter Two on the coffee table. Recalling her library due date for next week, she tucked her feet under herself on the couch and took off to British East Africa.

After an hour and a half, Eliza placed a scrap of wool in the book to mark the end of Chapter Five. Lost in the story as Beryl flew over herds stampeding across the Serengeti, she realized Ted hadn't returned home. Nothing good happens after midnight, she thought. The sirens had ebbed and disappeared, but the wonder of what had summoned them weighed on her. Driven by an innate medical training and motherly concern, she picked up the phone and asked the operator to connect her with Mass General. No, not an emergency, she told the woman.

"They'll be grateful to hear that! Although, I'm not sure anyone will pick up if I say it's not an emergency," said the operator.

"What do you mean, they'll be grateful?" Eliza's stomach began a slow churn.

"The fire. Mass General and Boston City. They've both taken in hundreds from the Cocoanut Grove. They're completely overwhelmed. I finished my on-call list about twenty minutes ago."

Eliza placed her palm on the counter's edge. Her hand trembled as it sought a solid surface to steady the mounting sway coursing through her body. "Did you say the Cocoanut Grove? The nightclub on Piedmont?"

"Yes. Terrible, tragic. I suspect it may go down as one of the worst in the city's history. So many young people. So many lives."

"STOP!" Eliza screamed. Her Ted, his life, her life.

She slammed the handset into the cradle. She ripped her nightgown edges apart. Small pearl-like balls flew across the room. She ran to her bedroom and threw on the closest clothes from the top of her laundry hamper. From the front closet, she reached for her medical bag on the top shelf. As she stretched for the bag, wool itched and chafed her nipples. Dear God. She'd forgotten a bra. She shook her head in vehemence. The hell with it. She wouldn't bother with a bra and the extra minute it took to insert two god-damn tiny metal hooks into two god-damn tiny metal eyes.

She hurried out the door, heading toward Mass General. She'd never find a cab at this hour. With her heart pounding and her lungs gulping in the smoke-tinged air, she ran down Joy Street. Her lips quivered as she murmured over and over the words she had skipped just hours before: *Remain strong, stay safe. We are with you, and you are with us. Remain strong, stay safe. We are with you, and you are with us.*

A calamity the size of a battlefield had arrived in the streets of Boston. She would not allow it to claim her son in the backyard of their home. Not near the spots where he had floated a wooden boat in the Public Garden lagoon or hidden from his brother beneath the tent of a weeping willow tree or laid on the banks of the Charles River painting with his father. Boston had held Teddy Shaw in its bosom as close as Eliza had. But it could not have him. He belonged to Eliza.

CHAPTER FORTY-THREE

E liza rushed through the swinging doors at Mass General, entering a triage scene which mirrored those across Europe. Bodies on stretchers lined the hallway. Manic screams from some echoed against the walls. Others remained silent in shock or death. A backward walking intern in his short white jacket bumped into Eliza as she stood frozen at the entrance. His partner at the other end of the stretcher nodded at her. "Please ma'am, can you move?"

She slunk back against the wall. The body on the stretcher lay motionless as they passed by her. A white sheet covered it from head to toe except for the left hand. Blackened splotches ringed by bright red blisters covered a man's hand. At the base of the thumb, pale and papery skin split open, exposing the gleaming white metacarpal bone. A glint of gold on the ring finger announced that somewhere, a bride had become a widow. If she was alive herself. Eliza said a silent prayer for the dead man and his widow before sending thanks that this corpse at least was not Ted. She could still hope for a miracle among the madness.

Before the first intern nudged a swinging door with his hip, Eliza asked, "Have they identified any of them?"

"No ma'am, we're just trying to make room for any more live ones we get," said the second one. "I'm sorry."

Diagonally across from where she stood, a crowd jammed in front of the admitting window. Other mothers, fathers, spouses, siblings, and friends sought information, too. Rare occasions had arisen in Eliza's forty years when she wielded her doctor title for benefit. This moment commanded her declaration. She elbowed her way through, lifting her medical bag for visibility and affirmation. "Excuse me. I'm a doctor. I can help. Let me through."

A path parted for Eliza to approach the window. A nurse raised her bloodshot eyes from the scattered forms on the desk behind the window. Her voice cracked, repeating the words she had uttered for the longest ninety minutes of her young life. "We are unable to release any names. Please take a seat."

"I understand the situation. I'm here to assist in any way possible. Dr. Eliza Edwards. Where can I find the hospital administrator?"

The nurse looked Eliza up and down, from her loafers to her auburn hair streaked with gray and pushed back by a thick, paisley cotton headband. "Really? A doctor? I'm sorry, but I can't possibly allow you to go any further than the waiting room."

"Miss," Eliza spied the woman's tag over her left breast, "Nurse Martin, I may be a licensed obstetrician, but I know how to assess and qualify the severity of a patient's situation. You have interns performing the work of an orderly. Surely you need help."

She opened her bag and extracted her license and AWH armband. After the debacle with the ambulance driver when Florence had taken her fall, Eliza made sure she kept her license and armband in her bag. As she pressed the identification pieces against the glass, a woman behind her said, "For crying out loud, nurse. Don't look a gift horse in the mouth. Let her through."

The woman tugged on Eliza's coat sleeve. "Go. Just go. Please, I think my daughter is back there. Rebecca Howard. She's wearing a strapless pink satin dress. A velvet choker. Her hair is…"

She stopped. Eliza feared the woman imagined her daughter's hair singed, burned, gone. Eliza patted the woman's arm. "If I find her, I'll let you know immediately. My son was at the Grove tonight and hasn't returned home. If you see or hear of a young naval officer in his dress whites, Lieutenant Commander Teddy, er, Edward Shaw, please let him know I'm here."

Mother to mother, they locked eyes and nodded in agreement.

The emergency ward on the other side of the barrier doors teemed with doctors, nurses, orderlies, and interns. Their bustle around each stretcher, however, carried a sense of order and control. With precision worthy of an army regiment, a group of four attended to each victim lining the corridor. Shouts came quickly through surgical masks over hacking coughs and labored breathing.

"DOA—orderly!"

"O-TWO! STAT!"

"Surface only. Okay for now."

"Plasma."

Awed by the orchestration, Eliza realized this staff had trained for a mass casualty event of this magnitude ever since Pearl Harbor. Their preparedness would save lives tonight, Eliza hoped, although in the five minutes she'd stood pressed against a wall to stay out of the way, she had heard DOA pronounced twice. At each one, she glanced over, searching for a man in a white naval uniform.

Like a fox low in the scrub brush of the Cumberlands, Eliza tucked her head into her neck, hunched her shoulders, and inched forward down the hallway. Each time her foot hit the tiled floor, she repeated her prayer: *We are with you, and you are with us.* As she passed another gurney, Eliza noticed the blush of pink satin beneath the covering sheet. Someone had placed a strip of black velvet in a neat circle on top of the chest area. An orderly arrived, taking the handles of the gurney. Eliza caught hold of his sleeve.

"Her name is Rebecca Howard. Her mother's in the waiting room. Please make sure she knows."

He nodded and moved ahead with his heavy transport.

Twenty-five feet ahead, the sign leading to the surgical ward hung suspended from the ceiling like a pall of contradictions. Beyond the doors, life or death hung in the balance. A blur of white shapes, one horizontal and one vertical, blended into the sterile wall next to the doors of the ward. As she neared, she saw the gurney first. A woman, with platinum hair matted and splayed across the pillow, lay still, her eyes closed and chest rising in quick jerks beneath a sheet pulled up to her neck. Below the chest and beneath the sheet, a fragile life strained.

Next to the gurney, a body leaned against the wall. Gray and black smudges smeared across white clothing. A fire victim, not an orderly or intern. A man in dress whites, his pants and jacket singed by smoke and ash. One of his hands fingered the black cloth board, adorned with three gold stripes and a star, on his left shoulder. The other hand rubbed up and down his leg in a rhythmic slide. Soothing tones filled the space from a voice trained by the Navy to remain calm during a storm or battle and by a mother who had instilled a sense of sympathy for the wounded.

"Ted-dy," Eliza said, his name escaping in a deep exhale.

"Mom." Teddy leaned down to the woman on the gurney. He repeated the same words Eliza had heard as she approached them. "He's coming, Shirley. Don't worry. He'll be okay."

He stepped away from the woman and wrapped his arms around his mother. As he laid his head on her shoulder, he blurted out the horrors of the night. "I tried, Mom. I did. I pulled the girls through a broken window."

Eliza held him.

"Rob trailed behind, keeping the girls between us. The ceiling broke into sheets. A huge, flaming piece came down on him. I can't tell her right now. She's in shock. Her sister's in there." Teddy raised his chin toward the closed doors. "She snagged her leg on the glass and ripped it open. They both lost consciousness..."

"You did everything right, Ted," said Eliza. "I'm so sorry about Commander Cole, but you saved the ones who could be saved."

From reading the newspapers and listening to the radio, Eliza knew what type of battles her son had seen. Troops landing on beachheads as he watched them disappear into the jungle; half of them never returning. Ships alongside his blown into steel nuggets with crew covered in flames jumping to the sea. A plane over-skidding an aircraft carrier's narrow landing strip and sinking like a great ocean leviathan. Hurricanes and typhoons tossing fleets like a child's tub toy. This was different. Rob and Ted had survived eleven months in the South Pacific. Death shouldn't find them in a spot where a band played dance music and gin and tonics flowed from glass tumblers while women in party dresses circled and dipped in their arms.

"What about Shirley?" she asked. "Any cuts or burns? How long before you got out? The smoke—I could smell it on Joy Street. It could be toxic. Has anyone examined her, or the baby?" She picked up Shirley's wrist, counting the beats against her wristwatch's second hand. Too fast. Way too fast.

"Ted. My bag." Eliza pointed to the worn, black leather bag she had dropped to the floor when she realized her son was the white blur against the wall.

Shirley's legs twitched. A guttural moan, one Eliza had heard thousands of times before, filled the space between them. Ted opened the bag and pulled out his mother's stethoscope. He handed it to her, knitting his brows into a dark line. Eliza moved aside the sheet and unbuttoned the front of Shirley's modest maternity dress. "Ted, could you..."

He turned his back away from the gurney-turned-exam-table. After checking Shirley's heart and lungs, Eliza rubbed her palms together to warm them before she commenced Leopold's maneuvers to assess the fetus's position. Muscle memory guided her fingers from Shirley's upper to lower abdomen, finishing by pressing her palm deeply against the womb. After finding the spot to place the stethoscope's diaphragm, she listened and timed the baby's heart rate. Too slow. She draped the stethoscope around her neck as she spoke softly to the expectant mother. "Shirley, I'm Dr. Edwards. Ted's mother. We need to move you to the maternity ward."

"Rob. Rob." Shirley reached out her hand, searching for the one who had held it at an altar. Tears dripped from the corner of her eyes.

Eliza looked up and down the empty hallway. "Ted, the maternity ward is on the second floor. The elevator is that way." She pointed further down the corridor toward the right. "I'll run ahead and let them know she's coming. You'll have to bring her but go slow. Any more jostling won't help the situation. Keep talking to her. She needs to stay calm."

She snapped her bag shut and hurried toward the stairs, thinking the elevator may be in full use transporting the fire victims. A weariness caught hold during her pause at the landing between the stair flights. The adrenaline surge which had sent her flying from her home and through the hospital lobby to the corridor where she found Ted and Shirley faded like a candle sputtering to the end of its wick. She gripped the handles of her bag in a firm squeeze. Decades of use molded the straps to her curved palm. Eliza's mother had given her the bag upon completing her residency. It meant as much to Eliza as her mother's graduation gift to her, a pearl necklace, and matching earrings, when she had told Eliza, "Pearls symbolize wisdom gained through experience. And pure white ones signify new beginnings. They're the perfect choice for the doctor who stands before me."

Eliza thought for a moment back to twenty-three years ago when her mother lay in a Mass General recovery room. Eliza had stood by her bedside, praying for a miracle after Charlotte had performed the double mastectomy. Her mother's surgery had come too late. The cancer had invaded with a furious force. On a gurney that Ted propelled toward the maternity ward, another woman lay waiting, unaware she may be a mother soon. If they weren't too late.

An unnatural quiet surrounded the maternity ward when Eliza emerged from the stairwell. A nurse flitted out of one room and headed toward another. Eliza grabbed her by the elbow, "Excuse me, Nurse? There's a woman on her way up, early labor at approximately twenty-eight weeks. I need to speak to the attending physician."

"Dr. Reingold and the rest are downstairs. They requested everyone available to help." The nurse hurried into the next room.

Even amidst an emergency, protocols must be followed. Eliza did not have admitting privileges at Mass General. Shirley Cole was not her patient. Her experience demanded that she act, while wisdom suggested that she should not.

The elevator doors opened to the sound of soft moans from Shirley Cole. Teddy pushed the gurney through, eying his mother for direction. Downstairs, lives had been lost. Others survived a few minutes or hours before succumbing to the results of burns, infection, and respiratory tract complications from smoke inhalation. Some were saved. The lives of two more hung in the balance on this evening of chaos. Beneath Shirley's legs, a fluid tinged with pink flowed and seeped into the gurney's sheet.

"Nurse!" Eliza called down the corridor. "I need a room. Stat."

Eliza watched Shirley come to from the nitrous oxide. The nurse handed a swaddled bundle to Eliza and stepped aside. Eliza placed the lifeless body of Robert Edward Cole on his mother's chest and turned away as Shirley brought her lips to the top of the fist sized head.

Of the one thousand men and women who were inside the over-capacity Cocoanut Grove nightclub on November 28, 1942, four hundred ninety-two perished in the deadliest fire in Boston's history. The tallied list of dead did not include the two-and-a-half-pound son of Commander and Mrs. Robert Cole.

CHAPTER FORTY-FOUR

January 1943

Ever since the bombing of Pearl Harbor thirteen months ago, Eliza resumed her practiced panic mode when she heard a knock at her front door. Teddy had reported to the Charlestown Navy Yard two weeks after the Cocoanut Grove fire. After leaving the Fore River Shipyard in Quincy, by now *U.S.S. LCI (G) 397* would be plying through the Pacific on the hunt for the Imperial Fleet of Japan. Eliza cursed the Navy. They may have declared Lieutenant Commander Shaw physically fit and able, but she worried about his mental and emotional state after the trauma of the fire and its aftermath. An unstable officer could cause more harm to himself and others with distracted decision-making. Since his departure, she added a round of prayers for her sons to her morning routine as well.

Eliza eased open the door. The edge of dizziness disappeared when she saw a white envelope in the hand of a man wearing a gray-colored suit on her stoop.

"Eliza Edwards? M.D.?" he asked, his eyes downcast to the doorsill.

"Yes," she said.

"You are hereby notified and delivered a summons from the Suffolk Superior Court of the Commonwealth of Massachusetts. The complaint against you is enclosed."

He extended his arm, pressed the envelope into her hand, turned on his heel, and left. His job demanded brevity with a quick confirmation of the recipient's identity. Nothing more, nothing less.

Eliza's mind raced through recent events, trying to isolate anything she had done which warranted a complaint. Since she and Olga had joined the American Women's Hospitals Reserve Corps six months ago, their work had focused on running first aid classes for civilians, collecting items for the endless forms of supply drives, and serving at the Charlestown Navy Yards' coffee canteens. What type of complaint could be lodged against her for the most benign and basic duties? She hadn't over-poured a cup of boiling coffee on a waiting hand, nor broken into a house to forage through a woman's lingerie chest for hidden nylons, nor accidentally tied a bandage too tight.

From inside, Olga pulled tight a sturdy knot around a stack of *Boston Travelers* newspapers. "Who was at the door? Doesn't the Paper Trooper kid pick up on Tuesdays?"

"I've been served a summons," said Eliza. She squared her shoulders as she continued to search for a cause.

"Well, don't just stand there. Open it."

In bold type, Eliza's name leaped off the page next to the primary complaint of NEGLIGENCE. Shirley Cole blamed her for the death of her baby. Her father had filed a lawsuit on her behalf. In it, he claimed Eliza had *failed to provide the Cole infant with appropriate treatment, such as cardiac resuscitation and the use of respirator equipment, which may have saved its life.* Further, *as a direct and proximate result of the negligence of Dr. Edwards, Mrs. Cole has suffered emotional distress, pain, and suffering, which has rendered her no longer able to sustain a physical and mental will to live.*

The complaint also listed Mass General for negligence in allowing Eliza, as neither a contracted nor approved member of the hospital staff, to deliver the baby.

Her hesitation from that night flooded back to her. Act and save lives or follow protocol—stand by with her credentials unconfirmed and potentially witness the death of two, the mother and child. As if she could shake the words on the page into oblivion, she waved the letter in the air. "Shirley Cole. The woman from the fire. She's suing me. Says her baby died due to my negligence."

Holding out her palms, empty of reasoning, Eliza said, "He was twelve weeks premature. Two and a half pounds! His heart was barely beating when I examined her forty-five minutes before the birth."

Her mouth hung open before sputtering, "Even if any help was available, he was too weak, too far gone. They had moved all the respirators down to the emergency ward for the fire victims. I...I...don't know what..."

Olga grabbed the letter from Eliza. She put on her thick-framed glasses and moved her finger down the page. "Bah. What is this FigNYAH? This nonsense?"

She tapped the section which named the parties, then shook her fist, her thumb pressed between the index and middle finger in a gesture Eliza knew that many enraged Russians used. Eliza peered over her shoulder to see what had set Olga into a tizzy. In her haste, Eliza's eye had flown past her name after seeing it listed as *Defendant*. She had missed the words, *Female* and *sixty-two years of age*. Beneath her name, the entry for the second defendant, Dr. Donald Reingold of Mass General, did not include additional descriptors.

"They don't note that Dr. Reingold is a man, nor his age," Olga said.

"No, they don't. Why me?" said Eliza. By including Eliza's gender and age, the Court and the plaintiff's counsel implied incompetence. Except for delivering Flora, she hadn't formally practiced her craft since leaving Jellico. But that didn't mean she would accept the title of scapegoat by ceding her right to practice medicine. When her practice closed, she took on the case of Kay Clark, traveling to Warm Springs. When she saw a need in Appalachia, she built a Maternity Shelter. When family responsibilities pulled her back to Boston, she decided Florence needed her care. Eliza controlled where, when, and how she defined herself as a medical professional. Six years ago, when an economic depression stripped that ability from her hands, she had laid on a bed with an ether mask over her face. She had worked too hard through her entire career to lose it to a father who allowed his and his daughter's grief to cloud their judgement. Dr. Edwards needed someone who could throw her a lifeline and pull her to safety. But who?

With twenty days to respond, Eliza wasted no time in seeking legal help. Albie, her oldest brother, with his law degree, offered little advice. He specialized in corporate affairs. "I can ask around. But that will take at least a week. You need a lawyer with experience in the civil courts, ideally someone who has tried a malpractice case," he said.

The next night, Eliza and Olga tossed ideas back and forth over dinner. Eliza pushed the creamed chipped beef around her plate in a clockwise circle. "Unfortunately, I made the mistake of burning a bridge with Dr. Miles at the Brigham when I asked for admitting privileges for Anne. I backed him into a corner which won me no favors. He may not even take a call from me."

"I'm afraid, dear Eliza, these leftover Puritans have deemed you as a new Hester Prynne with a scarlet A stitched to your dress. A for Accused. We've got to think beyond Boston."

Silently, Eliza pulled out drawers of information that she had stored in her mind over the decades. Like fingers walking through a library card catalogue, she called forth names from her past. Any connections who may be able to help. She nodded her head with a slight tick at each letter until she hit "L". Lovejoy, Esther Pohl. Oftentimes, the best place to start was at the top. Dr. Lovejoy had been supportive of building the Jellico Maternity Shelter and sympathetic to her reason for leaving. Eliza had no doubt she would find assistance again from the elderly, yet energetic female director of the AWH.

After waiting an unbearable five days, Eliza reached Dr. Lovejoy by phone upon her return to New York from Great Britain. Neither time nor travel could slow down the indomitable, seventy-four-year-old Lovejoy. Eliza had barely finished reading the entire complaint when Dr. Lovejoy interrupted her. "Dr. Edwards. This is a most unfortunate situation. From what you've told me, however, no basis for a claim of negligence exists. But be that as it may, you must respond and settle quickly. We need doctors such as yourself now more than ever. You will have this case dismissed if you can find two people. One: A woman lawyer like Dorothy Kenyon. If she wasn't tied up with our fight in Washington, I would send her to you. You need a smart and capable woman before a judge. I will ask her if she knows anyone in Massachusetts. The second person you need is a male doctor."

"But you just said we need a smart woman lawyer. Why a male doctor?" Eliza said.

"You will need him to testify as to your abilities. The judge will accept his opinion as an authoritative witness. He won't consider another woman doctor with the same level of credibility. The harsh truth must be faced and played. I'll be in touch if Miss Kenyon has any names for you."

Eliza thanked her and hung up the phone. Olga, who sat at her elbow to listen in on the call, smirked and let out a low chuckle.

"What's so funny? She was kind enough, but basically, not a lot of help," said Eliza.

"I am thinking of the scene for your next phone call."

"Finding a doctor to testify for me won't be impossible. There were a couple of them on shift when Flora was born. They were quite complimentary and helpful."

"No, it's the woman lawyer I'm thinking of."

"You know someone? Here in Boston?"

"Dah. Yes. You know her, too."

Eliza crinkled her eyebrows. Olga's smirk widened until she burst when Eliza realized she knew a woman lawyer. Helen Warner Shaw. A Massachusetts licensed lawyer with experience with civil cases and the widow of Eliza's ex-husband.

CHAPTER FORTY-FIVE

March 10, 1943
Washington, D. C.

Between March 10 and March 18, 1943, the Subcommittee on Military Affairs for the House of Representatives held testimonies in support of Bills submitted by Emanuel Celler and John Sparkman to amend the Act of September 22, 1941 (Public Law 252). They would argue that the term "woman" constituted a "person" and that women physicians should be appointed and commissioned in the Army of the United States or the Naval Reserve with the same rights, privileges, and benefits as members of the Officers' Reserve Corps.

CHAPTER FORTY-SIX

March 10, 1943
Boston, Massachusetts

"Your honor, today, counsel for the plaintiff would have you believe Dr. Eliza Edwards has committed a level of medical negligence which has caused undue suffering and distress for the plaintiff, Shirley Cole. We shall make the strong recommendation that this court dismiss the complaint against Dr. Edwards with expediency."

Dressed in a navy wool suit, belted loosely at her waist and with the collar and cuffs of a dove gray and pleated blouse peeking out at her neckline and wrists, Eliza sat at a wooden table in a small hearing room of the Suffolk Superior Court. Before leaving the house, Olga had fastened a silver brooch to each of Eliza's jacket lapels. On the right, she wore a set of wings with a propeller placed vertically across the mid-point. On the left, her Navy pin. Patriotism and sacrifice greeted the judge when Eliza stood for the reading of the complaint.

Eliza locked her stare on Judge Francis Webb as he watched her lawyer stand and read the opening statement. The ever so slight rise of his eyebrows belied his otherwise blank expression. This case may be a novelty for him, thought Eliza, but she had cast her die. She had hired Helen Shaw to represent her. Now, only time would tell if Helen Shaw's appearance in the courtroom would help or hurt Eliza. And ultimately, the outcome of the complaint against Eliza could direct the reputation of women doctors and lawyers for years to come.

After Harrison's death, Helen had joined the faculty at her alma mater, Boston's Portia Law School, the only law school for women in the country. In recent years, Helen had led a study group to prepare students for the bar examination. Eliza had noticed a small article in *The Boston Traveler* last year mentioning Helen's success. In the five years since she had started, all her female students passed the bar on their first attempt.

Helen had demonstrated her desire to help other women succeed. Yet, Eliza calling on Helen was different. Before she had picked up the phone six weeks ago, she had played out Helen's response in her head. *You want me to help you? You, the suffering wife who refused to divorce Harrison for sixteen years? The woman who denied me a life with the man I loved.* Click.

Regardless of what Helen may think of her, Eliza had made a promise to herself at Harrison's graveside that for the sake of her sons she would always be cordial to Helen. Debasing Helen in front of them would serve no purpose. She had made the right decision then, because today, at this moment, Eliza needed Helen Shaw in the defense attorney's chair: a smart and capable lawyer and staunch supporter of a woman's abilities. She made the call. Helen answered.

Now, in a Boston courtroom, Helen Warner Shaw stood before a judge on behalf of her husband's ex-wife. Upon completion of an opening statement, she turned the paper in her hand face down on the table and settled into the chair next to Eliza and leaned toward her. In a conspiratorial whisper, she said, "Let the games begin. *Veni, vidi, vici.* I have no doubt, we will win with a quick, decisive dismissal."

Eliza admired Helen's confidence, but worried about the lemony Jean Nate scent which lingered on Helen's wrists. Did Judge Webb return home every night to a happy homemaker, Mrs.

Webb, with an apron tied around her waist and a dab of Jean Nate at her ear, standing over a stove, a place most men believed women should stay? From where Eliza sat in the defendant's chair, she wasn't so sure quick and decisive were at hand.

Over the next twenty minutes, Eliza listened as the plaintiff's lawyer stated Shirley Cole's complaint. Each time the lawyer referred to Eliza as "the defendant," he shot a look toward her like a spotlight beam trying to blind her into submission and confession. Motionless, Eliza ignored him despite her urge to glare him down like a lioness stalking her prey. Helen's directive to remain calm and fettered to stoicism and confidence rang in her ears to the point of burning when he said "Female, sixty-two-years of age". Behind her in the audience section, Olga muttered under her breath, "FigNYAH". Eliza turned her head to check that Olga's hands remained in her lap. The last thing she needed was a raving Russian shaking her fist in a courtroom.

He then called the attending nurse. The nurse's remarks presented basic facts: the size and weight of the fetus, the gestational age, the lack of use of any resuscitative measures.

"Does the defense have any questions," said Judge Webb.

Helen rose. Eliza followed her gaze to the man seated next to the plaintiff's lawyer. David Stevens, Shirley's father, dressed in a black suit, wiped his forehead with a crisp, white handkerchief. The lines around his eyes tracked crevices of grief. Eliza knew he had suffered. He'd lost his son-in-law, his grandson, and to some extent, his daughter in the span of one night.

"Thank you. None for Nurse Fiske, but two questions for Mr. Stevens."

The judge dismissed the nurse. "Proceed," he nodded toward Helen.

"First, we ask if the Plaintiff would comment as to why his complaint included Dr. Edwards's gender and age and what relevancy the Court deems they have on this complaint?"

A silence fell across the room. Eliza watched Mr. Stevens shift from one buttock to the other. He lowered his head to whisper to his lawyer. The lawyer rose and said, "No comment."

"The defense requests the words 'female' and 'sixty-two-years of age' be stricken from the complaint. I ask that Dr. Edwards be referred to as *doctor* or *person*. Or, until this complaint is dismissed, we accept the use of defendant," said Helen in a clear and affirmative voice.

"Granted," said the judge. "Next question."

Veni, vidi, vici, thought Eliza. *I came, I saw*. They'd conquered the first hurdle. But Eliza would be the fool if she believed the rest of the judge's decisions would come as quick and decisive. Perhaps he simply had no interest in opening the hearing with a debate over gender and age.

"We understand Mr. Stevens filed the complaint on behalf of his daughter, Mrs. Robert Cole. Nowhere do I see a full and notarized statement taken from Mrs. Cole regarding her assessment of the delivery of the child and any presumed negligent actions taken by Dr. Edwards. Mrs. Cole is a vital witness in this case. Can the Plaintiff produce Mrs. Cole as a witness should this complaint proceed to a trial?"

"Your honor," said the opposing attorney, "Mrs. Cole's current mental and physical state make her unable to appear in court. As stated in the complaint, the negligent behavior is documented."

Judge Webb nodded toward Helen. "Any witnesses for the defense?"

"The defense calls Dr. Howard Orman," said Helen.

After having him state his name and credentials as the Chair of the Gynecology and Obstetrics Department at Boston University's School of Medicine and a practicing physician of thirty-two years at the Peter Bent Brigham Hospital, Helen asked Dr. Orman to provide his professional opinion on the complaint.

"Dr. Orman, I understand from your paper on the subject in *The New England Journal of Medicine*, there are six areas where negligence can be considered in a case where a child is delivered deceased. Please explain what constitutes those areas and your opinion of Dr. Edwards's actions as they pertain to each one."

"First, a fetus must be monitored for distress. Failure to check vital signs, such as heartbeat, would constitute negligence. From my review of the accounting of the situation, including a letter from Lieutenant Commander Edward Shaw, Dr. Edwards's extensive professional experience compelled her to examine the state of the patient immediately."

Eliza squeezed her fingers into a tighter clasp as she rested her hands on top of the table. A ship-to-shore telegram from Teddy, notarized by his superior officer, had arrived two days earlier, validating his testimony as witness to Eliza's first encounter with Shirley Cole and her evaluation of Shirley's condition.

"Please, continue," said Helen.

Dr. Orman listed four other actions which would constitute grounds for a claim of negligence. Eliza eased her clasp each time he finished the sentence with, "I see no basis of negligence by Dr. Edwards in this area, given the circumstances and conditions under which she was proceeding."

"What is the final area, Dr. Orman, which may constitute negligence?" asked Helen.

"A physician must at all times focus on the patient's well-being. For maternity doctors, however, there are two patients: the mother and the fetus. Failure to protect the mother must not be overlooked."

"Did Dr. Edwards fail to protect the fetus?"

"In my opinion, the delivery of a documented stillborn, as noted by Nurse Fiske—no pulse, no evidence of breathing, the size, and weight—and given the extraordinary circumstances at the hospital, operating in a triage situation which demanded use of all available respiratory equipment elsewhere, Dr. Edwards could not have resuscitated the fetus."

"Did Dr. Edwards fail to protect Mrs. Cole from any unnecessary complications?"

"No. On the evening of November 29th, there could have been one additional death at Mass General. Due to Dr. Edwards' adherence to the standard procedures for any delivery, she saved the life which could be saved, that of Mrs. Cole. Moreover, beyond the medical actions required of her, Dr. Edwards displayed a level of sympathy for her patient. As noted by Nurse Fiske, she placed the deceased infant in Mrs. Cole's arms and allowed her a chance to say goodbye to her child."

Olga reached over the bar and squeezed Eliza's shoulder. Eliza drew the care and concern through Olga's fingertips and into her heart. She kept her eyes, however, straight ahead on Judge Webb. Was that a blink in his eyes? A flutter to stem a tear?

"Thank you, Dr. Orman. Is there anything else you would like to add to your statements here today?"

"I met Dr. Edwards when she was temporarily on staff at the Brigham to deliver one of her patients. I observed her over the course of three hours during the woman's final labor. If my daughter should ever need a maternity doctor, I would recommend Dr. Edwards. In fact, I would like to see all our patients cared for by doctors like Dr. Edwards."

Eliza considered Dr. Orman's remark. She had done her job in the same manner she had practiced for forty years, with competence and compassion. That Dr. Orman had specifically commented on it made her wonder how male physicians performed their jobs.

Dr. Orman took a sip of water from the glass placed on the bar of the witness stand. He withdrew a folded paper from the inner breast pocket of his suit jacket. Unfolding it, he continued, "Last week, I received a call for my services by the United States Army. While I hardly think our wounded soldiers are candidates for Cesarean sections, I will bring my surgical skills with me to wherever my country needs me. If it's admissible, I'd like to have this letter added to the complaint file. Within it, you will find my request and recommendation that the Peter Bent Brigham Hospital immediately hire Dr. Eliza Edwards, should she be willing, for the full-time position to replace me."

An "Ohhh," loud enough to be heard in the back corner, escaped from Eliza. She covered her mouth and dropped her gaze to her lap, not allowing the Judge to view her complete reaction.

Judge Webb rapped his gavel once against the thick block on his desk. "Dr. Edwards, do you need a minute?"

Helen grabbed Eliza's wrist as Eliza moved to rise from her chair. "Your honor, my client is more than all right. She is outstanding. Thank you, Dr. Orman."

CHAPTER FORTY-SEVEN

A weak March afternoon sun filtered in through the single window of the courtroom. At the conclusion of Dr. Orman's statement, Judge Wells called a lunch recess. He would hear closing arguments after a break. Eliza, Olga, and Helen huddled around the defense table. Who needed a lunch break when stomachs bounced like a child on a pogo stick?

"You had no idea about Dr. Orman's letter?" asked Helen.

"None whatsoever," said Eliza. "I knew he would speak favorably on my behalf, but he hadn't mentioned his draft notice when I called him. I'm sorry I gasped like that; I hope I didn't look like some hysterical twit."

"Actually, I think it worked in your favor. It shows that we hadn't coached Dr. Orman. His statement was authentic, and your reaction was as well. Now, if you ladies will excuse me, I want to review the closing one more time."

Olga gestured toward the back of the room where Eliza's brothers stood waiting for her. "Let's get a breath of air. A brisk walk to the Common and back will clear your head." She reached for Eliza's arm.

Eliza bent her elbow away from Olga, saying, "Yes, good idea. Can you grab our coats from the coat check girl? I'll be right there."

Eliza watched Olga steer Albie and Freddy through the courtroom door, leaving the room empty save for the two Mrs. Shaws, the former and the widow. Helen peered down at a typed page, her lips moving silently as she skimmed the lines. Eliza waited. In the middle of the page, she watched Helen draw a straight line through one sentence. Satisfied with the change, she tilted her head up, seeing Eliza at the end of the table.

"Are you going for a walk?"

"I am. I mean, I will. I just wanted a quick moment to tell you, regardless of the outcome today, I owe you a tremendous thank you." Eliza wiggled her left foot in a semi-circle. The press of a bunion against the leather pump began to throb.

"When I received the complaint, at first, I was dumbfounded. In shock, really. Then I became furious. Then panic set in when I realized all that I could lose. All I've ever wanted is to put my training into good use by taking care of women. I've seen what havoc traumatic loss could have on a life. Before I went to Jellico, when I was out of work, I grieved over my lost profession. I wasn't ready then, and I'm not ready now, for someone else to tell me when I should end my career."

"I completely understand. I'm not ready either," said Helen, standing from her chair and facing Eliza full-on. "That's one reason I took your case. We should be allowed to work with the freedom, at any age, to have our individual qualifications be the only criteria for assessment."

"And for that I am grateful. Do you mind if I ask what the other reason is you took my case?"

"I must admit, I was shocked to hear from you. We haven't had many reasons to speak to one another over the years. But then, I looked around my living room and the bookcase which holds our law books, mine and Harrison's, and I thought of how Harrison would have answered your call."

Eliza thought back to the home she'd shared with Harrison on Mount Vernon Street. His law books had lined shelves in their parlor, too, intermingled with her medical texts and favorite novels. She raised her eyebrows as she also wondered how Harrison would have responded.

Helen continued, "There's no question. The two of you had your issues. God knows, I'm all too familiar with the struggles Harrison battled every day with his alcoholism and how that affects a relationship. It's a challenging disease for the person and those who love him. But I want you to know, I think he would have said yes, Eliza. He respected you and your work, even if he didn't tell you."

No, he hadn't told Eliza.

"So, I took your call for him, as much as for you. And for me. Women practicing law aren't much different from women practicing medicine. We face the same blatant disregard for our abilities. We've fought the same fight. If I can help you win yours here today, it will also help me and women lawyers in Boston. Two victories with one win," Helen said with a chuckle.

"Now, go on." She flicked her fingers toward Eliza to shoo her on her way.

Re-seated at the defense table, Eliza waited under a heavy cloak of uncertainty. The plaintiff's lawyer made his closing statement. No one could deny the fact that Shirley Cole suffered from her losses. Her inability to rise from her bed. Her selective mutism, making it impossible for her to discuss her grief. Her body and spirit weakening with each day that passed without an infant to hold in her arms. A sympathetic judge would rule in her favor to provide meager offerings of recompense. Yet, Judge Webb had sat expressionless throughout the entire hearing. Perhaps he played poker on Friday evenings in a dark paneled room of the Parker House, chawing on a cigar stub clenched between his lips and his fingers running up and down a tumbler of rye. If so, Eliza envisioned chips stacked in multiple neat piles in front of him.

Her breath quickened as she searched for a rhythm to calm her nerves. She drew a deep breath in through her nose. *And hold.* Next to her feet, a black leather purse's bottom sat upon the cold, tiled floor of the courtroom. Inside, she had placed her license awarded by the Commonwealth of Massachusetts, which declared her rights and abilities to practice medicine. She imagined her fingers transforming into tentacles, feeling in the dark abyss of her purse for the coveted object to relinquish it to fingers stained with cigar smoke and moist from sweat drops from a tumbler.

"...we also grieve with Mrs. Cole." Eliza exhaled. Helen Shaw had started her closing argument.

"Losing a spouse, a partner, rips apart a life. The loss of a child shreds one's life to pieces. We feel for her and extend to her not only our condolences, but also the hope that she will find a medical professional who can guide her to a place where she can find a reason for living. She deserves that type of care. But what we cannot offer her is Dr. Edwards as a scapegoat for her grief and current condition."

Helen crossed the room from the defense table to the plaintiff's and back to stand before Judge Webb. "The testimony from Dr. Orman is irrefutable. At no point during Mrs. Cole's labor and delivery did Dr. Edwards perform her duties in a negligent manner. Further, she followed the strict teachings of the training she received through four years of medical school and four years of a residency in one of Philadelphia's finest hospitals. And, in this situation, perhaps as equally important, as Dr. Orman noted, she brought forth to an extreme emergency a sympathetic approach to her patient, which has been a part of her practice for forty-two years."

Inhale and hold...

"Here today," Helen continued, "in a courtroom where facts and laws must be adhered to, we ask that you set aside the sympathy which is due to Mrs. Cole and dismiss this complaint against Dr. Edwards. Her services are needed at the Peter Bent Brigham Hospital. The mothers-to-be of Boston need her. Thank you."

Exhale. And wait.

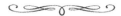

Twenty minutes later, all those in the courtroom rose from their chairs when the court bailiff called out, "All rise" as Judge Webb re-emerged from his chambers and settled in his chair on the raised platform.

"Dr. Edwards, please remain standing," said Judge Webb.

Eliza's right foot rubbed over the bunion on her left, the pain increasing from a dull throb to a pulsating pain. She steadied her hands against the table edge when her one-legged stance wobbled. She turned toward Helen, who gestured for her to direct her attention to the judge. Pinpoints of sweat formed in her palms. The pulsation from her foot echoed in her brain. The desire to hear a single word bounced between her ears.

"In the matter of Civil Action Number 00-4988G, filed by Mr. David Stevens on behalf of Mrs. Robert Cole, against Dr. Eliza Edwards, the Court finds insufficient evidence of negligence. This complaint is dismissed."

The rap of the gavel against the wooden block rang clear and true. A single word: *Dismissed. Vanished. Vanquished. Validated.* Eliza would settle for any one of them.

CHAPTER FORTY-EIGHT

April 16, 1943
Washington D.C.

P resident Franklin Roosevelt signed the Sparkman-Johnson Bill, thereby granting women who entered the Army and Navy Medical Corps to receive full military commissions and benefits. Dr. Margaret D. Craighill, Dean of the Woman's Medical College of Pennsylvania, became the first female physician to join the Army Medical Corps, commissioned as Major Craighill.

CHAPTER FORTY-NINE

February 1944
Boston, Massachusetts

Eliza collapsed onto the couch. She unwound the knit muffler from around her neck and pulled the end free. Stretching her legs out before her, she looked down at her worn rubber boots. She'd never find a new pair. All available supplies went into manufacturing life rafts, tank treads, jeep tires, and thousands of other uses as the United States began its third year of battling a world war. She may have to stick newspapers inside her boots on the next rainy day she trekked to the Brigham to care for a patient.

From the kitchen, Olga called to her, "Some days I'm not sure Dr. Orman did you any favors giving you this position. Can't you speed those kids along? Maybe add some caffeine to the gas they give the mothers? A little jump start wouldn't hurt. How about you? Coffee?"

Eliza sent a silent thank you. *Bless you, Mr. President, for ending the coffee rationing. The weary on the home front appreciate your benevolence.* As she bent down to unhook the boot buckles, a small pile of letters on the table caught her eye.

"Olga, mail? From both of them?" Her voice rose and caught in her throat.

"Dah. Will's letter came yesterday. Teddy's this morning. Famine or feast. I guess we'll take a feast any day, right?" She winked at Eliza, handing her a plate of toast. Eliza scrunched her nose at the pale-yellow goo smeared across the top.

"Sorry," said Olga. "We're down to the last of the butter. We should have points by next week for more. I had to whip up a bit of Knox Spread last night. It's better than dry toast. Open the letters. You won't even notice the gelatin mixed in with the butter."

Letters from Will came more infrequently than Teddy. Will had a wife who worried her days away in Connecticut. Eliza understood that any spare minutes he had should be spent on sending news to Anne and Flora. She tore open Will's letter.

January 26, 1944

Dear Mom,

We're back at Camp Griffiss in Middlesex to unwind and refuel. We desperately need this time after a raid to drift back to normalcy—whatever that is, since nothing, of course, is normal! There's a lot I've seen but will have to wait until there is no more censorship—then maybe I can give you some of the background to the big goings on behind the scenes. It should be interesting if I don't forget it all! And sometimes I wish I could. After special treats at Christmas, for the New Year we're back to corned beef hash—out of a can—and Lord help us if we lose the can opener! I hope you and Olga enjoyed the holidays. I'm glad you were able to visit my gals, making as much of it as you could. With all my heart, I hope we'll be able to make up for the dreariness that has marked 1943.

Please know that I'm keeping my eagle eyes sharp and my spirits up. You all help through your letters, cheerful, bright, and interesting. Suppose they were blue, moaning and groaning about how hard it is to be a civilian in a world gone mad. Naturally, such news would upset me, with a resultant loss of whatever efficiency I may have. Multiply that by all those in the service who might receive similar letters—what would the result be? A disillusioned, distracted army and navy. So, thank you for doing your share—you deserve just as much credit as those who have done the actual fighting.

Love,

Will

"All good?" asked Olga.

Eliza pressed the thin parchment against her chest and held it there. Big goings-on. What could be bigger than what the newspapers and radio reported? She murmured her twice-daily prayer, adding under her breath, "May a one-way route to Victory continue over Paris and straight on to Boston. And let it be soon."

"Yes," she said to Olga. "They had a short leave back in Middlesex. He alluded to some big initiative in the works. I wonder if it's all those raids on the German airfields near Paris? He says to keep writing, it keeps their spirits up. Our plans for a Victory Garden this spring should bring him a few chuckles. Picture it—two old lady doctors with a hoe and watering can."

Olga untied the apron strings at her back and let them drop. She pinched the edges and flared out the sides. "Well, I've already got the cameo and apron. Find yourself a pitchfork and borrow some overalls from one of your Tennessee friends and we'll send him a picture. It'll be a finer display of Americana than anything Grant Wood has painted."

Eliza sputtered, sending pieces of toast across the coffee table. She wiped the dribble from her chin, allowing other tableaus to develop in her mind. Chet's hand reaching for hers as they surveyed the garden together; young shoots pushing through the dirt primed to bring meals rich in vegetables to the mountain families. Ruth and the other women of Jellico walking in tandem lines toward the knitting mill with its re-fitted looms turning out everything from parachutes to mosquito netting. Kay Clark removing her arm brace as she settled in a chair to read a letter to her children about John's work with the Army Corps of Engineers. Each scene brought serenity. On the home front, amid war, life continued, guided by purpose and prayers.

"I'll get the coffee. Open Teddy's," Olga said, interrupting Eliza's wandering thoughts.

Teddy's letters always arrived in the same thin envelope, with two, three-cent *Win the War* stamps in the right corner and his ship, *LCI(G) Group 39* and home port of San Francisco, CA in the left. Inside, single-spaced lines covered the paper from margin to margin. While she knew Will left from and returned to Middlesex on a regular basis, Teddy's ship had island-hopped its way through thousands of nautical miles in the South Pacific. Next to the calendar on the kitchen wall, she had pinned a map to track the shipping lanes made by Amphibious Group 39.

January 14, 1944

Dear Mom,

I'm writing with hopes we are heading to Pearl Harbor. There will be a good supply of fresh food, but what I long for the most is freshwater showers! We need the reprieve—even if it takes us 20 days to get there—after mightily working over the Solomon Islands. The Japs are mighty stubborn, and even after we felt sure that the islands would sink from the sheer weight of steel that had been hurled at them, they still fought back. Those of us on the decks had to duck as shells, definitely unfriendly—although we didn't look closely enough to see the "Made in Japan" sign on them—zoomed over our heads. The jungles with their dense, entwined underbrush are also enemies to the marines and infantry that go ashore. If they finally release this DDT spray and powder that the govt. has developed, at least we'll win the battle of the bugs!

Once we get away from the battle isles, there are several beautiful spots. The views from the top are breathtaking, for the cliffs are sheer, and far below flat plains encircled with rugged ranges push out like fingers. There's one true thing about Navy travel—you get around at the government's expense!

We're coming into monsoon season. That means people going mad—banging their heads against the bulkhead—for, to have constant rainy weather on this overcrowded shoe box is a serious matter. No outlets for excess energy, and we can't keep scraping paint—the ship will eventually fall apart, and, when that happens, I would much rather be in friendlier waters. We've had enough Japs on suicide missions, swimming up to our ships with bombs strapped to their backs, to prove that point conclusively.

If we are headed to Pearl Harbor, I'll pick up mail. I wonder if the next pile will exceed the last record of sixty-five letters waiting for me. Please tell Bess, the Uncles, Helen, and Anne, to keep them coming. I'd love a new picture of Flora, too. Will is a lucky man. Those extra twenty points for two dependents will help him with a quicker release when this nightmare ends. Maybe I should have taken you up on your offer to meet one of those physios from Warm Springs you kept talking about!

Love from your son,
Ted.

Eliza lay the letter in her lap, smiling with a smirk. No mother needed to be prompted twice to introduce her son to a nice young woman. She'd shoot off a letter to a couple of the physios, asking them to write to Teddy. Across the country, citizens rallied, sending cheery notes to servicemen. Those lovely physios would be no different. Tomorrow. She'd do it tomorrow. For now, though, she needed to pour her body into bed. Last night and this morning's fourteen-hour labor had done her in as much as it had the new mother. Both her sons had survived the most recent rounds of warfare. She could rest easier, or at least until the next battle reports spanned the headlines of *The Boston Globe*.

CHAPTER FIFTY

March 1944
Philadelphia, Pennsylvania

The knock against the hotel's paneled wood door sounded loud and sure. Eliza patted the victory rolls over her ears, pushing the web of bobby pins deeper against her skull to hold the popular hairstyle in place. The soft glow of the Tiffany lamp refracted against the oval mirror. She studied her face. How much had changed in four years? She conceded that the extra creases across her forehead were well earned. Three and a half years of war worry had etched the grooves as smooth and deep as the ones on the lid of a wooden box. This weekend, she would turn her thoughts to a happier occasion. She reached for the glass-cut doorknob and whispered through the wood. "Chet?"

A baritone voice said, "Yes, Eliza, it's me."

Her heart pounded. She had told Grace she'd be staying at the Majestic Hotel and suggested that she tell Chet that he would find the hotel's location convenient to the train station and for the graduation exercises. She'd left a note addressed to him for when he checked in. Her simple words would be easy enough to read. *I'm in Room 402.* Amidst the bustle of a city hotel, a desk clerk managing three-hundred and sixty rooms could hardly bother whether the man he sent up to Eliza's room was her husband or not. There were plenty of "look-the-other-way" situations during send-offs and welcome-homes.

Eliza grinned like the Cheshire cat. She cracked the door to find Chet Wilson standing before her, a fedora hat in one hand and a small valise in the other. A grin to match hers spread across his face. His goatee had turned completely white, including the stubble above his lip from its faded blonde red. Otherwise, he hadn't aged a day. If anything, years had slid from his frame and face. She drank in his presence, remembering what a gift he was to her.

A double-breasted dark gray suit jacket, like the ones with an Edwards Wool Company tag sewn inside, was neatly buttoned over a crisp white shirt and a green and gold striped tie. He seemed to be doing well with his job.

"You came," said Eliza, opening the door wider.

He dropped the valise and tossed his hat to a chair. He caressed the wrinkles covering the blue veins spread across the back of her hand. "I did."

By 1943, many medical schools had instituted changes to their curricula to compress their academic year to graduate doctors quicker and deploy them for the war effort. Two months ago, Eliza had received the invitation to attend Grace's commencement, scheduled for March 16, 1944. She had beamed as bright as the sun shining against the yellow-gold leaves of the Cumberland Mountains. Grace Wilson had succeeded in every way Eliza knew she was capable of. From a one-room schoolhouse in Jellico to completing her college education in an accelerated three years while working at the Maternity Shelter. This morning, Grace would claim the crowning glory of four years of arduous study at Woman's Med.

Eliza spotted Grace at the far right. Upon hearing her name called, she looked out to the small audience, found Eliza and Chet seated next to each other, and waved. Chet squeezed Eliza's hand that he held in his lap.

"I sure wish her momma and granny could see her," he said.

The Class of 1944 formed a single line at the front of a small presentation hall in the College of Physicians. Forty-three years ago, Eliza had stood in a similar line, surrounded by her classmates, and cheered by her family. Her thoughts had gone to her grandfather, who had helped found the school with the belief that women had the right to test their intellect and be rewarded with accredited medical degrees. To become doctors.

Eliza returned his squeeze and said, "They can. Sshh, now. They're starting. It will be quick with only twenty-one of them."

What a tragedy, thought Eliza. She had learned through alumnae bulletins that although forty students had entered Woman's Med with Grace in the fall of 1940, less than six months later, tuberculosis had hit the campus with the force of an air raid. Despite strict adherence to germ-control protocols, for some unknown reason, the tuberculosis bacteria that the Woman's Med students encountered had been especially virulent. Over the next two years, nineteen students left the school. They traded bent heads over microscopes in labs for reclining bodies in chaises at sanitoriums or at home.

From the podium, the Toastmistress announced, "In our study of medicine, we often overlook the dangers that our students face with exposure to contagions during rounds at clinics and hospitals. Please join me in a moment of silence for two members of the Class of 1944 who dreamed of studying medicine and are not here with us today."

Eliza added her own silent prayer. *Bless those poor souls who will never wear the coveted white coat. They paid a sacrifice as great as the ones as our armed forces in their fight against other evils.*

Major Margaret Craighill, M.D., the college's dean who had taken a leave from the school to serve in the Army Medical Corps, had returned after her most recent European tour to confer the degrees. Halfway through the list, she read the name of Grace's roommate. "Miss Toshiko Nakamura, of McGill, Nevada. Bachelor of Science degree from the University of Utah. Congratulations, Dr. Nakamura."

Up and down the rows of other family members and reporters in the audience, Eliza noticed hands remaining in laps, folded and tight. She shook her head in disgust. Eliza nudged Chet with her elbow, encouraging him to join her in clapping harder and louder for Toshiko to make up for the silent hands on either side of them. Toshiko should not be denied the recognition of her accomplishment the way her country had denied the rights of her family.

While Eliza was disappointed that Toshiko had declined their invitation to join them for a celebratory lunch, she understood. Too many people in a public restaurant would see only the color of her skin, not the diploma in her hand. Toshiko, like Kay and John Clark, chose her battles. She would rather board a train heading west, head and eyes down, to return to Nevada.

After the ceremony, Grace, Eliza, and Chet started in the direction of Snockey's Oyster and Crab House. It may not rival Boston's Union Oyster House, but it would give Chet a taste of the delectable fresh-shucked oysters with their salty brine, dash of hot red pepper sauce, and a squeeze of tart lemon juice over the top. Grace looped her arms through Chet's and Eliza's and tightened them to her like the clamps of a vise.

"I can't tell you how much it means to me that you both came," she said.

"I wouldn't have missed it for the world," said Eliza, squeezing her elbow against her side, bringing Grace's arm closer. "Not only did I get to watch one of my favorite gals realize her dream, but what a wonderful excuse to visit this special city. I've been away too long."

"It's a mighty fine city, with mighty fine folks. 'Course it's the first one I've seen, but if they're all like this, I'd say impressive indeed." Chet pointed toward the William Penn statue atop City Hall. "Who's that chap in the clouds? He's got the best view of anyone."

Eliza launched into a history lesson, including how, when she was a young girl, she and her brothers had watched the workers climb five hundred and forty-eight feet into the sky to install the statue. Chet let out a low whistle. "Whew-ee, but that's high. Don't think I could've done that."

"Don't sell yourself short, Mr. Wilson." Eliza nodded toward Grace. "Where do you think her bravery comes from? I think it's the Wilson genes, starting with you. Descending into those coal mines or logging timber, even now, working at the mill. All those jobs required specialized skills, hard work, and the courage to tackle each one."

"Not unlike you, Dr. Edwards," added Grace.

Chet added, "Exactly right, Gracie. You were brave too, Eliza. You left Boston to come help Dr. Fairbanks. You stayed on in our hillbilly hamlet, traipsing through the woods by yerself. Building our Maternity Shelter. Heck, you even learned how to ride ol' Ollie. That took guts."

"Which one? Coming to Jellico? Or riding Ollie?" Eliza said with a wink.

"Maybe both," said Chet.

"Don't forget the chickens!" Grace said. "You clucked at them and tossed them grain before the first snowfall."

All three of them burst into laughter. Those hustling past them on the sidewalk turned to see the trio, who found a reason for levity in their afternoon walk. Laughter healed. They would need to lock those chuckles away, pulling them out to savor when dark days descended. And they would. Eliza was sure of it, especially with Second Lieutenant Grace Wilson heading to England at the same time that Will had hinted that a big initiative was in the works. Before starting her residency in pediatrics at the University of Tennessee, Grace had flipped her plans upside down when she announced she would join Major Craighill in the Army Medical Corps. During a brief phone call in February, she had shared her plans with Eliza, "A rotation in pediatrics may be child's play after serving in a European war front hospital. We've earned the right, thanks in part to doctors like you and Dr. Povitsky who wrote to Congress to petition for women doctors' commissions into the armed forces. I intend to exercise that right."

As they neared the restaurant, Eliza said to Grace, "Do you mind trotting ahead and double checking our reservation?"

With a sideline glance, Grace nodded. *She's a smart one,* thought Eliza, *knowing I'd like a moment alone with Chet.*

Eliza reached for his hand, her fingers entwining his in silent appreciation which went miles beyond *thank you* for coming to her room last night. He gripped her hand and moved closer to her. On a city sidewalk, as cars and trolleys raced by, time halted.

"When I left Jellico, I thought I'd never see you again—any of you—but you came last night and you're here now. Chet Wilson, someday, maybe tomorrow, maybe five years from now, when all of heaven's faith and peace is with us again, when the sun shines across your mountains, and you're alone drinking in their glory, I hope you'll think of the lady doctor from Boston and know what you've meant to her. You completed me at a time when darkness and uncertainty lay at my feet. I'll forever remember you with a loving fondness as a bright moment in those days."

"I will, Doctor Ma'am." He pressed his lips to her cheek and guided her through the restaurant door.

CHAPTER FIFTY-ONE

August 1944
Boston, Massachusetts

The poster on the brick wall outside the market reminded millions of mothers like Eliza that *This is No Time to Let Go!* The Fifth War Loan Drive was underway. As she had done previously, Eliza purchased a twenty-five-dollar bond. The Allies couldn't ease up on the throttle. Too many lives and limbs had been sacrificed and scarred on the beaches of Normandy.

The metal cans clanged as they rolled against each other in Eliza's shopping basket. By six o'clock on Saturday night, the grind of can-openers would release salted clumps of Spam and Friend's Baked Beans into sizzling pans across Boston. Next to the cans, Eliza placed the butcher paper-wrapped ground pork. "More pink than gray, please," she had told the meat-cutter, remembering a childhood lesson from her mother.

"Not much pink in the neck bones, ma'am, that's all we've got today," he'd replied.

She wished that a couple of rib-eyes sat in her basket. Will loved thick red slabs quartered into portions large enough to hang over the edge of a plate. Sautéed buttons of mushrooms strewn across the meat. Puffs of potatoes whipped with real butter, not margarine or Knox Blend, and the steak's juices dribbling in a puddle on top.

At least the rhubarb betty would be a cheery dessert. The sturdy plants in her Victory Garden had ripened last week. A sprinkle of the sugar she had saved from their June allotment would sweeten the tart stalks. *Wouldn't it be divine if this was the end of rationing?* Eliza thought. She'd more than settle and prepare another concocted way to serve Spam, however, in exchange for her thankful joy that Will was home.

Her Will. The boy who would run away from her in parks, pick up a bat, or kick a ball whenever he found a chance, would be forever sidelined. Her Will. The proud father who would long to run alongside Flora's bicycle, wobbling as she found her balance with the training wheels removed. Her Will. The competitive tennis player who hated to admit losing a set to his cousin. Her Will. Airman Shaw whose name appeared among the casualty list of ten thousand on June 6th, the lower half of his right leg in a heap outside a British surgical room.

When Eliza and Anne had met him at the Charlestown Navy Yard, Eliza had looked beyond his mask of happiness. *A mother always knew.* He would need her now as much as the wooden crutches he leaned upon. She would ensure he wasn't alone on his journey. Through patience and understanding, she would provide him with a haven of hope amid his fractured world. She would keep a watchful eye, too, on the levels in the Scotch bottles, lest the amber liquid mark against the glass disappeared quicker than one glass a night. She knew what type of ugliness arrived on two-or-more Scotch nights.

In the days and weeks that followed D-Day, as the assault had been named, Eliza, Olga, and her brothers' families had gathered around radios tuned to ceaseless broadcasts about the invasion. Repeated reports detailed the first waves of the Army Air Corps. Pilots and navigators in cockpits, tail gunners in the rear, and paratroopers lining the planes' bellies poised to assist those whom the Navy landed on the beachhead. A full-on assault, in the works for months, had finally arrived. Servicemen and women, wherever they served in the European theatre, turned their attention to a six-mile stretch of France's northern coast along the English Channel. Every American also sent their thoughts and prayers to a thin strip of white sand, soon to turn a deadly red.

Eliza had doubled up her prayers that day. She hadn't heard from Teddy in two months. But by the end of every evening, when neither a Western Union delivery boy nor a uniformed officer had shown up on her doorstep, she dropped to her knees and gave thanks. With the announcement of D-Day, she'd channeled her attention to England where Will climbed aboard a B-17 bomber, while her dear niece, Bess, sheltered in London, waiting to interview those who returned to the Army's Hospital Units. Will had been one of them, arriving in a Red Cross airlift.

Before the Army had contacted Eliza with news of Will's casualty status, Bess had found him in one of the beds, post-surgery with a stump at his knee. She had sent a telegram to her father, giving him instructions to alert Eliza that Will was alive. And, most of all, he would be on his way home as soon as they stabilized him after amputating his mangled right leg. Tonight, at her brother Freddy's home, Eliza and her family would celebrate. If only Teddy sat in his own spot at the table, too, then her heart would be full.

Eliza sat to Will's left, cradling a sleeping Flora in her lap. She rested her head on top of her three-year-old granddaughter's downy strawberry blonde hair. Anne sat to Will's right, her hand resting on his throughout the entire meal. Behind him, leaning against the chair rail of the formal dining room, a pair of wooden crutches stood sentry. Over coffee and the rhubarb betty, Will retold the tale of his final mission. "We headed out in the first wave. Our paratroopers hit the ground before the landing craft reached the beach. After the drops, we circled back over to give them cover when the Germans discovered the onslaught. My Iron Hornet took a direct hit from one of those damn Messerschmitts. We'd escaped them for two years, but with the sheer number of us in the sky that day, the odds were against us. The next thing I knew, we spiraled in a nose-dive from 23,000 feet down to 12,000. It was a free-fall to the dunes below. Our radio guy was on the floor with half his side blown out..."

Anne let out an injured puppy-like welp. Eliza closed her eyes to the terror her son had lived through and wondered what scenes unfolded in front of Teddy at the same moment.

"...the rest of us bailed to have any chance. We already saw other planes going down in fiery balls, smashing into smithereens. So many. So many..."

He stopped.

Across the table, Bess jumped from her chair. She quick-stepped over to Will and encircled him around his shoulders. She leaned over him. "But you made it, Willy Boy. And yowza, I've never been so happy to see a guy in a bed. Well, er, I mean..."

"We know what you mean," laughed Olga.

Eliza winced, looking over at her brother Freddy. A father didn't want to imagine his daughter's bedroom tussles with a man. Especially a yet unmarried daughter, whose tastes in men seemed to range from the athletic Viking type of Jack Hansen, now stationed in the Pacific as a war photographer, to the everyday man type of Jimmy Stewart.

Bess returned to her chair and resumed the story of how she'd found Will. Within a week, over two thousand patients lay in hospital beds, giving Bess plenty of material to keep her busy. She interviewed the injured soldiers, transcribed their dictated letters, and began the next day with another row of troops. The bodies blurred together. Bandaged limbs and heads peeked out from starched sheets tucked in tight around their maimed bodies. As severe as their injuries may have been, Bess said she found comfort in gazing out at rows of live bodies covered in white sheets rather than white crosses. These men would be returning home to lives they'd left behind. Farm boys from Kansas. Teachers from Maine. Movie set grips from California. And a textile company manager from Massachusetts.

"While I was searching for status updates on the men I'd interviewed the prior day, the name on the records sheet stopped me cold." Bess continued, explaining how she measured a good day as when there was a higher ratio of RELEASED over DECEASED. Airman William Shaw's name appeared in the ACTIVE column. After wrangling information from the clerk in the main recovery room, Bess raced out the door toward Building C. She burst through the entrance. Respectful of the rules sanctioned for the comfort of the patients, she refrained from screaming. Inside her head, however, four letters pounded, W-I-L-L! W-I-L-L!, until she couldn't contain herself any longer.

Will interrupted her, taking over the narration. "You should have heard the guys' hoots and hollers when they saw her flying across the ward like she was skimming the fields of France on the hunt for Krauts." He reached for the cup of coffee and took a gulp. Anne shot him a look, nodding toward Flora stirring in Eliza's arms.

He lowered his voice. "When she called out, 'Will, Will Shaw, where the hell are you?' even the most banged up guys ripped loose. And then, I knew. No one else but my cousin Bess would tear through a hospital like a bat out of hell. I was the luckiest guy in the ward that day. That morning, Dr. McDonough had told me that I would be going home soon. And then, our Bess appears like she had dropped from the heavens, ready to take my hand and whisk me onto the first flight heading to the States."

Eliza's sister-in-law, Bea, poked her head into the dining room. "Eliza, phone call. It's the hospital. One of your patients is on her way in. Sounds like they need you. You're on call tonight?"

Eliza's shoulders sagged, melting into the curve of Flora's neck nestled at her bosom. "Yes. It's Ellen McPhearson. She's two days overdue. First child. Her husband's out west in some intelligence work. She's done well so far. I hope I won't be long."

She rose and eased Flora into Anne's outstretched arms. Once a doctor, always a doctor. A baby ready to make his entrance didn't care that your son had returned from two years of flying bombing missions. He didn't care that your granddaughter had finally broken into a smile of recognition after not seeing your face since Christmas. A woman who had thrown all her trust into your training and experience to deliver her child couldn't control when that baby decided his turn had come. Those patients' needs trounced your own personal desires. Like how you'd rather sit all night, fixing your eyes upon your son's and granddaughter's faces, faces that shared the same button nose. Searing them into your memory. Touching them to make sure they were sitting next to you in flesh and blood, not in picture frames and creased photos tucked into the side pockets of a purse and medical bag. Inhaling and savoring the sweet scent of baby powder and after-shave. Hearing Flora giggle when Eliza tickled her under her chin. Or Will's boisterous laugh when Olga arrived waving a full bottle of vodka in the air and proclaiming, "Time to find the bottom of this one. Freddy, get the glasses."

Eliza kissed the top of Flora's head. "Happy dreams, my sweetheart. Your daddy is home."

She squeezed the top of Will's shoulder, bending down to whisper in his ear, "I know you've got a few more battles ahead. But you're strong and those smaller victories will come, too. I'm sorry I've got to go. Get some rest. Hug your beautiful girls. I'll see you tomorrow."

Will reached up his hand to grab hers. He pressed it against his cheek. "I know, Mom. Lots of victories are coming now. We've turned the tide. And then we'll have our Ted home, too. I promise."

With a catch in her throat, Eliza couldn't stop the tears from slipping. Grateful and fearful, the emotions dueled in her heart.

This moment, however, she would let grateful triumph. She picked up her medical bag and left the embrace of her family. Tonight, she would help create a new family. As she walked toward Joy Street to hail a cab, she thought, *May Ellen McPhearson never have to send her child off to war. May the madness end once and for all.*

Teddy's last letter in May, however, indicated that her worries wouldn't end any time soon. The enemy in the Far East held on as fierce and furious as a bulldog chomping a hambone. On her way to the hospital, in case she didn't have time once she met up with Mrs. McPhearson, Eliza bent her head and clasped her hands together and recited her nightly prayers with a re-doubled tenacity for Teddy on one front and Grace Wilson on the other.

CHAPTER FIFTY-TWO

May 1945

All three lamps blazed in the living room. *More money for Boston Edison*, thought Eliza as she let herself in through the front door. An ashtray on the coffee table, besieged by stubbed butts, added a layer of staleness to the room's stagnant air. One cigarette rested in the notched groove of the glass. Its ember and once-defined white edges dissolved into a delicate, crumbly gray length of ash. Next to the ashtray, a half-empty glass of vodka sweated droplets of condensation. Beneath it, a dark ring formed on the cherry wood. Why bother owning a fine set of cork coasters if Olga still failed to use one?

On the couch, a new issue of *LIFE* magazine lay open at the three-quarter mark. On the left page, a red Pegasus, its wings spread as if in flight, dominated the page. Boston drivers could rejoice at the arrival of Mobilgas, now available to fill tanks with *Flying Horsepower*. Well, good for them, she mused, but at sixty-five-and-a-half, Eliza still had no intention of buying a car. The advertisement held little interest for her. The facing page, however, piqued her curiosity. Even behind faces half-covered in white masks, there was no doubt that an audience comprised completely of women filled an operating room gallery. Each head was bent toward a table positioned beneath a large domed light.

They focused on the instruction coming from the skilled hands at the table.

As she reached the headline beneath the large black and white photograph, Eliza yelled toward the back bedrooms, "Olga, have you seen this FigNYAH? An article about Woman's Med's ninety-fifth year, yet the headline reads *Girls' Medical School*. The students are women for crying out loud, and it's a college, not a grade school."

No concurring echo of "FigNYAH" sounded. An unsettling stillness enveloped Eliza. Leaving the magazine on the couch, she walked toward the bedrooms. "Olga?" she called out, looking into Olga's room and then her own. Behind the closed lavatory door, she heard rushing water. She knocked on the door, "Olga. Are you there?"

Silence, except for the faucet's gushing stream, gripped her. She turned the doorknob and gingerly pushed it open until it stopped only two inches wide. A swath of maroon blocked the door's swing. Speaking to the black and white tiled floor, she said the name of the woman who had shared her bathroom and worn the same maroon terry cloth robe for the last four years. "Olga."

Her voice rose as her heart sped toward a panicked pace. "OLGA!" she screamed, lowering her shoulder into the door. She pushed until she felt the weight against it give and moved with the door. She dropped to her knees and crawled toward the motionless body. Water spilled over the sink's edges and soaked Olga's hair into gray mop-like clumps. Eliza placed the tips of her index and middle fingers on Olga's neck as she gazed into Olga's eyes, their emptiness magnified by the thick lens of her black-framed glasses.

"No, no. Oh, no. Please. Please. Olga, please."

Sobs reverberated against the tiled walls and floor. She cradled Olga's head in her lap. Sitting on the floor, puddles seeped through Eliza's white coat, sending a numbing chill through her body. The realization of causes and effect battered her mind as she slowly shook her head. Olga Povitsky, M.D. had never diagnosed a silent killer which lurked in her veins, creeping through clogged arteries and smoke-filled lungs until it crept no further. Eliza stretched one arm up to the sink and shut off the running faucet.

Life would never be the same without Olga by her side, offering sharp-witted quips and steady frankness which had always steered Eliza along the right path. As she hung up the phone after calling Olga's sister in New York, Eliza eased herself onto a kitchen chair. Snatches of all she and her dear friend had achieved flashed before her eyes. Together, it was more than she had ever dreamed possible. She stepped back forty-eight years to the moment she crossed the threshold of Room 204 at the Woman's Medical College of Pennsylvania. Next to her in a row of desks sat a young, quiet woman with a tight blonde braid twisted into a bun. Eliza later learned that the silence came from the woman's limited English, not a lack of enthusiasm for studying medicine.

Over their sixteen years of practice, a flood of accomplishments swam forward in Eliza's mind. How many wombs had they saved from unnecessary hysterectomies through careful explanations of the stages of menopause and what to expect? How many breasts filled women's brassieres, rather than succumbed to double mastectomies? How many women averted an unplanned pregnancy, secure to enjoy sexual relations with a diaphragm properly in place? How many children born with challenges went home from a maternity ward wrapped in the embrace of family love instead of sent to sterile institutions to languish, cry, and die? How many women and children were whole, fulfilled, and cared for, thanks to Dr. Edwards and Dr. Povitsky?

A bittersweet ache seized Eliza's breath. In her palm, she caressed the profile of a woman etched in ivory. The gold filigree encircling the cameo glinted from the ceiling light. A jewel of memory and moments would hang forever on the chamber wall of Eliza's heart. "My dearest Olga, my sister. What will I do without you?"

She closed her hand into a fist, covering the cameo brooch and brought it to her lips.

CHAPTER FIFTY-THREE

June 1945

The June evening remained light. In two days, the summer solstice would occur. Many civilizations celebrated the date as the start of planting season. Festivities revolved around the feminine elements as the human embodiment of Earth. The longer days gave fields time to yield their soft earth to seeds feeding a future. On a crowded sidewalk, amidst the throngs of servicemen spilling across the streets, restaurants, and bars, three women elbowed their way through the North End of Boston. Doctors Eliza Edwards and Grace Wilson, and war correspondent Bess Edwards matched their stride to the rapidly setting sun. Their futures figured prominently in each of their thoughts, especially Eliza's. Over the past month, life changes had hurled themselves at her with the ferocity of a gathering storm bearing down on the earth beneath her feet.

"Really, Grace, you're welcome to stay with me," said Eliza.

"Oh, thank you, but I don't want to put you out," Grace said, her eyes widening with each block they passed. They saw Italian delicatessens with odors wafting out their doorways as foreign as the dialect upon many of the tongues of the people seated at sidewalk tables, couples in tight embraces on black wrought-iron balconies and fire escapes and listened to the peal of bells from the Old North Church as the hour struck seven. "I should take advantage of the Army's offer to stay at the Park Plaza. I've never been in such a fancy hotel."

"Well, I won't deny you the chance to soak in their over-sized tub as a special treat. At least come in for a cup of coffee. Maybe I can find some bath salts in my closet for you," Eliza suggested.

Grace had disembarked from the most recent troop ship to pull into the Charlestown Navy Yard. Ships tied up to the docks while others remained anchored outside the protected harbor awaiting their turn to deliver home the millions of Americans who had served in the European theatre. With the surrender of Germany in May, servicemen and women vied for a spot on those ships, longing to place their boots upon American soil as soon as possible.

Bess chimed in, "Knowing my aunt, I bet the bath salts I gave her for Christmas are still in the box. Plus, I'd love to finish my interview with you. And if you need one more enticement, I think I smelled gingersnaps baking in the kitchen this morning."

"In that case, absolutely yes. I love those gingersnaps," said Grace.

Eliza wrapped her arm around Bess's shoulder. Her niece knew an offer of bath salts and coffee was a mere ploy. Returning to an empty home unnerved Eliza each time she walked over the threshold to Five Smith Court. Inside, Grace and Bess settled in the living room while Eliza started the coffee. Her ears perked up when Bess asked about Grace's last rotation with the British Emergency Medical Services in Warwickshire.

"After visiting with Will there, I wanted to write a piece about his doctor. You know— an Irishwoman, treating one of the Yanks in a British hospital. But my orders came to return to the States before I got to meet her. Any chance you met Dr. McDonough? She was wonderful with Will, making sure he was as comfortable as possible considering the amputation, and diligent over infection control."

Doctor. Ireland. Eliza couldn't hear those two words in the same breath without thinking of Patrick Callahan. Her heart, which had lost its urgency ever since losing Olga, quickened. She saw him in front of her, looking just as he did the first time he showed up on her doorstep in Philadelphia, full of apologies and a hang-dog expression. He had left her too many times. She slid the blue-checkered dish towel from the stove door handle and dabbed at the corner of her eyes. *Damn you, Patrick Callahan.*

She put the mugs of coffee and a plate of gingersnaps on a tray and carried them into the living room. Grace and Bess reached for the same cookie, laughing as their fingers rubbed the coveted sugar crystals off the top. Bess broke the snap in half and handed a piece to Grace.

"Goodness ladies. I can make another batch tomorrow. No need to fight over them," Eliza chuckled. She lowered herself to the needlepoint-covered chair next to the table.

"I could polish off the whole plate, yes I could!" said Grace. She nibbled the edge before finishing her answer to Bess. "Dr. McDonough. Erin? From County Cork? Oh yes. They assigned me to shadow her for surgical rounds. She's a real spitfire."

Bess blew on the top of the coffee, sending ripples through the black liquid. "That's fantastic. Maybe you can help me with some of her backstory. I always start with probing their inspiration to study medicine, especially as a woman."

Pulling a small memo pad and pencil from her hip pocket, Bess flipped a few pages to find a blank one.

"Well, that's an easy enough one to answer," Grace started. "Erin and I spent many meals together, if you can call slop out of a can a meal, and we swapped lots of stories. She couldn't imagine what my life looked like in Tennessee—the mountains, the creek, my little Rosie Ray of Sunshine, the mountain laurel, even old Ollie, our mule. Then when I told her about meeting Dr. Edwards and how she encouraged me to go to Woman's Med, well, she nearly keeled over like when the air raid sirens sounded."

"Why's that?" asked Eliza, her eyebrows rising as she leaned in closer to the story of Dr. Erin McDonough from County Cork, Ireland, the last known address of Patrick Callahan.

"When Erin told her stepfather she wanted to study medicine, he encouraged her. If Trinity accepted her, he promised he would help her throughout her studies. Until that day, she never knew that he had taught at Woman's Med, many years ago, before massive ship liners sank to the bottom of the sea. That's how he had phrased it to her. She went on to tell how he was supposed to be on the *Titanic*, but missed the sailing and decided to stay in Ireland and then took a job at the Queenstown cottage hospital."

Eliza slapped her hand over her mouth as every ounce of color drained from her face. She looked like the ghost that entered her living room. The ghost of Patrick Callahan, stepfather to a Dr. Erin McDonough.

Bess said, "Aunt Eliza, are you all right? Did you know that teacher from Ireland?"

"Yes. Dr. Callahan. He..." she stopped.

Would she, could she, share the fractured fairy tale story of Eliza and Patrick? All the women—Florence, Olga, her mother—who had their misgivings about her relationship with Patrick, were gone. Her brothers, most likely, wouldn't recall or be bothered with their sister's long-ago beau. She had suffered enough in recent weeks. Teddy's most recent letter indicated he didn't expect the war in the Pacific would be over until sometime in 1946, at the earliest, despite V-E Day. Her agony and worry over him continued to have no end in sight. Losing Olga had knocked her as low as when she'd lost Florence and her mother. If she kept the tale to herself, Patrick would remain hers alone, forever, and ever.

"He taught Anatomy, as I recall."

When the last gingersnap disappeared and Bess had finished six pages of notes from Grace on the workings of the British convalescent hospital, Grace gathered her suitcase. Her eyes drooped and fluttered. "Thank you again, Dr. Edwards, but I really should get going. Would you be able to call me a cab?"

Poor thing. Look at her, thought Eliza. Utterly exhausted, yet she's sat here and visited with us when she's desperate to burrow beneath the feather quilt of a hotel bed after months of sleeping on an Army cot.

"Of course. I'm sorry we've kept you so late. Bessie, would you call the cab? I need to grab something."

Eliza headed toward the bedrooms. At the door to Olga's, she steadied her trembling hand before turning the knob and entering. From books stacked two feet high on the floor to open journals, pages flagged with paper clips, strewn across a bureau and nightstand, the evidence of a researcher lived. A framed diploma from Woman's Med hung on the wall over the twin bed. Eliza had made up the bed after calling Taniya. Regardless of four years of sharing a room in Philadelphia during medical school and years living together in Boston, Olga had never yielded to Eliza's request that she make her bed in the morning. *Why bother?* she'd say. *It's my tired bones that will fall back into the same spot tonight. Why waste time messing up that spot?*

In the top bureau drawer, Eliza felt for a small piece of green velvet amidst a tangle of hair clips, knotted necklaces of glass beads, scented sachets, and wrinkled handkerchiefs balled and stuffed into the corners. The same principles applied to beds and handkerchiefs, in Olga's opinion. *Why waste your time ironing them? They're getting jammed into a pocket. Who cares? Who'll see them except my snotty nose?*

Eliza found the soft, crushed fabric. She drew it out and carefully untied the bow. She had discussed her plan with Taniya, then Bessie. They agreed. The cameo, which had started as a gift between sisters—Eliza's Aunt Maria to Eliza's mother—became a symbol of something more when Eliza's mother passed it on to Olga in honor of her friendship with Eliza. Sisters could form without a drop of blood between them. Love bloomed wherever two people stood next to one another with only respect and shared values to fill the space between them.

Grace had her hat on. Her suitcase rested against her leg. Eliza reached for Grace's hand, opening her fingers to lay Grace's palm flat. She placed the velvet pouch in Grace's tender hand. "Dr. Wilson, I'd like you to have this. Just like Olga, even if you're closer to being the age of a granddaughter, you're my sister. My sister from Woman's Med. It doesn't matter that our classes were nearly forty years apart. We understand and appreciate what each of us went through to earn that degree. I am honored we met. I know you will achieve great things at the University of Tennessee and beyond. You'll make us all proud. You already have."

Grace peeled back the velvet. Gold filigree shone around the ivory. Eliza pulled Grace to her bosom and recited a chant that she and Olga and their classmates had sung at their graduation festivities.

"Where, oh, where, are the loving memories
Of all that has gladdened us here?
Laid away in our heart's deepest niches
To blossom for many a year."

CHAPTER FIFTY-FOUR

September 1945

The end had come. One month ago, Eliza and the world laid down their fears. They stepped into houses of worship and knelt on kitchen floors. They gave thanks to whatever being they believed had guided the Emperor of Japan to surrender.

She looked down at the envelope. Teddy had left the South Pacific. Both her boys had survived the nightmares which had plagued her and their country for four long years. Her shoulders released. Her breath drew steady. And with Anne's due date less than a week away, they would add another Shaw to celebrate life after millions of deaths. She had thanked Dr. Orman for allowing her to stay on at the hospital to see Anne through her second delivery. He had returned to his position but told Eliza that if she wanted to remain as an on-call physician, the choice was hers.

Inside the entry table's drawer, Eliza reached for a wooden hand-carved letter opener etched with the North Star. Slicing open the thin airmail envelope, she pulled out a single sheet and stretched her arms away from her chest. The words demanded reading this minute, to hell with the glasses on her night table.

September 7, 1945
Dear Mom,

My correct address is now Staff, Phib Group 5. *I haven't been aboard* LCI(G) 397 *since the middle of July. I consider myself fortunate and can finally tell you what my new job WAS! I was transferred to the* USS Blue Ridge *under Admiral Wright's command, working on plans for a landing on Japan's mainland when the news came through. A day we thought would never come, for the Japs don't quit, or surrender. They take the bullet or put the bullet in their head themselves. It's been a long, tough, and bloody war out here, but I've never been happier to be tossed out of work.*

I suppose you are as relieved as we are that this war is over. Some days it hardly seems possible, and probably won't seem real until I set foot on the dock in Oakland. Still no firm arrival date, but I'll wire you as soon as I know. Hallelujah and amen – I'm coming home.

Love always,
Ted

Her boy was coming home. *Hallelujah and amen.* Eliza's glow beamed back to her in the mirror which hung over the entry table. She returned the sheet to its envelope and picked up the rest of the mail. This week's *New England Journal of Medicine* cover called out an article on *Diagnosis and Treatment of Cystitis in Women and Children.* Eliza made a mental note to read it before seeing her patient tomorrow morning. The monthly statement from Boston Edison. With one less room being used, her electricity charges had dropped in the past four months. She would pay those higher rates without hesitation if it meant that Olga burned the lightbulbs all night long.

A small note-sized envelope addressed to Olga Povitsky, M.D. halted Eliza's shuffle. The return address read Corning Glass Works. A business correspondence of some sort, Eliza surmised. She wouldn't be crossing any privacy concerns if she opened the letter. She'd need to find out who mailed it and inform them of Olga's passing.

September 1, 1945
Dear Dr. Povitsky,
We thought you might like to learn that Corning has received a large order for your five-litre bottle from Dr. Leone Farrell at Connaught Laboratories of the University of Toronto. You may be familiar with her work to increase penicillin production, which was desperately needed for the war effort. We have not been informed of Dr. Farrell's purpose in her use of the bottles. However, if her research is anything like what she has done with the strains of penicillium, it will be likewise momentous. You may want to watch for her name in published papers, knowing that your bottles are contributing to her work, and ultimately, what we expect will be another success.
Sincerely yours,
Philip Nash, Manager, Canadian Sales Division

Eliza savored the news of learning that Olga's expertise and dedication to her research would carry on, contributing to advances in bacteriology for years to come. She would write to Mr. Nash this week and ask that he continue to send her any other similar updates on the "Povitsky Bottle."

The last envelope in her pile carried the familiar seal in the upper left corner. A mother and child on the left, with another woman on the right lighting a lamp. The Woman's Medical College of Pennsylvania seal symbolized the light which shone through medicine. Eliza expected it held another funding plea from Woman's Med. The alumnae formed the glue of the Woman's Med family. Their support would direct its future. Discussions of co-education or a merger with Jefferson loomed again. War on the heels of the Depression gravely struck the College's financial viability.

Eliza had contributed each year since 1901, some years more than others, but always a check signed by Eliza P. Edwards, M.D. made its way to Philadelphia. The appeal generally included a progress report as well. Best to see what this year's situation held. She slit it open, spilling its contents onto the table. A thin envelope and a single note card fell out.

Sept. 4, 1945
Dear Dr. Edwards,
Enclosed please find a letter received by the college with a request to forward it on to you. Please accept our apologies for its delay. It arrived last spring during our graduation activities, and we misplaced it during the summer recess.
Sincerely,
Katherine Weldon, Secretary to Dean Marion Fay

Eliza's eye moved to the return address of the airmail envelope bearing her name centered in the middle. The hand script was shaky, but familiar. She clenched her hands tight. The tremors which had disappeared on Victory in Japan Day re-emerged from the hidden depths in her heart and pulsed until her temple throbbed. She pressed her arms against her body like a wooden soldier.

5 Bishop Street
Cobh, County Cork, P24 AY26 Ireland

Eliza inched her fingers toward the envelope. His fingers had touched their edges. His tongue had licked the stamp and sealed the flap tight. After thirty-three years, he'd found the courage to write to her. She would find the courage to open it and read his words.

May 15, 1945
Dear Dr. Edwards,

A line ran through the salutation.

~~Dear Mrs. Shaw,~~

Another cross out. She laid the letter down. Her hands, right over left, went to her breast. She pressed deep against her thin cotton blouse. In his last letter from Ireland, before the *Titanic* was to sail, he had written to her: *Seeing these lush fields makes me want to jump off the train and search for the luckiest of shamrocks and bring it home to you. I'd press that four-leafed clover close inside your chemise, tucked against your bare breast to keep the luck of the Irish with you always.*

But he hadn't tucked a four-leafed clover against her breast. Her luck, and love, had run out when he never returned.

Dear Eliza,

I'm unsure how to address you. Unsure how to begin. In my last letter, I begged for your forgiveness. Here I am, thirty-three years later, an old man at seventy-six struggling to kneel. Struggling to find the strength to ask for your forgiveness once again.

I assume by now you've heard from Grace Wilson that she met my stepdaughter, Erin McDonough, at the convalescent hospital in England. When Erin told me about the fine, smart, ambitious, young woman who had graduated from Woman's Med, I couldn't help but think of you. As Erin continued with Grace's story that a Dr. Edwards had found her in the mountains of Tennessee, had mentored her, and directed her into medicine, I had no doubt. Her Dr. Edwards had to be my Eliza.

I write from Cobh, formerly Queenstown. I've stayed in the same spot since the Titanic's *sinking. Who could have imagined three years later this port city would be called upon again to muster its fortitude when we pulled survivors of the* Lusitania's *sinking and brought them here? Erin's father, a crew hand on the ship, was among those rescued. I treated him for hypothermia for two days. I lost him on the third day, the day Erin and her mother arrived searching for him. I never intended to marry. Our marriage developed from a mutual need to bury our respective griefs. We settled into a pleasant life, and I came to love Erin as my own daughter.*

As I learned more about Grace and through her, your work these past years, it appears you have continued to apply your quiet manner to your doctoring work. I can't help but wonder that if I had returned to Philadelphia, would you have achieved as much as you have? We may have settled into a comfortable routine and never ventured to places like Georgia and Tennessee.

Grace spoke highly of you to Erin and even shared your support of her roommate, the Japanese girl. It reminded me of the morning you spoke to Mr. Silvestri about baby Salvatore. Your complete desire to accept those who are different from us and care for them captured my heart. And never let go.

Eliza, I never stopped loving you. I stopped loving myself. I let my fears consume me and deny my passions—my passion to love you and become your husband. I won't ask for you to travel to Ireland, and at my age, I cannot board an airplane any more than I could board a ship. My fears continue to consume me as much as the cancer which has claimed my pancreas. I hope this letter is enough for me to tell you I am proud of all your achievements. I love you still.

Yours,
Patrick

Eliza clutched the letter to her mended heart. *Patrick, it is enough.*

EPILOGUE

May 1947
Boston, Massachusetts

The maternity ward at the Peter Bent Brigham Hospital sounded with cries and wails as one infant after another announced their arrival. Fierce competition to be heard abounded with every bassinet occupied and the overflow moving to Pediatrics. The birth rate had exploded, affecting nearly every young couple in the city of Boston. Will and Anne Shaw had done their fair share of contribution. After the arrival of Billy in September 1945, another girl joined the family twenty-one months later.

Eliza felt a tug on the pocket of her white coat. Her six-year-old granddaughter, Flora, said in a voice loud enough for the elderly couple next to them to hear. "Nana, isn't my sister the prettiest baby you've ever seen?"

"Well Flora, you didn't get to see yourself as a baby. I'll just say you're both beautiful. Billy, too," Eliza said, bending over her granddaughter who was perched on a chair. She drew Flora closer to lean into her side. Together, they stared at the blue and pink swaddled bundles.

"Boys aren't beautiful, Nana. They're handsome."

"I'd say they're the same. But what's most important, Flora, is how beautiful you are on the inside. You're a big sister now. You have a very important job. Billy and Susan will watch everything you do and will try to be just like you. Aren't I the lucky Nana to know that you are kind and smart, so they will be, too?"

Flora waved her small hand toward the glass separating her from her new sister. "Susan! Susan Anna Shaw. I am your sister, Flora Ellen. F-L-O-R-A. Nana, how do you spell Ellen?"

"That's a lesson for tomorrow. Send a kiss to your sister. We've got to get home now. Cousin Bess has probably collapsed on the floor, running after Billy all afternoon."

Flora smacked her fingertips, held out her palm, and blew the moist droplets toward the bassinet in the middle row, far left, Baby Girl Shaw, seven pounds, two ounces, nineteen inches long.

Eliza gestured for Flora to hop off the chair. Flora slid her hand into Eliza's as they headed down the hallway. The steps Eliza took resonated with familiarity. She had walked this hall and others like it for nearly forty-six years. She had comforted laboring mothers and calmed anxious fathers. She had tended to the halest and frailest of infants. The sounds of mothers laboring in rooms at the other end of the corridor faded to soft echoes of pain and joy. Eliza tightened her grip on Flora's hand. This would be the last day that she would button a white coat over her dress. Her journey had been a testament to her fortitude and training, garnered and enriched by the women who had supported her along that long and winding road. They'd learned how to act and hold their own in a profession dominated by men. They had proved themselves over and over and would continue to with each subsequent generation. Through their common womanhood, they wove a tapestry which belonged to all, rich in experience and triumphs, with broken threads of disappointments re-tied and strengthened with determination. They were M.D.s—medical doctors.

"Are you ready, hon?" Will called to Flora who stood at a makeshift home plate.

"Keep your eye on the ball," Eliza instructed from the green and white webbed, aluminum, folding lawn chair.

Will lobbed the softball towards Flora. Using his new prosthetic leg would take time for him to adjust, but today he stood steady, his sole focus on his daughter. He had gained strength and confidence each day from the sessions Eliza spent with him. After consulting with his doctor and referring to her mental notes of working with Kay Clark at Warm Springs, Eliza assumed charge of Will's physical therapy to strengthen his leg muscles.

Phwwatt. The bat in Flora's hand made contact.

"Run!" said Bess, as she emerged from the back door, Billy on her hip.

Flora looked from Bess to her grandmother. "That way," pointed Bess, toward the maple sapling to the right of Will on the pitcher's mound. A peal of laughter rang across the yard, reverberating against the white clapboards of Will's new mail-order house. With a promotion to Operating Manager at the Edwards Wool Company and assistance from the G.I. Bill, Will purchased a home in the suburbs of Boston. The house kit included two extra rooms, designed to move Eliza in with him and his growing family.

Bess plopped onto the grass next to Eliza. She pointed to Eliza's lap. "Go, you little urchin. Sit with your Nana."

Eliza gathered Billy up and breathed deeply, his sandy brown hair sweet from the baby shampoo. "Can't keep up with the men, anymore, Bess?" Eliza chuckled.

"Not ones with the energy of a two-year-old! But I'll let you know if I find one in Newport this weekend."

"I hope you can drag your cousin out with you. He desperately needs a night out with some energetic young people."

Teddy, still married to the Navy, had proved his intellect and aptitude with Admiral Wright at the end of the war planning the invasion of Japan. His appointment as an instructor at the Naval War College in Newport kept him close by. If Bess failed in her assignment to steal Teddy away to a tennis match or party, perhaps Eliza could convince Teddy to join her for a trip to Jellico to visit Grace before the young resident returned to Knoxville for her third year.

The cardboard box slipped from Will's hands and thumped to the floor.

"Damn it," he said.

"Don't worry," said Eliza. "It doesn't sound like anything broke."

Will shrugged and left her to finish unpacking. Eliza watched him leave with the hitch in his gait. She opened the folded flaps and peered into the box. The wrapped frames remained intact; no shards of glass had ripped through the pages of last week's *Sunday Boston Globe*. Page six covered the top edge of the wrapping. An advertisement from Chandler's encouraged summer brides to imagine their bridesmaids a misty study in pastels. Eliza looked closer at the black and white drawing of the dress, trying to imagine it in tea rose pink, candied pale green mint, or Easter egg blue. The style with its floor-length gown, high bodice and capped sleeves resembled the choice of many of Eliza's high school friends when they made their debuts. A dress which Eliza never slipped over her head to walk through a receiving line at the Presentation Ball in Philadelphia.

She had chosen a different path. With each step she took, her path widened into a journey down a road of uncertainty. Yet, it had become her path beneath her feet, defined by the choices she had encountered at each waypoint along the way. Like disembarking at a train depot in Warm Springs, Georgia. Or veering into the mountains of Appalachia. Or facing down a catastrophic crisis at Mass General. Her journey began in her grandfather's library when she had sought a freedom to discover her purpose and live it. She'd reached out and embraced those experiences without fear. She'd claimed them as her own, as a life well lived.

The empty boxes stood stacked in a corner of Eliza's sitting room next to her writing desk. A jewelry tray rested on the top shelf of the desk, waiting to be tucked away into her bureau drawer. Nestled into one of the tray's sections, a string of pearls lay curled in a loop of concentric circles: each bead could be the beginning or the end. On the wall over her desk hung her diploma. A gilded scroll ran around the edges of the frame. Woman's Medical College of Pennsylvania emblazoned across the center. Amidst the printed sentences, on the lines reserved for handwritten script, read the name, *Eliza Pearson Edwards*, and the date *nineteenth day of May in the year of our Lord, one thousand nine hundred and one.*

Eliza sat at the desk, looking at the statement of her first triumph. Fifty years ago, she convinced her mother to allow her to attend Woman's Med, the school which had given her a place and the confidence to unfold her soul. Classrooms where a family of sisters formed among classmates; women who cared for each other whether they sat at an adjacent desk, held a hand during life's tragedies and trials, or treated her family as their own. The school where she had met Patrick, the man who believed in her, supported her desire to care, and who had affirmed that his love had never waned. Love, in all its forms, could transform a life. It shaped joy, strength, and resilience. It drove heartbreak and loss. It connected and shredded. It nurtured, and most of all, knit together a life's narrative.

She opened the desk drawer and pulled out a sheet of note paper, monogrammed at the top with curling "E's" and a "P", and her grandfather's pen.

May 19, 1947

Dear Dean Fay,

Best wishes for the upcoming conferring of degrees on the ninety-fifth class of Woman's Medical and congratulations to the graduates. I am heartened that Woman's Med continues to maintain its vision of educating women and providing them with role models and support to help them realize their dreams of entering our noble profession.

I'm sure the Class of 1947 is as well-prepared and filled with confidence as my classmates and I were forty-six years ago.

I am writing to you with an update on Olga Povitsky's estate which has finally made it through probate. As the executor, I am pleased to inform you that she has bequeathed a sizeable sum to Woman's Med with the directive that the funds are designated to offer financial assistance to other international and first-generation students. I would like to recommend Ruby Inoyue as the first award recipient. Learning of her background as a student who had to petition for her rights to be released from an internment camp in 1943 to continue her undergraduate studies at the University of Texas indicates she is exactly the type of student who Olga would have chosen. Woman's Med's acceptance of Ruby exemplifies the teachings of the school—to strive to help those who cannot help themselves. She will be an incredible asset to the school. I have no doubt she will join the ranks of the women among us who have the empathy and sympathy to triumph in the practice of medicine.

I am also enclosing my contribution to the planned Olga Povitsky Scholarship Fund. Thanks to Secretary Perkins and her work in establishing Social Security benefits, my small pension provides me with the opportunity to honor Olga, my classmate and friend, in this manner. You may plan for the same amount from me for each year until my death, upon which a lump sum will be distributed, as I have declared within my will.

A new day has dawned. May the rays of hope and success continue to shine upon the graduates of the Woman's Medical College of Pennsylvania.

Most sincerely yours,
Eliza Pearson Edwards, M.D.
Class of 1901

THE END

AUTHOR'S NOTE

When I began my writing journey, I had intended to use the timeline of my paternal grandmother's life to guide my first novel. That period of sixty years, coming of age in 1897 and passing away in 1957, provided rich history to craft a story which would educate and entertain. With a flourish of keystrokes, I wrote THE END for *The Unlocked Path*. I packed the manuscript and set off for a writer's conference, where I had planned to pitch the story's premise to a panel of agents and editors. From my first meeting, I received the best advice for a debut novelist. "Are you crazy?" asked author/agent, Paula Munier. She pointed out that a novel covering sixty years would require 900 pages to do justice to that much time in history. *Did I think I possessed the talent or notoriety of a Ken Follett or Diane Gabaldon?* No one would invest their time or money in a 900-page book by an unknown author. Instead, she suggested I identify a logical stopping point and set my readers up for a sequel.

In the years since that conference, additional ideas formed for a sequel in my restless writer's brain. I gave myself time to linger with Eliza's early beginnings. What did I want Eliza and the other characters to accomplish next? Which historical events and issues did I want to cover to educate more readers? Two pieces of information I had gleaned during my original research stayed with me.

First, the real work of Olga Povitsky, M.D., Woman's Med 1901. I had fictionalized a good part of her life in *The Unlocked Path,* and felt that I owed it to her memory to celebrate her forty-year career with the NY Department of Health in bacteriology as well as her design of a culture bottle used for cultivating toxins. The abstract which opens Chapter 10 comes from a 1932 article in *The Journal of Immunology,* submitted by Dr. Povitsky, Erla Jackson M.D., and Minnie Eisner M.D. I adjusted the date to fit my story. A Canadian team, including Leone Farrell, M.D., used Dr. Povitsky's culture bottle design in the 1950s, which eventually led to its use by Jonas Salk's team to produce the polio vaccine on a large scale. Foxx Life Sciences, a manufacturer of laboratory equipment, currently offers an Olga™ Povitsky Culture Bottle.

The connection to polio, and Olga's indirect contribution to the vaccine, planted the idea that Eliza, a maternity doctor, would also be touched by that horrific pandemic. In *The Path Beneath Her Feet*, Kay Morrison Clark is a fictional character. I do not know if any pregnant patients traveled to Warm Springs for treatment. Kay's father, the Congressman Morrison, was inspired by Arthur Mitchell, the first African American to be elected to the U.S. Congress as a Democrat (Illinois). A Black patient at Warm Springs would have been highly unlikely in the 1930s due to segregation. Despite Eleanor Roosevelt's request that separate housing and treatment facilities be built for them, the Administrator argued it would be too costly to build. They would also have needed to hire colored nurses and physios to a sum of $2,000 per patient per year—costs that he claimed colored families couldn't pay. (*Living with Polio, The Epidemic and its Survivors* by Daniel J. Wilson). Many of the therapists were trained at Peabody College in Tennessee and answered Roosevelt's call for help as "physios". The *Kenny Method*, mentioned later in the book, was developed by Sister Kenny from New Zealand, and was used widely until other methods emerged for easing the pain from paralyzed limbs.

Second, the work of the American Women's Hospitals in Appalachia. The AWH formed when women doctors volunteered during World War I and traveled to France. Denied by the US Army to treat American soldiers, the women turned to the needs of French civilians. After the war, the AWH provided medical care in other war-torn areas. By the early 1930s when the Depression heightened the need for services in the States, they turned their attentions to "South America"—the rural communities of the

South and Appalachia where professional medical care was nearly non-existent. Doctors Esther Lovejoy, Hilla Sheriff, and Lillian South were instrumental in opening clinics, creating healthmobile units, and maternity shelters in places like Greenville and Spartanburg, SC, Jellico, TN, NC, FL, and VA. For more on the work of the AWH and the formation of AMWA, I highly recommend *Oregon's Doctor to the World, Esther Pohl Lovejoy & A Life in Activism* by Kimberly Jensen and *Twenty Years with the American Women's Hospitals: A Review (1916-1936)* by Esther Lovejoy. Dr. Lovejoy directed the AWH until her death in 1967 at the age of ninety-eight.

In the same vein that books like *The Giver of Stars* by Jojo Moyes and *The Bookwoman of Troublesome Creek* by Kim Michele Richardson presented packhorse librarians bringing literacy to Appalachia, I hope that *The Path Beneath Her Feet* showcases the work of the AWH in bringing medical care to those same poverty-stricken areas. The accomplishments of their health education programs and medical services contributed to significant decreases in pellagra cases and maternal and infant deaths, as well as provided widespread vaccinations for typhoid, diphtheria and polio.

During a research trip to Drexel University's School of Medicine, which maintains the archives of Woman's Med, I discovered the existence of Toshiko Toyota and Ruby Inoyue, both Woman's Med students who were affected by the internment camps of Japanese Americans during World War II. They both graduated from Woman's Med and went on to lengthy, successful careers working within their communities. I changed Toshiko's last name due to the modern-day familiarity of Toyota with the car company.

Within the archives, I also found the written documentation of the hearings before the Committee on Military Affairs which sought to amend Public Law 252 to provide for the appointment of female physicians in the Medical Corps of the Army and Navy with the same full commissions, pay, rank and benefits as their male counterparts. After reading that the War Department had ruled that where the word "person" or "persons" was used, only a man or men were intended, I knew that I had to include information of this blatant example of sexism against women in medicine. Dr. Emily Barringer of the AMWA led the petitions to Congress, directed by legal advisor Dorothy Kenyon. Congresswoman Edith Nourse Rogers (Massachusetts) also spoke on behalf of the AMWA. Over fifty pages of the document include statements and positions from other woman doctors and their supporters arguing for the acceptance of the amendment. Dr. Margaret Craighill, Dean of Woman's Med, became the first woman doctor commissioned, as a Major. Each one of these strong and determined women inspired the development of my composite, fictional character, Eliza Edwards, M.D.

At the time of the hearings, Eliza battles for her right to continue to practice medicine in the face of a negligence charge. Helen Warner Shaw is a fictional character inspired by my father's stepmother, Helen Bradlee Robinson. A graduate of the Portia Law School for Women in Boston, she was admitted to practice at the U.S. Supreme Court in 1923. In 1926, she founded a bar review. I wish I had been old enough before she passed to have appreciated all her work and what she must have faced as a woman lawyer beginning her career just after the passing of the 19th Amendment. She continued to practice real estate law on Cape Cod until her early nineties.

The Cocoanut Grove Nightclub Fire in Boston on November 28, 1942, claimed 492 lives making it the deadliest fire in Boston's history. A memorial to mark the spot in Boston's South End is underway with hopes for an unveiling in September 2024. To learn more, visit www.cocoanutgrove.org. Robert and Shirley Cole are fictitious characters. I am not aware if any pregnant women were at the nightclub that fateful evening.

The article in *LIFE* magazine about the *Girls' Medical School* appeared in the December 1945 issue. I purchased a copy off eBay. If anyone wants a good chuckle over some of the advertisements, contact me through my website and I'll email you some photos.

The letters which Eliza's sons, Will and Teddy, wrote to her during WWII are based on, and in many spots lifted verbatim, from letters that my father, Lt. Commander Eliot H. Robinson, Jr. (USN, Retired) wrote during his twenty-two months in the South Pacific aboard *LCI(G) 397* (Landing Craft Infantry). I found the letters in my parents' attic. My father had passed fourteen years earlier. Neither I nor my brothers knew the letters existed. They were written to a family friend, sharing his sentiments and the experiences that he felt he could write about without the risk of being censored. His mention of suicide swimmers and his sentiment about the treatment of Japanese Americans is verbatim. The incident in Mt. Hood, however, happened in 1945. Eliza's worry about her sons, I believe, mirrored, what most women faced during those war years. My mother endured a two-year engagement while my dad was in the South Pacific and watched her only brother, at age nineteen leave his full college scholarship to join the Army Air Corps, becoming a tail gunner in Europe. My family is fortunate that both my dad and uncle came home. I can't imagine how those on the home front survived year after year without dropping from panic attacks every day.

The Path Beneath Her Feet is a work of fiction. The amazing work of the AWH and AMWA is very real. Since 1915, the AMWA has been *the vision and voice of women in medicine.* Their mission to *advance women in medicine, advocate for equity, and ensure excellence in health care* benefits us all.

- Janis Robinson Daly, September 5, 2024

READING GROUP DISCUSSION QUESTIONS

Questions and a more complete book club kit, including recipes for dishes mentioned in the book can be found on the author's website, www.janisrdaly.com/book-clubs. Daly is also available to join book clubs for an author chat, in-person or over Zoom. Contact her through her website.

1. Eliza is a more mature protagonist, age 57, when the story opens in 1936 and age 68 by the epilogue in 1947. Can you think of other books which have a mature protagonist? What were the similarities / differences between Eliza and those other characters?

2. Eliza finds her strength from the women in her life, Aunt Florence, Charlotte, Olga, Bess, Kay, Grace, and Helen. Do you have a favorite among the other characters? Were you surprised by their paths? Which one? Why?

3. How familiar were you with FDR's rehabilitation center for polio patients in Warm Springs? Did you learn anything about the center or the patients? Do you know anyone who contracted polio before the development of the vaccine? How were their lives affected?

4. Racism was a theme in this book, from Kay Clark's treatment in Warm Springs to Toshiko's experience at graduation. Why is it still important to bring these instances from history to light today?

5. Two popular books in recent years introduced readers to the packhorse librarians of Kentucky. Have you read either? (*The Bookwoman of Troublesome Creek* and *The Giver of Stars*). Like those books, *The Path Beneath Her Feet* introduces readers to the work of the American Women's Hospitals in Appalachia. Were you aware of those medical outposts before reading? How do these centers compare to the access to healthcare today?

6. Eliza grew up in Philadelphia and moved to Boston when she married, and remained there until the opportunity arose to travel to the rural spots of Warm Springs, GA and then Jellico, TN. Have you ever made a drastic move for your career or a relationship?

7. Olga advises Eliza: "The few times I left you on your own, you fell in love with the wrong man…A third time isn't always a charm." Were you surprised by the letter from Patrick? Was it the correct ending to their love story? Was Chet, a mountain man with little education, "wrong" for Eliza? Do opposites attract?

8. All forms of dementia destroy not only the one with the disease but also affect their caregivers. Eliza must choose to leave behind the Maternity Shelter she built to care for Aunt Florence. How have caregiver roles changed in the past 90+ years? Do you think the health care industry has made enough progress with the cure and treatment of dementia or caregiving?

9. Opinions on Eliza's actions to deliver Shirley Cole's baby during the chaos at the hospital on the night of the Cocoanut Grove nightclub fire. Was she negligent? What would you have done? Were you surprised that Eliza reached out to her ex-husband's widow, Helen Shaw, to be her lawyer?

10. Letters throughout the book depict the primary means of communication in the first half of the 1900s. When was the last time you wrote a letter? To whom? When was the last letter you received? From whom? (Not a card or a thank you note, a handwritten letter covering at least one page). What have we lost with the demise of letter-writing?

11. The author dedicated *The Path Beneath Her Feet* to her parents, members of The Greatest Generation: "who came of age during the Great Depression and served upon the seas and at the home front during World War II. Their history is ours. Let us not forget it. Let us learn from it." What can we learn from the people who lived during the tumultuous landscapes of 1930s and 1940s America?

I love hearing from book clubs. Submit highlights from your group's discussion through the contact form on my website, www.janisrdaly.com to receive a free gift.

ACKNOWLEDGEMENTS

Anyone who thinks writing is a solitary art form has not moved typed words on paper into a published book. Although I spent countless hours alone at my laptop drafting *The Path Beneath Her Feet*, seeing these words on a printed (or digital) page would never have transpired without the help of many. Historical fiction requires extensive research. Whenever possible, authors should gather firsthand information and visit the locales of their settings. My facts and detailed accounts came to life with a visit to Warm Springs, GA. I am especially grateful to have met National Parks Services guide, Carol Ann Blynn, who shared her parents' story of meeting at the rehabilitation center, she as a patient and he as a "push-boy". Their relationship proved how normal the "cripples" could be, finding love and compassion amidst their pain, and how a woman using an arm brace could become a mother and raise children like any other woman.

Although I have not visited Jellico, TN (yet!), I have driven along the Blue Ridge Mountains in VA and TN and spent a week in the Great Smoky Mountains in NC on a family vacation to witness the natural glory of the region. I also have my grandfather's black and white photo scrapbook from a visit to Kentucky (Troublesome Creek area!) on a fact-finding trip in the 1920s as part of his work to inspect the building of a community center, funded by a Boston philanthropist. My grandfather, Eliot H. Robinson, Sr., was also a novelist. He set a trilogy in that part of the Cumberland Mountains in a series about a Boston doctor visiting the area and meeting a young woman, named "Smiles", who he encourages to become a nurse. As a woman of the 21st century, I wanted to modernize the story and have a woman doctor encourage a young woman to become a doctor. The two books in the cover photo are original copies of his "Smiles" books.

The team at Drexel University's archive department is amazing. Matt Herbison and Kiernan McGhee, thank you for compiling two carts of material for me to dig through to learn more about Woman's Med and the AWH. Knowing I could always email you after my visit with follow-up questions was extremely helpful, too. We found Toshiko Toyota's story during some of our follow-up exchanges.

To authenticate many parts of my writing, I am thankful that my writer friend, Judge Dennis Blackmon of Coweta County, GA read my manuscript to provide feedback from a male perspective, as a legal professional, as a native to Georgia, and as a former airman in the Air Force. Thank you to my reader friend, Georlen Spangler, Esquire, for letting me bounce off the ideas for a malpractice suit against Eliza. For medical references, I am indebted to Dr. Eileen DiGregorio for providing feedback amid busy winter days when an overflow of patients visited her family practice and Mollie Marr, M.D., PhD, while in the middle of her residency at Massachusetts General Hospital/McLean.

Writers also lean on other writers as experts in finding plot holes and character development misses. Thank you to fellow Black Rose Writing authors, Kerry Chaput and Karen E. Osborne for taking time away from your writing days to pore through my manuscript and pinpoint spots I needed to strengthen. Deb Kiley, a lover of history, found details which needed more explanation. I am also humbled that the talented historical fiction authors, Amanda Skenandore and Kathleen Grissom, read my manuscript and provided blurbs which go a long way to help lesser-known authors gain recognition.

In addition to beta readers, a special thanks to Cate Perry for her keen editing eye and taking me on as a new client, Fran Weiner for copy editing, and Susan Phillips for proofreading. I think we caught all those stubborn typos!

I would never have seen *The Unlocked Path* published, let alone this second novel, without the guidance and support of award-winning author and Wheaton College sister, Ashley Sweeney. Not only did she pause in the middle of finishing her fourth novel, *The Irish Girl* (SheWrites Press, December 2024), to read mine, critique, and direct me towards deeper scenes, but she has mentored and uplifted me every step of the way since I reached out to her blind via email with a "Do you have any tips for a beginner?" The rest of my Wheaton sisterhood and classmates have also been at my elbow every step. Thank you, dearest ones, for your unwavering support. 1-4-3.

To the team at Black Rose Writing, led by Reagan Rothe. Thank you for believing in my writing, encouraging me to try new marketing ideas, and for nurturing all your authors.

For my dynamite cover and title, thank you to the talented Marjorie Warnick, who photographed the still life shots for both *The Unlocked Path* and *The Path Beneath Her Feet*. In addition to the books on the cover, the framed photo is of my dad and his brother, circa 1928, another family heirloom. While it took me four years to come up with the title for *The Unlocked Path*, *The Path Beneath Her Feet* came to me while listening to author Libbie Grant (Olivia Hawker) deliver the keynote address at the Historical Novel Society's 2023 conference. Upon my request, she sent me her entire transcript so I could ensure that I quoted her correctly with her statements about paths to publication: *Sometimes the path doesn't even exist until you begin walking. But if you keep moving forward, if you take whatever next step presents itself to YOU, by and by you'll discover that a path is creating itself beneath your feet.*

My path to publishing my second novel has also taken twists and turns I never expected, like using only ten percent of the first manuscript draft in this sequel. At each step, however, I found the courage to continue, embraced by the love and support of my family. Once again, my brother Mark pulled out his red pen and attacked my miserable first draft and provided enough comic relief with some of his editorial notations to make me laugh through all the red. My other brother John, and my sons, Peirce and Brendan, asked about and read through a novel that they would never have picked up unless my name appeared on the cover page. And, to my husband, Jim. Thank you for listening to Eliza's continued story, two chapters at a time, to help me find my voice in hers.

ABOUT THE AUTHOR

Janis Robinson Daly. *Reading, Discussing, Researching, Writing Books.* Splitting her time between Cape Cod, New Hampshire, Florida, and hotels along Route 95, a tablet becomes Daly's library and desk, packed into a travel bag for reading and writing, wherever she might land. Inspired by the discovery that an ancestor was the founder of the Woman's Medical College of PA in 1850, Daly wrote her first novel, *The Unlocked Path* (Black Rose Writing, August 2022), which celebrates the early graduates of the college and women doctors at the turn of the 20th Century. Its sequel, *The Path Beneath Her Feet* (Black Rose Writing, September 2024), honors the work of the American Women's Hospitals in rural America during the 1930s.

The Unlocked Path was named a #1 New Release for US History on Amazon in August 2022, received an Honorable Mention for General Fiction from the 2023 New England Book Festival Awards, and at the time of this printing, is a finalist for the 2023 Goethe Awards of Late Historical Fiction from the Chanticleer International Book Awards.

Daly graduated with a B.A. in Psychology from Wheaton College, at the time, an all-women's college. At Wheaton, she developed a fond appreciation of the supportive relationships established between students, faculty, and alumnae, and a heightened awareness of female-centric issues. She is an active member and moderator for three book clubs and offers author chats to clubs that read her books. A presentation of how her genealogy research inspired her to take up novel writing has made Daly a sought-after speaker for women's and writers' groups and libraries, including the American Medical Women's Association, the Historical Novel Society, the Historical Society of Pennsylvania, and Soroptimist International and American Association of University Women chapters.

To learn more about Janis Robinson Daly, including book club tips, her curated lists of #31titleswomeninhistory, and information on other forthcoming novels, connect with her at www.janisrdaly.com

OTHER TITLES BY
JANIS ROBINSON DALY

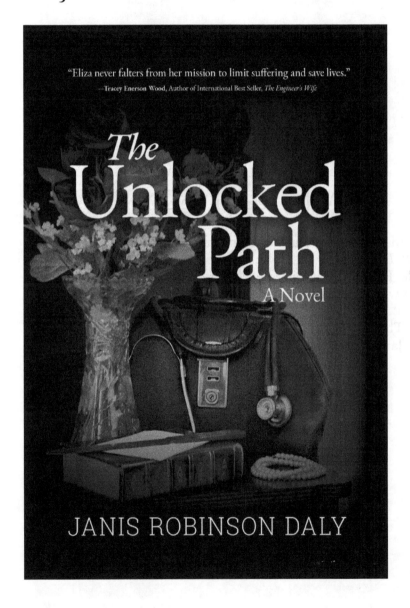

"Eliza never falters from her mission to limit suffering and save lives."
—Tracey Enerson Wood, Author of International Best Seller, *The Engineer's Wife*

The
Unlocked
Path

A Novel

JANIS ROBINSON DALY

NOTE FROM
JANIS ROBINSON DALY

Word-of-mouth is crucial for any author to succeed. If you enjoyed *The Path Beneath Her Feet*, please leave a review online—anywhere you are able. Even if it's just a sentence or two. It would make all the difference and would be very much appreciated.

Thanks!
Janis Robinson Daly

We hope you enjoyed reading this title from:

www.blackrosewriting.com

Subscribe to our mailing list – *The Rosevine* – and receive **FREE** books, daily deals, and stay current with news about upcoming releases and our hottest authors.
Scan the QR code below to sign up.

Already a subscriber? Please accept a sincere thank you for being a fan of Black Rose Writing authors.

View other Black Rose Writing titles at
www.blackrosewriting.com/books and use promo code
PRINT to receive a **20% discount** when purchasing.

Printed in the USA
CPSIA information can be obtained
at www.ICGtesting.com
LVHW041802110924
790683LV00009B/82

9 781685 134723